Blythewood

Blythewood

CAROL
GOODMAN

Viking

An Imprint of Penguin Group (USA)

VIKING
Published by the Penguin Group
Penguin Group (USA)
375 Hudson Street
New York, New York 10014, U.S.A.

USA + Canada + UK + Ireland + Australia + New Zealand + India + South Africa + China
Penguin Books Ltd, Registered Offices: 80 Strand, London WC2R 0RL, England

For more information about the Penguin Group visit www.penguin.com

First published in the United States of America by Viking, an imprint of Penguin Group (USA), 2013

LIBRARY OF CONGRESS CATALOGING-IN-PUBLICATION DATA
Goodman, Carol.
Blythewood / Carol Goodman.
pages   cm
Summary: "After a summer locked away in a mental institution, seventeen-year-old
orphan Ava Hall is sent to Blythewood, a finishing school for young ladies
that is anything but ordinary."—Provided by publisher.
ISBN 978-0-670-78476-9 (hardback)
[1. Supernatural—Fiction. 2. Boarding schools—Fiction. 3. Schools—Fiction. 4. Identity—
Fiction. 5. Love   Fiction. 6. Social classes—Fiction. 7. Triangle Shirtwaist Company—Fire,
1911—Fiction. 8. Hudson River Valley (N.Y. and N.J.)—History—20th century—Fiction.] I. Title.
PZ7.G61354Bly 2013   [Fic]—dc23   2013011236

Printed in U.S.A.

1   3   5   7   9   10   8   6   4   2

Book design by Nancy Brennan
Set in Haarlemmer MT

The publisher does not have any control over and does not assume
any responsibility for author or third-party websites or their content.

For Maggie, my fiery girl

1

I HEARD THE bells that morning as I was entering Washington Square Park. I stopped just past the arch and looked south to see if the sound might be a streetcar but I didn't see one. Then I looked north, through the arch and up Fifth Avenue, listening for the bells of Grace Church playing the quarter hour—but it wasn't the tune they played. And if the bells weren't from Grace Church or a streetcar, that meant they were *my* bells, the ones I heard inside my head, the ones I'd been hearing for the last six months whenever something bad was going to happen.

I felt a tingling on the back of my neck and knew there was someone behind me. I whirled around to find Tillie Kupermann's laughing face, her fresh-scrubbed cheeks rosy in the cold winter sunlight, her red curls already escaping from her Gibson Girl pouf. With her starched white shirtwaist tucked neatly into her slim dark skirt, you might have taken Tillie for a Gibson Girl, until you noticed the darning stitches on her collar or that instead of a tennis racket or a golf club she was carrying a tin lunch pail.

"Listening to the angel on your shoulder again?" she asked.

"How do you know I'm not listening to the devil on my shoulder?" I replied.

"Wrong shoulder," she chirped, slipping her arm in mine. "Everyone knows the devil sits on your left shoulder. And besides, I know you, Avaline Hall. You're on the side of the angels."

I laughed at that and let myself be led by Tillie through the park, past a group of young men—law students, I thought, from the books under their arms and the rumpled look of their tweed coats and trousers, on their way to the law library next to our building. One doffed his hat, revealing hair slicked back with a quantity of brilliantine pomade, and called out to Tillie as we passed by:

"I enjoyed your speech last night at the union hall, Miss Kupermann. You've converted me to your cause."

Tillie's mouth quirked into a smile. I tightened my grip on her arm and tried to keep her walking, but she swirled around to face the men, her skirts swishing above her ankle-high boots to reveal a provocative glimpse of red stocking. "So the next time we strike, you'll be on the picket line with us?" she asked with a brazen smile.

The pomaded young man clutched his hat to his breast. "On the picket lines, in the Jefferson Market courts, to the very depths of the Tombs themselves, I vow to defend your honor, m'lady."

Tillie tilted her head back, her slim throat gleaming white in the morning sun. "I don't need anyone to *defend* me, sir. But if *you* are ever in a scrape don't hesitate to call on me!"

His companions hooted like owls at Tillie's comment as she turned smartly on her heel, and I heard the pomaded gentlemen mutter something in Yiddish that sounded like *farbrente mayd-*

lakh. Tillie laughed out loud and kept walking, so quickly I had to skip to keep up with her.

"Tillie," I hissed, "talking about striking could cost you your job! I thought the strike was settled last year. And what's this about you giving a speech last night?"

"The strike was settled without us getting half our demands. We still don't have a union shop . . ." Tillie listed off her grievances as we crossed Washington Square and headed down Washington Place past peddlers selling shiny copper pots and pans, and food carts hawking roasted potatoes, chestnuts, and pickled herring. "There's still work to be done! You should come to the meetings."

I shook my head. Tillie knew I would never go to her union meetings or Marxist classes. Mother had raised me to keep my head down and never talk to strangers—especially young men, whom she'd regarded with deep suspicion. I would never banter with the young law students as Tillie had just done. They might spend their days just one building away from the factory where Tillie and I worked, but they were worlds away from girls like us, and I didn't have Tillie's hope that those worlds could be bridged.

"What was that he called you?" I asked as we neared the factory on the corner of Greene Street.

"*Farbrente maydlakh*," she said, fingering a lock of my chestnut hair, a far less dramatic shade of red than Tillie's own. "He meant both of us, *bubbelah*, because of our hair. It means 'fiery girls.'"

⇥ ✦ ⇤

There was a line for the freight elevators; we weren't allowed in the passenger elevators.

"Come on," Tillie said, pulling me toward the staircase. "If we're late Mr. Bernstein will lock the doors on us. I'll race you."

She was off in a flash of red stockings that stayed just out of reach for nine flights of stairs. We were out of breath and bent over with cramps of laughter, gasping, but we managed to slip through the door a minute before Mr. Bernstein, the foreman, closed the door, locking it behind us. We hung up our coats in the dressing room and hurried to our machines. Tillie was at the end of the back row, a much better place than my spot against the wall below the windows overlooking Washington Place for getting out early at closing time, when all the girls bunched up at the door waiting for Mr. Bernstein to check their purses for stolen lace or ribbons. When I was settled, I spared a moment to look down the long sewing table to where Tillie sat. She was helping a new girl find her place—a tiny malnourished sprite in an oversized dress. Her hands were shaking as Tillie put the scissors in them.

"Don't worry, Etta, I'm going to look after you," she told the girl, with a smile that warmed the unheated loft. They were the same exact words Tillie had said to me on my first day here four months ago.

I'd been even more of a mess than little Etta, driven to take a job in the loud, crowded factory after my mother had died. The only work I knew was trimming hats. Mother had had clients among the richest women in the city—"the four hundred," as she called the cream of New York society. She'd had a deft hand and keen eye for knowing just where to add a feather and tweak a brim and which ribbon suited which color of felt. We didn't have a lot of money, but we managed. Mother always said it was better to be a pauper than a slave to money, and although she sometimes lapsed into melancholic silences, she always rallied herself when she saw me looking worried.

Until the day she saw the man in the Inverness cape.

It was my sixteenth birthday. Mother had promised me a walk in Central Park after we delivered one last hat to a client on Fifth Avenue. As we were leaving, my mother abruptly halted on the sidewalk, staring across the avenue at the entrance to the park. Following her gaze I'd seen a man in an Inverness cape who'd lifted his Homburg hat in greeting. His face, dappled by leaf shadow, was indistinct but I could feel the intensity of his gaze. I found myself unable to look away. As I stared at him I heard a bell begin to toll. I thought it might be coming from Saint Patrick's Cathedral. My mother grabbed my hand and dragged me toward an approaching omnibus. She'd pushed me on, despite my protestations that she had promised me a walk in the park. She had refused to answer when I asked who the man was. "No one," she insisted, and then repeated, "No one."

Each time she said "no one" I heard the bell toll. It kept tolling as we rode the omnibus down Fifth Avenue, and eventually I realized that the sound wasn't coming from one of the churches—it was coming from inside my head. It faded after we'd ridden south of Fourteenth Street, leaving a faint ringing in my ears.

That night my mother had complained of a chill in her chest and sent me to the chemists for a bottle of laudanum. From that day on, she began to drink it regularly. She went out less and less, sending me to deliver hats to our clients, but always warning me not to talk to strangers. Before she got sick, my mother would spend hours in the local libraries—the Astor, the Seward Park, the Hudson Park branch—looking through strange and obscure books while I read the histories, novels, and poetry she recommended, and also as many of Mrs. Moore's novels about girls' school as I could find. But after she got sick, she sent me out for books and then spent her days reading on a chaise longue in front of the window. No matter how many times we changed apartments she always managed to find one that overlooked the river, which she said reminded her of her beloved Blythewood, the girls' boarding school she'd attended north of the city on the Hudson. She kept an engraving of the school on her bedside table, where another woman might keep a photograph of her husband. But my mother had no photographs of my father, nor would she ever tell me anything about him.

Nor would she tell me who the man in the Inverness cape had been. "No one," she repeated when I asked. "No one."

When I told her that I had heard a bell in my head when I looked at him, she looked frightened, but then she squeezed my hand and said, "That's because you were born at midnight on New Year's Eve. You're a chime child. The bell will warn you when you're in danger." I'd thought she was raving from the laudanum—after all, the time on my birth certificate was 12:15. But one day about a month later I was delivering a hat to a client and I heard the bell again. I rushed home and found my mother on the chaise longue, an empty bottle of laudanum and a long black feather from one of her hats lying by her side, her body as cold and lifeless as the winter wind coming in through the open window.

When I told Mother's clients that she had died of consumption, they closed their doors on me and found someone else to buy their hats from. If I'd told the truth—she'd died of an overdose of laudanum—they would have done the same, even if drinking laudanum wasn't catching.

Though maybe it was.

In the weeks after she died I'd sometimes pick up the empty green bottle that I'd found lying beside her and turn it over in my hand, looking into its mouth as if it were a green pool on a hot day. What oblivion had my mother sought there? Might I find relief from the bells I heard?

I knew well enough where to go and what to tell the chemist—I'd done it often enough for Mother—but so far I hadn't. Instead, I'd put the bottle away, along with the black feather, which didn't seem to go with any of the hats she'd been trimming, and found work at the Triangle Waist factory.

On my first day I was so clumsy with the scissors it was a wonder I didn't cut off my own fingers. I don't think I'd have made it through the day if Tillie Kupermann hadn't taken me under her wing and shown me how to trim the loose threads without nicking the fabric. Later, when I was promoted to the sewing machines, she taught me how to sew a straight seam. She covered for me when I had my spells—as I'd come to think of the moments when I heard the bells—and never asked what caused them. I heard them less when I was with her.

When little Etta was settled in her work, Tillie looked up, saw me, and stuck out her tongue and crossed her eyes. Suppressing a laugh, I ducked my head and picked up a sleeve from the basket at my feet, smoothed it out on my machine, and focused on sewing a straight seam. When that one was done I dropped it in the trough that ran down the middle of the table and picked up another. And another, and another. I sewed the same seam on hundreds of sleeves each day, as if I were a girl in one of mother's stories, condemned by a jealous goddess to perform the same silly task over and over again—sorting barley from millet or gathering fleece from bloodthirsty sheep to break the curse and win back the handsome prince. But at the end of each day all I had for my labors were calloused fingertips and a constant ache in my back.

Besides, how would a prince find me here? Even if I could bring myself to defy Mother's rules about not speaking to boys, the only males here were the arrogant cutters on the eighth floor, the stoop-shouldered tailors, and the runners who delivered the baskets of unfinished sleeves—raw-boned lads just off the boat from Italy or Poland who hardly spoke English. I rarely spared the time to look up when they dropped off my basket. Today, though, one got my attention by knocking it over.

"Clumsy boy!" I cried, bending over to retrieve the fallen sleeves. "If those get soiled Mr. Bernstein will take it out of *my* pay." As I grabbed for them, he seized my hand. A vibration went through my entire body, an electric current that flared and sparked like the wires that ran above the streetcars, and a bell sounded inside my head—not the deep bass note I heard when something bad was about to happen, but a sweet, high treble bell.

"You have to go," he hissed in my ear, his warm breath, which smelled like apples, spreading heat through my body.

I looked up into dark eyes flecked with gold, skin the color of a fresh peach, and black ringlets falling over a high, sculpted forehead. My whole body shuddered like a bell that had been struck. My hand, which looked small in his, was trembling. For a moment the din of the factory—the whirr of the sewing machines, the shouts of the foreman to hurry up, the street noise from the open windows—all receded. I felt as though the two of us were standing alone in a green glade starred with wildflowers, the only sound the wind soughing through the encircling forest. . . .

But then the sounds of the factory came rushing back and I remembered where I was—and *who* I was. A poor girl who made seven and a half dollars a week at the Triangle Waist factory. I wasn't *going* anywhere.

"I'm not the one who has to go—you are!" I snatched my hand out of his and glanced quickly around the room to see if Mr. Bernstein was near, but he was on the far side of the room talking to Mr. Blanck, one of the owners, who had brought his daughters in today to see where their papa made all the money to keep them in pretty frocks and lace pinafores. The sight of these girls, with their smooth, untroubled faces and clean soft hands, steeled me. I turned back to the dark-eyed youth who— *idiot!*—was still crouched beside me.

"We're lucky that everyone's looking at the pretty girls, but in a moment Mr. Blanck will look over here and see that precious seconds are being lost in the production of his fortune. I will be fired and then I will starve to death—but before I do, I will track you down and sever every one of those silly curls from your head. And"—I picked up a pair of scissors—

"I can't guarantee I'll spare your scalp. Understand?"

I snapped the scissors for emphasis and he started back, his mouth gaping. I bent my head down to my sewing machine and, willing my hands to stop shaking, sewed another seam. And another and another, until the shadow he cast was gone.

I worked steadily until lunchtime, when Tillie came to share her stuffed cabbage with me. I told her I had to work through lunch to make my quota because the idiot new boy had put me behind.

"There's a new boy?" Tillie asked through a mouth full of cabbage.

Usually Tillie's undisguised interest in the male gender amused me, but I had no time for it today. "Dark-haired lad," I answered, biting the words off as I tossed a sleeve into the trough. "Italian, I think, or maybe Greek. A right proper idiot."

"Oh," Tillie said. "I'll keep an eye out for him. Did you see Mr. Blanck's daughters? They had such lovely dresses." She sighed. "And their hats! One had an entire bird on the crown! Do look at them if they come through again. Maybe you can copy it for me."

I owed Tillie much more than a copied hat, but the longing in her voice reignited the longing I'd felt when I looked at those girls, not for their dresses or hats, but for the lives that I imagined went with them. Time to read a book, or sketch a picture, maybe even go to school. My mother had tried to educate me with her old books and trips to libraries and museums, but I knew it wasn't the same as an education at a real school like the ones Mrs. Moore wrote about. And my mother had told me enough stories about her beloved Blythewood to conjure images of girls in white tea dresses and straw boaters having tea in a garden or studying in deliciously cool rooms lined with books. . . . But now that my mother was gone, whatever faint dream I'd ever had of going to Blythewood had faded to ashes.

"A knock-off hat won't make you look like those girls," I said, the words escaping my mouth before I knew I was going to say them aloud.

"Oh," Tillie said, sounding like a wounded bird. "Of course not. . . . I didn't mean . . ."

And then she was gone. I looked up to see her retreating back, an uncharacteristic stoop in her slim shoulders, and felt a sharp pain in my own back, just below my ribcage. I started to go after her, but then remembered that if I didn't make my quota today I wouldn't have the money to pay this month's rent. I'd make it up to her after work. I'd make her that hat out of Mother's old trimmings.

I bent back to my work, my head full of feathers and ribbons, and let the rhythm of the machine lull me into a stupor that shut out the bells and the idiot runner and Tillie's hurt voice. The next time I looked up at the clock on the wall it was half past four. Only fifteen minutes to closing time. I had only two more sleeves to make.

As I looked down from the clock I noticed a man standing beside the Greene Street door speaking with Mr. Bernstein. A tall man in an Inverness cape and Homburg hat. A man who looked just like the one whose appearance had heralded my mother's decline into laudanum addiction and death.

2

NO, I TOLD myself, *it can't be. I must be falling into my mother's habit of suspicions.*

The man turned away from Mr. Bernstein and caught me staring at him. Beneath the brim of the Homburg, I glimpsed glittering black eyes, as cold and hard as lumps of coal. I tried to look away but I was transfixed, unable to move. The deep bass bell began to ring in my head, a steady toll like a funeral dirge. As I stared, horrified by my immobility, he raised his hat to me and smiled. Then, without taking his eyes off me, he tilted his head toward Mr. Bernstein and said something to him. Mr. Bernstein looked toward me, a frown creasing his heavy, bland face.

Good Lord, they're talking about me. My heart began to race. Desperately, I tried to look away, to go back to sewing, but my eyes and hands were frozen. The man in the Inverness cape began to walk down the aisle between the sewing tables and the airshaft. At the very least I would lose my job, but I already knew something even worse was about to happen. The bells in my head told me so.

My mother had been so frightened by this man that she'd had to drug herself into oblivion. He was coming to take me away to the workhouse, or prison . . . or an insane asylum. I sat frozen to my seat as the man in the Inverness cape turned down the aisle between my sewing table and the next, the deep bass bell ringing madly in my ears. He'd reach me in a few seconds. . . .

The man juddered to a halt like a piece of cloth that's gotten jammed in the pressing machine, but it was as though *he* were the machine. His limbs jerked and spasmed like those of an automaton that has run down or a puppet's when the puppeteer's hand slips. He wheeled around to see what had halted his progress.

It was Tillie. She had caught a fold of his cape in her machine. I saw her assembling her features into a semblance of innocence, but when she looked up at the man all the blood drained from her face. I'd seen Tillie talk boldly to Mr. Blanck himself when she thought a new girl's wages were unfair. I'd heard stories of her facing down the thugs hired to break the picket lines during the strike. I'd never seen her look afraid before. Now she looked not just afraid but horrified.

I started to get up to draw the man's attention away from Tillie, but someone yanked me back down. It was the dark-eyed runner, crouched below the sewing table. *"You see,"* he hissed, *"I told you to go."*

"How . . . ?" But there wasn't time to ask how he had known about the man in the Inverness cape—or *what* he knew about him. "Where?" I asked instead.

He grabbed my arm and shoved me under the table, behind a row of workbaskets. "Keep crawling to the dressing room. I'll take care of *him.*"

I couldn't imagine how this boy was going to "take care" of a man who had frightened Tillie Kupermann, but I did as he said. I crawled on my hands and knees beneath the tables, sure that at any moment I would be seized by the nape of my neck like a mouse plucked up by a hawk.

As I crawled I heard the quitting bell ring, and then a stampede of feet as all the girls hurried to be first to leave. When I reached the end of the tables I looked up and saw that they were all crowding around the Greene Street door. The man in the Inverness cape was pushed toward the door by the crowd of girls. He was scanning the room, those hard, coal eyes sweeping the air like the wings of a carrion crow. Where was that boy who said he'd take care of him . . . ? Then I saw him. He was right behind the man in the cape. A terrible thought occurred to me: perhaps the boy worked for the man in the Inverness cape and his message had been a ploy to make me lose my job.

I watched as the boy whispered something into the man's ear. Whatever he said, it immediately drew the man's attention. His head whipped around, moving with the speed of a striking snake, his neck twisting farther than it should have been able to turn. Seeing that gave me a sick feeling inside, but I used his momentary distraction to make a run for the dressing room. I saw out of the corner of my eye a swirl of dark cloak as the man fled the room, pursuing the dark-eyed boy. So maybe the boy wasn't working for the man. . . .

There were a dozen or so girls inside the dressing room, putting on their hats and coats, gossiping about their plans for the evening. Esther Hochfield was boasting that her fiancé was going to meet her at the factory door and take her out to dinner. Yetta Lubitz was looking at her paycheck and sighing that she didn't have enough to buy the hat she wanted. Then Tillie grabbed my arm and whispered into my ear.

"Who *is* that man?" she asked, her face pale and her hand trembling.

"I don't know," I said. "But my mother and I saw him once and she was frightened of him."

"Of course she was frightened of him! There's something . . . *wrong* about him. My papa used to tell me stories about an evil spirit that could take over a man's body. That's what this man feels like—like he's been taken over by a dybbuk. But somehow your friend managed to lead him out into the stairwell. We'll take the other stairs."

I was about to protest that the dark-eyed boy wasn't my "friend" as Tillie steered me out of the dressing room toward the Washington Place stairs, but as we came into the loft, I noticed a commotion. A flock of girls was running toward the Greene Street door, their voices excited and . . . *scared*. The deep bass bell was gonging inside my head so loudly I couldn't tell what they were saying, but when Tillie spoke I heard her clearly.

"*Fire!*"

As if the word had conjured the thing itself, the airshaft windows shattered and a blaze of flames burst through them. The blaze looked like a swarm of fiery rats pouring over the sill and across the factory floor. I stared at it transfixed until Tillie's voice in my ear broke my trance. "We have to get out!" she cried. "The Greene Street door is blocked—we have to try this one!"

She pulled me across the room toward the Washington

Place door, but I couldn't take my eyes off the fire, which was spreading across the examining tables below the airshaft windows, snatching at the piles of shirtwaists. The ignited scraps floated into the air and drifted across the room like firebirds spreading their destruction. They landed on the workbaskets beneath the sewing tables and set each one ablaze. The smoke that rose from the smoldering baskets looked like flocks of black crows.

I blinked, trying to clear away the illusion, but when I opened my eyes the room was thick with smoke. Frightened girls ran from door to door to window to window, wheeling around the room like birds beating their wings against a cage. The fire roared like a rabid beast, hungry for our flesh. A small figure flitted by, which I recognized as the new girl whom Tillie had been helping before. She was running with a group of girls toward the dressing room.

"Etta!" Tillie cried, yanking her hand out of mine and running after the girl. I followed them both into the dressing room. Tillie crouched down in front of a low cubby. "I can't leave her!" Tillie cried. "I promised I'd look after her today."

It was the same promise she'd made to me on my first day. I'd believed it then, little knowing how far she'd take that promise.

I knelt down beside Tillie and looked into the cubby, straight into the girl's terrified eyes. As I willed calmness into my voice, I heard the clanging bass bell in my head slow to a steady toll that reverberated through my body and vibrated on the surface of my skin.

I'd never felt this before. Since the bells had started they had always sounded wildly when I was frightened or when something bad was about to happen. I'd never tried to control them. But I did now, for Tillie and Etta's sake. I reached into the cubby and put my hand on the girl's arm.

"It's all right," I said, measuring my voice to the now steady, slow beat of the bell inside my head. "Tillie won't let anything happen to you. Come on out and we'll all go home together."

Etta's eyes widened—I wasn't even sure she spoke English—but under my hand I could feel her muscles relax and her small hand slip into mine. I closed my hand around hers and pulled her out of the cubby. She came out like a cork popping out of a bottle and immediately latched onto Tillie, wrapping her arms around her neck and her legs around her waist. Tillie stood up and looked at me over Etta's shoulder, then down at the other girls huddled on the floor.

"Are we going to wait here like lambs to the slaughter?" she cried in a clear strong voice. "Or are we going to save ourselves? I'm getting out of here. Who's with me?"

Not waiting for a response, Tillie strode out of the dressing room straight through the smoke to the Washington Place door. A few of the women in the cloakroom roused themselves to follow her, but when we reached the door we found it locked.

I turned to look across the room. The flames already blocked the airshaft by the fire escape and the Greene Street door. The fire was pushing us toward the tall windows that overlooked Washington Place. They stood open, beckoning us with the sight of blue sky unstained by smoke. One of the women climbed up on the window ledge and cried "Fire!" as if that could be news to anyone. I looked out the window and saw that the street was full of horse-drawn fire engines and crowds of spectators all looking up at us. Their mouths were open, shouting something, but I couldn't make out what.

I turned around and saw that in the few seconds I'd turned my back on the fire it had stolen closer. I could feel the heat of it on my skin now, doubly hot after the coolness of the outside air. Another woman climbed up onto the ledge. "They're holding out nets!" she cried.

"That won't help!" Tillie shouted. "We're too high up—"

But the woman was gone, vanished from the window as if she'd been plucked from the sky. I looked out the window and saw her plummeting to the ground, her skirts billowing in the air, her arms pinwheeling as if to keep her balance. She hit the net and went straight through to the pavement with a horrible, sickening thud. The crowd let out a groan and then began shouting again.

"No!" they were shouting "No! Don't jump!"

But what other choice was there? The fire was steadily advancing across the floor, pinning us between the flames and the deadly drop like butterflies pressed between panes of glass. Another girl climbed up on a window ledge. She turned and handed me her purse—as if she were at a dance and wanted her hands free—and daintily stepped off the ledge.

I didn't watch this time. I shut my eyes.

You always have a choice, my mother had once said to me.

But what kind of choice was this—burning to death or smashing on the pavement? It felt like my whole life had been driven by impossible choices—rent or food? Factory or sweatshop? Living as Mother had us live, never trusting anyone, or taking a chance and caring about a stranger, like Tillie? I opened my eyes and looked for her, but saw instead another figure at a window on the Greene Street side. I thought it was another girl jumping. She spread out her arms and for a moment I thought I saw wings. Then the figure jumped *into* the room and flew toward me, resolving into a black winged creature cleaving the smoke and flames. Just before the wings swept around me, I blinked and saw they were a blanket, and the figure who held it over my mouth was the dark-eyed boy.

"Come on," he said. "The stairs going down are full of smoke. We have to get to the roof."

He began pulling me toward the Greene Street door, but I twisted out of his grip and turned to find Tillie. She was at the Washington Place door, still holding Etta, and banging on the locked door. "Not without Tillie!" I cried.

Still keeping hold of my arm with one hand, he put his other arm around Tillie's shoulders. "Come on, then, both of you. We're making a run for the Greene Street door."

Before we could object he threw the blanket over both our heads and shoved us straight toward the fire. I heard Etta whimper and Tillie scream, but the boy barked at us, "Just close your eyes! It will be all right."

The certainty in his voice compelled me. Besides, what other choice did we have? I closed my eyes and let him push us into the fire. He must have found something else to throw over our heads because I heard a rustling noise from above and, although I felt the heat of the fire all around us, the flames seemed not to touch us. It was as though we were moving through the fire inside a protective bubble.

Then we were through the Greene Street door and in the smoke-filled stairwell and struggling up the stairs, past the tenth-floor showroom and out onto the roof. The fresh air felt like heaven, but when I looked up I saw a dark cloud hovering over us. I could see shapes in the smoke, a roiling mass of crows circling the burning building.

"*Don't look at them,*" the boy hissed in my ear.

"You can see them?" I asked, not sure if I should be relieved I hadn't lost my mind or terrified that the crows were real.

He said something that sounded like it might have been Latin—*tenebrae*—and then he was pulling me to the west side of the roof where two ladders had been set up between the skylight and the taller building to the west. A group of young men in shirtsleeves were helping terrified girls up the ladders. I recognized the law students from the park earlier—had it only been this morning? Just one building over, I had thought, but worlds away. But here they were bridging that gap. I felt a swelling in my chest at the thought, an unfamiliar pang that I dimly recognized as an emotion I hadn't felt in a while: hope.

The dark-eyed boy squeezed my hand and I looked into his face. The peachy down was streaked with soot and his eyes were wide and shining.

"No matter how dark the shadows," he said hoarsely, "there's always good." A flush of red swept his face and he looked away. He shouted toward the law students, "I've got three more for you, lads!"

"That'll make a round dozen you've brought us, boy-o, but we'll take 'em all!" one of the young men shouted with a graceful bow. I recognized the dandy who had flirted with Tillie this morning. His pomaded hair stuck up in spikes and his once-white shirt was torn and streaked with soot. When he saw Tillie he grinned and bowed. "I told you I'd defend your honor one day!" he said.

Tillie made a gasping noise in her throat but didn't move. "*Now* is not the time to be shy," I said, pushing her forward.

"I can't climb that ladder with Etta!" she cried. "And I won't go without her."

"We're all going," the dark-eyed boy said, gently prying Etta from Tillie's arms. "Come on, doveling," he cooed to Etta in a gentle voice. "It'll be just like climbing a tree. Have you ever climbed a tree?"

Etta shook her head, staring wide-eyed at the boy. "No?" he said. "Well, there's a first time for everything. One hand on this rung, then . . ." He kept up a soothing patter as he coaxed Etta onto the ladder and kept his hands on her until the law student had her in his arms. Then he turned back to Tillie and me.

"Who's next?"

"Tillie."

"Ava."

We said each other's names at the same time.

"Right then, Ava it is." He put his hands on my hips, his fingers so long they nearly circled my waist. I felt the blood rush to my face as he lifted me bodily up onto the bottom rung of the ladder. I looked over my shoulder for one more glimpse of those dark eyes for courage—but he was looking up, into the maelstrom of crows . . .

Which were diving down toward the ladder. They fell on us in a clawing mass, their weight bowing the thin wooden slats.

One flew at the law student holding the top end and savagely clawed at his eyes. He let go of the ladder and I felt it sway under my feet.

"Ava!"

I heard Tillie's voice and looked back to see her on the edge of the roof reaching for me . . . and someone emerging from the smoke behind her. It was the man in the Inverness cape. He was looking up at me, but he had his hand on Tillie's back. His lips parted and a wisp of smoke curled out of his mouth. He smiled wider, revealing a gullet full of smoke and flames, and then he pushed Tillie off the roof.

I screamed and reached for Tillie. The ladder cracked beneath my feet. I was falling. I felt the air billowing around me, tugging at my clothes, my shoulder blades tingling as if they wanted to break through my skin, as if I'd already hit the pavement and all my bones had shattered. The sky stretched out above me.

And then I felt those strong hands around my waist again, and instead of sky I was looking into dark eyes flecked with gold and, beyond those eyes, black wings spreading over us like a mantle. Like the blessed oblivion of sleep. I closed my eyes to fall into that darkness and was instead lifted into a blinding light.

3

I AWOKE INTO that light—light so bright that every time I tried to open my eyes I had to close them and I was pushed back down into the dark. . . .

Smoke-filled dark. I was back on the ninth floor of the Triangle Waist factory, trying to find my way out, but the smoke was so thick I couldn't see where I was going. Horrible shapes emerged out of the smoke: Esther Hochfield, holding her engagement ring up for me to admire, her hair on fire; little Etta flitting by like a bat, leathery wings stitched to her thin arms; a white, bloated face bobbing out of the smoke like a pickled egg that, horribly, I recognized as Tillie. I clutched her arm, relieved to find her no matter how awful she looked.

"Tillie!" I cried. She opened her mouth—I saw her lips forming my name—but a spume of smoke gushed out like lava from a volcano. It was pouring into my mouth, choking me . . .

I awoke into the light again, gagging on the smoke.

"Shall I administer more ether, Doctor?" someone said.

Blinking against the light, I saw figures hovering over me. One, dressed in white, blurred into the surrounding aura of light; the other was a dark shape, a looming figure like an elongated mushroom . . . or like a man in an Inverness cape. I screamed as he leaned over me, and struggled to get away, but my hands and feet were bound. The white-garbed figure leaned over me with something bell-shaped in her hand. As she fitted it over my mouth, a sickly sweet smell flooded my mouth and throat and I felt my tongue growing thick—like a bell's clapper muffled in wool gauze as church bells were muffled for a funeral toll. I was the bell and I was being muffled for all those who had died in the fire. For Esther Hochfield and Lucy Maltese and Jennie Stern and Tillie Kupermann. I heard their names as I sunk back into the dark.

And into the smoke, where the dead girls waited for me. They no longer ran, looking for a way out. They sat at their sewing machines, heads bowed over their work, hands smoothing white cotton even as the flames crept up their skirts and caught in their hair and the smoke rose from the baskets at their feet. The girl at the end of the row lifted her head up.

"The strike's been settled," she said. "If you want to keep your job you'd better get to work. We've saved a place for you." She nodded to an empty machine at the end of the table. I started walking toward it, down the long row of girls—a row far longer than any on the ninth floor of the Triangle Waist factory. This sewing table stretched on forever and seated hundreds of girls, all bent over their work. I had only to sit down beside them to take my place and I'd never have to worry again about rent money or having enough to eat or having to beg on the street. I'd have this job *forever*.

I tried to pull out the empty chair in front of the empty machine but found it was bolted to the floor. As I angled my body to fit into the narrow space I looked down at the girl at the next machine, at her hands busily feeding cloth into the bobbing needle . . . and saw with horror that the needle was moving in and out of her own flesh. I looked down the row and saw that all the girls were sewing their own flesh, binding themselves to this place forever. Their blood trickled down into the trough that ran along the middle of the table, merging into a stream that flowed to the end of the table where, his mouth open wide to catch the gory spill, sat the man in the Inverness cape.

I woke up screaming. The white-garbed figure was there with her bell, but I knocked it out of her hand.

"No!" I cried, my voice creaky, but audible at last. "That man is drinking their blood. He caused the fire. I saw him push Tillie off the roof. I would have died, too, but the winged boy caught me . . ."

Once my tongue had been loosed I couldn't stop talking. The nurse—of course that was what she was—called the doctor and he sat down beside my bed and wrote down what I had to say. I told him everything, from the first time I saw the man in the Inverness cape and heard the bells to when I saw him at the factory and my last glimpse of him on the roof when the dark-eyed boy sprouted wings to save me.

"You have to find him—the man in the Inverness cape, I mean, not the boy, although you should find him, too. He might know where to find the man."

The doctor—Dr. Pritchard, as he introduced himself—assured me that inquiries would be made, but that I must not worry. I was going someplace safe.

I felt a sharp prick in my arm and then a rush of warmth flooded my body. I could taste something sweet at the back of my throat that reminded me of my mother's green bottle, and then there was darkness. Smoke-free darkness. I was in the cool green pool I'd spied inside my mother's laudanum bottle.

When I awoke I was in a clean white room. I was no longer tied to the bed, but there were bars on the window and the door was locked. When the nurse came later, it took her several minutes to unlock all the locks. She wore a ring of keys affixed to a chain around her waist and a watch pinned to her starched white shirtwaist (I wondered if it came from the Triangle factory) and the words "Bellevue Pavilion for the Insane" stitched neatly across her breast, just above a nameplate that read "M. Rackstraw, R.N."

Nurse Rackstraw came three times a day with a tray of food and my medicine, her face as pinched and closed as an oyster. Once a day, Dr. Pritchard came with his notepad. He asked me questions about the bells I heard inside my head and the smoke-breathing man in the Inverness cape and the boy with wings. He told me that Tillie Kupermann had been identified among the dead. I had been found lying by her side on the pavement, unconscious but curiously unhurt. Someone had brought me to the hospital.

"Was it the winged boy?" I asked Dr. Pritchard, sniffing back tears at the thought of poor Tillie's broken body. "Or the man in the Inverness cape?"

"The man who breathed smoke out of his mouth?" Dr. Pritchard asked, looking up from his notes. When I said yes he wrote something down and asked Nurse Rackstraw to give me my medicine. As I sank into the green pool I heard him say, "We'll try water therapy to see if the delusions stop."

Water therapy sounded more pleasant than it was. Some time later—I'd lost track of days—two stout, muscular women walked me to a tiled room. They stripped off my nightgown and left me standing naked in the middle of the cold floor as Nurse Rackstraw ordered one of them to aim a canvas hose at me while the other one turned an iron wheel. A geyser of ice-cold water struck me so hard I fell to the floor, where I crouched, covering my head against the relentless wall of water. The pummeling went on so long I must have lost consciousness. I awoke in my bed, hair soaked, wrists and ankles tied again. Dr. Pritchard was there with his notebook.

"So tell me more about the man in the Inverness cape."

"There was no man in an Inverness cape," I said through chattering teeth.

Dr. Pritchard looked up from his notes. "You mean you imagined him?"

I nodded.

"Then why were you hiding under the table when the fire broke out? And why didn't you get out right away?"

"There was less smoke near the floor," I said. "And the Washington Place door was locked."

Dr. Pritchard shook his head sadly. He had pale green eyes, the same color as the green pool, thin sandy-colored hair straggling across his egg-shaped scalp, and yellowish fingernails. "Mr. Blanck and Mr. Harris have told the papers that it wasn't."

"I'm sure it was locked," I said, trying to keep my voice calm.

"You're sure the door was locked but you're not sure whether you saw a man in an Inverness cape? What about the boy with the wings?"

"It was a blanket!" I cried. "He put a blanket over our heads to shield us from the fire. I only imagined the wings when I was falling."

"But, Miss Hall, if you imagined the wings when you were falling, how did you survive the fall?"

I had no answer for that. Dr. Pritchard gave me another sad look and wrote a note in his book. As he was leaving I overheard him telling Nurse Rackstraw to increase my dosage. "I'm afraid she's begun to dissemble. We may have to move her to another facility, and since she appears to have no living relative it will have to be the state hospital for the insane."

The words struck a chill in my heart colder than the icy water in the hydrotherapy room. *The madhouse.* I'd heard my mother talking about such places. She'd made me promise not ever to let her be taken there.

But who would keep *me* from ending up there?

I tried from then on to answer Dr. Pritchard's questions as best—and as *sanely*—as I could, but the increased dosage of medicine made my brain so foggy it was harder to concentrate. I'd fall asleep for a moment and wake up to Dr. Pritchard saying, "So the bells started the first time you saw the caped figure?" or "The winged boy called the crows *tenebrae*?" I began to doubt everything I remembered. If the dark-eyed boy didn't really have wings, did he even exist? If he did exist, had he saved me or was he working for the man in the Inverness cape? Because if he had saved me, why would he have let me end up here?

No matter how hard I tried to keep the delusions to myself they bubbled out of my mouth. No matter how hard I tried to convince Dr. Pritchard that I didn't believe the things I'd seen in the fire—the wings, the crows, the smoke coming out of the man's mouth—I *did* believe that all those things had happened. Worse, I was *still* seeing things. I saw wisps of smoke lurking in the corners of my room and writhing against the glass panes of the window. I probably did belong in a madhouse.

One day—I'd lost all track of time and my only window faced a brick wall, giving me no sense of the season—Dr. Pritchard came to see me with a smile on his face. For a moment I thought he'd decided I wasn't insane and was going to let me out.

"I have good news," he said. "I've found a benefactor for you."

A benefactor? Could it be my grandmother, whom my mother had always refused to turn to? They'd never spoken during my lifetime, but my mother had never said anything really bad about her. I was willing to forgive my grandmother almost anything if she'd get me out of here.

". . . he's willing to pay for you to go to a private institution," Dr. Pritchard was saying.

He? Could it be my father? I'd always assumed my father was dead, but perhaps my mother had been keeping him from me. And what did Dr. Pritchard mean by a private institution? Could he mean Blythewood?

". . . he just wants to have a word with you to determine the best course of action."

"Now?" I asked as Dr. Pritchard signaled to Nurse Rackstraw to open the door. Frantically, I tried to smooth my hair down with my one untied hand. If I looked like a madwoman I'd be sent to a madhouse. I smoothed the front of my coarse gown and tried to sit up, willing my heart to stop beating so loudly.

Only it wasn't my heart. It was the bell. The deep bass bell tolling a death knell in my head. *Not now!* I silently pleaded. *Don't let me start raving about bells now. I need to at least* appear *sane.*

The door opened. I closed my eyes for a moment, willing the bell away. I'd been able to slow it when I needed to calm Etta. Shouldn't I be able to do it for myself now? But the bell clanged away like a fire engine. I would just have to ignore it. I opened my eyes . . .

And looked into the swirling smoke-filled eyes of the man in the Inverness cape.

I screamed and kept screaming while Dr. Pritchard held me down and Nurse Rackstraw jabbed a needle in my arm, all while the man in the Inverness cape loomed over me, a smile parting his lips and smoke trailing out of them like a fat, black slug. The smoke slug slithered across the floor toward me.

"What a shame!" the man said in an oily, unctuous voice. "I'd hoped she could be rehabilitated. I'm afraid it will have to be the insane asylum for her." As I began to slide down into the green pool, I saw the smoke slug snaking up onto my bed, twining around my arm, sniffing its way to the needle marks in the crook of my arm, trying to find a way in. . . .

When I woke up next the room was filled with smoke. I blinked, and the smoke dispersed into the murky gray light of dawn. The man was gone. In his place was a gangly, long-limbed blue wading bird standing in front of the gray square of the window. Black shapes writhed against the windowpanes—the smoke-things trying to get inside—but the blue bird raised a talon to the window and inscribed a shape on the glass. The smoke-things fled, vanishing into the gray dawn.

They were right. I *was* insane. Anyone who saw giant blue birds and smoke monsters belonged in the madhouse. But then the feathered creature turned and resolved itself into a slim woman in a snug blue suit and straw hat crowned by a long blue ostrich plume. As she came toward me I saw that her face was enormously freckled.

"Ava?" she asked, leaning over me. A red curl escaped the brim of her hat. It reminded me of Tillie. Blinking back tears, I asked, "Are you my guardian angel?"

She laughed. It was the first time I'd heard laughter since the morning of the fire. "In a manner of speaking," she replied. "My name is Agnes Moorhen. I am personal secretary to Mrs. Throckmorton van Rhys Hall. Your grandmother," she added when I failed to react to the name. "I am here to get you out of this place."

"Are you taking me to the insane asylum?" I asked.

She clucked her tongue. "Of course not! You're no more mad than anyone would be after being locked up in this infernal place for five months!"

"Five months! I've been here for five months?" The thought made me dizzy. I knew that between the drugs and dreams I'd lost track of time, but to have lost five months of my life to delirium and delusion felt like having a limb lopped off.

Miss Moorhen's eyes widened. "I'm afraid so. We've been looking for you since the fire—well, since *before* the fire, actually."

So my grandmother *had* been looking for me. Had she sent the man in the Inverness cape after me? But I didn't want to ask Miss Moorhen lest she change her mind and decide I *was* mad.

"But you've been well hidden." She looked back at the window—where the smoke-things had been—but I wasn't going to ask her about those either. When she turned back to me I saw that her eyes were wet but her jaw was firm. "There's no use crying over spilt milk. Let's get you out of here. The first thing to do is get you dressed. Here . . ." She picked up a capacious carpetbag from the floor and put it on the bed. She pulled out of it a clean white chemise, a dark skirt, and a white shirt-waist. The sight of the crisp white cotton reminded me of the dream of the dead girls sewing their hands. I shook my head to clear away the image.

"Oh my," Miss Moorhen said, noticing my restraints for the first time, "let me untie these . . ." Her voice faltered when her cool fingers touched the rope burns on my wrists. "What monsters! The board of directors will be receiving a strongly worded letter from me, I can tell you that! And I will have a word with my friend at the *World* . . ."

She kept up a stream of invective, listing all the newspapers and agencies she would notify of my mistreatment as she untied my restraints. When she was done she handed me the clothes and turned to the window to give me privacy. After months of being handled like a piece of meat, the gesture brought tears to my eyes, but I bit the inside of my cheek to keep them from falling and stripped the coarse nightgown off and put on the fine clothes she'd brought. They were a little too big for me, but the crisp, clean cloth felt like cool water on my skin.

When I slid my bare feet onto the floor, she turned and looked at me. "There!" she said, dashing a tear from her cheek. "You look just like Evangeline in those. I knew they'd fit."

"You knew my mother . . . ?" I began to ask, but the sound of the door creaking open interrupted me. Nurse Rackstraw stood framed in the doorway, her thin-lipped mouth a round O.

"Who are you?" she demanded. "And how did you get in here?"

Miss Moorhen squared her shoulders and tilted her chin up, the feather on her hat quivering like the crest on a warrior's helmet. "I am Miss Agnes Moorhen, personal secretary to Mrs. Throckmorton van Rhys Hall, grandmother and legal guardian to this woefully mistreated child. Who are you?"

Nurse Rackstraw opened her mouth but, without saying a word, fled. We heard her calling for Dr. Pritchard as she ran down the hall. Miss Moorhen sniffed and withdrew a pair of boots and stockings from her bag. "You'd better put these on so there's no delay," she said.

I hurriedly pulled on stockings and boots, my hands shaking. What if Dr. Pritchard wouldn't let me go? What could one woman—even one as clearly forceful as Miss Moorhen—do against a man of authority?

Doctor Pritchard returned with Nurse Rackstraw as I was tying my laces. His eyes flicked from me to Miss Moorhen standing at the window with her carpetbag in one hand.

"I don't know how you got in here, young lady," he boomed at Miss Moorhen, "but I know how you are going out. I have called the guards—"

"And I have called the police, sir. They will be curious to know why you are holding Miss Hall without notifying her grandmother. Here is a copy of the writ of complaint Mrs. Hall's lawyer has drawn up against you"—Miss Moorhen withdrew a sheaf of papers from her bag—"and forms releasing Miss Hall into my custody. Mrs. Hall's lawyer and two employees of the Pinkerton Detective Agency are waiting for me outside in Mrs. Hall's automobile. They have instructions to go straight to the mayor's office in . . ." Miss Moorhen withdrew a pocket watch from her vest pocket. "Ten minutes, if I have not exited the premises with Miss Hall."

Dr. Pritchard's light green eyes bulged and a vein at his temple throbbed. "In my expert medical opinion it is dangerous to remove this patient from care at this time—"

"Oh," Miss Moorhen chirped. "Is that the same medical opinion that kept a sixteen-year-old girl drugged and bound for five months? No, I don't believe we will be requiring *your* medical advice anymore, Dr. Pritchard. Now, if you will please step out of the way, Miss Hall and I will be going."

Dr. Pritchard's hands curled into fists. The bass bell inside my head rang once. I got ready to hurl myself at him should he attempt to throttle Miss Moorhen, but then his hands went limp and he let out a breath. He smiled and stepped to one side, bowing and waving his arm in the air toward the door. He looked at me.

"You are, of course, free to go, Miss Hall. I wish you luck in your new home. But remember, if you ever require my services again, I will be here waiting for you."

He smiled at me, and a thin wisp of smoke dribbled out of his mouth. I shuddered at the sight, but forced my eyes away from him and focused on Miss Moorhen.

"I'm ready to go," I said. She linked her arm through mine and together we walked out of the Bellevue Pavilion for the Insane.

4

AS MISS MOORHEN had promised, there was an automobile waiting for us just outside the massive iron gates of Bellevue—a long sleek silvery automobile with a figure of a winged woman at its prow—but it wasn't full of Pinkerton detectives. A uniformed driver sat at the wheel, and a nervous-looking young man in a rumpled linen suit paced in front of the car, raking his hands through his hair and muttering to himself.

When he saw us coming out of the gates he rushed toward us, looking as though he were going to fling his arms around Miss Moorhen, but then satisfied his urges by flapping his arms up in the air once and grabbing the ends of his hair. The hair and plain, homely face looked familiar. It was the law student who had flirted with Tillie the morning of the fire.

"Another thirty seconds and I was going to call the police," he told Miss Moorhen. "I thought you'd been swallowed up by that damned place."

"We very nearly were, Mr. Greenfeder," Miss Moorhen said, casting a look back over her shoulder and shuddering. It was the first sign she'd shown that she was afraid, and it made me afraid, too. I looked back at the great hulking mass of the hospital and noticed that the sky above it was filled with crows. One landed on the iron gates and cawed at us.

"Let's get going before they change their minds and come after us," Miss Moorhen said.

Mr. Greenfeder opened the door for us and we climbed into the plush interior of the automobile—the first one I'd ever been inside. Mr. Greenfeder sat on a jump seat across from us and spent the first few minutes of the drive anxiously peering out the back window. As did Miss Moorhen. I looked back and saw the lone crow on the gate flap back toward the hospital.

After we'd turned west on Twenty-Ninth Street, Miss Moorhen and Mr. Greenfeder settled back in their seats and switched their attentive gazes to me.

"Well!" Mr. Greenfeder slapped his knees with his hands. "We found you at last! It's been quite the Herculean task!"

"Yes," Miss Moorhen agreed. "I'd never have succeeded without your help, Mr. Greenfeder, and without your assurances that she was alive." Turning to me, she said, "You see, your name was listed with the dead. That is how it first came to your grandmother's attention that you were at the Triangle Waist factory on the day of the fire. Imagine our grief, to be looking for you for so long only to think we had lost you in such a horrible tragedy. Mrs. Hall sent me down to the piers where the bodies had been laid out for identification."

Miss Moorhen shuddered, the feather on her hat trembling. "If I live to be a hundred I will never forget what I saw there. All those poor souls burnt or smashed to death—some no more than children! All victims to the rapacious greed and neglect of Misters Blanck and Harris."

"You blame the owners for the fire?" I asked.

"Not for starting it. They think it was a cutter carelessly tossing a cigarette into the scrap pile, but if there'd been an alarm system and the new water sprinklers the fire would have been put out. If the door hadn't been locked and there had been an adequate fire escape most of the victims would have lived." Miss Moorhen shook her head again.

"They will stand trial for their conduct," Mr. Greenfeder assured her. "They have been arraigned and charged with six counts of manslaughter."

"We shall see," Miss Moorhen said. "Men like them often manage to evade their fates because of their money and their influence."

"The law will hold them accountable," Mr. Greenfeder countered. "I'm sure of it."

Miss Moorhen held up a gloved hand. "Dearest Samuel, your faith in the law is admirable, exceeded only by your zeal to discover the truth." She turned to me. "It was his insistence that the body identified as Avaline Hall was not yours that led us here today. I found him mourning beside the body of your friend, Miss Kupermann, which lay next to the poor unfortunate who had been identified as Avaline Hall. He told me that he had seen Miss Kupermann's friend Ava the morning of the fire and that you were wearing a navy skirt, not black, and that your hair was chestnut, not brown. Remembering the color of your mother's hair, I believed him."

"*That's* the reason you believed me?" Mr. Greenfeder asked, aghast.

Miss Moorhen smiled. "That and your obvious powers of

observation. His description of the fire was so detailed and thorough, despite the obvious emotional impact it had had on him, that I felt sure he was right that the body in question had been misidentified. Also, he said that he had seen you on the pavement unconscious but unhurt after your fall. Though he could not explain how you could have fallen ten stories without injuring yourself."

I swallowed and waited anxiously for what would surely come next. Would they ask me to explain how I had survived? How could I do that without mentioning the boy with the wings?

"I do have a theory about that," Mr. Greenfeder said, holding up one finger as if proving a point before a jury. "When the ladder broke it swung against the side of the law building. The last thing I saw before being overcome by a gust of smoke was that young bloke who had saved so many girls making a mad dash toward you through the air. I thought for sure he must have died in his attempt, but I didn't see him among the victims. I believe that when the ladder swung down against the law building you were thrown into a window and that the young fellow dived through that same window and then carried you down to the pavement. From there you must have been transported to the hospital—"

"Where of course we took up our inquiries right away. We checked all the local hospitals, including Bellevue, but no patient fitting your description was listed among the wounded."

"They kept me hidden," I said, anger replacing the craven fear I'd felt for so long. The thought that while Dr. Pritchard

CAROL GOODMAN   39

had been telling me that I had no living family, Miss Moorhen and Mr. Greenfeder had been searching for me turned my stomach. "But why?"

Miss Moorhen looked anxiously at Mr. Greenfeder and sighed. "We don't know," she admitted, "but perhaps you witnessed something that would be incriminating to Misters Blanck and Harris."

"The scoundrels!" Mr. Greenfeder exclaimed. "You can be sure that I will continue investigating the connections between the owners of the Triangle Waist factory and Dr. Pritchard. I won't rest until I find out why they held you against your will for so long."

"Thank you, Mr. Greenfeder," I said, tears springing to my eyes at the unaccustomed kindness. "And thank you for all you did the day of the fire. You and your friends were very brave."

"I only wish I could have saved your friend Miss Kupermann. She was the one who was brave." Mr. Greenfeder blushed, making him look suddenly very young, and glanced furtively at Miss Moorhen, who in turn blushed and looked out the window. Then he looked out the window, too, and clapped his hand to his forehead. "I forgot that I have to make an appearance in court. Could the driver let me off here?"

Miss Moorhen signaled to the driver to stop at the corner of Twenty-Ninth Street and Madison Avenue. As he was getting out I thought of a question.

"Mr. Greenfeder," I called. "The boy who saved all those girls—have you seen him since the fire?"

Mr. Greenfeder shook his head. "No, I've looked all over for him—even advertised in the papers so he could testify at the trial—but there's been no sign of him." He shook his head. "It's like he vanished into the smoke. Sometimes I think I imagined him." Then, with another furtive look at Miss Moorhen, he left.

I watched Miss Moorhen watch him go, a faraway, dreamy look in her eyes, which I suspected wasn't her habitual expression.

"What a nice man," I said as the car turned north on Madison Avenue.

"Oh! Mr. Greenfeder is a *fine* young man!" she declared as adamantly as if I'd said the opposite. "In the months since the fire he has been tireless in his efforts to promote regulations to prevent such a tragedy from ever occurring again—motivated, I believe, by his . . . er, *fondness* for your friend Tillie. She must have been quite extraordinary."

"Yes, she was . . ." I began. I wanted to tell her that while Tillie *was* extraordinary, I wasn't sure that she still held Mr. Greenfeder's heart—not after seeing the way he had looked at Miss Moorhen. But I didn't have a lot of experience telling girls that boys liked them, and before I could try it, Miss Moorhen shook herself briskly, like a bird shaking out wet feathers.

"But enough of Mr. Greenfeder! You'll want to know more about your situation, I imagine."

"My situation?"

"Yes. I hope you'll forgive me for speaking frankly, but I always find it's best to lay all one's cards on the table. Don't you?"

I swallowed and glanced nervously out the window. As we drove north the streets were decidedly less crowded than those downtown. "Fashionable people," I recalled my mother telling me, "flee the city during the hot summer months."

My mother had always known such things—what grand

hotels the rich visited in Europe, when the season began in New York, and which families were from "old money" and which were the nouveaux riches. I had always suspected that she came from a wealthy family, but the reality of entering one of the great mansions we were passing now on the wide deserted avenue—through the front door instead of the service entrance—was suddenly terrifying. What if my grandmother took one look at me and was so appalled by my disheveled appearance that she sent me back to the madhouse? It would be better to wind up on the streets.

"I don't expect anything from Mrs. Hall," I said, squaring my shoulders and lifting my chin. "Mother always said it was better to be a pauper than a slave to money."

"Evie was very proud," Miss Moorhen said fondly. "A trait she inherited from her mother, I'm afraid. The two of them fought after your mother was expelled from Blythewood."

"My mother was expelled?"

Miss Moorhen looked startled at my question. "I'm sorry. I didn't realize that you didn't know. Yes, your mother was expelled from Blythewood a month before her graduation. We were all shocked. No one ever knew why, but there were rumors that it had something to do with her going into the Blythe Wood, which was strictly off-limits. But it never made much sense to me that a girl of such accomplishments as Evangeline Hall would be expelled for such a trifling matter. Later, when I came to be employed by your grandmother and I learned that you had been born that following autumn . . ."

Her voice trailed off and I realized she was leaving me to reach my own conclusions. It took me a few moments to do so.

"Oh! You mean my mother was expelled because she was . . ." I searched through all the euphemisms but then heard my mother's voice telling me it was always better to use the correct word. "Pregnant with me?"

Miss Moorhen looked a little taken aback by my bluntness, but then patted my hand. "I want you to know I never thought any less of her for it. I'm sure she must have loved your father very much—whoever he was—and that there must have been a good reason why they couldn't marry." Her voice faltered when she saw my face color. "Oh my land, I'm sorry. I thought you knew. Evangeline was so forthright."

"I knew that my father had vanished before I was born, but I'd assumed . . ." My mother, who had been so frank about everything else, had never told me that she was not married. I wasn't sure what was more shocking—the fact itself or that my mother had kept it from me.

"Your mother was the most honorable woman I ever met," Miss Moorhen averred fiercely. "You must never be ashamed of her."

I shook my head, unable to explain that I wasn't ashamed of my mother. I was ashamed that I had been the cause of her expulsion from her beloved Blythewood. "And that's the reason she had been estranged from her mother?" I asked.

"I suppose so. Mrs. Hall will never speak of it, but I have watched her these last few years regret the pride that kept her separated from her only daughter. She was devastated when she heard of Evangeline's death and became obsessed with finding you. She's not so bad, Mrs. Hall. Only a bit lonely rattling around in that drafty mausoleum."

She gestured to a great glittering white sarcophagus that we had just pulled up in front of. It was one my mother and I had passed many times in the course of delivering hats to our wealthy clients, I realized, but not once had my mother given any hint that her own mother lived behind the spiked iron gate and ornately carved façade.

"And set in her ways—the *old* ways." Miss Moorhen's ears were twitching beneath the brim of her hat and her voice betrayed an edge of anger. I wondered what *the old ways* had ever done to her. She tucked a stray curl under her hat and gave me a level look.

"Part of the old ways is doing right by your blood relations. She'll do right by you . . . or she'll have my resignation."

I was so startled and touched by this fervid promise I wasn't sure what to say. "Thank you, Miss Moorhen . . ." I began.

"Call me Agnes," she said, squeezing my hand. "We working girls have to stick together, don't we?" Then she got out of the car and led the way up the marble steps between two marble bloodhounds. My skin prickled as I walked between them, as if they might pounce on me if I made a wrong move.

At the top of the stairs a footman in black, red, and white livery held the door for us. We crossed the threshold onto a floor inlaid with black and white diamond tiles. A grand staircase rose beyond to a landing with a stained-glass window depicting a classically robed woman drawing an arrow back in her bow: Diana at the hunt. *Well, at least all the stories Mother told me will come in handy,* I thought, noticing two more mythologically themed works of art in the foyer. A sculpture of another Diana—this one perfectly nude—stood at the center of a fountain. Her bow was aimed toward a second statue of a cowering boy being torn apart by wild dogs. The wild eyes of the boy looked up at me with an imploring expression that reminded me of someone. I stepped closer and saw that deer's antlers sprang from the boy's head.

"Actaeon," I said aloud, shocked by the brutality of the statue. "Diana punished him for seeing her naked and turned him into a deer. His own hunting hounds tore him apart." I recalled now where I'd seen that expression before—on the face of the dark-eyed boy when he looked up at the crows massing above the roof of the Triangle Waist factory.

"I see you've learned your mythology."

The voice, which came from beyond a set of open French doors, interrupted my thoughts. At a nod from Miss Moorhen, I passed through the doors into a long dim room. After the brightness of the foyer it took a moment for my eyes to adjust to the gloom, and then another moment to locate among the tapestry-covered divans, purple satin chairs, tables covered with bric-a-brac, statuary, stuffed birds, and enough palm trees to shade a desert oasis, the woman who had spoken.

It didn't help that she was entirely dressed in black, in a dress so fitted that she appeared to be armored. Nor that she was so still she might have been one of the ebony statues of Moorish servants that knelt on either side of the fireplace before which she sat. Only the slight motion of her chin that made her jet earrings tremble distinguished her from the décor.

"Here she is, Mrs. Hall," Agnes said, giving me a little shove with the tip of her umbrella. "Mr. Greenfeder was right. They were keeping her at Bellevue in a private ward."

I made my way toward Mrs. Hall—I couldn't quite think of her as my grandmother—my ankles wobbling on the thick carpet. Her eyes, which glittered as darkly as her jet beads, remained fixed on me. When I was a few feet away she raised one gloved hand, palm out, and motioned for me to stop. Then she lifted a lorgnette, which was attached to a long chain around her neck, to her eyes and looked me up and down.

"Are you sure you found the right girl, Miss Moorhen?" she asked in a lofty, imperious voice. "This one doesn't look a bit like Evie." At the mention of my mother's name her chin seemed to quiver the tiniest bit. "She's so . . . *thin*."

"I suspect they didn't feed her very well at Bellevue," Agnes, who had crept up silently behind me, replied tartly. "But I'm quite sure this is Evie's daughter. Look at her hair, Mrs. Hall. It's just like Evie's."

Agnes gave me another little push and I found myself inches from Mrs. Hall. She lifted a trembling hand toward my hair and fingered a lock that had come loose. Her mouth crumpled for a moment, then she looked up into my eyes. "Hm . . . it's duller than Evie's, but yes, I see the resemblance now. She certainly doesn't have Evangeline's figure. These clothes are hanging on her like rags."

"Do you want me to make an appointment with Miss Janeway?"

Mrs. Hall sniffed. "You might as well. She's too tall to fit into Evie's old things. Go on now," she ordered Agnes, who gave my hand a squeeze before she left the room. "Tell Carrie she must be fit in *immediately* so as to have suitable clothing for her interview."

My interview?

As Mrs. Hall looked back up at me, lorgnette poised on her long narrow nose, I took courage from Agnes's hand squeeze.

"Actually," I said, "I'm exactly the same height as my mother. She measured me on my birthday." The thought that it had been the last birthday I'd ever spend with my mother sapped all the courage out of me and froze my throat.

Mrs. Hall lowered her lorgnette and stared at me. "Well, perhaps it is I who have shrunk. You look like a giant looming there. Sit down before I strain my neck looking up at you."

She waved her lorgnette toward a footstool beside her feet. I sank down on it, next to the statue of the kneeling Moor whose eyes seemed to say, "Watch out or you'll end up like me, frozen for all eternity at Medusa's feet." The notion that all the statues in the room were live creatures petrified by my grandmother's glittering black gaze only increased my terror. What if I began raving about such notions to her? She'd think I belonged in the madhouse. Was that what the "interview" was for? Another insane asylum?

"Well," Mrs. Hall said after she had examined me thoroughly. "You haven't got Evie's beauty, but perhaps that's for the best. Have you had any education?"

I tried not to show that I minded being told I wasn't as beautiful as my mother. Of course I knew *that*. Instead of my mother's rich chestnut hair, mine was a paler, washed-out version. Instead of my mother's emerald-green eyes, mine were a murky hazel that shifted between gray blue and olive green as if they couldn't quite decide what color they wanted to be. Even the bones of my face were a little vague, lacking the sharpness of my mother's classical profile. But at least my mother had bequeathed me *something*.

"My mother taught me Latin and Greek, and we read books together and talked about them. She had a subscription to the Astor Library even though we could ill afford it, and we spent our spare time reading there, or in the Seward and Hudson Park branches of the New York Public Library . . ." My voice trailed off as I recalled the strange books that my mother would ask for, often causing the librarians to stare. But I didn't mention that to my grandmother.

"In the evenings while she trimmed hats I read aloud to her." I recalled my mother's slim white hands flitting deftly among the ribbons, beads, and feathers of her craft and felt a sudden pang when I realized that the box of her trimmings I'd kept after her death must be gone now. My landlady had no doubt sold it when she saw my name among the dead.

"But you've had no real schooling?"

"We moved too often for me to attend a regular school."

"No doubt to keep your whereabouts a secret from me. It wasn't until my detective saw your name listed among those who had died in the fire that I even knew you were in New York. Imagine, a granddaughter of mine working at a shirtwaist factory with common laborers!"

I bristled at this, thinking of Tillie and all the other girls I'd worked beside. "It was honest work," I said, "and the other girls I worked with weren't *common* at all. Some of them were quite extraordinary."

Mrs. Hall jerked her chin back, surprised as I was at my outburst, but then a faint smile appeared on her face. "Ah, I see you've caught the reformist fever. Just like Evie! I only meant that I would never have willingly let my daughter and grand-daughter live in poverty. Is that what your mother told you?"

"No, she never spoke of you at all," I said quickly—too quickly to think what effect my words would have on her. I watched as the color leached out of her cheeks and her lips thinned. She looked shrunken, suddenly, and as lifeless as the carved Moor at her feet.

"Well," she said at last, "well. I always did teach her that if one doesn't have something pleasant to say, one shouldn't say anything at all." She laughed a dry, bitter laugh. "So Evangeline did heed my advice about *something*. Did she speak of her past at all?"

"She spoke very fondly of Blythewood," I replied, wrack-ing my brain for some shred of comfort I could offer up. I had always assumed that it had been my grandmother who had sev-ered ties with my mother, not the other way around. I knew my mother could be sensitive—and proud. In recent years she'd become suspicious and fearful, and in the last few months of her life her eyes had taken on a hunted look. Perhaps the fault hadn't all been on my grandmother's side. And so I added, "I'm sure she was very grateful that you sent her there."

Her face froze as if she were Medusa, and Perseus had just held up his shield to freeze her with her own reflection. In the silence that followed even the carved Moor seemed to shrink lower into his crouch, and the ormolu clock on the mantel seemed to miss a beat.

"If she had been truly grateful," Mrs. Hall said at last, speaking through a clenched jaw, "she wouldn't have disgraced me by leaving as she did." She lifted her lorgnette, regarding me through its crystal lenses as if I were a rare species of insect. "Perhaps you shall do better there. But we shall speak of that later."

She raised her gloved hand, palm out, as she had before, to forestall the questions bubbling up inside me. "Here's Agnes, come to show you to your room. Let us hope you are right about being the same height as your mother so you'll find something in her closet to wear—and let us hope it is the *only* trait you have in common with her."

❋ ⟶ ✦ ⟵ ❋

I left the drawing room feeling as though I had been drained of every ounce of vitality. Agnes steered me up the grand staircase and down a long hall lined with portraits of stern-looking men and women who glared at me with disapproval.

The room we entered woke me up. Unlike the dim and cluttered drawing room, this one was light and airy, its walls papered in a yellow floral print, the furniture and bedstead painted white, the windows lightly swathed in white lace and open to an interior courtyard with a pretty garden. A book lay open on the window seat as if its reader had just lately left the room. I picked it up and saw it was open to Tennyson's "The Lady of Shalott," my mother's favorite poem.

"Mrs. Hall kept the room just as Evangeline left it," Agnes said, picking up a framed photograph from a grouping of many on the desk.

I looked at the photographs. Girls in white shirtwaists, long dark skirts, and straw boaters frolicked around a maypole, wielded hockey sticks, drew bows, or posed like Greek statues in a garden, all of it like something out of Mrs. Moore's girls'-school books. I picked out my mother because she was the tallest in every group, but I wouldn't have recognized her carefree expression otherwise. In one she stood arm in arm with a blonde girl below an arched doorway engraved with the words "Blythewood Academy—*Tintinna vere, specta alte.*"

Ring true, aim high. It was Blythewood's motto, which my mother had often quoted to me.

I noticed a box sitting atop the dresser. Looking into it, I saw it contained books, ribbons, a blue-and-white willow-pattern teacup, an untrimmed straw hat, feathers—a long black feather among them—and a familiar-looking green bottle.

"I got your address from the Triangle Company and went to your lodgings," Agnes said. "I hope you don't mind that I took the liberty of collecting your . . . things. Some of them looked like mementos of your mother. I thought you'd want them."

I held up the green bottle. It looked wrong in this yellow-and-white room. How had the girl who grew up here ever ended up as the woman who drank from it?

I looked around the room. A pink-and-gray pennant hung above the bed. A bow and quiver of arrows leaned against the bureau. Bronze trophies for archery, Latin, falconry, and "bell ringing" lined the bookshelves. Everything in the room referred somehow to Blythewood.

"Mrs. Hall mentioned an interview," I said, almost too afraid to ask the question. "Did she mean . . . ?"

"An interview for Blythewood," Agnes replied. "Now that you're sixteen you're just the right age. The interview is in three days. You'd better get some rest. The next few days are going to be trying. We have a lot of work to do to get you ready."

I breathed out a sigh of relief that the interview wasn't for an insane asylum, but then, looking at the pictures of happy, smiling girls, I wondered if the gulf between them and me wasn't even wider than the one between the girl who had grown up here and the woman who'd died drinking laudanum. A gulf far too wide to bridge in three days.

5

AGNES WAS RIGHT about the next few days being trying. I felt as if I were trying out for a part—and one I wasn't even sure I wanted. It had always been my dream to go to my mother's alma mater, but without her here to see me realize that dream, going there seemed cruelly ironic. And while the pictures of frolicking girls certainly made the place look like fun, when I studied those girls—as I did closely for the next few days—I saw the cosseted daughters of wealthy families. It wasn't their dress, which seemed to be some sort of uniform, but their carefree expressions. Even though Agnes assured me that Blythewood was a finishing school for girls ages sixteen to nineteen, the girls in the pictures looked younger to me. I couldn't imagine any of these girls working in a factory or delivering a hat by the back door or explaining to the landlady that the rent was late again. How would I, with my work-coarsened hands and haphazard schooling, ever hope to fit in?

Even at the dressmakers' I felt as though I were being measured for more than a wardrobe. Miss Janeway's establishment was a small first-floor shop off of Stuyvesant Square with elaborately feathered hats displayed on wire forms in the window, and white paneled cabinets, mirrors, and robin's-egg-blue hangings and carpet in the discreet showroom. I could hear the hum of sewing machines and women's voices coming from a workroom in the basement, a sound so familiar from my days at the Triangle Waist Company that I felt a pang for those lost girls.

But this was a very different sort of place from the Triangle. It was exactly the kind of smart establishment my mother sometimes dreamed of running, but I was surprised that Mrs. Hall didn't patronize one of the more glamorous French dressmakers.

"All the Blythewood women use Miss Janeway," Agnes explained in a whisper as a shop girl escorted us into the dressing room. "Caroline Janeway went to Blythewood on a scholarship, as I did, and she still practices the old ways—at least when it comes to clothes," she added, her lips quirking.

The *old ways* again. What did that mean in a dress shop? I wondered. Was I going to be outfitted in leg-o'-mutton sleeves and stiff crinolines? I was expecting an antiquated fossil, but Miss Janeway turned out to be quite young and pretty. She wore a crisp white smock, a slim gray skirt, and a red beret pinned jauntily over her smooth dark hair. When Agnes introduced me to her, Miss Janeway held out her hand and shook mine briskly, then folded it in both of hers.

"I was very sorry to hear about your mother, Miss Hall. Evangeline was a legend at Blythewood. I'll make you a dress to do her proud—I think a French blue tea dress with white lace trim for the interview, don't you, Agnes?" She snapped her fingers and a shopgirl appeared with a little gold notepad affixed to a chain around her neck, identical to the one that hung from Miss Janeway's neck.

"Mabel, check that we have enough of the white feather-patterned lace and the French blue serge. I heard you worked at the Triangle Waist Company, Miss Hall," she added, as though it were an afterthought.

"I did," I said, holding my chin up, determined not to be embarrassed. "I was a sleeve fitter."

"A difficult job," Miss Janeway said, making a note in her little book and turning to Agnes. "Shall we also make three Blythewood skirts and matching shirtwaists with the Bell and Feather?"

"Leave off the Bell and Feather for now," Agnes said.

"Of course, we can add the insignia in a trice. You know, Miss Hall, I worked as a seamstress in a factory before I went to Blythewood," she said, leading me toward a raised platform in front of a set of triple mirrors and unceremoniously helping me strip off my dress down to my loose cotton chemise.

"Really?" I asked, encouraged that someone from my own background had made the transformation to Blythewood.

"Yes," she replied, a smile quirking her lips. "Not *all* of us Blythewood girls come from the four hundred. I remember only too well the dreadful conditions in the factory, the long hours with no breaks, the stifling heat, the humiliating searches at the end of the day. When I think of those poor girls locked in, unable to escape the fire, forced to jump from the windows . . . Well, it makes me so angry I could spit! And how many women among us are forced every day to make such horrible choices?

Without the power to determine our own fates we are like those poor girls, choosing between fire and the street, which is really no choice at all, now is it?" She looked up at me and I realized she was waiting for an answer.

"I thought the same thing," I said softly, my voice quavering, "when I saw the girls jumping . . . that they were like butterflies trapped between panes of glass."

"*Exactly*, Miss Hall," she said with shining eyes, "butterflies trapped between panes of glass. I couldn't have said it better myself. It's high time we broke that glass, don't you think?" Then she turned to Agnes. "You're right, Aggie, she has the fire in her. She'll make a fine Blythewood girl. Maybe she'll shake things up a bit there. The bells know the old place needs it." She snapped her fingers and another shopgirl appeared with a measuring tape and began taking my measurements.

"You'll scare Ava with your radical talk, Carrie," Agnes said. "She hasn't even gotten through her interview yet."

"Nonsense," Miss Janeway said briskly. "A girl who's survived the Triangle fire won't scare easily. And it's time things changed. If we continue adhering to the old ways simply because of tradition we will end up preserved like old Euphorbia Frost's specimens behind glass, as Miss Hall has so aptly put it."

I started to object that I hadn't been talking about Blythewood, but Agnes was heatedly replying. I had a feeling that this was an argument that the two women had had before.

"You know I want the same things you do, Carrie, but I believe we have to work from the *inside*. These things take time. Violent measures will not win our cause. We must be patient."

Were they talking about the vote for women? I'd heard such debates between Tillie's friends, some advocating the rock-throwing violent measures that the British suffragettes had adopted, others maintaining that peaceful, decorous protest was the best way to persuade the men in power to give women the vote.

"How can we be patient when so much is at stake?" Miss Janeway objected. "Have you heard about—"

Glancing down I intercepted Agnes giving Miss Janeway a warning glance. "Perhaps we should discuss this later," she said, sliding her eyes from Miss Janeway back to me.

"Of course," Miss Janeway said, "you're right as always, Aggie. Now, what do you think about an archer's costume?"

"But I don't know how to shoot arrows!" I pointed out, distracted from their argument by the idea that I might be expected to shoot arrows at my interview.

"You'll learn, my dear," Miss Janeway said, snatching the tape measure away from her assistant and stretching it across my back. "You've got the shoulders for it and"—she stretched out my right arm to the side—"the arms." Leaving my arm extended midair she pulled back my left shoulder with one hand and turned my chin to the right. "There! You have the natural stance of an archer."

Out of the corner of my eye I stole a look at myself in the triple mirror. Three Avaline Halls drew three invisible bows. In my loose white chemise I looked like the statue of Diana in my grandmother's foyer. I looked, I dared think for a moment, like a Blythewood girl. I could see from the expressions on Agnes's and Miss Janeway's faces that they thought the same. All their disagreements seemed to vanish, replaced by fond memories of their school days.

I began to turn to them to share Agnes's triumphant smile, but a movement in the mirror drew my attention back to its reflective surface. A blur of wings, as of a black bird flying through the dressing room, passed over each of the three panes and then vanished. I whirled around, nearly knocking over the shopgirl still taking my measurements, to see where the bird had gone.

The only feathered creature in the dressing room was Agnes's plumed hat, which bobbed as she bent over a pattern book with Miss Janeway. But that feather was white. The black bird had been as much an illusion as the image of myself as brave hunter and Blythewood girl.

⤞ ✦ ⤝

Before we left her establishment, Miss Janeway and Agnes slipped into "the office" to settle the bill and, I suspected, finish in private whatever they'd been arguing about earlier. Perhaps they were discussing my chances of getting into Blythewood with such a checkered past. Even if Caroline Janeway had also been a factory girl, she probably didn't have a mother who drank laudanum.

We went from Miss Janeway's to Ladies' Mile, where we ordered a puzzling assortment of items, including a bow and quiver and set of arrows, a falconer's glove, and a hand bell. Many of the establishments we visited seemed to be owned by Blythewood alumnae, but Agnes was careful to squelch any conversation concerning *old ways* in my presence and contrived to have a private word with each of the Blythewood women before we left.

We spent the next two days "swotting" for my exam, as Agnes put it. We had the mansion to ourselves. My grandmother had been called upstate on a "delicate matter."

"But I leave you in capable hands. I am sure you will acquit yourself as befits a Hall."

The last bit sounded more like a threat than a hope. She was right about Agnes, though. She drilled me in Latin declensions, historical dates, passages of English literature, and, most curiously, collective nouns. My mother had had a fondness for these that I had always thought strange, and now it turned out that they were part of the Blythewood tradition.

"It's part of the archery program," Agnes said vaguely. "Ladies are expected to attend the hunt. Thank goodness that Evangeline taught them to you."

"I don't see how knowing the collective noun for *badgers* is going to make me fit in at Blythewood," I said the morning of the interview as Agnes gave me a last-minute drilling over breakfast. "Perhaps Miss Janeway would consider taking me on as an apprentice?" I'd been thinking since our visit to Miss Janeway's that I'd feel more at home among the girls at their sewing machines than on the archery fields and in the tearooms of Blythewood.

Agnes frowned with disapproval.

"I *can* sew," I said defensively. "My mother taught me that. Not everything she taught me was useless. She just somehow neglected archery."

Agnes reached across a platter of kippers and squeezed my hand, her kind, honest face stricken. "Oh, Ava, it's not that Miss Janeway wouldn't have you, it's that you're destined for so much more!"

"I hope I'll never think myself better than a dressmaker . . . or secretary," I added, sneaking a look at Agnes, who smiled at the inclusion of her profession. "Is it really so important I go to Blythewood? Do I have to go? From how you and Miss Janeway were talking it sounded like not everyone is entirely happy with the school."

"We shouldn't have been arguing about those things in front of you. Please don't tell your grandmother—or the admissions board—that I said anything against the school."

"Of course not," I assured Agnes, surprised and alarmed to see her so rattled. "But if Blythewood is so mired in tradition, will they really accept a girl who's worked for a living—"

"Blythewood does not disapprove of work," Agnes cut in, her freckles standing out on her face as they did when she was angry. "We're all encouraged to find our proper role in the world—whether as the wife of an earl or a dressmaker or a secretary. We all serve Blythewood in our own way."

"Even a woman who bore a child out of wedlock and took her own life?" I asked, my voice trembling. "That's what you've been talking about with all those women, isn't it? Whether Blythewood will take me after my mother disgraced herself. Well, maybe I don't want to go to a place that wouldn't have my mother." I didn't know that I felt that way until the words were out of my mouth.

"Oh," Agnes said, her mouth a round O and her eyes wide.

"My dear, that's not what we've been talking about at all! There are other things happening at the school which I'm not at liberty to tell you. I'd never gossip about your mother behind your back like that. It's perfectly natural for you to feel aggrieved on your mother's behalf. I don't blame you at all." She looked down, her brow knotted and her head bobbing as she silently mouthed something to herself, something she did, I'd noticed, when she was trying to work out a problem. Then with a final nod that whipped the feather in her hat to attention, she looked up and nudged her chair closer to mine.

"By George, if you don't want to go to Blythewood you shan't go! I won't let anyone make you, not even Mrs. Hall. If need be we can live with Carrie Janeway above the shop and we'll *all* trim hats for a living! Don't worry, Ava, you and I shall be great friends whether you go to Blythewood or not. That is, if you'll have me as a friend after I've behaved like a fool."

"I'd be honored to have you as a friend, but you haven't behaved like a fool."

"Yes, I have. I didn't even consider that you might not want to go to Blythewood after how they treated your mother. And I don't blame you. It wasn't fair. Other girls have . . . well, let's just say that other girls did far worse than Evangeline and weren't asked to leave. I've always thought that Evangeline must have said something to the Council that made them want to be rid of her or that she knew something that frightened them.

"You see, Blythewood is full of mysteries, and because of that, the Council thinks they have to keep us in the dark. Things can get . . . complicated. Rumors, whispering campaigns, even *factions*. But in the end we're all loyal to Blythewood and all the layers of traditions and secret rites that are slowly revealed to the new girl as she makes her way through her years there. I can't tell you them." She tapped her ring. "We all take an oath by the Bell and Feather not to reveal the secrets of Blythewood, nor do I know the very deepest secrets. Those are always reserved for the Dianas—the chosen girls. But I wonder if Evangeline learned something even beyond what the Dianas were told. And I suspect it was a secret that had something to do with your father."

"My father? Do you know . . . ?"

"No, I don't know who he was. I don't think Evangeline ever told anyone. But hasn't it occurred to you that your best way of finding out who he was—and why your mother was really expelled—lies in going there yourself?"

I didn't answer right away. The secret of my father's identity was one so long veiled in mystery I had long ago given up ever penetrating it. Whenever I had tried to ask my mother any question about him she looked so pained that I had learned to shy away from any reference to *fathers* at all.

"Do you really think I might learn who he was at Blythewood?" I asked at last.

"I think," Agnes said, gripping my hand tightly, "that if you put your mind to it you will be able to learn everything you need to know there."

I covered Agnes's freckled hand with mine and looked into her deep brown eyes. "What time is the interview, then?"

⇥ ✧ ⇤

The next morning I dressed in the French blue serge dress with inserts of white lace and matching hat and veil that Caroline

Janeway had made for me. Agnes escorted me to the Italian Renaissance palazzo on Forty-Second Street, not far from the new public library, which housed the Bell & Feather Club.

"A lot of Blythewood alumnae, including Mrs. Hall, belong to this club," Agnes told me at the doorway. "The selection committee conducts their interviews in the Oak Library on the second floor. The secretary at the front desk will be able to direct you to it."

"You're not coming in?" I asked, suddenly feeling frightened.

She shook her head. "I'm not a member. But here, I know what will help." She reached into her pocket and took out the black feather that had belonged to my mother. She ran her fingers along the long curved vane of the black plume so that it gleamed in the sunlight and then tucked it into my hat. "You saved this for a reason—I imagine because it reminds you of your mother. Think of how proud she would be of you today."

I thanked Agnes and gave her a brave smile. When I turned to go in I felt a breeze tug at the feather, lifting my chin, which *did* make me feel braver. But as I turned to enter the building, I thought of how I'd found the black feather beside my mother's lifeless body and wished that Agnes had chosen something else to remind me of her.

⇥ ✦ ⇤

I stepped into an elegant entrance hall paved in pink marble, the walls painted a soothing dove gray. An elaborate gilt-edged desk stood opposite the front door, behind which sat a Chinese man in a gold silk embroidered jacket. I crossed the foyer toward him, holding my head up high, and explained why I had come. He bowed and, without a word, got up and motioned that I should follow him up the curving staircase. I did, staring at the long braid that hung down his back and marveling at how little sound his feet, appareled in thick sandals, made on the marble steps. Halfway up the stairs, I switched my attention from him to the oil portraits of stern-looking women that lined the staircase.

"Is the Bell & Feather only for women?" I asked when we reached the top.

But he only bowed again and opened a heavy wooden door that was labeled "The Oak Library." I stepped through the doorway and gasped. The room, which must have taken up the entire second floor of the palazzo and was three stories high, was lined with books. Brass balconies ran around the second and third stories allowing access to the upper levels of books. I was immediately drawn to the shelves and to the gilt titles stamped on old leather bindings.

Travels to Faerie and Back Again, Arbarrati's Atlas of Other Worlds, The Great Sky Castle of Doctor Ashe—each title was more alluring and fanciful than the next. Were the members of the Bell & Feather fans of the scientific romance made popular by Mr. Jules Verne and Mr. H. G. Wells?

"Ahem."

The sound of someone rather exaggeratedly clearing her throat drew my attention away from the books. I turned, feeling the feather in my hat snap at the movement, reminding me to lift my chin, which was good because I might otherwise have cowered at the sight before me. At the far end of the library was a long black-and-gilt table, behind which roosted a murder of crows.

I blinked, and the giant crows resolved themselves into three women in black attire. The impression of crows came from their hats, which sported not just a few black feathers but the bodies of entire birds, their preserved heads peering over the hat brims with hard, glittering eyes.

The woman seated in the middle cleared her throat. "While we admire your enthusiasm for the written word, the Council does not have all day. We have other interviews to conduct. Many young ladies are eager to attend Blythewood, though few are chosen."

I started forward with lowered eyes until the feather tugged my chin up and I found six sets of eyes on me—those of the women and those of the birds atop their hats. I wasn't sure which were more intimidating. The women wore dresses that might have been in style at the turn of the last century: stiff, glossy black silk encrusted with lace, embroidery, and beading. Were they all in mourning, I wondered, perhaps for the same lost relative? They looked, with their pale skin, light-colored eyes, and silver hair, as if they might be related; only the woman in the center was larger and more formidable than the two women flanking her.

As I got closer I noticed a fourth woman sitting in a chair to the right of the table. She was younger, blonde, and dressed in a navy-blue suit and a flat tricornered hat trimmed with yellow feathers. When I looked in her direction she smiled at me and then looked down at the notebook in her lap. Perhaps she was a secretary. Her smile gave me courage. I looked back at the triumvirate of crows. The middle one indicated I should sit in the low straight-back chair in front of the table.

"Avaline Hall?" she asked, looking down at a sheet of paper before her.

"Yes," I said, "only I go by Ava—"

"Here you will go by your correct name. I am Mrs. Ansonia van Hassel and these are my associates, Miss Lucretia Fisk . . ." The needle-nosed woman on the left slightly inclined her pointy chin. "And Miss Atalanta Jones." The woman on the right scowled at me. "Miss Vionetta Sharp, who has lately been hired to teach English at Blythewood, will be observing the proceeding and taking notes."

I glanced at the slim blonde in blue and received another shy smile.

"However, she will have no vote," Mrs. van Hassel added, glaring at poor Miss Sharp. "Together we three will decide if you are suitable for Blythewood. The school is most selective. Family legacy alone will not gain you admission, nor will consideration for your recent bereavement, although I personally would like to say that you have the Council's condolences for your loss."

The three women briefly bowed their heads, which left me looking into the hard beady eyes of the three crows atop their hats, who didn't look the least bit sorry that my mother had died.

"Now," Mrs. van Hassel said, "we will move on to the examination. At Blythewood we follow a rigorous regimen of classics and athletics. As you appear to be physically fit—"

"She's a bit thin," Mrs. Jones said with a hungry look in her eyes that suggested she might like me fattened up a bit before having me slaughtered for dinner.

"And pale," Miss Fisk added, tilting her head at me like a robin listening for worms in the ground.

"I'm sure she'll tone up with a regular regimen of archery and bell ringing," Mrs. van Hassel asserted. Clearly she was in charge here. She might even be the one to decide whether I went to Blythewood. "Would you like to ask the first question, Lucretia?"

Miss Fisk cleared her throat and asked me to conjugate the verb *incipio* in all tenses, moods, and voices. I took a deep breath and launched into the conjugation, grateful my mother had quizzed me on my Latin every day over tea. When I was done Mrs. van Hassel informed me that I had *slaughtered* the pluperfect subjunctive and instructed Miss Sharp to award me a seven out of ten. Then she asked me to recite the story of Niobe as given by Ovid. And so the examination went on, containing a great deal of Latin, Greek, mythology, English poetry, and etymology, including an entire section on collective nouns.

"An exaltation of larks. A parliament of owls. A cete of badgers," I responded, glad and surprised that my mother's strange fascination with "the language of the chase," as she'd referred to such terms, was finally coming in handy. As I answered each question successfully it came to me that she had spent my lifetime preparing me for this exam. Did that mean she had wanted me to attend Blythewood?

After I answered the last question, Mrs. van Hassel asked to see Miss Sharp's notebook. She ruffled through the pages, Miss Fisk and Miss Jones peering over her shoulders, their heads bobbing so that it seemed again as if the three crows were picking over my answers like seeds of grain.

"Not bad," Mrs. van Hassel concluded, handing the notebook back to Miss Sharp, "but there's more to being a Blythewood girl than intelligence and learning. There's character. Miss Sharp, would you mind stepping outside for a moment?"

Miss Sharp looked up from her notebook, an expression of surprise on her face that was immediately extinguished by what she saw in Mrs. van Hassel's face. She glanced at me and then quickly turned and knelt to gather some books that lay beside her chair on the floor. A sound drew my attention behind me. Only as I was turning did I realize that the sound came from inside my own head. It was the bass bell tolling danger. Were the three women in danger? But when I turned I found that they were no longer women.

Three enormous feathered creatures perched on the long black-and-gold table. As I watched, one of them spread its wings and launched itself at the tender white nape of Miss Sharp's neck. Without knowing I was going to, I leapt to my feet and threw myself between the bird and Miss Sharp. I heard the sound of wings thundering in my ears, felt the brush of feathers against my cheek and the scrape of talons on my wrist . . . and then I felt nothing but air. I stumbled into Miss Sharp, who looked up, surprised, and steadied me with her hand. I whirled around to face the creatures, but found the three women again, sitting sedately, their eyes coolly watching me.

"Excellent, Miss Hall. We think you will do very nicely at Blythewood. We'll expect you on campus tomorrow at noon sharp."

6

I WALKED OUT with Miss Sharp, whose calm demeanor suggested she had experienced nothing unusual in the library. Her open, cheerful countenance belied any suspicion of a subterfuge. Had I imagined the giant crow attacking her? Was I hallucinating as I had at Bellevue? The thought made me feel sick. I'd hoped those visions had been a result of the shock of the fire, the blow to my head from the fall, or the drugs Dr. Pritchard had given me. But if I were still hallucinating . . .

"Congratulations, Miss Hall," Miss Sharp said as we came down the stairs. "I'm sure you'll do very well at Blythewood. You have an admirable command of classics and mythology. Your mother taught you well. She would be very proud of you."

"It seems she was preparing me for that exam all along."

"Perhaps." Miss Sharp paused at the bottom of the stairs and turned to me, a troubled look on her smooth elegant features. Had she seen the crow attack after all? I wondered. "Or perhaps she was only sharing with you what she loved. At its best Blythewood instills a love of learning in its girls, and a wish to share that knowledge with others."

"You attended Blythewood?"

She smiled—a sad smile, I thought. "Most faculty are

alumnae. I did my bachelor's degree at Barnard College and I've been teaching at Miss Spence's school, but I've missed Blythewood terribly. I can't tell you how pleased I was to get this appointment. I'm afraid there is one flaw in Blythewood." She touched my arm and looked at me gravely. I wondered if she was going to tell me that the school was *mired in the old ways*, but instead she leaned closer and whispered, "It's so perfect that no place will ever measure up. You'll always long to go back."

⋺→ ✦ ←⋼

Agnes was waiting for me outside. When she saw Miss Sharp her face lit up.

"Vi!" she cried.

"Aggie!"

The two women threw their arms around each other and twirled around on the sidewalk, nearly colliding with a stout businessman in a bowler hat and eliciting disapproving looks from a clutch of ladies exiting a dressmaker's. They were oblivious, though, to anyone but each other—even to me—as they traded particulars of their lives since graduation. When Agnes learned that Vionetta Sharp would be teaching at Blythewood, she turned to me. "Now I haven't any reservations at all about you going, with Vi there to look after you. That is if . . ."

"She got in," Miss Sharp announced. "She did brilliantly on her exam."

"I knew she would," Agnes said, pulling one of her oversized hankies from her bag and dabbing her eyes. "Evangeline taught her well."

Both women were sobered by mention of my mother.

"I was very sorry to hear about your mother," Miss Sharp said gravely. "She was a few years ahead of me at school and I admired her greatly." I saw a shadow pass over her face and I wondered if she was thinking about the circumstances of her expulsion, but instead she said, "What I said earlier about Blythewood being so perfect that no other place would measure up—I didn't mean that we should just accept the way things have been done there forever. There are those of us who think there should be changes—especially after this most recent occurrence."

Agnes made a strangled sound and pulled Miss Sharp abruptly away. They bent their heads together and whispered while I stood a few feet away feeling foolish. After a few minutes they returned to me.

"I'm sorry, Ava," Agnes said, her face pale beneath her freckles. "Vionetta and I had a few . . . er . . . details to discuss about what you'll need for school."

"Yes," Miss Sharp concurred with a bright but brittle smile. "The place has changed so much since we went there . . . is still changing. . . . But I'm sorry to prattle on so when you must be exhausted after your exam. Congratulations again. I look forward to seeing you in my literature class. And you"—she turned to Agnes—"come visit! You can always stay at my aunts' house in town."

Then she took her leave of us, hurrying toward the Grand Central Station, while Agnes and I walked over to Fifth Avenue and turned north.

"I'm so pleased that Vionetta Sharp will be your teacher. She was top of our class, but never the least bit conceited about it."

Agnes kept up a bright, happy chatter as we walked back to my grandmother's house, opening her enormous umbrella as rain began to fall. She was so happy that I couldn't bear to tell her about what I had seen at the end of my interview. I must have imagined it, I concluded, and if I were imagining such things, how long would it be before I was having the sort of delusions I'd had at Bellevue? What if Dr. Pritchard had been right and I really did belong in an insane asylum? After all, my mother had had delusions and had killed herself by drinking laudanum. What if there was some family history of insanity and these were the first signs? No, I decided as we entered the marble foyer and Agnes ran to tell my grandmother—returned from her trip upstate—the good news, I wouldn't ruin the celebration and my chances of going to Blythewood by telling anyone what I had seen.

⇥ ◈ ⇤

The news that I was expected to report to Blythewood the next day threw my grandmother's household into turmoil. Servants were dispatched to Ladies' Mile to collect the items we had ordered. A large trunk was hauled out of the attic and deposited in my room. The dresses and skirts that had come from Miss Janeway's were packed into the trunk folded in layers of tissue paper. Since there was no time to send my blouses back to Miss Janeway's to have the Blythewood insignia added, Agnes volunteered to sit up with me and teach me how to sew it myself.

I was glad for some occupation. Since we'd come back from my interview with the Council, it had been raining so heavily we couldn't go out for our usual walk in the park. The rain filled my grandmother's luxurious mansion with shadows and made it feel like a mausoleum. Even my mother's cheerful yellow-and-white bedroom felt gloomy.

As I bent over my sewing, I thought I spied things moving in the corners—wisps of shadows like the smoke-things I'd seen at the hospital—but whenever I looked up there was nothing there but the shadows of the curtains moving in the breeze. Agnes looked as nervous as I felt, jumping whenever a gust of rain hit the window.

"Is there something wrong, Agnes?" I finally asked. "Is it anything to do with what Miss Sharp was saying? About the 'recent occurrence'?"

Agnes's needle slipped and she stabbed her finger. A drop of blood fell on the lace trim of the blouse she'd been embroidering. "Vi shouldn't have said anything," she said, jumping to her feet to douse the blouse in the washbasin. "It's nothing you need to concern yourself with. You'll be fine at Blythewood," she added, scrubbing furiously at the spot of blood as if erasing it could banish whatever dark thoughts she'd been entertaining, which I suspected had to do with whatever she and Miss Sharp had been whispering about.

Agnes gave me a smile that was as artificially bright as the silk flowers women were wearing on their hats this season as she hung the damp blouse from the curtain rod to dry. Then she picked up a shirtwaist I had just finished embroidering.

"You've caught on to the feather stitch brilliantly!" she said, obviously determined to change the subject. "There's nothing to worry about at all!"

⇢ ✦ ⇠

I went to bed early, but I didn't get a good night's sleep. I had dreams in which I was running through a dark nighttime wood pursued by I knew not what. Hounds bayed and horns trumpeted as I scrambled through thick thorny underbrush that tore at my bare feet and arms. I could hear the dogs getting closer, their howls growing wilder as they smelled me.

An arrow whizzed past me, the hard edge of its fletch scratching my cheek, the tip striking a tree trunk with a *thwonk* just ahead of me. The air was suddenly full of arrows flying past me like a flock of birds flushed from the undergrowth. *A spring of teals*, I found myself gibbering crazily, *a flight of sparrows, a tiding of magpies.* I was crying out the terms as if they could save me from the approaching hounds (*a sleuth of hounds . . . no, a howl of hounds*), as if they were magic spells, but they did no good. I could feel the heat of the hounds' breath on my heels and hear the gnash of their teeth . . . and then, through the thick bramble a hand was reaching for me, pulling me to safety.

I looked up and saw a face lit by moonlight—the face of the dark-eyed youth who had rescued me from the fire, his dark ringlets a wild halo around his face, a halo that seemed to burst into a corona of black wings silhouetted against the moon.

I felt that same spark I'd felt when I first saw him, only now it swelled into a flame as he took my hand and pulled me up out of the bramble, the hounds snapping at my feet as we rose in the air. He held me tightly against his chest and we flew high above the forest. I looked below and saw a silver river unspool beneath us, swathed in long strands of fog, and beside the river, a stone tower rising out of the silver mist. My heart raced at the sight of the long fall, but then I heard, beneath the beat of wings, the beat of his heart and felt steadied by its slow, dependable rhythm and the strength of his arms.

I won't let you fall.

I heard the words in my head but I knew they came from him, just as I knew he meant what he said.

But then something flew past my face and I heard the awful sound of iron hitting flesh and his cry . . . and then we were falling, the silver mist rising to meet us, the bells in the tower tolling our death knell. I reached out for him but came away with only a handful of feathers.

I startled awake, flailing my arms out to break my fall, and found myself in my bed in my grandmother's house, clutching the black feather—which I'd taken to keeping under my pillow—in my sweaty hands. The rain had stopped, and moonlight poured through the open window, a chill breeze rustling the lace curtains with a sound like wings. The bells of a nearby church were tolling midnight. I got up to close the window. As I crossed the room I noticed a strange pattern on the walls and floor—a pattern of black feathers splayed over the moonlight.

Black wings against the moonlight, the face of the dark-eyed youth who had become a winged creature . . .

I held up my hands and saw the imprint of feathers on my white skin and, looking down, the same pattern on my white nightgown and bare feet. I was covered in feathers, a creature like the youth in my dream.

Something banged against the windowpane. I ran to the window and looked down. Below in the courtyard I saw a figure standing beneath a tree looking up at me. *The winged youth!* I thought. At the thought that he'd come back for me I realized how much I'd been longing for him, how much I wanted to believe he was real. That he had saved me—and that he had a good reason for leaving me on the sidewalk and letting them take me to Bellevue. Because I didn't want to believe that he had delivered me into Dr. Pritchard's hands and that he was in league with the man in the Inverness cape.

A bell began to toll. But hadn't the church bells just tolled midnight? I looked back down and caught my breath as the figure removed his hat and bowed to me. It wasn't the winged youth; it was the man in the Inverness cape, standing below my window, watching me. The bass bell was tolling inside me madly now, as he straightened up and smiled at me, ejecting a wisp of smoke from his mouth.

Something brushed against my hand and I jumped. I looked back down and saw that the man had vanished. Had he ever been there? I saw it was only my lace blouse brushing my hand, the damp one Agnes had hung from the curtain rod. That's what had cast the shadow feathers across the room. That, and the noise of it rustling like feathers, had created my dream. But what had created the vision of the man in the Inverness cape? Had my dream about the winged boy summoned him? Were they somehow connected?

The bell inside my head had quieted now. I closed the window, hung the blouse in the closet, put the black feather away in my trunk, and went back to bed. But it took a long time before I could close my eyes and not feel like I was falling.

7

THE RAIN BEGAN in the night and followed me upstate to Rhinebeck.

"Sit on the left side of the train," Agnes had told me at the Grand Central Terminal, "so you can see the river."

But the river was cloaked in fog, a white gauzy layer that muffled the landscape like a funeral shroud. I felt muffled myself, numb to any excitement about starting at Blythewood. That had been quelled when Agnes told me she wouldn't be accompanying me on the journey.

"Mrs. Hall needs me right now for the fall Council meeting at the Bell & Feather club. But don't worry, Gillie will pick you up. You'll get on with Gillie."

I didn't want to "get on" with Gillie. I wanted to cling to the only shred of familiarity I had left, and that was Agnes. I'd even felt sad saying good-bye to my grandmother. When I thanked her for all my new clothes and for sending me to Blythewood, her eyes had watered. She'd become so flustered searching for a handkerchief that I'd handed her one of my new ones embroidered with my initials and the Bell and Feather insignia. She waved it off impatiently and complained of late-summer allergies, then squeezed my hand and admonished me to "uphold the family name at Blythewood."

"Always remember you're a Hall. The Hall women have always gone to Blythewood."

But not always graduated, I thought sourly now, staring out at the mist-shrouded river. What if that was all they saw at Blythewood—the illegitimate daughter of a girl who'd gotten herself pregnant senior year and gone off to live in poverty, then died of a laudanum overdose? The daughter of a madwoman, a girl who'd worked in a factory and spent five months in Bellevue? Although Agnes had promised me that no one would know how I'd spent my summer, still I was afraid that they'd be watching me for signs of madness.

They wouldn't have far to look. That hallucination at my interview of the Council women turning into crows, the dream I'd had of being borne aloft by a winged dark-eyed youth, the appearance of the man in the Inverness cape below my window—all could be signs of madness. My mother's delusions had begun when she saw the man in the Inverness cape on my birthday and believed herself followed. And then I had seen the same figure at the Triangle Waist Company and Bellevue hospital. Dr. Pritchard had told me that I had imagined him at the factory the day of the fire. Certainly I had imagined the smoke coming out of his mouth. I had hoped that the delusions had been caused by the drugs I was given in the hospital, but then why had I seen him again last night?

I was so mired in these dreary thoughts that I didn't hear the conductor call my station. Only when the sign flashed out of the mist did I rouse myself to leap to my feet and wrestle my carpetbag out of the overhead luggage rack. Would my trunk be taken out of the luggage compartment automatically? Why hadn't I asked Agnes about that? Oh, why wasn't Agnes with me?

Departing passengers were pushing past me in the aisle as the train slowed. I tried to squeeze past a stout woman in purple bombazine whose wide-brimmed hat spanned the entire aisle.

"Pardon me," I said as she glared at me from under a beaded veil, "I just want to make sure the porter knows to get my trunk."

"If you gave the proper orders at boarding there will be no problem," the woman in bombazine announced in loud, ringing tones, not moving an inch. "If not, it is not for the rest of us to suffer for your lack of preparedness. You will just have to wait."

"But my trunk . . ."

"We all have trunks, young lady, but apparently not all of us have manners."

Squelched by her imperious tone and unable to navigate past her broad bustle (*Who wears bustles anymore?* I wondered irritably. *They went out in the nineties!*), I waited until the matron in bombazine descended from the train. We were the last ones down. I was relieved to see my trunk waiting on the platform, but less happy to see my companion commandeer the last porter to carry her trunk up the long flight of stairs. The platform was at the bottom of a steep cliff next to the river, but apparently the station was at the top of the cliff. Seeing no way to transport my trunk up the steps by myself and not being willing to leave it, I sat down on it and stared out at the river—or rather at the fog. The only sign of the river was the lap of water and the low moan of foghorns.

Whoever Gillie was she could bloody well find me here, or I'd take the next southbound train back to the city. I'd go straight to Miss Janeway and beg her to make me an apprentice. I didn't need Blythewood for that. I didn't need Blythewood at all.

"Hall! Hall!"

A loud, booming voice that I at first took for a foghorn coming from the river penetrated my bout of self-pity.

"Hall! Hall!"

I looked up and saw a small, dark and very damp figure emerging from the fog. My first startled impression was that one of the kelpies from my mother's stories had risen from the Hudson to drag me into the water and drown me.

"Hall?" It boomed, advancing on me with a clinking sound as if it were dragging the anchors of drowned ships. "Miss Avaline Hall?"

As the figure came closer I saw that it was a neat, compact man in a long, black waxed raincoat and a wide-brimmed hat of the same waterproof material that shadowed his face. Water streamed off his hat and the shoulders of his coat. The clinking came from an enormous ring of keys hooked onto his belt. I was pretty sure that kelpies didn't carry keys.

"Are ye Miss Avaline Hall?" he asked in a thick Scottish brogue.

I admitted I was.

"Gillie," he said, reaching for my trunk.

Did he think I had Gillie in my trunk?

"Gilles Duffy, that is," he added when I didn't budge from

the trunk. "But the girls all call me Gillie." He tilted back his hat, revealing a deeply lined face and eyes as dark as mountain tarns. Despite the worn look of his face, his hair was pitch black without a hint of gray—it almost seemed to have a dark-green sheen to it, as if in his damp state he had grown moss. His expression dared me to laugh at the girlish name, which I thought now oddly suited for a creature who looked like he might have gills. "If you like I'll carry you with the trunk, but you might find the ride a bit bumpy."

"Oh!" I cried, leaping to my feet at the thought of entering my new school slung over the shoulder of the stern Gilles like a sack of potatoes—an image made all the more ridiculous by his small stature. He hardly looked strong enough to carry my trunk. "I beg your pardon. Shall I get a porter to bring it up?"

But Gillie, despite his diminutive size, was already hauling my trunk up on his shoulders as if it were a box of feather pillows. He turned to climb the steps.

"Miss Moorhen told me a Gillie would be meeting me, but I thought you'd be a girl," I said as I hurried to follow, hardly able to keep up with his pace even though he was weighted down by my heavy trunk.

Gillie snorted. "If I know Agnes Moorhen—and I figure I do—she was playing a little joke on you. The girls think it's funny to call me Gillie, but it doesn't bother me. Where I'm from a Gillie is the man that watches over the land and manages the hunt. And that's what I do at Blythewood. I tend the hunting falcons and keep an eye on the creatures of the river and woods. It's an honorable job."

We'd come to the top of the stairs where a black glossy

coach emblazoned with the Bell and Feather insignia waited for us. Gillie tossed my trunk up on top as if tossing his hat on a coat rack.

"My mother said that all work is honorable if you do it with honor," I said, remembering that she'd told me that when I complained about the calluses on my fingertips from sewing or that we had to deliver our hats to the servants' door.

"Your mother was a kind soul. Mayhaps too kind for her own good," Gillie said gruffly, tugging his hat over his eyes so I couldn't see his expression. Before I could ask how well he'd known my mother and what he meant about her being too kind, a sharp rapping from inside the coach interrupted us.

"It is rude," a trilling voice announced, "to engage in personal conversation when a third member of your party waits."

Gillie's mouth quirked into a crooked smile. "Begging your pardon. Miss Avaline Hall, may I introduce Miss Euphorbia Frost, Mistress of Deportment."

A veiled face appeared at the window of the coach. I recognized the woman in bombazine from the train. "You most certainly may not! It is customary when making introductions to name the most important person first."

Gillie looked as if he might have a different opinion as to who was most important here, but he obligingly repeated the introduction, ending by mentioning that I would be sharing the coach with her.

"That is completely unacceptable. I believed that this conveyance had been sent exclusively on my behalf. How am I to preserve the proper distance necessary for the relationship between teacher and pupil if I am forced to be crammed in with that rather damp individual?"

It was true that I was getting damper by the minute. A peek inside the coach revealed that Miss Frost's ample skirts occupied half of the interior; her hat and carpetbag the other half.

"I willna leave her here," Gillie growled. "Not with what's been goin' on. And she can't ride outside on the box with me. It's raining auld wives and pipe staves out here."

Miss Frost sniffed. "All the more reason to make haste. This abominable river climate is giving me the vapors."

Beneath the shadow of his hat Gillie's face grew darker. His eyes, black a moment ago, flashed green—the color of the sky before a thunderstorm. The color of the sky above us now, I noticed, my eyes drawn up by the sound of wind. The trees beside the station were thrashing in a sudden gust, the rain was spitting like an angry cat, and the air smelled like singed wires. I had the feeling that if we stood here a moment longer we'd all be blown away into the river. I reached out and touched Gillie's gloved hand. He startled at my touch and I was afraid I'd broken some unspoken Blythewood rule. Inside the coach, Miss Frost sniffed.

"I don't mind riding outside," I said. "I've got a waterproof on and I'll have a better view of the school this way."

"Perfectly correct," Miss Frost said. "If a bit wordy. A simple 'I am happy to accommodate Miss Frost' would have done."

"I am happy to accommodate Miss Frost," I parroted, my eyes still on Gillie. Had I offended him? He might be a servant at Blythewood, but I was just an ex–factory girl and once-upon-a-time hat trimmer. I likely had more in common with Gilles Duffy than the girls I was about to meet. I somehow knew that if I started out on the wrong side of Gillie, nothing would go right at Blythewood.

Gillie narrowed his eyes at me, the green fading to black, and grunted. "I don't mind sharing the box with you if you don't. As long as you promise not to scare the horses."

I couldn't imagine what I could do to scare the enormous workhorses yoked to the coach, but I eagerly nodded. "I'll be very still and quiet," I promised.

Gillie grunted again. "That'll do, then," he said, offering me his hand to help me up onto the box. Though he didn't smile, he squeezed my hand as he helped me up—probably just to keep me from falling, but it made me feel better. When I took my seat on the hard, uncushioned "box" (really just a plank of wood) I noticed that the rain and wind had stopped. And *that*, I decided, was at least a good omen.

8

ALTHOUGH THE RAIN had stopped, the fog had not. It had moved from the river to envelop the road—River Road, a sign looming out of the fog informed me. It seemed, indeed, a road turned into river, one of thick curdled murk out of which stray objects bobbed like driftwood floating on the incoming tide: stolid, wide-eyed cows, tumbled stone walls, gnarled branches, and once, startlingly, a crow, cawing as it briefly alit on Gillie's shoulder and then flew away without eliciting any reaction from the man.

We rode in silence, the only sound the clap of the horses' hooves and water dripping from the invisible trees on either side of the road and from the brim of Gillie's hat. He hunched over the reins, his face impassive, still as a stone.

Maybe he wasn't supposed to talk to students, I thought, or maybe he didn't *like* to talk to them. But then I remembered that reassuring squeeze and his refusal to let me stay at the station, and I remembered something Tillie once said. "Sometimes people are so shy they wall themselves up in their silence. A kind word can open up a chink in those walls." I didn't know if Gilles Duffy needed his walls unchinked, but I knew that I did. I was approaching an unknown place that would be my home for the next three years. I felt cold and alone and scared. If I didn't talk to someone the cold would settle in my bones and stay there forever.

"Thank you for not leaving me at the station," I said, breaking a silence that felt like ice.

"Aarrghh." He made a garbled sound like he was clearing his throat and spit into the road. "'Twouldn't have been right, to leave a girl alone in this fog. It's my job to make sure you girls are safe."

"Oh, so you don't just watch over the animals, then?"

"I watch over Blythewood, the house, and the woods and all that dwell in 'em," he said with a firm nod and a cluck to the horses, who picked up their ears and walked more briskly at the sound of their master's voice.

"That must be a big responsibility," I said.

"Aye," he grunted.

"Er . . . how long have you worked at Blythewood, then?"

"Since they brought 'er over."

"Brought who over?" I asked, confused.

His green-black eyes slid warily toward me. "Y'mean you don't know the history of the place? Your mother never told you?" He sounded almost angry.

"No," I admitted. "My mother talked about Blythewood, but it often made her sad and she would stop suddenly. And sometimes if I asked her a question . . ." I paused, remembering my mother's lapses into silence and melancholy. I'd always assumed that she grew sad talking about Blythewood because she missed it, but perhaps she had been thinking of something bad that had happened here. "Well, you know how it is," I croaked.

"Sometimes it's hard to talk about a place—or a person—you've lost."

He turned and looked at me, his eyes level with mine so that I could really see them for the first time. They *were* green—a deep moss green, the color of a forest at night. *So* that's *where he goes,* I thought, looking into Gilles Duffy's eyes. *He has a forest inside him.*

"Aye," he said, "I know well what that's like. I know about lost things—and it happens I'm fair good at finding them. Would you like me to tell you the story of how Blythewood found itself here on the banks of the Hudson and the legend of the seven bells?"

"The seven bells?" I asked warily, feeling a chill travel up my spine as I thought of the bell I had been hearing in my head. But I didn't hear the bell now and "the legend of the seven bells" sounded like one of the stories I'd read in Mrs. Moore's books, the sort of tale my new schoolmates might tell around the fire at night over cocoa and biscuits. Perhaps a little bit scary, but basically harmless. "I would love to hear a story," I said finally. "Is it one of the Blythewood mysteries? Agnes told me there were lots of them."

"Aye, it's the *first* Blythewood mystery. The one at the root of all the rest and the oldest of 'em.

"It started back in the old times, in a village in the Borders, that is, the lands near the border between England and Scotland—on the edge of a dark forest. There was a bell maker in this village who was famous all over the world for the bells he made. All the grandest cathedrals wanted him to make the bells for their towers because it was said his bells had the purest chime. Some said he added the blood of falcons to carry the sound far and wide. Some whispered he used the blood of fallen angels. But that was nonsense, of course, because . . ." Gillie snorted. "Everybody knows angels—fallen or otherwise—have no blood."

I shivered, recalling the dream I'd had of the winged boy, who had looked, it occurred to me now, rather like a fallen angel. Perhaps my mother *had* told me this story after all.

"But *I* think," Gillie went on, warming to the story, his shyness ebbing away, "that the rumor of angel blood arose afterward on account of what happened to the bell maker's seven daughters."

Gillie chose this moment to bend over to untangle a knot in the reins and I cried out impatiently, "What happened to the bell maker's daughters?"

He straightened up and adjusted his hat before continuing, as if he were addressing an audience more impressive than one wet schoolgirl and the backs of two horses. He looked straight ahead as he told the story, his eyes on the road as if on the lookout for something that might come suddenly out of the fog.

"The bell maker's wife had had a dream that she would have seven daughters, each as beautiful as a star, and so when she did she named them after them seven sisters who became stars."

"The Pleiades?" I asked.

"Aye, a strange choice if you ask me, but no one ever asks old Gillie. When the youngest girl was born her mother named her Merope, and then died. The girls all grew up to be beautiful as their namesakes, but also hardworking. They helped their father by gathering wood in the forest for the foundry fires, and when they were old enough they helped pour the molten bronze into the molds for the bells. They could all ring changes on the bells and it was said their voices were as sweet and clear as their father's bells."

Lulled by the sway of the coach, I relaxed into the rhythm of the story—a fairy tale, I thought—wondering what fate waited for the bell maker's daughters. Would there be princes vying for their hands or magical balls in underwater kingdoms or might they all turn into swans?

"One autumn a wealthy prince . . ."

Ah, I thought, *so there* was *a prince!*

". . . commissioned the bell maker to forge seven bells for the bell tower of his castle that lay beyond the forest. The bells had to be ready in time for Hogmanay—that's what they call New Year's Eve in the auld country. There was hardly enough time, but the pay was so generous that the bell maker would be able to give each of his daughters a handsome dowry. All of the girls were happy at this prospect, except for the youngest daughter, Merope, who worried that her father was working too hard."

Of course it was the youngest daughter, I thought. *It always is. She'll be the one who marries the prince at the end.*

"When she could not convince her father to give up the commission, she worked extra hard to help him work the forge and pour the molds. Her father let her help mold the last and smallest bell herself, the treble bell, and named the bell after her—and then so his other daughters wouldn't be jealous he named each bell for one of his daughters and that's how the bells came to be named for them stars. Each one is stamped with its name, which you can see on the bells to this day. There's Maia, Electra, Taygete, Alcyone, Celaeno, Sterope, and Merope. Only Merope's no longer in the tower, but I'll get to that in time.

"Despite the girl's help the bell maker worked himself so hard that when the bells were finished, he fell ill—too sick to bring the bells himself to the prince's castle. The girls would not risk losing their dowries, though, so they agreed to take the bells themselves. Merope begged to stay home to nurse her father, but the oldest sister, Maia, thought that the appearance of seven sisters delivering seven bells would make a pretty picture, and she hoped to gain the prince's admiration by the show. She even composed a seven-part peal for the sisters to play on the bells when they were installed in the bell tower.

"When the bells were packed in straw and loaded on the cart the sisters dressed in their best dresses and cloaks and set out for the prince's castle. Merope urged her sisters to take the longer route around the forest, because not only were the woods full of wolves and wild boars but also it was whispered that they were the abode of the fairies and that many a traveler had gone missing in the fog never to be seen again."

Gillie turned to me and looked me in the eye. "Only a foolish girl goes wandering in the woods by herself."

"But the oldest sister insisted they go through the woods," I said, sure I saw where the story was going now, but also to distract myself from the thought of those creatures that came out of the fog . . . which might even now be lurking in the fog that surrounded us.

"Aye," Gillie agreed. "Because she wanted to be there by nightfall when the prince would attend mass. And they would have been if they hadn't been caught in a fog bank that swept down out of the mountains and swallowed up the whole forest. The girls couldn't see where they were going . . ." Gillie turned to me again, black-green eyes flashing like sparks off a forge. "No more than we can now, Miss. Who can tell if we're still on River Road heading toward Blythewood School, or if we haven't slipped off our path and gone astray. There's them that believe a fog like this is sent by the fairies to trick the unwary traveler into fairyland, where she may wander for a hundred years without finding her way out. There are places a girl can wander where even auld Gillie won't be able to find her."

I knew Gillie was only warning me to keep me out of the woods, but still I looked anxiously around for any sign that we were still on River Road. But the fog was so thick I couldn't even see the stone walls that edged the road. We might already be traveling through fairyland, a place I knew about from my mother's stories. I felt in my pocket to stroke the black feather for reassurance. It seemed to curl around my hand like a cat seeking warmth.

"Is that what happened to the bell maker's daughters?" I asked. "They wandered into fairyland?"

"No," he answered. "Far better for them if they had. Instead they heard a rustling from the woods on either side of them. At first they tried to convince themselves it was only deer or foxes, but the creatures making these sounds were larger, and soon they heard the yip and bay of wolves calling one to t'other.

They were surrounded by a pack of wolves. And not just any wolves—*shadow wolves*." Gillie gave me a look that made my blood run cold.

"What are those?" I asked, my mouth dry.

"They're not natural animals made out of blood and fur. Natural animals can be dangerous, Miss, but they've got no evil in them. Shadow creatures are made up of pure evil. The horses knew what they were. They bolted and the reins fell out of the oldest sister's hands and the horses ran wild—right into a ditch. The wagon pitched sideways and dumped the sisters and the seven bells out into the snow. As they broke free from their straw packing, the bells made a huge and terrible clamor. When it ended the forest was silent around them.

"'The bells have scared the wolves off,' Merope whispered. They could hear the baying of the wolves in the distance. Then they heard it coming closer.

"'But not for long,' another sister said.

"'We should run,' another suggested.

"'Where to?' another asked. 'We'll only get lost in the woods and the wolves will pick us off one by one.'

"They could hear the wolves coming closer . . . and then they heard a terrible scream that they knew was one of their horses, who'd broken free of his traces, brought down by the wolves. Some of the sisters began to cry. Merope looked at her sisters and the seven bells that lay scattered in the snow. She ran to one that lay on its side—which was the treble bell, the one that had been named for her—and reached inside to grab the clapper. Then, with all her might, she struck the clapper against the inner rim of the bell. A clear chime rang through the forest, so pure that it silenced the wolves . . . for a moment, at least.

"'Find a bell,' Merope called to her sisters. 'We'll ring to keep the wolves at bay until the prince hears it and sends help.'

"'How will he know it is us?' the oldest sister asked. 'If I heard bells coming from this forest I would think it was the fairies and run as far away as I could.'

"'We'll ring the changes we practiced for the prince. Who else but the bell maker's daughters know how to do that? They will know it is us and come.'

"Before the oldest sister could argue, Merope began to call out the orders for the peal." Gillie shifted his weight on the perch and looked at me. "Have ye ever rung changes, girl?" I shook my head. "Aye, well your arms are a mite skinny now to pull the bells, but a few months of good exercise and you'll be up to it. 'Tis a wonderful thing to be part of. The music of the bells takes you over and your blood thrums with the vibrations and it's like you're a part of the sound. You feel hollow, but also full. You feel part of something bigger'n yourself. To tell the truth, I don't know if Merope thought the bells would keep off the wolves or if the prince would come, but she did know that if her sisters were ringing the changes they wouldn't be afraid any longer. And so it was. They rang the bells through the night, Merope calling out the changes.

"In the castle the prince heard the bells. At first he thought it were the fairies playing their tricks, but the prince listened and counted the bells to seven and said to his knights, 'Those are the bell maker's daughters ringing my bells. Whoever will come with me to save them shall have one of these brave girls for a bride.'

"And so the prince and six of his knights rode into the forest, following the sound of the bells through the deep fog. As they grew closer, though, they noticed that one of the bells had dropped out of the peal. One of the sisters must have grown too tired to strike her bell. The prince spurred his horse on and urged his comrades to ride faster. Another of the bells fell out as they rode, and then another and another, until only one bell—the treble bell—rang. It rang clear and steady. The prince pledged to his knights that whichever sister rang that bell, she would be his bride.

"They reached the sisters just as dawn was breaking. As they entered the clearing their horses scattered the ring of wolves and the fog with them. Over each of the bells lay one of the sisters, their arms too weak to ring anymore, but still alive. The seventh bell, the treble, which lay farthest from the overturned wagon and hidden in the last scrap of fog, still rang. But as the prince dismounted and walked toward it the bell tolled its last chime. The air was still ringing with the sound when the prince reached it, but there was no one there. He looked around the woods, which were full of sunlight now, but there was no sign of the youngest sister. No sign but a single black feather lying on the ground where she had knelt beside the bell."

"What happened to her?" I cried, my hand clenched around the feather in my pocket—a single black feather that had lain beside my mother's body. Is that why my mother had kept a black feather? Because of the story? Gillie held up his hand and brought the horses to a stop.

"Listen," he said.

At first all I heard was the drip of water from the trees on either side of the road, but then I heard it: bells. First one and then another . . . and then a chorus of them.

"They're ringing us home, Miss. Showing us the way through the fog. See, the horses know."

The horses' ears were indeed twitching toward the sound. Gillie snapped the reins and we veered left, off the road, toward the sound of the bells.

A black iron arch loomed out of the fog. I could just make out the words "Blythewood School" and below "Tintinna Vere, Specta Alte" as we passed below the gate. The road went steeply up, the fog lightening as we climbed and the sound of the bells growing louder. Even from this distance I could feel what Gillie had meant. The bells seemed to make my blood thrum. They seemed to be inside me, the way the bass bell rang inside me, but these bells didn't make me afraid. They made me feel as I had when I'd slowed the bell inside me to calm Etta. Safe.

When we reached the top of the hill I looked down and saw that below us the fog still clung to the ground, but rising up out of the white mist, as if floating in midair, was a square tower hewn out of honey-colored stone. As the bells stopped ringing, the mist scattered, revealing first the outlines of a turreted castle—the same castle as the one in the engraving my mother had kept by her bed. It looked like a castle in a fairy tale, and I wondered if Gillie's story had somehow transported me into a fairy-tale land. Then, listening to the bells as they, one by one, ceased to ring, I noticed something.

"There's only six," I said to Gillie.

"Aye. For hundreds of years the seven bells rang in the prince's bell tower. The knights and the six bellmaker's daughters installed the seven bells in the tower and turned the prince's castle into an abbey, with a monastery for the knights, and a convent for the sisters, who together founded the Order of the Bells. Young men and women from all over the world flocked to the abbey drawn by the sound of the bells. They believed that the tolling kept the wild creatures and fairies of the woods at bay and that so long as the seven bells rang from the tower the demons would stay in their own land. The Order of the Bells became a great abbey, famous for the learning of its sisters and monks. Some of the men and women who were educated there chose a monastic life, but others went out into the world and became great leaders. The Order spread throughout Europe, founding schools wherever there was evil to fight.

"But eventually the Order did its job so well that folk no longer saw a need for them. The Order's power faded, and the abbeys fell into ruin or were destroyed in wars. Even the original abbey in Scotland, Hawthorn Abbey, was ransacked during the Reformation. The last remnants of the Order came together from all over Europe and decided to bring the original bell tower and the convent over here and found Blythewood.

"Three barges it took to bring her up the river. The last barge held the tower and the bells packed within it on account of the legend that the bells must always stay in the tower, but as the barge came around that bend there"—Gillie pointed to the river where a high cliff protruded from the western shore—"a storm came up. They say you could hear the bells ringing out in the storm, even though they were packed in straw, and that they could be heard as far away as Albany. The ship listed hard to port and the tower began to slide into the water, but at the last minute the ship righted itself and only one bell from the tower was lost."

"The smallest bell?" I asked. "The treble?"

"Aye, the one named Merope. She fell to the bottom of the river, where she remains today. But some say that when her sister bells ring out you can still hear her. Listen."

The last of the bells had finished chiming now. There was a silence and then, faint, but clear, the chime of another bell. It seemed to come from the river. Perhaps it was just an echo, I told myself, but would an echo pierce my heart as this bell did? I could feel it vibrating through my blood and the marrow of my bones. I'd heard this bell before. It was the treble bell I'd heard when the dark-eyed boy had touched my hand.

9

WE CLIMBED THE hill and came into a circular driveway crammed with vehicles, trunks, shrieking girls, and muttering moving men. I saw right away that most girls had arrived at Blythewood in their own conveyance, either horse-drawn carriages gilded with old family crests or long, sleek automobiles, their prows adorned by silver figures like the mastheads of ocean-going vessels. One such leviathan barreled past us on the drive, horn blaring like the call of a sea monster, nearly sending us careening over onto the lawn. Gillie muttered under his breath in Scots, his face darkening under lowered brows.

"The Montmorencys still act like they own the place even though the house was made over to the Order years ago."

The long black vehicle plowed through the crowd like the *Lusitania* coming into port. When it reached the front door a figure emerged, a girl swathed in a velvet coat like a cocoon, topped by a cloud of rose-gold hair that caught the sunlight as if the sun had come out especially to alight on it. Two other girls standing at the doorway dropped their bags into the arms of their servants and screamed "George!" in one shrill voice.

George?

A small crowd quickly surrounded George, moths to the

flame of her Gibson pouf, blocking the entranceway. Liveried servants stood weighted down by trunks while the girls called to one another.

"Fred!"

"Wallie!"

The names—did all the girls have boys' names here?—fluttered through the air like brightly colored birds. Of course, I realized, they would all know each other. Even the new girls must have grown up together and gone to the same dances and teas. With a pang I remembered spotting Tillie's bright red head across the park and hearing her voice calling my name, or looking across the rows of sewing machines and catching a smile from her. I remembered what it felt like to have a friend. Would I ever find that here among these bright, carefree girls?

"Och, you'd think it had been a year they haven't seen each other, not just the summer," Gillie muttered as he helped me down from the box. And then, in a lower voice, he added, "Don't worry, Miss, they only sound like the hounds of hell. Most of them are all right . . . though *some . . .*" He broke off to stride over to the knot of girls blocking the entrance, scattering them like geese. They did sound like geese—which, come to think of it, was what the hounds of hell were supposed to sound like. I was bracing myself to plunge into the melee when a rapping from inside the carriage brought me up short.

"It is only polite to assist your elders when disembarking from an elevated vehicle," Miss Frost drawled.

"Oh . . . here." I opened the door and held out my hand to help Miss Frost. She clutched my hand with a pincer-like grip. Her skirts rustled as she stepped down. I started to withdraw my hand, but she tightened her hold and drew me toward her, so close I could smell her tea-rose perfume and, beneath it, a bitter smell that was somehow familiar.

"Congratulations on getting Mr. Duffy to unburden himself," she hissed between yellowed teeth. "I haven't heard him string that many words together in the twenty years I've taught here. But he left something out."

The thought of Miss Frost crouched inside the carriage like a black spider, listening to our conversation, was unnerving.

"When the knights found the seventh bell," she went on, "there was an impression in the snow of the girl's body. It had filled with blood. But there were no signs of her body being dragged away."

She reared her head back like a snake about to strike and tapped her lorgnette case against my forehead. "What do you suppose *that* signified?"

"That she wasn't dragged away by wolves?" I suggested tentatively, the image of a girl's body drawn in blood in the snow making me feel slightly faint.

"Exactly!" Miss Frost rewarded me with another tap of her lorgnette case. Then she leaned forward, releasing a whiff of the bittersweet smell again, and whispered, "She was taken *from above*. Never forget, '*Tintinna vere,*' but most of all . . ." She tapped the lorgnette case against the underside of my jaw, jerking my head up so abruptly that I heard my teeth click. '*Specta alte!* Girls who keep their eyes on the ground have a habit of disappearing," she hissed. Then she whirled around and swept past the servants with their trunks and a covey of giggling girls whom Miss Frost glared into silence.

My own trunk lay on the bottom step. A thin girl in a black skirt, white shirtwaist, and plaid sash stood next to it, a marbled notebook folded against her flat chest. Her brown hair was parted severely on the side and pulled back into a tight bun. She reminded me of one of Tillie's socialist friends.

"Don't worry about Miss Frost," she said, walking toward me. As she moved I heard a faint chiming sound coming from her, as if she had been belled like a cat. "Our theory is that she was a naturalist's experiment gone terribly wrong—an attempt to preserve a specimen of genus Old Biddy circa 1893. Hence the aroma."

"She did smell as if she'd been . . . *pickled.*"

The girl smiled, revealing a dimple in her left cheek and lessening the severity of her expression.

"It's to do with her specimens. Lucky me, I'm to be her assistant this term. I'll probably end up smelling like her." She made a face, and then seeing my confusion, said, "Sorry, your head must be positively spinning and I'm *supposed* to be your orientation. Everything's in a bit of a kerfuffle this last week because . . . well, never mind. I'm Sarah Lehman." She held out her bare hand. I took off my glove to shake hers. "But everybody calls me—"

"*Lemon!*"

The summons came from the rose-gold girl with the unlikely name of George. She had moved slightly to the side of the doorway at Gillie's command, but she was still taking up a lot of space on the stairway, surrounded by her suite of matching oxblood leather trunks, half a dozen pale blue hatboxes, and her admiring throng of friends. I could tell by the dilation of her nostrils and a stiffening in her shoulders that Sarah had heard her, but she remained facing me.

"*Sour Lemon!*" George said more loudly. "I'm talking to you."

"As I was saying," Sarah said to me, ignoring the girl named George, "everyone calls me Lemon. But only one girl is rude enough to call me *Sour*." Sarah turned on her heel to face George, who had taken a step forward at the same time and so was forced to take a step back, backing into her trunks and toppling over the hatboxes on top.

The two girls who had greeted her first—Fred and Wallie?—went running after the hats that tumbled out of the boxes in a flurry of feathers. They looked like they were chasing after a brood of wild turkeys—a sight so comical I burst out laughing.

"Do you think it's funny?" George rounded on me, violet eyes flashing, rose-gold hair smoldering like a just-lit fuse. Those violet eyes were roving over my rain-drenched hat, damp waterproof, soaked skirt hem, and muddy boots, all of which screamed out the fact that I'd traveled here on a public train and not in a private car. But it was my hand her eyes fastened on—bare because I'd just removed my glove to shake Sarah's hand.

"Oh," she said. "Don't you have the wrong door? I believe the servants' door is around back."

Blood rushed to my cheeks and I heard the bass bell tolling in my head. *Ridiculous*, I scolded myself, *this ninny is no danger!* Tillie would knock her down with a right hook.

Suddenly George doubled over and pressed her hands over her ears as if she were in pain. The moment I saw her cringing my anger faded—and with it the bell. She looked up, her violet eyes wide with disbelief. Her friends fluttered around her, but she kept her eyes on me.

I forced a smile on my face. "No, this is my door, but . . ." I cast a glance down at the trampled assortment of hats. "I believe hat deliveries are made at the rear."

Then before she could reply Sarah was pushing me past her and through the front door. "Oh my!" Sarah cried. "Georgiana will be in shock until teatime. Alfreda and Wallis will have their hands full."

"Why do they all go by boys' names?" I asked as Sarah steered me past another clutch of reunited best friends crowding the foyer.

"They were named for their fathers—George Montmorency, Alfred Driscoll, and Wallace Rutherford, the three richest men in America and benefactors of Blythewood—"

She was interrupted by a blur of feathers hurtling through the air followed by a high-pitched shriek. I ducked under the missile, which nearly knocked my hat off. A breathless girl, skirts hiked up, followed in pursuit. She wore a single heavy leather glove with leather straps hanging from it.

"Did you see a peregrine falcon go by here?" she cried.

"It went into the hall, Charlotte. You're supposed to have him tethered, you know."

"Of course I know that, but he slipped his jesses, the confounded creature! Swift will have my head." The girl turned and ran into the hall in pursuit of her falcon.

"That's Charlotte Falconrath. The Bells know she only got picked as a Diana because the Falconraths are an old family. Their name even means 'keeper of the falcon'! The Dianas have to train their falcons before school starts by staying awake with them for three days and nights. By now falcon and girl should be bonded, but it doesn't look as though Charlotte's bird wants to bond. Not that I can blame it."

"So only Dianas get to have falcons?" I asked, feeling a sudden stab of desire. Even though I'd only caught a glimpse of the peregrine, it had given me a curious feeling of elation to see it streaking by me.

"Yes," she said with a wistful sigh, "and *somehow* the Dianas are always girls from the oldest and richest families. . . . Oh, but that won't be a problem for you, will it?"

I blinked at her, more confused than ever, until I realized that she was including me among the ranks of the privileged. I noticed now the telltale marks of darning around Sarah Lehman's shirt cuffs and the worn spot on her belt where she'd had to pull it one notch tighter. To her, I must look like a rich girl in my new clothes.

"Oh, I'm not rich!" I blurted. "I used to work in a factory!" I didn't add that I'd spent the last five months in the Bellevue Pavilion for the Insane.

"Really?" Sarah's eyes narrowed as she looked down at her notebook. "But you're not listed as a scholarship student here."

"My grandmother is sending me to Blythewood. So there are still scholarships?" Why hadn't my mother ever mentioned that?

"One for every class, 'for young ladies who show exceptional talent despite their *unfortunate* circumstances.' By unfortunate circumstances they mean quite literally being born without a fortune. In my case, to poor Polish immigrants . . .

but you don't need to hear my hard-luck story. We're encouraged not to dwell on our familial circumstances once we have been lifted out of them and elevated to the role of Blythewood girl—even if we have to do half a dozen jobs to supplement our scholarships while we're here. We're supposed to be all united in our grand mission here at Blythewood, but you'll find girls like Georgiana Montmorency are rather unforgiving when it comes to social status. I suggest you leave out the *factory* in your background."

"I think the secret's out," I said, holding up my callused palm.

Sarah took my work-worn hand in hers. "Then you and I will stick together," she said, squeezing it. "It's good to know there's another girl like me here."

I nodded gratefully. I'd been so worried about fitting in with the carefree girls in their white dresses that I'd seen in my mother's pictures that it hadn't occurred to me I might look like one of those girls to someone from my own background. It was a relief to know there was at least one girl at Blythewood I could be myself with, even if she had just confirmed my suspicion that I would have to hide that self from my other classmates.

"Come along," Sarah said, leading me out of the narrow foyer and into a huge vaulted space. My head tilted back so far my hat nearly fell off once more. The only place I'd ever seen approaching this in grandeur was Saint Patrick's Cathedral on Fifth Avenue in New York City, where my mother had sometimes taken me to sit and rest between delivering hats to the mansions north of the cathedral.

But this wasn't a church. The long room ended not in an altar but in a raised podium on which stood a long table upon which sat seven hand bells. Nor were the stained-glass windows that lined the west wall overtly religious. In each one a graceful female figure stood, armed with bow and arrows and holding aloft a hand bell.

"The Great Hall," Sarah said from behind me. "Don't worry, you'll be seeing plenty of it. Dinner will be in here tonight."

I noticed now that a flock of girls, their black skirts covered by white starched aprons, were covering the long tables that filled the hall with white tablecloths.

"Come along, we've got four flights to go up. The nestlings—first-year students like yourself—room on the fourth floor of the South Wing. Second years, or fledglings, on the third floor, third years—or falcons—on the second floor. In other words," Sarah added as we reached the first landing and she paused to let me catch my breath, "you have to earn a room closer to the dining hall and classrooms. That is, all except the Dianas, who room in the North Tower Room. By the time you're in your third year like me you're used to climbing stairs. Frankly, I miss the views from the upper floors. I think they should reverse the order of floors, only I suppose they're afraid—"

Sarah was interrupted by the sound of male laughter echoing in the stairwell.

"It can't be," she muttered under her breath, hurrying up the next flight of stairs. She was right about getting used to the stairs. Even though I had been accustomed to the walk-up tenement buildings I had lived in with my mother, my time in Bellevue had weakened my legs and Sarah easily outpaced me. By the time I reached the third-floor landing, Sarah was remonstrating with a tall flaxen-haired beauty in a frilly blue silk tea dress and a large feathered hat tilted coquettishly over her delicate features.

"You're supposed to be in your room unpacking, Helen," she was telling the blonde girl. "I am acting warden this term and can assign you demerits for rule infractions. You haven't even changed yet!" I noticed that though Sarah had identified herself as a social inferior to the other girls, she had no trouble speaking up to them. She reminded me of Tillie in her forthright manner—if Tillie had ever had the chance to go to a fancy boarding school.

"Don't be a bore, Lemon," the girl said with a toss of her pretty curls. "My cousin Sophronia told me that the warden job is just a sop to give scholarship girls an extra few pennies. Besides, Nathan says this blue brings out my eyes."

Both girls turned toward the window. I followed their gazes to a young man who was lounging along the window seat, hands in the pockets of his striped trousers, his legs crossed. The sun caught his fair hair and turned it silver, but threw his face in shadow so it was impossible to read his expression. His pose suggested boredom, and so did the languid drawl with which he addressed the girls.

"So I did. It's bad enough I'm going to spend the next nine months looking at women dressed like nuns." He gave Sarah's neat skirt and shirtwaist a disparaging look. "You can't begrudge me a last bit of color before the veil drops over us all."

"What do you mean, nine months?" Sarah asked, her voice so icy I felt the chill of it three feet away. "You don't mean to say you've been kicked out of yet another school? I thought you'd been sent to Hawthorn."

"Please don't ever mention that beastly place to me," he remarked, shamming a shiver. "D'you know they get you up at dawn to run bare-chested over the moors?" He shuddered and recrossed his legs, moving a fraction of an inch forward, enough so I could see that he possessed the finely carved features of a Greek statue, his skin pale as marble, his eyes the weathered gray of worn granite. And a heart as hard as stone, I wagered, from his indolent manner. But then those eyes looked up from beneath a fringe of silver lashes and lit up with a flicker of life. It was like striking a match to kindling. What had seemed cold was now warm—or perhaps the warmth had been kindled in me at the thought that he'd lit up at the sight of me.

"This must be the new girl everyone is talking about. The one whose mother—"

Helen drove the toe of her boot into the boy's shin. *That's* why he was looking at me with so much interest. I was a bit of scandal.

"No wonder Hawthorn gave you the boot, Nathan Beckwith," Sarah said. "You haven't the sense the Lord gave a toadstool. Go make trouble elsewhere. Even if your mother *is* headmistress, I can't believe she's given you free reign of the girls' dormitory."

Ah, so that explains his presence here, I thought as Nathan peeled himself off the window ledge, tipped an imaginary hat to Sarah and Helen and then bowed low to me. *And his sense of entitlement*. He was acting as if he were the lord of the manner, not an interloper. As he passed me on the stairs I heard him say, low enough for only me to hear, "You should blush all the time; it becomes you."

Blushing all the more, I hurried up the stairs to Sarah and Helen, who were too busy glaring at each other to notice my discomfiture.

"Helen van Beek, must you find the only male within a ten-mile radius to throw yourself at? You're as bad as your cousin Sophronia."

"I was not throwing myself at anyone, Lemon. It is not my fault men find me attractive. Just because you'll end up a spinster—"

"I'd certainly rather be a spinster than married to a reprobate like Nathan Beckwith—"

"Gillie is male," I interjected. Both girls stared as though a piece of the furniture had spoken. "You said Mr. Beckwith was the only male in a ten-mile radius," I explained, "but there's Gilles Duffy."

Helen tilted her head back, exposing a strong throat encircled by a pearl choker, and laughed. "I'm not even sure that Gillie is *human*, but your point is well taken. You must be Avaline. We're to share a room." She extended a dainty gloved hand.

I hesitated. I could ignore what I'd heard Nathan Beckwith say, but then I'd always wonder. I'd already faced down Georgiana Montmorency. If this girl was to be my roommate I couldn't start out by pretending I hadn't heard what I'd heard. "Avaline Hall," I said, taking her hand. "It seems you've already heard of my mother."

Sarah made a strangled noise while Helen blushed. Her blue eyes widened and she bit her lip. I was afraid I'd made another enemy, but then she shook her head, blonde curls trembling, and grasped my hand in both of hers.

"I owe you an apology, Miss Hall. Nathan was passing on a story he'd overheard from his mother. I should have told him I wasn't interested in gossip, but at least I can tell you that the only thing he heard was that your mother disappeared once while she was here."

"Disappeared?" I repeated, my voice echoing shrilly in the stairwell. Sarah put a finger to her lips to silence me and looked anxiously around to see if anyone had overheard me. Then she stepped closer to me and in a hushed voice said, "There have been various disappearances over the years at Blythewood, girls who have gone . . . *missing*. Now the stories have been revived because of this recent occurrence."

"What recent occurrence?" I asked, recalling that it was the same phrase Miss Sharp had used to Agnes after my interview. "Do you mean a girl has gone missing?"

"Yes—" Sarah began, but Helen interrupted.

"I'm sure she's just run off. Who can blame her for fleeing this place?" She shook her head, making the feathers on her hat tremble like an agitated bird. "I'd rather disappear than be trapped in this nunnery. Nor can you blame the poor inmates here from making up stories to relieve the tedium. I would wager that most of the so-called missing girls are home enjoying the season or on the grand tour.

"Anyway, Nathan wanted to know if I knew anything about the story. I answered him quite truthfully that I didn't know anything about your mother disappearing. So there, that's the whole truth." She squared her slim shoulders as though she were facing a firing squad. "You'll find I have many"—she cast a sideways glance at Sarah Lehman—"*many* faults, but flattery isn't one of them."

Sarah made a strangled noise, as if she were repressing a laugh. Helen was still looking at me, waiting for my reaction to her confession.

"Thank you for telling me what he said," I told her. "My mother's circumstances were difficult—" I caught a warning look from Sarah and remembered what she had said about not telling anyone about my background. I could well imagine what Helen van Beek would say if I told her I had spent my youth trimming hats like the one she was wearing or that I might very well have stitched Sarah's shirtwaist myself. "But she never told me anything about disappearing from Blythewood." Of course there was a lot my mother never told me about her time at Blythewood, but I managed a reassuring smile to show Helen I forgave her for gossiping. Instantly her shoulders relaxed and her face dimpled.

"Then you do forgive me!" she exclaimed. "Thank the Bells! I'd hate to start the year out with an angry roommate. Come along, we've got one more waiting upstairs for us."

Helen gathered up her voluminous skirts and proceeded up the next flight of stairs with Sarah and me trailing behind her, staying far enough back not to trip over Helen's skirts—or for Helen to overhear Sarah's comment.

"You did well to call Helen out on her gossiping. You mustn't let her get away with any untoward behavior. I knew her cousin Sophronia when she was here. All the van Beeks are impetuous, bull-headed, vain and lazy—and *they* all say that Helen is spoiled rotten by her father. It will be a miracle if she gets through her first term at Blythewood without getting herself—and her friends—in serious trouble. Especially with Nathan Beckwith in attendance."

"Is Mr. Beckwith really such a bad influence?" I asked.

"Incorrigible!" Sarah declared. "He was expelled from half a dozen boarding schools throughout the Northeast before being sent to Hawthorn. That's our brother school in Scotland. I have heard it's a bit strict, but if you ask me that's what Nathan Beckwith needs after growing up without a father, surrounded by women."

I was about to ask what had happened to Nathan's father, but Sarah put her hand on my arm and leaned close to whisper into my ear. I thought she was going to tell me about Nathan Beckwith's childhood, but instead she said, "If there's anything you need to talk about, don't be afraid to seek me out. I'm afraid Helen won't be the most sympathetic confidante and Blythewood can be . . . *overwhelming*. There are other ways to disappear here than to go missing in the woods."

Her words, although meant to be kind, conjured an image of an empty impression in bloodstained snow that chilled me to the bone. But surely that was not the kind of disappearing that Sarah meant.

"Thank you," I said, through chattering teeth. "I'll do that."

Sarah smiled and then turned to walk briskly to the end of the hall. "At least you got one of the very nicest rooms," she declared, sweeping into a large, drafty, irregularly shaped room. "This was my room when I was a nestling." Tucked under the eaves of the roof, the room was made up of sharp angles and cozy nooks and a large fireplace. Two narrow iron bedsteads were pushed against the walls at either side.

Still chilled from that image of bloody snow, I moved into a patch of sun at the far end of the room where a third bed was fitted into an alcove. The window above the bed afforded a view of the river that reminded me of the view from the apartment I had shared with my mother on West Fourteenth Street. I stood breathing in the warm air, trying to regain my composure. *Blythewood can be overwhelming,* Sarah had said. Suddenly even the idea of sharing a room with two strangers made me feel crowded.

"Oh, do you want this bed?" A flat, nasal voice interrupted my thoughts.

Startled, I turned to find a slight girl with brown hair pulled severely back from her pale oval face, standing in a shadowy nook, her hands clasped tightly before her. She was wearing a faded calico print dress that nearly blended in with the wallpaper, which must have been why I hadn't noticed her.

"Oh no," I said quickly. "You were here first, you should have first choice."

"*Technically,*" Helen interjected, coming up behind me, "I was here first. I only went out because no one was here yet and I felt lonely. This *is* the best bed. You've got privacy, a river view—oh, and look, there are these darling built-in drawers!" Helen was already moving her hands over the cabinets in a proprietary manner—as if she owned them. I suspected she was used to getting whatever she took a fancy to.

"You should spin for it," Sarah suggested. "That's the fairest way. Here." She reached into her hair and retrieved a long arrow-shaped pin. "You sit in a circle and spin the arrow. Whoever it points to gets the bed. That is, if that's all right with you, Miss . . ." she added, looking to our third roommate.

"Moffat," the girl replied. "Miss Daisy Moffat from Kansas City, Kansas."

Helen's lip quirked and Sarah gave her a little kick. "Well, then, Miss Daisy Moffat from Kansas City, Kansas, are you agreeable to spinning for the bed? It's really up to you since you were here when we all arrived."

"Oh!" Daisy squeaked, wringing her hands. "Really, I don't mind *where* I sleep. I've got seven sisters at home and I sleep in the cupboard. It's up to the other ladies."

Sarah raised an eyebrow at Helen. "It's fine by me," Helen said, "but I don't see what all the fuss is about. It's just a bed, for Bell's sake, not a suite at the Plaza Hotel."

"So Helen's in." Sarah turned to me. "And what about you, Ava?"

"It seems fair," I replied. I suppose I could have feigned indifference like Helen—or abject humility like Daisy—but the truth was I really wanted the bed in the window alcove. Just five minutes with my two new roommates had exhausted me. If I didn't have a little privacy I wasn't sure I'd survive here at Blythewood. *There are other ways to disappear here.* I could already feel myself fading into the shadows.

Sarah shoved aside Helen's trunks—there were four of them, all with marks from European cities—and instructed the three of us to sit in a triangle an equal distance apart. Helen insisted on dusting the floor with her handkerchief first and complained that her skirts would be crushed.

"That's why you should have changed into your school clothes already," Sarah chided.

When we were all seated, Sarah placed the arrow on the floor between us. "We say a little rhyme when we do this at Blythewood:

Round and round the arrow goes,
where it stops nobody knows.
Now it points to she who wins,
but it may strike one who sins.

"Ew," Helen mewed. "What a sordid little rhyme! Let's get this over with. Shall I spin?"

Without waiting for an answer Helen reached into the middle of the circle and grasped the shaft of the arrow with her long, elegant, be-ringed fingers. What pretty hands Helen had, I thought with a pang of jealousy as the arrow spun in a golden blur and we all said the strange little rhyme. Those hands had never sewn hats late into the night or slaved over a machine at a factory. Even Daisy's tightly clasped hands did not look as if they had seen much work. Would I really fit in with either of these girls—or any of the girls at Blythewood? It had taken Georgiana Montmorency not more than three minutes to see that I didn't belong here. How long would it take others?

The arrow was slowing to a stop. I saw it was going to come to rest pointing at Helen. Of course, I thought, she was the sort of girl—pretty and rich—who would always be noticed by boys like Nathan Beckwith, who would always get the best of everything, who would never disappear. The anger I'd felt at

Georgiana before was back and with it the bass bell. I deliberately made it slow in my head, and as I did the arrow abruptly jerked and stuttered to a stop, pointing at me. Three sets of eyes also fastened on me.

"That was odd," Helen remarked. "It seemed to move on its own there at the end."

"We could do it over," I suggested.

"No," Sarah said, retrieving the arrow and getting to her feet. "The bed belongs to Ava, fair and square. Now you'd better unpack and change for dinner. Six sharp—lateness for meals is not tolerated. You'll hear the bells."

She tilted her head, looking at me. "That's one bit about Blythewood you'll have to get used to—all the bells. They can drive you mad sometimes. They say there was girl a few years back who fell from the belfry while trying to muffle the bells." Then she smiled and hurried away, leaving me with the thought that the bells inside my head were already driving me mad.

10

"DON'T MIND SOUR Lemon," Helen said after Sarah had gone and we had all started to unpack our trunks. "My cousin Sophronia says the scholarship girls only take all those jobs so they can lord it over us."

"I imagine they take the jobs for the money," I said, still chilled by the thought of the girl who died trying to silence the bells. "And I didn't think she seemed sour. I like her very much."

"Do you think that story is true?" Daisy asked, her eyes wide.

"Nathan says that Blythewood is full of such stories—girls going mad, going missing, or just suddenly going . . ." Helen blushed, no doubt recalling that Nathan had been asking about my own mother's disappearance.

"How do you know Nathan Beckwith so well when you only just got here?" I blurted out.

"Oh!" Helen looked up from folding a stack of pristine white shirtwaists. "The Beckwiths and the van Beeks have known each other for generations. Our townhouse is around the corner from theirs in Washington Square and our summerhouse is just south of here in Hyde Park. Our fathers were friends before Mr. Beckwith died. And of course the van Beek women have always gone to Blythewood. Daddy says we give so much to the school that it will ruin us." She laughed, as if the possibility of ruin for the van Beeks was absurd.

"At any rate, Nathan and his mother have come for tea since I was little. We children would be sent outside while our mothers reminisced about their school days. Nathan always wanted to explore the woods or the riverside. Once he talked me into playing pirates with Daddy's dinghy and we tipped over in the middle of the river! I couldn't swim so Nate had to rescue me."

Helen's dainty hands idly stroked the polished cotton of her shirtwaists, her blue eyes gazing out the window toward the river as she spoke. Looking at the crisp white blouses, I thought of the girls who had sewn them for a few dollars a week. Then I thought of those girls burning . . . and saw smoke rising from the stack of shirts. I looked away quickly, toward the river, but the pretty view was now smeared over by smoke. Smoke was rising from the river and curling over its bank, stealing across the lawn, heading toward the castle.

"Oh, dash that infernal fog!" I turned to find Helen behind me. She was looking over my shoulder toward the river, seemingly unconcerned by the approaching smoke. "It's always worse in this bend of the river, something about the cold water from the mountains meeting the warmer tide from the bay. Nathan was explaining it. Whatever its cause, though, it'll soak the lawn and ruin any chance of a walk after dinner . . . which we'll be late to if we don't hurry. It's almost six o'clock."

I turned to look at the river again. Of course, it wasn't smoke, I realized now. It was only fog. I turned to join Helen and Daisy, but as I did I saw, out of the corner of my eye, a long tendril of fog swirl into a shape. For a moment it looked like the man in the Inverness cape, but then the tower bells began to ring, dispersing the fog and the illusion at the same time.

»→ ✦ ←«

By the time we got downstairs, the Great Hall was full, the din of a hundred girls' excited voices rising to the rafters like a great exaltation of larks. It reminded me of the closing-time clamor at the Triangle, but the snatches of conversation I caught as we threaded our way through the tables were far different.

"The count's yacht was simply divine."

"Mama says our new Newport cottage will be even grander than the Vanderbilts'."

"I simply explained to Papa that he couldn't expect me to catch a husband on such a skimpy dress allowance. Imagine..." The girl—Alfreda Driscoll, I realized as we drew closer—named a figure that was more than all the salaries of all the girls at the Triangle for an entire year.

Georgiana waived a delicate hand at the figure as if shooing away a moth, the yellow diamonds on her fingers catching the candlelight from the tall candelabra that stood on each table. "You were right to put your foot down, Freddie. Men! What do they know of dresses?"

All the second-year girls at Georgiana's table tittered as if she had said something witty.

"Did that girl really mean she spent that much on dresses?" Daisy whispered into my ear. "Why that's more than we spent feeding our draft horses last year!"

Helen snorted. "Better spent money than outfitting Alfreda

Driscoll in French couture," she quipped as we sat down at the table next to the one where Georgiana Montmorency held court. "No amount of Peau de Chine and Chantilly lace would make that face look any less like a horse's."

"Oh!" Daisy cried, looking anxiously to see if Alfreda had overheard the remark. "I didn't mean . . . why . . . I wasn't comparing . . ."

"Don't worry," Helen drawled, unfurling a thick white linen napkin. "Freddy *likes* horses. And with her dowry and family lineage she can marry anyone she pleases. I believe she's set her cap at Georgiana's brother."

"Is everyone so rich?" Daisy asked, staring at the gilt-edged china and the baffling array of polished silverware.

Helen blinked at the directness of the question and then laughed. "Why, yes, except for the scholarship cases, I guess so. Most of the girls come from the One Hundred."

"You mean like the Four Hundred," I said, recalling that was how my mother referred to the New York aristocracy.

"Oh, the Blythewood One Hundred are ever so much more exclusive than that! We're descended from the original founding families. Of course the school takes in girls from all over now. . . ."

"Yes, like stray cats," Sarah Lehman said as she sat down at the head of our table.

"What are *you* doing here?" Helen asked.

"I'm your head girl. Every nestling table's got one to show you how things are done." She smiled sweetly. "And to make sure you stay in line. Oh, look, watercress soup. My favorite!"

A girl dressed in pale gray had brought a tureen and a covered basket that smelled deliciously of freshly baked bread, but since no one at the other tables touched theirs, we didn't either. Three other girls sat down across from us.

"Hullo!" A girl with short dark hair and a heavy fringe stuck out her hand. "I'm Cam, short for Camilla, Bennett, and these are my roommates, Dolores and Beatrice Jager. They're twins, in case you haven't noticed."

It was impossible not to notice. The girls were not only identical in features—long sallow faces, aquiline noses, deep-set brown eyes—but they also wore their thick brown hair in identical plaits piled high on their heads and the same horn-rimmed glasses balanced on their long noses.

"Jager?" Helen inquired. "What kind of name is that?"

The girls exchanged a guarded look. The girl on the left—Beatrice, I thought—answered for both of them. "We are Austrian on our father's side. Our mother was English. Our father was just given the appointment of professor of natural sciences."

"Oh, the new science professor." Helen leaned across the table and we all leaned in with her to hear her whisper, "I hear the old one just up and vanished. The rumor is she eloped with a traveling Bible salesman. Imagine!"

The two sisters regarded each other soberly and again Beatrice answered for them. "Scientists are just as likely to fall victim to the tender emotions as anyone else. Our father fell in love with our mother while employed as her instructor. They ran away together and lived in a cottage until she died giving birth to us. My sister and I . . ." she gave her sister Dolores a baleful look, "have concluded it is best to avoid the romantic emotions altogether."

"Oh!" Helen remarked, her blue eyes gone wide at this story. "How extraordinary! I've never met—"

We didn't get to hear the types of people Helen van Beek had never met—a list that would have been, I guessed, quite extensive—because at that moment a bell rang, a clear sweet chime that pierced through the cacophony of a hundred girls' chatter. It came from the front of the hall, where a figure in a hooded cloak stood on the dais holding a gleaming gold handbell aloft. With a flick of her wrist she sounded the bell again and the sound swallowed every last scrap of conversation and shuffle of feet as if the bell were a dark pit that absorbed sound and transformed it into ringing silence. Then an echo of the first bell rang from one of the tables, and then from another and another, until the hall was filled with the sound of bells.

"One of you must ring our bell," Sarah said, pointing to the gold bell in the middle of our table. I looked to Helen, expecting that she would seize this honor, but before she could reach for the bell, Daisy had grabbed it. She held it up and gave it a firm shake when it was our turn.

"Brava!" Cam said, reaching across the table to clap Daisy on the shoulder. "Thatta girl!"

"Yes," Helen conceded. "Well done, Daisy." But then she added under her breath, "It's the quiet ones you've got to watch out for."

While the tables were ringing their bells, a procession filed out onto the dais. I recognized Vionetta Sharp, her blonde hair and violet eyes set off by her purple robe. She was followed by a tall, gangly man whose robes flapped loosely over tweed trousers. He ducked his head when he came onto the dais as if embarrassed to be the center of attention, but when one of the students shouted "Bellows!" he looked up, brushed back his hair, and grinned boyishly.

"That's Rupert Bellows," Sarah whispered. "Our history teacher. All the girls have crushes on him. It's quite ridiculous how they swoon over him." Despite her professed indifference to the history teacher, Sarah's eyes were fastened on him, as were the eyes of all the girls in the hall. The very temperature in the hall seemed to warm when he smiled, but that warmth vanished with the appearance of the next teacher. Euphorbia Frost steered onto the dais like a great ship coming into port, her bulk under layers of robes soaking up all the light in the room and all but swallowing up the slight, nervous-looking man following in her wake.

"Martin Peale," Sarah whispered. "The bell master."

"Peale?" Cam giggled. "D'you think he went into that profession because of his name?"

"Possibly," Sarah answered seriously. "The Peales have been bell ringers at Blythewood since its founding. Just as Matilda Swift is the third Swift to be archery mistress." Sarah tilted her chin toward the next teacher arriving on the dais, a tall slim brunette with an angular face, hair scraped back unfashionably tight, and keen dark eyes that scanned the farthest corners of the room as though alert for prey.

"How old *is* Blythewood?" I asked as a slight elderly woman, whom someone identified as Mrs. Calendar, the Latin teacher, tottered across the stage.

"The castle was brought over in the eighteenth century by Scottish and Dutch settlers," Sarah replied promptly. "The school opened in eighteen sixty-one, so we're celebrating our Golden Jubilee this spring."

"But that's impossible," I said. "Gilles Duffy told me he'd been here since the castle was brought over."

"I'm surprised you got more than two words out of Gillie," Sarah said. "You must have misunderstood him. What did he—?"

She was interrupted by Beatrice crying out, "There's Papa! Doesn't he look dignified in his robes?" Mr. Jager looked more somber than dignified, I thought. He was a large man with abundant gray hair, unruly eyebrows, and a face lined with woe. His heavy-hooded eyes looked out at his new pupils with an expression of unutterable sadness as if he saw a church full of mourners instead of girls on the first day of school.

"Poor Papa," Beatrice said. "You can tell he's thinking of Mama. She was his student here at Blythewood. I'm afraid being here has brought back painful memories of the first time he met her."

Mr. Jager glanced around the room, no doubt seeking out the table where his daughters sat. He smiled sadly when he saw them, but when he saw me his eyes widened with surprise. Perhaps he had recognized my resemblance to my mother. I leaned over to ask Beatrice and Dolores what years their father had taught at Blythewood, but was interrupted by a gasp from Daisy.

"Why is that woman wearing a veil?"

Looking up, I saw that the last teacher to reach the stage was a slim woman wearing a close-fitting bell-shaped hat with a short-netted veil.

"That's Lillian Corey," Sarah whispered. "She's the librarian. No one knows why she wears that veil."

"Really?" Daisy asked, "Do you think—"

But Sarah shushed Daisy. "No one talks about it. Now quiet, Dame Beckwith is ready to address us."

The woman who had first appeared on the dais stood now in front of the teachers. She held aloft the golden handbell, but she didn't need to ring it to command silence. With one hand she drew back her hood, revealing silver hair piled high over a smooth white forehead and gray eyes the same color as her son's. She had only to look at a whispering girl to silence her. Her gaze seemed to take in all of us, and when it reached me I felt she was looking into my very being. I sat up straighter, squared my shoulders, and lifted my chin as if her eyes were magnets drawing me upright. I felt that same magnetic pull on my soul—and a desire to be *better.*

After her gaze moved on I glanced around to see that she had had the same effect on all the girls—but not on the one boy in the room. Nathan Beckwith was standing in the rear of the great hall, leaning against a tapestry of a hunting scene. He was giving his mother the same look with which the hunter in the tapestry regarded the stag he was about to spear. As if he'd finally caught his prey.

"Girrrls of Blythewood," Dame Beckwith began, rolling the *r*, "new and old, welcome. It does my heart good to look out and see so many of you returned safe and sound." Someone made a sound like a half-strangled laugh. I turned to see Nathan Beckwith leaving the hall. Dame Beckwith resumed, with a deeper note of sadness in her voice. "I am reminded, though, of those who have not returned to us, those who have lost their way in the dark."

My throat tightened as I thought of Tillie Kupermann and all the girls who had died in the fire. But she couldn't be thinking of them. Was she referring to the girl who had recently gone missing from Blythewood? Had the girl really just run off, as Helen thought, or had something terrible happened to her?

But then Dame Beckwith's eyes fell on me and I wondered if she was thinking about my mother, who, if Nathan was right, had gone missing from Blythewood but had come back. Where had she gone, and for how long? And why would Dame Beckwith have been telling Nathan about it? Maybe, in a way, Mother had never completely come back from wherever she'd disappeared to. She had always seemed like a lost soul, but I'd thought that was just her nature. Now I wondered if she'd seen something—or someone—that had changed her.

I lifted my chin, intending to meet Dame Beckwith's gaze with defiance, but the look of pity in her eyes melted my resolve to a fervent desire to succeed at Blythewood and remove the apparent tarnish of my mother's memory.

"Here at Blythewood we begin each year by pledging ourselves to the light," she continued. "We pledge by the bell." She held up the gold bell, her hand so steady that the bell remained silent. "Our forebears knew that the power of the bell is to warn of evil's approach and to ward it off. No matter what differences we may have"—here I thought I saw her eyes fall on the veiled librarian, Lillian Corey—"we must remember that our mission unites us. Let us now recite the Blythewood oath with one hand over our hearts and one hand on the bell."

I'd read about school oaths in Mrs. Moore's books about girls' schools. But still it seemed a queer practice to pledge to a bell. Or perhaps it felt queer to me because of the bells I'd been hearing in my head. Did I want to pledge an oath to *that*? True, the sound had warned me of danger, but it had also made me fear for my sanity. All around the room girls placed their right hands over their hearts and their left on the bells on their tables. Helen, eager to show she knew what to do, was the first one to touch the bell on our table, followed by Cam, Beatrice, Dolores, and Daisy. Only Sarah and I hadn't touched it. I saw Sarah's eyes on mine, as if she guessed my hesitation. She gave me an encouraging smile as she lifted her own hand. We touched the bell at the same instant. I thought I felt a faint vibration.

"For the new girls you have only to repeat after me," Dame Beckwith said in her loud, ringing voice. "I solemnly swear to uphold the honor, traditions, rules, and mysteries of Blythewood."

As I repeated the words the vibration under my fingertips seemed to grow. Was my hand trembling—or the hand of one of the other girls? But all our hands appeared to be steady.

"To stand by my sisters in peril and adversity, to lead my life in a fashion that will be a shining example to all."

I stared at the bell, willing the vibration to cease. There were etchings in the metal that went around the circumference of the bell: "Maia-Electra-Taygete-Alcyone-Celaeno-Sterope-Merope"—the names of the seven sisters who had made the original bells. I focused on the names to keep my hand from trembling.

"And I swear to hold the enemies of my sisters as my enemies," Dame Beckwith concluded. "Amen."

That was the last of it. I repeated the words hurriedly, glad to be at an end, but as I spoke, the bell beneath my fingers began to chime. The rest of the girls were so startled that they drew their hands away from the bell. All except me. I looked up and saw Daisy staring. I quickly withdrew my hand.

"Which bell was it that rang?" Dame Beckwith demanded, her voice urgent. I knew instantly that to make the bell ring must mean something bad. It must mean that my first guess was right—I did not belong at Blythewood with these beautiful and educated girls. The stain of my parentage and the taint of madness had signaled me out. Somehow the bell *knew* I didn't belong here and it was ringing out to unmask me just as the magic harp sang out in "Jack and the Beanstalk." At the next table Georgiana Montmorency leaned over to whisper into Alfreda Driscoll's ear. There was no way to hide. I had to admit that I had made the bell ring.

I opened my mouth, but Helen spoke first. "It was our bell, Dame Beckwith. I accidentally pushed it."

Daisy's eyes widened at the lie. "That's not so," she began. Helen glared at her, but Daisy went on firmly. "We *all* pushed it."

Dame Beckwith sighed. "Be more careful next time. The bells are only to be rung at the correct times. But since this is your first day"—she smiled—"we shall say no more about it."

11

WHEN DINNER WAS over—a delicious meal of roast fowls and savory pies, baked apples, and pudding—and we were dismissed to our rooms, I drew Helen aside on the stairs.

"Why did you say you pushed the bell?" I asked. "You know you didn't."

Many of the older girls had rushed into the Commons Room for a card game they called flush and trophies, but Sarah had gently hinted that the nestlings traditionally repaired to their rooms on the first night for cocoa parties. She had dispatched Daisy to pick up the supplies in the kitchen and Helen and me to go upstairs to start a fire in our fireplace.

Helen shrugged. "My cousin told me about a girl who was thrown out of Blythewood on her first day because her touch made the bell ring. I didn't want you thrown out. Who knows who I'd wind up with as a roommate?"

I blinked at her, surprised that I already rated high enough in Helen's estimation that I was preferable to an unknown. "But why do you suppose it rang for me?"

Helen leaned closer, even though there was no one in sight, and whispered.

"They say the bells—even the small handbells—can sense an intruder. Personally I think it's total rot. How can a metal bell sense anything? I've been catching dribs and drabs of these Blythewood superstitions since I was a baby. I think all of it—including the stories of the missing girls—is a bunch of nonsense designed to give the place an aura of mystery so we don't all die of boredom walled up here like nuns studying Latin and bell ringing while *other* girls are dancing at balls and finding husbands."

Her blonde curls trembled with genuine anger. Blythewood was so lovely—and so much finer than any place I had ever been before going to my grandmother's house—that it had not occurred to me that some of the girls here would have preferred to be elsewhere. "So if you ask me, that bell rang because one of us bumped into the table. I'd wager it was that awful galumphing Camilla."

"Well, thank you for taking the blame anyway," I said as we reached our floor. "I would have hated to be expelled on my first night."

"Expelled on your first night? *That* would be an accomplishment even for me."

The disembodied voice startled me all the more for being male *and* for coming from an open window.

"Nate!" Helen cried, rushing to the window. "Are you trying to break your neck?"

I followed Helen to the window and craned my head out beside her to see Nathan Beckwith sitting cross-legged on a narrow cast-iron catwalk that hugged the west side of the castle. His fair hair and pale skin looked ruddy in the light of the setting sun, which was just sinking behind the mountains on the other side of the river.

"Not at all," Nathan replied. "Although I am touched to hear your concern about my neck. Oh, hullo," he said, noticing me. "You're the girl who made the bell ring, aren't you?

I colored deeply. "Is that what people are saying?" I asked.

"I don't know about people," Nathan replied with a sniff as if the general herd of humanity was beneath his notice. "I was in the kitchen cadging leftovers from Cook when I overheard my mother say to old Peale that he should keep an eye on you when you handle the bells. Capital of you to step in like that and take the blame, Helen."

Beside me Helen blushed and dimpled, trying not to smile. "Well, I couldn't let her get kicked out, could I? We'll both be, though, if anyone sees us talking to a boy in dormitory." Helen glanced nervously behind us. The landing was still empty, but on the stairs we could hear voices of girls making their way up.

"Come on out here, then," Nathan suggested. "No one will see you and you can watch the sunset with me. Don't you want a breath of fresh air before you're stuck inside all night with a bunch of giggling girls drinking cocoa?"

A moment ago I'd been looking forward to the cocoa party. It was another detail I'd read about in Mrs. Moore's books—nighttime dormitory feasts where girls sat around in their nightgowns braiding each other's hair and telling ghost stories—but now I wondered if rumors of my making the bell ring were spreading around the school. How well would I fit in with the other girls if they thought I was an intruder? Suddenly I felt as though I were suffocating.

"That sounds lovely," I said, edging past a startled Helen and picking up my skirts to climb through the window. Nathan Beckwith's gray eyes widened with surprise. Apparently, he hadn't thought we'd be brave enough to join him.

"Well, shove over," I said, "unless you want us both to end up cracked like eggs on the flagstones below."

Behind me, Helen yelped and exclaimed, "Well, I suppose *one* of us has to get the fire going for cocoa." When I looked back she was gone.

"That's funny," I said, settling myself on the catwalk. "Why would she go?"

"Fear of heights," Nathan explained, grinning.

"Really? I wouldn't have thought Helen van Beek was afraid of anything."

"That's what she likes people to believe, but when we were ten I dared her to climb up to the roof of her house and she froze there. I had to carry her down."

"Are you sure it wasn't an excuse to get you to carry her?" I asked, remembering what it had felt like when the dark-eyed boy had caught me in the air, his arms around my waist. But I had only imagined that.

"I suppose . . . but would she have spit up all over my shirt, then? You don't seem at all afraid of heights, though. You look as comfortable as an eaglet in its cliff-side aerie."

I smiled at the image. Perhaps it wasn't the most flattering comparison a boy could make—weren't boys supposed to compare your skin to milk and your cheeks to roses?—but then, what did I know of boys? Mother had always forbidden me to talk to them. And yet here I was, sitting only a few feet away from one with no one else around. I smiled, thinking that while my mother might disapprove, Tillie would be proud of me.

And I hardly felt awkward at all. In fact, I felt peculiarly comfortable—snug in the nest of wrought iron with the river valley spread out below us. The sun had slipped behind the mountains, turning their dark, undulating slopes purple and blue. The banks of the clouds beyond them could have been another range of mountains—lilac and pale blue and silver in the distance. The Hudson shimmered with a mysterious glow, as if it held secrets below it that it was carrying swiftly toward the ocean. It was strange to think that it was the same river that I'd seen from the windows of the city apartments where I'd lived all my life. I understood now why my mother had always found us lodgings with a view of the Hudson: the river was the thread that connected her to Blythewood. Now it was the thread that tied me to my old life.

To Nathan I said, "I guess I'm just accustomed to heights. I used to climb the fire escape onto the roof whenever I needed a breath of air. In the city it's the only place where you can be alone and think."

"Yes, fire escapes also come in quite handy if you need to make a quick escape from a police raid or a jealous husband."

I glanced over at him. He was rolling a cigarette, his eyes cast down. Now that the sun had set, his face had turned pale again and I noticed lavender smudges beneath his eyes. "What kind of places do you frequent that the police raid, Mr. Beckwith?"

"Well, Miss Hall, it's not really a subject for a lady's ears, but there are certain establishments that purvey the most illuminating elixirs."

"Opium joints, you mean."

He was so startled that he dropped the cigarette paper he had been rolling. It slipped between the slats of the metal grate, was caught by the wind, and fluttered toward the river like the first pale moth of evening. "What do you know of those places?" he asked.

"There was an opium den in the building we lived in one year. Fancy coaches and hansom cabs pulled up in front all night long, and men and women, cloaked to disguise themselves, would slip into the building. Later, when they came out, they wouldn't bother to hide their faces. They always looked as if they were walking in a dream. I watched the same ones come and go for months until their faces changed and they began to look like they were in a nightmare . . . then they would stop coming altogether. Sometimes an ambulance would arrive—"

"Stop!" Nathan cried, holding up his hands. "I'll never go to one again. You're worse than the settlement house reformers."

"I wasn't trying to reform you, Mr. Beckwith," I said, trying not to smile as I glanced at his flushed face. "What you do is your own business. I'm sure if you frequent the opium joints you have a reason. My mother always said we should pity the poor souls who came there because something in their lives had caused them a terrible pain and this was what they did to forget that pain. . . ." My voice trailed off as I thought about my mother drinking laudanum in the last months of her life. What pain had *she* been trying to forget?

Slowly I became aware that Nathan was staring at me with eyes so wide they looked like silver disks reflecting the lilac evening light. In the fading light I saw that the smudges under his eyes were a deep mauve, the same color as the shadows under his cheekbones and in the hollows of his throat exposed by his unbuttoned shirt. The evening shadows seemed to be creeping over his skin, threatening to take him. A breeze from the river, as chill as if it had traveled straight from its icy headwaters in the northern mountains, ruffled his fair hair and we both shivered.

I recalled what Sarah had said about Nathan's fatherless childhood at Blythewood being the cause of his bad behavior at all his schools. What had he seen here? And why had he been interested in my mother's disappearance from the school? He looked as if *he* were disappearing into the shadows. I was tempted to reach out and grab him to keep him from slipping away, but then he spoke in a voice as cool as the evening air.

"What an extraordinary imagination you have, Miss Hall. I can assure you I only visit those places for *larks* . . . much like the cocoa party you will be late for if you do not hurry."

"Oh yes," I said, taking his hint. I'd managed to shock even the resident reprobate. Sarah Lehman had been right: I had better not reveal my lowly origins to anyone else here at Blythewood. I gathered my skirts and crawled back through the window. When I was on the landing I looked back to say good night to Nathan Beckwith, but decided not to disturb him. He now looked entirely lost to the shadows.

⇥ ✦ ⇤

After that wind on the catwalk, the roaring fire was a welcome sight as I entered my room—as were the faces of the five girls gathered around the fireplace.

"There you are!" Helen cried, scrambling to her feet and rushing across the room to pull me into the circle. "You must have gotten lost looking for Cam and Beatrice and Dolores. And look—you didn't need to go invite them to join us. They invited themselves!" She squeezed my arm and widened her blue eyes at me. Clearly Nathan was to remain our little secret—as was the fact that she'd had no intention of inviting the three girls to our cocoa party.

"We just figured the more the merrier, right-o, Dolly?" Cam said, clapping Dolores on the back and jolting the frail-boned girl so that she spilled milk from the pail she was hanging over the fire. "And this way we can pool our booty. Bea and Dolly have got some lovely chocolates from Vienna and I have the tin of biscuits my mother packed for my train ride. I hardly ate a bite I was so excited to be on a train for the first time. Do you want to hear the states I went through?"

"We were just telling how we all came to be Blythewood girls," Helen interrupted. I could see that she was put off by Cam's blunt manners. "Camilla's from a ranching family in Texas. She's been telling us how very rich they are." She widened her eyes, obviously aghast at the idea of someone talking so openly about money. "Of course Ava and I are *legacies*, and so are Dolores and Beatrice, but Daisy here was *discovered* by a teacher at her school. Isn't that interesting?"

Daisy paused from spooning cocoa into the milk pail and

looked up, blushing. "I wouldn't say *discovered* exactly. My music teacher, Miss Baines, was an alumna of Blythewood. She thought I would do well here, and so a committee of Blythewood women came to Kansas City to interview me. It was a most peculiar interview."

"How?" I asked eagerly, wondering if Daisy had seen her interviewers turn into crows as I had.

"They asked me a lot of questions about Latin and such— I've always been quite good at languages, Mother says because I have a musical ear—but then they blindfolded me and had me listen to a series of bells and describe to them what the sounds reminded me of."

"Crickets!" Cam exclaimed. "They blindfolded me, too, and had me shoot arrows. I'm a crack shot, if I say so myself, but I'd never tried it blindfolded. Queer thing was, I hit the bull's-eye on every single one."

"Most curious," Beatrice said, narrowing her hooded brown eyes at Cam. "Papa says that the selection committee recruits for particular skills to enhance the student body. If only the children of alumnae were allowed to attend, Blythewood would become quite stale. You are new blood."

"My mother says old blood is the best," Helen said. "Mmmm . . . the cocoa smells almost done. Shall I pour? I always do for tea."

No one objected to Helen pouring the steaming frothy chocolate into teacups bearing the Bell and Feather insignia.

"We're all here for a reason," Beatrice opined somberly, blowing on her hot cocoa.

"I can't imagine what the reason could be for me," Helen moaned. "I'll be missing the season in New York. I don't know how I'll ever find a husband here when Ava's gone and taken the only eligible young man on the premises."

I opened my mouth to object that I certainly hadn't taken anyone, but Helen was on to a new idea. "I know, let's find out who will marry first! We'll toss hazelnuts into the fire. Here—I stole a bunch from the kitchen just for this reason."

"My aunt Lucille always says that divination is wicked," Daisy said. "We shouldn't try to know what the Lord has in store for us."

"Then whyever did God make hazelnuts?" Helen replied promptly. "Or give us minds to wonder? Here." She handed a nut to Daisy. "All you do is toss it in the fire whilst reciting this poem:

"A nut I throw into the flame,
to it I give my sweetheart's name.
However flares this nut's bright glow
so may my sweetheart's passion grow."

Daisy looked hesitantly down at the shiny brown nut in her hand, her cheeks turning pink. *Did* she have a sweetheart? Curling her fingers into a tight fist she recited the rhyme dutifully, as she might have said her Latin declensions, and then flung the nut into the fire as if it were already burning her hand. We all leaned forward to stare at Daisy's nut where it lay among the coals. Within moments it began to glow.

"A nice steady glow, Daze!" Helen exclaimed. "That means your beloved has a true heart and will be faithful to you. Come on, do tell, who is he?"

"Roger Appleby," Daisy whispered, her eyes lit up by the flames. "He works in the Kansas City Savings and Loan."

"Well, I bet he's thinking of you right now. Who's next? What about you, Beatrice?"

"As I mentioned," Beatrice said solemnly, "my sister and I have sworn off romantic—" Before Beatrice could finish, her sister Dolores snatched a hazelnut from Helen's hand and lobbed it into the fire, silently mouthing the poem. The hazelnut instantly burst into flames.

"Aha!" Helen crowed as Beatrice stared appalled at her sister. "I knew it! Let me guess, you're in love with a Russian count who was forced to go back to his motherland but promised one day to return to you!"

Dolores covered her mouth to hide a smile and emitted an incongruous-sounding giggle. Beatrice grabbed a nut and tossed it disdainfully into the fire, where it was immediately lost in the flames. "Ah," Helen said wisely, "you will fall in love with a man who goes missing in war. It will be a grand passion that nearly kills you, but that in the end makes you stronger. You will do great things in his memory."

"Well," Beatrice sniffed, looking secretly pleased, "I suppose the doing great things part might be true."

"My turn," Cam said, flinging a nut into the fire so forcefully that it bounced off the fire screen and fell into the half-full pail of milk.

"Ah, you know what that means, don't you?"

Cam shook her head.

"It means you'll refuse all offers for your hand in order to devote yourself to a very important cause, but just when everybody has given you up for an ancient spinster you'll have a wild and dramatic affair."

Cam hugged her knees to her chest and stared. "Really? Will it be a happy love affair?"

"No," Helen said, touching her hand, "but it will be heroic."

Cam nodded solemnly. "Like Abelard and Heloise?"

"Exactly."

Cam bit her lip and looked strangely pleased. Helen, I saw, knew exactly what to tell each girl. I wondered what story she would spin for me. I certainly didn't believe there was anything to this silly game. At least that's what I told myself as I took one of the last two nuts from Helen's hand.

I didn't even have a sweetheart to think about. I supposed I could think about Nathan Beckwith, but as I said the rhyme, an image of the dark-eyed, dark-winged boy rose in my head. I saw his face hovering above mine, felt his strong arms wrapped around me, heard the thunder of wings beating overhead . . .

I tossed the nut into the fire. It landed on top of the flaming logs. For a moment it lay still and dark, and then it split in two, each half catching fire and soaring upward on a gust of flame so that for a moment it looked like two wings spreading out over the fire.

"Oh my!" Daisy said. "Does that mean that Ava is going to fall in love with an aviator?"

"Perhaps it means she will *be* an aviatrix," Beatrice said. "Like Miss Harriet Quimby."

"Oh, she's marvelous! The Aero Club of America awarded her a pilot's certificate this summer. The first time ever it was given to a woman!" Cam said. "Pa says if I do well in school he'll buy me an airplane."

Cam and Beatrice began a spirited debate about how exciting it would be to fly a plane. I was glad to have attention diverted away from me, but I noticed that Helen kept looking at me strangely. And I noticed that she never threw her hazelnut into the fire.

12

WE STAYED UP talking and drinking cocoa until the eleven o'clock bells alerted us that it was time for lights out. Cam and the twins went back to their room and we got into our beds. I thought it would take me a long time to fall asleep in this strange, new place with its odd rituals and the murmur of two strangers talking quietly to one another. I felt a pang that since I'd gotten the bed farthest away I was excluded from their conversation. Helen had seemed friendly enough at first, but would she freeze me out now that she thought I liked Nathan Beckwith? Would she take sides with Daisy against me? I'd read about such things in Miss Moore's books. If only my hazelnut hadn't exploded quite so vehemently—like flaming wings.

As I drifted into sleep I felt myself falling. Then I was caught up in the arms of the dark-winged boy, as if he'd been there waiting for me all along. We climbed through the clouds into the pure blue ether of the upper stratosphere. His face was limned with a halo of red from the setting sun, as were his great dark wings. We were climbing toward the sun.

Too close to the sun. I remembered the old story of Icarus, the boy who flew too close to the sun. His wax wings melted and he plummeted to earth and died for daring to reach too high. *Stop!* I wanted to scream, but he couldn't hear me above the sound of his wings beating the air. He was flying straight into a raging inferno. Each feather was tipped with fire now, a fire that spread with each beat of his powerful wings. I felt the heat on my face, heard the roar of the fire, the glare of flames blinding me . . .

I awoke blinking into a bright flame floating above me, a face haloed by light. But it wasn't my dark-winged boy. It was a tall girl in a white dress holding a lantern, her long hair falling loosely around her shoulders.

"Avaline Hall, if you would be one of us, arise now and come with me to join your sisters."

"What?" I asked groggily. "I thought we already did the initiation at dinner." Had they discovered I was the one who had made the bell ring? Were they offering me another chance to belong? If that was it, I should be getting up to take their offer but all I wanted to do was close my eyes and go back to my dream, to be carried away by my dark-winged boy.

"Ava!" Helen's voice hissed. "Wake up! It's the Blythewood initiation. We have to go!"

I opened my eyes again and saw Helen and Daisy standing in their nightgowns behind the tall girl holding the lantern. "Here." Helen shoved a pair of slippers at me. "Wear these— my cousin warned me about this, so I've got an extra pair."

She could have told me earlier, I thought crankily as I reluctantly sat up and stuffed my feet into Helen's too-small slippers. Did I have time to put on clothes? But our escort was already urging us out into the hall, where I saw other bleary-eyed nestlings in nightgowns stumbling behind girls with lanterns. Beatrice and Dolores, their braids hanging down to their knees, were huddled closely together. Cam, her hair sticking up in spikes, looked like a newly hatched chick eager for her first flight, but Daisy, I noticed, looked frightened.

"It's all right," I whispered, taking her by the arm. "It's probably just another silly oath taking. We'll read some ghastly rhyme, spin around three times, and be back in bed before we know it."

Daisy gave me a tentative smile, but still looked frightened. I had to admit it was an eerie sight: two dozen girls, all in white nightgowns, following the seven lantern-bearing sentinels. It reminded me of the scene in Mr. Wells's novel *The Time Machine* when the peaceful Eloi deliver themselves over to the flesh-eating Morlocks. I became even more worried when we reached the first floor and instead of passing into the Great Hall were led outside into a moonlit world of mist and shadow.

The lantern bearers walked through the fog as if they would know their way blindfolded. I noticed now that they also bore bows and quivers strapped over their shoulders. *The Dianas*, I realized; ushering the nestlings to initiation must be part of their duty. We followed them, any hesitation quickly replaced by the fear of losing sight of the lanterns, the only light once the fog enveloped us. *River fog*, I thought, remembering the thick mist that had covered River Road on my journey from the station.

I recalled the story Gillie had told me of the bell maker's seven daughters and the journey they had made through the fog-ridden woods—a wood much like the one we entered now. Ghostly trees loomed out of the mist, branch tips reaching out like skeletal fingers. We were entering the woods on the north side of the school . . . or were we? Gillie had said that fairies sent a fog like this to lure unwary travelers into fairy land. Perhaps the lights that floated before us were not the lanterns held by the Dianas, but will-o'-the-wisps luring us into bogs to drown. Perhaps the rustling I heard in the underbrush came from the shadow wolves that preyed on the bell maker's daughters.

"Where are they taking us?" I whispered to Helen, who hung on to Daisy's other arm.

"To the Rowan Circle," Helen whispered back. "My cousin told me about it. There's a clearing there surrounded by rowan trees. Look—" Helen reached out her hand and plucked a branch seemingly from the fog itself. She handed it to me and I could see that the branch was heavy with red berries. My mother had told me something about rowan trees once.

I lifted my eyes from the branch to ask Helen if she knew, but the question died on my lips as I saw what lay in front of us: a clearing ringed round with flames. For a moment I thought the woods were on fire, until I saw that the flames came from torches plunged into the earth. Beside each torch stood a dark, robed figure. As the last girls entered the circle each figure lifted an arm and held aloft something that gleamed in the firelight.

A peal of bells sounded through the fiery circle, playing a tune I hadn't heard before, a mournful dirge like something medieval church towers would have rung to announce the coming of the plague. The very fog seemed to flee before the sound, creeping out of the circle and into the woods, uncovering as it went a solitary hooded figure standing in the center of the circle. When the bells had ceased the figure lowered her hood.

Dame Beckwith, her silver hair billowing loosely about her face like a swath of fog that had wound itself about her head, turned in a slow circle to look at each of us. In the firelight her pale gray eyes shone yellow, like the eyes of an owl sweeping the forest floor for prey. When she had made a complete circuit, she spoke.

"Girls," she said, her voice ringing with the same carrying force of the bells, "you have come here tonight to be initiated into the mystery of Blythewood. In a moment I will tell you a story that will change the way you see the world and alter the course of your life. We have tried to ensure that only those who are strong enough to face this moment have made it this far. I believe that every one of you has it in her to be a Blythewood Girl."

She turned again, resting her eyes on each of us. "But I have been wrong before, and there may be some among us who are not ready to commit to this undertaking. It is not a covenant to enter into lightly. Much will be asked of you. You may find yourself in grave danger. Although we will train you to face the dangers ahead, even the best trained among us have been lost."

Her voice wavered and I imagined she was thinking about the girl who had disappeared. In the flickering torchlight her face seemed to quiver, as if a gauzy veil had been dragged across her features. But when the flame steadied her face appeared calm and she continued in a sure and measured voice.

"If any of you wish to leave now, you may. You will go home on tomorrow's train with no reproach from me or from any of us here. Many are called, but few are chosen. To make it easier for those who wish to leave, you may do so under cover of darkness."

At her signal the torches and lanterns were extinguished and the circle was plunged into darkness. I heard the rustle of one or two girls leaving, accompanied by one of the Dianas, who lit her lantern once they were outside of the circle. As I watched the light of that lantern fade into the fog, I thought of going myself. It would only be a matter of time before it became obvious that I did not belong here. I wasn't like the other girls with their smooth hands and carefree smiles. I could feel my difference—my *wrongness*—like an itch on my skin that threatened to spread into an ugly rash for everybody to see. Wouldn't it be better to skulk off in the dark before anyone could see how different I was?

But then I thought about what Agnes had said to me before I left—that coming to Blythewood would be my only way of finding out what happened to my mother and who my father was. Dame Beckwith had told Nate that my mother had disappeared once while at Blythewood. I burned to know where she had gone, what had transpired, and how she'd returned, as it sounded like the other vanished girls hadn't. Perhaps if I could find out the truth about my mother's past, I would understand her life and why it turned out the way it had.

Thinking about my mother gave me the strength to stay. After all, whatever was going to happen to me at Blythewood, she had gone through it once, too.

When the sound of retreating footsteps had faded, the torches were relit and Dame Beckwith began her story.

"This is not a tale told round the fireside to delight and entertain," she began. "This is a story of the very real dark things that lurk in the shadows and the sacrifices each and every one of us—" She laid her hand over her breast and I thought I heard a slight catch in her voice. What had *she* sacrificed? I wondered. But when she went on her voice was steady. "Must make to keep those shadows from destroying all that is good.

"Our story begins with the tale of the bell maker's daughters . . ."

Oh good, I thought, as I listened to the story Gillie had told me earlier today, *I know this already*. But she didn't stop with Merope's abduction.

"After their sister was taken from them, the six daughters brought the seven bells to the prince's tower at the edge of the woods. The shadow wolves followed them."

She paused, letting that last sentence sink in. I remembered Gillie had said the shadow wolves were made of the bits and scraps of what was left of the dead. Outside the circle, the gray fog billowed like floodwater held back by an invisible dike. One could imagine creatures like the shadow wolves taking shape inside it, but it was just a story. Wasn't it?

"By the time they reached the prince's tower they were surrounded by the shadow wolves and other creatures who had come out of the woods, because in those woods lay a door—a door to hell, some might call it, although some of a more fanciful mind might call it Faerie."

It was obvious what Dame Beckwith thought of those possessed of a fanciful mind. I felt a pang at the thought of my mother and her love of fairy tales. Was this story supposed to cure us of a childish love of stories? If so, I was doubly sure I'd never fit in here. Besides a stray feather and an empty laudanum bottle, the tales my mother had told me were all I had left of her.

"But let me assure you," Dame Beckwith continued, "that the creatures who came through that door, though they may have looked innocent, were not. They were bloodthirsty scavengers that preyed on humankind. They stole babies from their cribs and wives from their husband's beds and replaced them with changelings. They assumed pleasing shapes to seduce women and then drained them of their vitality and beauty, leaving dry, withered husks behind. They lured unwary travelers to their deaths and pulled fisherman from their boats down into the bottom of the sea. They waged war on humankind and would have destroyed us all if they were not stopped.

"The sisters found that if they rang the bells correctly they could keep the creatures away. By trial and error—grievous error that cost many lives—the sisters learned how to ring the bells not only to repel these beings but to summon them. You see, it is not enough to merely evade evil. One must seek it out and destroy it. And so the sisters learned how to lure the demons into traps and how to shoot them down with arrows. They founded the Order of the Bells to pass down their skills to the next generation. The good knights who served them were the first knights of the Order and have faithfully served them since. Together the sisters and the knights brought the Order to wherever the evil creatures dwelled and fought them back. They fought so well that the doors to Faerie fell into disuse and closed. The old ways were forgotten by all but a very few. Many thought the war was over and that evil had been defeated. But evil is never entirely vanquished; it just goes underground and emerges somewhere else."

She held out her arms by her sides, her fingers splayed wide.

"It bubbled up here," she said, raising her arms. The fog outside the circle seemed to rise with the motion. I felt a tingle at the back of my neck and I began to realize that this wasn't a story that took place once upon a time in a faraway land. This was a story about *here* and *now*.

"The remnants of the Order heard of evil rising up on America's shores. They scoured the country looking for the root of that evil, and when they found it, they knew what they had to do. At great personal cost and danger they brought the bells—and the bell tower that held them—stone by stone to Blythewood. The evil creatures that came through the door were so threatened by the bells that they summoned a storm to destroy the boats carrying them. Many lives were lost battling the dark forces. Sacrifices were made. But the Order prevailed and we established a stronghold here on the banks of the Hudson and on the edges of hell.

"That is the tradition to which you girls are heirs. That is the mystery of Blythewood. Tonight you will be welcomed into the Order of the Bells."

The chime of bells filled the circle. The peal the hooded figures played was surprisingly sprightly after Dame Beckwith's frightening speech. Perhaps it was a fairy tale after all, a parable meant to teach us a lesson, and now we'd sing a song to celebrate our union. My body swayed and my feet tapped. On either side of me I felt Daisy and Helen caught up in the tune, too. It made you want to dance, to fling yourself into a circle. But then the hooded figures raised their torches and we saw what ringed our circle.

A multitude of faces peered in at us. My first thought was that they were children—wide-eyed, elfin-faced starvelings. I'd seen faces like this staring out of tenement windows on the Lower East Side, children so malnourished their bones stuck out and their eyes were too big for their faces, but I'd never seen children who had starved until their ears were pointy, or their faces wrinkled like old men, or their feet cloven. Or ones who had grown long rat-like tails.

"*What are they?*" Daisy whispered, her fingers digging into my arm.

"I don't know," I managed, my throat so tight it hurt to speak. "They look like . . ."

"*Goblins,*" Helen hissed. "Goblins and elves and fairies. It's true. I'd heard the stories but I didn't believe them."

I stared at the creatures, desperately looking for some other explanation. They had to be children in costumes cleverly made up to look like the fairy creatures that decorated the margins of the storybooks my mother had read me. One of the creatures pressed itself up against the edge of the circle, its fox-like face sniffing low to the ground, a ridge of brindled fur raised along its spine, long tail twitching in frustration. Some invisible barrier seemed to be keeping it out of the circle. It lifted its sharp nose, sniffed, and licked its lips with a dark-blue tongue the length of my forearm.

Daisy screamed. The creature arched its back and snarled, baring sharp, pointy teeth. Its delicate pale blue ears quivered.

"Some of them look almost human, don't they?"

Dame Beckwith's voice seemed to float over the circle. My

eyes were glued to the creature—*the goblin,* I said to myself, scarcely believing it. I thought of the lines in Miss Rossetti's poem:

> *One like a wombat prowled obtuse and furry*
> *One like a ratel tumbled hurry-scurry . . .*

This one cringed and skulked along the perimeter of the circle, its sharp claws scrabbling over the ground, its tail lashing like a snake.

"Or like some harmless animal," Dame Beckwith said.

I didn't think the creature looked particularly human *or* harmless. I had gone past the point of doubting the evidence of my eyes. These creatures—at least two dozen of them now ringed the glade—were not of this world. I had always wondered how my mother had made her stories so vivid, and now I knew. She had seen these creatures firsthand.

"Some even look quite lovely." Dame Beckwith held out her hand and whistled a long trilling note. One of the lights outside the circle detached itself from the fog and floated toward her outstretched hand. "Don't be alarmed," Dame Beckwith said. "Only the ones I summon can breach the circle." When the blur of light alighted on Dame Beckwith's hand I saw it was a diminutive winged person—a sprite clothed in blue and green flames.

"Oooh," Daisy cooed beside me. "She's so pretty!"

"Yes, isn't it," Dame Beckwith said, turning her hand so that the creature revolved slowly, like a ballerina pirouetting on a spot-lit stage. "Genus: *Fatae*; species: *lychnobia*; subspecies: *ignis fatuus*. Commonly known as a will-o'-the-wisp, Jennyburnt-tail, Kit-in-the-Candlestick, or lampsprite. Collectively known as a conflagration of lampsprites. Their favorite trick is leading unwary travelers into bogs and marshes and then laughing while they drown."

The lampsprite tilted its head and blinked its wide yellow-green eyes innocently at Dame Beckwith. "And if that was all they did we might leave them be, but they also have another nasty trick up their sleeves."

Dame Beckwith brought her hand closer to her face, pursed her lips, and blew as if she were extinguishing a candle. The flames surrounding the lampsprite eddied in the gust and shrunk around the tiny figure like scraps of crumpled silk. Then a high-pitched whine, like the buzz of a mosquito magnified a thousand times, filled the circle and the tiny delicate creature exploded into a living, breathing fireball. Enormous wings veined with lightning stretched over our heads. The pretty face was transformed into a snarling mask of rage, pointed teeth and long, sharp talons poised to tear Dame Beckwith apart. It hissed and dove, but before it could reach Dame Beckwith, one of the cloaked figures stepped forward, lifted a bow, and shot an arrow into the creature's breast. The creature crumbled to the ground at Dame Beckwith's feet.

"Look at it," Dame Beckwith commanded. "This is its true face."

Drawn by her voice—and a horrible curiosity—we all gathered round the wounded creature—all except the robed figures and the seven Dianas, who stood guard around us, bows drawn. Blue flames still flickered over its body, but the figure was no longer the pretty thing that we'd seen a minute ago. Its face was seamed with blue veins, its ears pointed and tufted with coarse fur, its eyes bloodshot and bulging. A hideous monster.

"Like all creatures of Faerie the lampsprite assumes a pleasing mien to lure you astray. And that is exactly what they will do: lead you astray. Members of our own Order have been led astray by the most beautiful of these creatures—the Darklings.

"They were so beautiful some among us forgot they were not human, that they were *demons*. There have even been those foolish enough to enter into an alliance with them, but their trust has always been rewarded with betrayal and destruction. You must never forget that these creatures are monsters. It is our duty to protect the world against them. That is what you have come to Blythewood to do. You will learn here the secrets of these monsters. How to recognize their wiles and disguises and—"

Dame Beckwith touched the toe of her boot to the sprite's ribs and, like an ember stabbed by a fire poker, its body collapsed into a pile of gray ash.

"—how to hunt them down and destroy them.

"So, girls, now that you know the Blythewood mystery, I ask you: Are you ready to take up the fight against evil?"

My fellow nestlings stirred. I looked at the faces of the girls I'd come with. Cam, with her hair sticking up in spikes, Daisy with her lacy high-necked nightgown and wide innocent eyes, Helen with her snobbery and entitlement, Beatrice and Dolores with their world-weary melancholy—all these differences seemed to have fallen away. I saw a dozen sets of burning eyes, lifted chins, and firm jaws. I thought of Tillie suddenly, of how she looked when she stood up to the bosses, and I thought of what Mr. Greenfeder had called us: *farbrente maydlakh*. Fiery girls. If Tillie were here, how eagerly would she take up this fight!

"Yes," Cam burst out. "I want to *do* something. I want to make a difference."

An answering murmur swept through the circle. *Yes, me too!* It was impossible not to be swept up in the enthusiasm. Who wouldn't want to fight evil, to push back the tide of darkness?

"Then join me in your second oath of the night. You have already sworn yourself to Blythewood. You now may swear yourselves to the Order of the Bells."

Dame Beckwith held up the golden handbell. The robed figures on the edges of the circle each held up a handbell as well and lowered their hoods. I saw the faces of our teachers illuminated by torchlight, glowing with a fervor that transformed them from ordinary schoolteachers to knights and ladies in a medieval stained-glass window. Even Euphorbia Frost's heavy face shone with passion. Only Lillian Corey's face remained unseen behind her veil.

"You have only to say, 'I pledge myself to the Order of the Bells.' But to be sure, we ask that you repeat the words seven times to the chiming of the bells." She rang her bell—as did all the teachers—and we all repeated the words, once for each time the bells rang. Each time I said the words I felt them sinking deeper inside of me, reverberating with the chimes, the vibrations clearing away all other thoughts and doubts. *This* was why I had always heard the bells in my head! I had always been meant to come here. When the bells rang the seventh time I felt sure that I truly belonged to the Order.

I began to say the oath for the seventh and last time, but as I did I saw something stir in the fog. Something with black wings and a flash of eyes that looked . . . familiar. Could it be one of the Darklings Dame Beckwith had spoken of? I gasped and looked around to see if anyone else had spotted it, but all my classmates were looking at the bell in Dame Beckwith's hand, their eyes shining as brightly as its gold in their fervor and certainty.

I was the only one who was looking into the shadows—and the only one, I suspected, who had failed to finish her vows.

13

WE WERE ESCORTED out of the grove, our teachers ahead ringing their handbells and the Dianas bringing up the rear with their bows drawn. The ghastly goblins scattered at the sound of the bells, but I still heard rustling in the underbrush and caught glimpses of the floating lights amid the fog-bound trees. I didn't see any sign of the Darkling. Perhaps I had imagined it.

"Perhaps it was all a dream," Daisy whispered, echoing my thought about the Darkling. "Perhaps we'll wake up in our own beds and realize it was all a dream."

"I only dream of *nice* things," Helen insisted. "Of cotillions and dances, lace dresses and diamond earrings. I would never, *ever* dream of horrible slavering monsters!" She swatted angrily at a low-hanging branch and swore in a most unladylike fashion when it snapped back and hit her in the face.

"You must keep up with the others," admonished the Diana behind us, a stern-looking girl with spectacles and sharp chin whom I recognized as the girl who'd run by me chasing a falcon yesterday. "You're already the last in the queue and I'm not allowed to linger behind."

"You needn't take that tone with me, Charlotte. Everyone

knows the Falconraths are only chosen for the Dianas because they own the land that borders on the school."

"You're a fine one to speak, Helen. The van Beeks are only tolerated here because of your mother's friendship with Dame Beckwith."

"How dare you! My mother would never presume on India Beckwith. Why, I didn't even *want* to come here. I begged Mother and Daddy to let me stay home, and Dame Beckwith herself came to implore me to come."

"Then why don't you leave," Charlotte Falconrath suggested, jutting out her sharp chin. "You were given a chance before the initiation. Why don't you just slink off in the dark like the other cowards?"

"Dame Beckwith said there was no shame attached to those who left," Daisy cut in. Charlotte and Helen both turned to stare, as startled as I was to hear Daisy speak up. Charlotte recovered from her surprise first.

"*That's* what we tell the girls who leave, but of course it's not what we say amongst ourselves. You wouldn't know that, not being one of our kind."

"Leave her out of this," Helen growled. "Daisy has just as much right to be here as you or I do."

"Maybe, but what right does *she* have"—Charlotte's eyes raked me with undisguised disdain—"after what her mother did?"

The words were hardly out of her mouth before Helen was upon her, fists flying. Charlotte was so shocked at the attack that she automatically drew back her arms, releasing the arrow she'd been holding ready. It shot into the woods and hit something that yelped. We all looked at each other.

"Now look what you made me do—" Charlotte began, but then her eyes widened with terror. Something was coming out of the woods toward us. Something *big*.

"Draw another arrow!" I yelled at Charlotte, but she had already turned and fled, running toward the house—which is what we all should have done. But when I grabbed Daisy's hand and pulled, she was frozen to the spot. Helen grabbed a stick from the ground and brandished it. I did the same and stood, prepared to meet the thing that was coming for us. From the noise it was making in the underbrush it seemed to be as large as a rhinoceros. It broke through the fog with a crash, fair hair flying, arms pinwheeling, spraying blood. Helen cocked back her stick to strike it, but I grabbed her arm.

"It's Nate!" I shouted, recognizing the pale, drawn face just before Helen struck him.

"Nate?" Helen cried, falling to her knees beside him as he fell to the ground. He was clutching his shoulder, from which protruded Charlotte's arrow. "What are you doing here?"

"I followed you . . ." he gasped. "They told us about the fairies at Hawthorn, but I wanted to see it for myself. Mother forbade me—she said the initiation was only for girls—so I snuck out."

"But if you were outside the circle, why didn't the goblins and sprites attack you?" I asked, appalled at the thought of being outside with those creatures—and then realizing that we were outside the circle with them *now*.

"I climbed a tree and hid," Nate said. "Besides, they didn't look so fearsome until Mother provoked that fire thingum. And look—it was one of her amazons that mortally wounded me."

"Pshaw!" Helen clucked. "It's only a scratch." She pulled his shirt back to uncover the place where the arrow was lodged an inch into his skin. "I suppose I can pull it out."

"No!" Nathan screamed. "Are you daft? I'll bleed to death!"

"Well, then we'll take you to your mother and she'll see to it," Helen said. "She was a nurse in the Second Boer War."

"But then she'll know I was out in the woods and she'll send me away again. No, I suppose you had better take it out, but let me brace myself—" Before he could finish, Daisy reached out her tiny hand and wrenched the arrow cleanly free of Nathan's shoulder. Nathan screamed and grabbed his arm.

"Well done!" I told Daisy. "Now let's wrap his arm. Here." I tore off the ruffled flounce at the bottom of my nightgown and handed it to Helen to wrap around Nathan's arm. We each had to sacrifice a ruffle from our gowns to staunch the blood, but when we were done the bleeding had stopped and Nathan, although pale, was still conscious—and speaking.

"Are you sure I don't need a few more lengths of bandage?" he asked, ogling our bare ankles.

Helen swatted him. "The only cloth I'm going to sacrifice for you is a gag for your mouth, Nathan Beckwith. Now if you can walk, we'd better be getting back to the house or we'll be punished for breaking curfew."

"I think we have a worse problem." Daisy's voice, hardly louder than the creak of branches, made me look up from Nathan's face to hers. She was staring into the woods behind my back, her eyes huge as a startled deer's. The hair on the back of my neck rose and a cold chill crept down my spine. The bass bell was tolling inside my head and had been for several minutes, I realized, only I'd been too busy tending to Nathan to notice it. I turned, slowly.

There were dozens of creatures: the rat-faced goblin men, the glowing lampsprites, and others we hadn't seen before—hairy dwarfs with bulbous noses, green-scaled lizard men, goat-horned women—all creeping stealthily closer to us.

"We're surrounded," Daisy whimpered. "What can we do?"

What *could* we do? We had no weapons—no bell, or bow and arrow, or lantern fire. I saw one of the lizard men lick its lips with a long forked tongue, drool dripping off sharp fangs. It opened its mouth wide. I was sure it meant to lunge and bite us, but then it did something even more frightening. It spoke.

"Hunn . . . gree!"

"Did it just say it was hungry?" Daisy asked, wide-eyed.

"Well I don't think it's asking us for tea!" Helen cried. "I believe it means to eat us."

"Not if I can help it," Nathan growled, his good hand curling around a stick. "I'll beat them back while you girls run."

"No," I said, the word coming out of my mouth before I'd known I was going to speak. "We'll stand together." I found the stick I'd dropped and grasped it. I rose to my feet slowly and the others followed. I could hear Helen's quick, shallow breaths and a soft whimper from Daisy and a creak of wood as Nathan shifted the stick in his hand. Back in the circle, while the rest of my classmates took their oaths, I'd felt like I was on the outside looking in, but now I felt like I belonged—maybe not to Blythewood, but to this little group of four. I clenched my arm and swung back the branch and braced myself for the attack.

But it came not from the woods but from above. A great whoosh of wind and roar of wings crashed into the clearing like a black whirlwind descending from the clouds. The creature landed a few feet in front of us, its back to us, huge black wings beating the air. One of the goblins darted beneath its feet but the winged creature grabbed it and flung it against a tree, where it slid limply to the ground. The goblins, sprites, and other creatures scattered, evaporating into the fog as suddenly and stealthily as they had appeared. Then the winged creature turned to face us.

I heard Helen and Daisy gasp. My mother had taken me to the Metropolitan Museum once and we'd seen a Greek sculpture of Adonis. This young man, dressed in only loose trousers, had the same beauty, the same fine white limbs and muscular chest—all the whiter against the ebony gloss of the enormous wings spread out behind him. His wings were the same color as his tumbling dark hair and bottomless black eyes—eyes I had seen before, on the day of the Triangle fire and nearly every night in my dreams since then.

"You!" I cried, the word escaping from my lips. His lips parted, but before he could speak Nate ran at him with his stick raised. The dark-winged boy flexed one wing and swatted Nate away like a fly. Then he turned back to me, and his eyes locked on mine. He took a step forward. As his wings beat, the air stirred around me like warm water lapping against my skin. I should have felt afraid, but I didn't. The bass bell was no longer ringing in my head. Instead the treble bell chimed sweetly as a crystal chandelier swaying in a breeze. He tilted his head, as though listening.

He heard them. The dark-eyed boy could hear the bells inside my head. The thought filled me with joy. Because if someone else could hear the bells inside my head it meant I wasn't crazy.

But then the tinkling was replaced by a solemn knell, the leaden bells of Blythewood ringing midnight. The boy looked up, his white profile a cameo carved against the ebony of his wings. When he turned back his eyes were as fearful as when he'd seen the crows swooping down on us on the roof of the Triangle building. I felt the same tingle of electricity flowing between us as I had then. I took a step forward, my hand raised, but he flexed his wings and took off, the force of his wings' draft knocking me backward as he rose into the night.

Something fluttered down to earth in his wake. I knelt and picked it up. It was a long black feather, identical to the one I had found on the floor beside my mother on the day she died.

The boy who had saved me from the fire, who haunted my dreams, was one of the Darklings Dame Beckwith had warned us about. And a Darkling had been with my mother when she died.

14

WE WERE ABLE to sneak back into the house because Nathan knew of a back door near the scullery that was never locked.

"Won't Charlotte have told them we were left behind?" I asked.

"And get herself in trouble for abandoning us?" Helen scoffed. "Not her. The Falconraths are notorious cowards. One of her ancestors was executed for desertion in the Revolutionary War."

"My bet is that she told the others that you returned," Nathan added. "Otherwise there'd already be a search party out looking for us."

"Won't your mother know you were gone?" I asked him, unsettled by the idea that we all could have gone missing with no one the wiser.

"Mother stays up all night in her study working. I doubt she'd notice if the castle burned down around her—and besides, my room is two floors below hers in the North Wing." He shrugged and then winced at the pain in his shoulder.

"But won't she notice that you've been hurt?" I asked.

"Not unless I fling myself between her and her books and

drip blood over some priceless ancient manuscript. Honestly, I'll be fine, but you three will get kitchen duty for a week if anyone catches you outside your room. You'd better hurry up."

Daisy plucked at my sleeve, anxious to go. Helen was watching Nate and me warily.

"You've certainly become chummy with Nathan in a short time," Helen remarked when we'd left him.

"I'm worried about his injury. And not only that. He seems . . . haunted somehow."

Helen snorted. "Haunted by gambling debts and jealous husbands, perhaps. Don't let Nathan fool you. That *sensitive soul* pose is just an act to make girls fall for him. Clearly it's worked with you. You obviously have a crush on him."

"I do not—" I began, but Daisy, who was ahead of us on the stairs, stopped dead and wheeled around.

"Are the two of you really arguing over a boy when we have just learned that the world is populated by fairies and monsters—which is definitely *not* what I was brought up to believe—and *we* are the ones supposed to protect people from them?"

"Of course it's a shock—" Helen began.

"Did you really not know?" Daisy demanded. "Even with all the van Beek women who have gone here?"

Helen shook her head. "I'd heard stories, but nothing like this."

"And you." Daisy turned to me. "Your mother went here. She never told you?"

"No," I said. "Whenever she spoke of Blythewood it was with fondness and longing. I knew there were secrets she wasn't telling, but I thought they had to do with my father."

"Perhaps your father was killed by one of those monsters," Helen suggested.

"I'll bet it was a Darkling," Daisy said. "One of the creatures that Dame Beckwith told us were so beautiful they tricked the Order into believing they were good. You can see why." Daisy's voice grew faint. "The one we saw *was* beautiful."

"But deadly," Helen said.

"But he saved us!" I blurted out. I couldn't tell them that it wasn't the first time he had saved me.

"I thought he was going to abduct one of us from the way he was staring." Helen shivered and wrapped her arms around herself.

"He was staring at Ava," Daisy said. "It looked like he was going to grab her, but then the bells rang. That's what saved us from him. Remember what Dame Beckwith said—the fairies can make themselves look beautiful to fool us. Who knows what that Darkling *really* looks like. He could be a monster. And it's up to us to protect the world from his kind. I feel . . ." Daisy lifted a hand and placed it over her heart. She was shaking so hard she swayed on the steps. I reached out a hand to steady her, afraid that the shock had been too much for her and she was going to faint or have a convulsion of some kind, but when she spoke her voice was steady and strong as the toll of the bells in the tower. "I feel as if, for the first time in my life, I have found my purpose."

⇥ ◈ ⇤

Only when I was in bed did I allow myself to think about what I had seen. Daisy and Helen likely assumed that my quiet while we got into bed came from the shock of "the revelation of the Rowan Circle (as, we would learn on the morrow, the Blythewood girls called the first night's events). They couldn't know it came from the shock of discovering that the boy who had saved me from the Triangle fire was a Darkling—the sworn enemy of the Order.

But maybe he hadn't been trying to save me. He'd shown up at the factory just before the man in the Inverness cape had. And then I'd seen him whispering in the man's ear—to distract him, I'd thought at the time, but what if he'd really been working with the man in the cape? After all, I'd woken up in Bellevue after the fire. Mr. Greenfeder said he thought the boy had left me on the pavement, but maybe he was the one who had carried me to Bellevue—right into Dr. Pritchard's and the caped man's hands.

Knowing what I now knew about the dark-winged boy and the other creatures that were part of our world, I wondered what other symptoms of my madness were real. Had smoke really poured from the mouth of the man in the Inverness cape? Had he followed me to my grandmother's townhouse? What about the bells inside my head? Were they somehow connected to the Blythewood bells that scared away the boy?

And then there was the black feather I'd found lying on the floor beside my mother's body. Had a Darkling visited my mother just before she died? Or even killed her?

My thoughts spinning in a dizzying cycle, I fell into an uneasy slumber . . . straight into the dark woods, where I was running, chased by slavering goblins and vicious firesprites. I heard their angry growls behind me, coming ever closer. I tripped on a root, fell to the ground, and felt their claws on my legs, their hot, fetid breath on my face.

And then *he* was there, his great black wings beating away all the fearsome creatures, his arms wrapping around me, lifting me up. I looked up into his face: as always, a rim of fire from the setting sun haloing noble features stamped clean as a coin. Then he turned his face and the line of fire spread in a network of veins, just as lightning had spread across the face of the fire-sprite. The flame crawled from his face down the fine white skin of his throat and across the carved sinews and muscles of his chest. It spread like cracks in an old China teacup when you pour hot water into it, only these cracks were made of fire and burned away flesh, changing him before my eyes from the beautiful boy of my dreams into a horrid monster.

I lifted my hand to ward off the sight and saw something even more terrifying. The cracks had spread to me. My own skin was dissolving along with his.

I woke, drenched in sweat, sheets tangled, to the sound of bells. I held my hand up to my face, terrified that I'd find those cracks in my skin. After last night who knew what was a dream and what was real? Morning sunlight limned my fingers with fire, but my flesh remained whole. Still, as I rose and dressed for the day I felt as if the cracks were there, just as in an old teacup that hides its flaws until hot water reveals them. Sooner or later they would show up for all the world to see.

⇥ ✦ ⇤

I discovered at breakfast that I wasn't the only girl who had been visited by bad dreams. There were empty places at the tables in the dining hall. Passing Georgiana's table I heard her say, "At least *some* of the chaff has been separated from the wheat. Notice that the girls who have left are not legacies. Breeding will out."

By my side, Daisy flinched. "I have half a mind to tell her what I think," she muttered under her breath, but just then a girl at another table began screaming about "boggarts in the sugar bowl" and had to be escorted from the hall.

"Irish," Helen said with a sniff as we sat down at our table. "We had an Irish maid once who had to be dismissed because she said she'd heard a brownie in the chimney."

"Does it occur to you now," Beatrice asked drily, "that she may have been correct?"

"Just because there are real fairies in the world doesn't mean we should credit every fool who believes in them," Helen tartly replied, and then added, "You certainly look nonplussed. Did you know?"

"Father told us there would be surprising revelations in store for us here," Beatrice commented as she spooned brown sugar into her oatmeal. "I thought it might be *something* of this nature. We have always been quite sure that father had a more important role in world affairs than he was letting on." Dolores nodded encouragingly and Beatrice went on as if she were conducting a conversation with her mute sister.

"Wherever we have lived, men and women of the most exalted rank and position have come to consult with him—the Emperor Franz Joseph himself consulted Papa on the Serbian question. And of course this explains father's grave and serious demeanor. How could one be frivolous once one knows of the great evil threatening the innocent unknowing masses? We are most gratified that we will now be able to take our places beside him in this fight against evil."

"*This* must be the important cause the hazelnut predicted for me last night," Cam announced, her eyes burning with a fervor I'd seen in the young women who worked at the Henry Street Settlement and marched in the suffrage parades.

None of my tablemates questioned the evil nature of the creatures we had seen.

"Are *all* the creatures of Faerie evil?" I asked Sarah Lehman when she joined us.

"Oh, yes," she answered, briskly buttering her toast. "The Order has done exhaustive study on all the creatures of Faerie. You'll learn the classifications in science class, hear about the horrible things they've done to mankind in Mr. Bellows' history class, and"—she shuddered—"see the specimens in Miss Frost's class. Of course there are always naysayers in any group." She lowered her voice and leaned across the table. We all leaned in to hear her whisper.

"There have been rumors that there's a faction in the Order arguing for greater tolerance for the creatures and renewed negotiations between the Order and the Darklings, but . . ." She looked around anxiously before continuing. "Dame Beckwith has strictly forbidden any discussion of this topic in class. Personally, I think—"

A phlegmy cough interrupted Sarah. We all looked up into Miss Frost's imposing bosom.

"It is not the duty of the head girl to share her personal opinions, Miss Lehman. Nor to model inappropriate table manners by leaning across the table and whispering like a parlor maid gossiping about her employees. Unless that is the line of work you would prefer to pursue."

"No, Miss Frost," Sarah said, meekly leaning back in her chair and coloring deeply. "I apologize for my behavior."

Miss Frost sniffed. "Perhaps you are in need of a private etiquette tutorial."

Sarah's shoulders slumped at the suggestion. I could hardly imagine anything more disagreeable than being shut up with the overbearing Miss Frost.

"It was my fault," I said quickly. "I asked Sarah if all the creatures of Faerie were evil and she was explaining to me—" I caught a panicked look in Sarah's eyes. Clearly the talk about factions proposing more tolerant treatment of the creatures was *not* something she should have been sharing with me. "That they most certainly are all evil. Every single one of them," I finished. Sarah breathed a sigh of relief.

"Of course they are!" Miss Frost exclaimed, her face turning the same purple as her dress. "What fool would question such an obvious notion after all you saw last night?"

"That's what Sarah said," I replied. "I imagine she lowered her voice to spare me the embarrassment of everybody else knowing what a silly question I'd asked."

Miss Frost lifted her lorgnette to her eyes and regarded me critically. I held her gaze, aiming for a neutral, bland mien, the same expression I would employ when my landlady came to ask for the rent or the foreman at the factory would criticize a seam I had sewn. As I met her eyes I heard the bass bell tolling in my head and I knew that if I didn't do something Miss Frost would assign me some terrible punishment. I forced the bell to slow in my head as I had when when I calmed Etta and got her to come out of the dressing room. As it tolled inside my head I saw Miss Frost's eyes glaze over.

"Well, then," she said, lowering her lorgnette and blinking like a baby owl. "That's another matter." She looked around the table as if she had forgotten why she had come. "I see they're serving kippers," she remarked. "Do remember not to swallow any bones." Then she turned and drifted away, zigzagging across the dining room like a sailboat tacking across a windy harbor.

"How did you do that?" Daisy asked when Miss Frost was out of earshot.

"Do what?" I asked. "I only apologized . . ."

"Euphorbia Frost has never been swayed by an apology in her life," Sarah said. "You *bell-manced* her. It's a technique we learn for mesmerizing our quarry in a hunt, but it's not taught until the fledgling year and it's usually done with bells. How did you know how to do it?"

I shrugged, uncomfortable now. All the girls at our table were staring at me. "I don't know," I said. "I'm sure it was an accident."

"Papa says each of us is chosen for Blythewood because we have some inherent power," Beatrice said. "This *bell-mancing* thing might be Ava's. I'm hoping for *bibliosmosis*, the ability to absorb the contents of any book by merely holding it in your hand."

"But wouldn't that ruin the pleasure of reading?" Daisy asked. The two girls were quickly engaged in an argument over the purposes of reading, which was joined by the other girls at the table—all except Sarah, who smiled and laid a hand on my arm.

"Thank you for saving me from a private tutoring session with Miss Frost. It's bad enough I have to dust her specimen cases. I shan't forget it."

I returned her smile, glad to have won Sarah's gratitude even though I had no idea *how* I had done it. Only later, when the bells had rung for class and I was hurrying with the rest of the girls to our first lecture, did I realize I'd never gotten to hear what Sarah thought about the factions that thought the fairies weren't all evil. I wondered which side she fell on.

Our first class was in the North Wing lecture hall, which resembled the Third Street Vaudeville House, only the seats that rose in a semicircle around the stage were uncushioned and the performer wasn't a dancer in spangles and feathers but an earnest young man in a tweed suit, which was much too heavy for the warm weather, and gold-rimmed glasses. Still the story he told was as fabulous as anything I'd ever seen on a vaudeville stage (including Varney the Sword Swallower and the magical feats of the Amazing Houdini).

Rupert Bellows took off his glasses, gripped the podium on both sides, leaned forward, and told us that the history of the world was "one long story of the fight between good and evil."

"Last night you encountered the face of evil, but it is not always so plainly disclosed. In this class you will learn how evil forces have been secretly at work behind the scenes for centuries. The barbarians that overran the gates of Rome? Mongolian centaurs! The bubonic plague? Spread by goblin-rats! Napoleon's attack on England? Instigated by a succubus! And wherever evil arises, the Order has been there to strike it down. The Order established their schools throughout the world: Mont Cloche in the Pyrenees, the Glockenkloster in Vienna, the Gymnasium Klok in Holland. That is the tradition you are heir to. . . . Some of you are *literally* heirs to the men and women who created those schools."

His voice full of emotion, Mr. Bellows paused and took off his glasses to rub the fog that had clouded them. I looked around the room at the assembled girls in their white shirtwaists and dark skirts and noticed that although many of them were from the Dutch and English families of Old New York, some were from other countries, like the Jager twins, or a Russian girl named Grushenka whom I'd heard someone whisper was related to the Tsar's family, or a shy Spanish girl named Fiamma who spoke hardly any English. They were all riveted by Mr. Bellows's lecture, their eyes burning.

Only one student didn't seem to be under Mr. Bellows's spell and that was the only boy in the class. Nathan Beckwith sat in the last row, his chair tipped back, a straw boater tilted over his eyes. "Is it all left to the women, then?" he drawled. "Doesn't seem quite sporting."

Mr. Bellows put his glasses back on and regarded Nathan coolly. "The prince who rode to the aid of the bell maker's daughters sacrificed himself for their safety. His knights founded a knighthood to serve the sisters of the Order. Those accepted into the knighthood train at Blythewood's brother school, Hawthorn. I believe you're familiar with the institution, Mr. Beckwith."

Nathan snorted. "I didn't see any evidence of knighthood training, only a bunch of boring old men lecturing on obedience and service."

Mr. Bellows colored deeply and gripped the podium as though he wished it were Nathan's neck. "Perhaps you'll feel differently when you learn whom we knights serve." He went on to tell us that the women of the Order had learned the four elemental magics of the fairies—the magics of earth, air, fire, and water—and how to communicate with the falcons and train them to aid us in the hunt against the most brutal creatures, the goblins and trows. "They learned from the master hunters themselves—the Darklings."

Mr. Bellows pronounced the name in an ominous voice that created a rustling in the room as girls shifted uneasily and rubbed their arms as if they were suddenly cold. I felt a shiver, too, but not of fear. I was remembering how the dark-winged boy in the woods had looked at me and how his eyes had made me feel warm. I'd wanted to lean into his arms and let him carry me up. . . .

"They studied the Darklings because they were their worst enemies. It was a Darkling who abducted and killed Merope."

The words broke into my head like the lash of a whip. What was I doing daydreaming about one of these monsters? If the other girls knew what I was thinking they would shun me—worse even than if they thought I was mad. I would be a pariah.

There was a sharp cracking noise behind me. Startled, I turned, half expecting that my thoughts had summoned the

Darkling, but it was only Nathan, who had tilted forward on his chair and was now following with full attention as Mr. Bellows retold the story of the bell maker's daughters—only this time explaining that it was a Darkling who had stolen the youngest daughter.

"After Merope's abduction, the Order of the Bells was founded to protect the world against the fairies and the Darklings. We study our enemies to learn how to hunt them down and we use the bells, made of iron and our own blood, to keep them at bay."

"And what about the girls they steal? What do we do about getting them back?"

The question came from the back of the room. I knew it was Nathan because he was the only boy here, but I hardly recognized his voice. Gone was the bored, upper-class drawl he'd first affected—gone, too, the excited boyish voice I'd heard in the woods last night. There was an anger and gravity to his voice now that made him sound years older. I glanced back and saw that he'd taken off his hat and raked his hair back off his forehead. His pale gray eyes flashed silver. A muscle twitched above his clenched jaw.

"That is not my area of expertise," Mr. Bellows began in a faltering voice totally unlike the one he'd used to lecture us.

"Then what good are you?" Nathan demanded. "What good is it to learn the history of these bastards"—several girls gasped—"if we don't do anything about them stealing our own?"

There was a stunned silence as Mr. Bellows put his glasses back on and stared back at Nathan.

"Now we know why he got kicked out of Hawthorn," Helen whispered under her breath.

But Mr. Bellows didn't throw Nathan out. Instead he said, "You make an interesting point, Mr. Beckwith, and I sympathize with your outrage. Why don't you stay after class a moment to discuss the issue with me. The rest of you—read the first hundred pages in Claveau's *History of the Order of the Bells* and write a three-page *pensée* on the doctrine of bell magic for class tomorrow. Class dismissed."

We gathered our books and filed out past Nathan, who sat fuming in his seat. I tried to catch Nathan's eye to show him I wouldn't ostracize him, but he stared straight ahead in such a rage that I doubted he saw any of us.

"Why is Nathan so angry?" I asked Helen when we were in the hall.

Helen looked around and then pulled me into an alcove. "Nathan's sister Louisa disappeared a week ago. Dame Beckwith said she went to a sanatorium in Switzerland, but I overheard Mother tell another Blythewood alumna that she *vanished*."

"Nathan's sister is the girl who went missing?" I asked, appalled. "Dame Beckwith's own daughter? Why didn't you tell me? Why is everybody keeping it a secret?"

Helen looked puzzled at the question. "Well, it would seem rude to talk about the headmistress's daughter like that."

"Rude?" I barked, startling both Helen and myself. "A girl's gone missing and you're all worried about the rules of etiquette?"

"You needn't get yourself all in a twist about it. You sound like one of those suffragettes! Actually, you sound a bit like Louisa the last time she was at our house for tea. Honestly, when I first heard she'd gone missing I was sure she'd run off to England to march with Mrs. Pankhurst, but when I saw Nathan here I knew it must be more serious than that, and after last night . . ."

Her voice faltered. In the brief time I'd known her Helen hadn't looked unsure about anything, but right now she looked worried.

"You think he's come back to find her?"

"Yes," she admitted, "but if she went missing in the woods he must realize it's hopeless. No one could survive alone in those woods, except . . ."

"Except who?" I asked.

"Except your mother. I think that's why Nathan was asking me about her. She disappeared into the woods for a whole month and *she* came back."

15

I WALKED TO our next class—science with Mr. Jager—in a daze, trying to make sense out of what Helen had told me. My mother had gone missing in the Blythe Wood for a whole month. What had happened to her there? I tried to imagine what it would be like to be all alone in those woods with the fearsome creatures that roamed through them. How had my mother survived? Had she seen something so awful there that she'd never been able to recover? Was that why we moved so often, why she begged me not to talk to strangers? Was she running from something she had seen in the woods—the source of the hunted, shadowed look in her eyes? It was the same look, I realized now, that Nathan had in his.

Growing up alone with my mother, isolated from all family, moving too often to make friends, I sometimes daydreamed about what it would be like to have a sister or a brother, someone with whom I could share my thoughts—and the responsibility of looking after my mother. After she died and I went to work, I saw other girls walking to the factory with, or met after work by, their brothers, and envied them. But now I imagined what it would be like to have a sister and lose her. Worse, to know she was lost in those woods with the monsters we'd seen last night.

Poor Nathan. Those shadows under his eyes, his brittle, hard way of talking—it was all because he was walking around with a hole inside him.

I reached the laboratory, a long narrow room that ran along the north side of the castle beside the conservatory, and stood for a moment in the doorway. The room was arranged with long high tables that reminded me of the layout of the Triangle factory, except that instead of sewing machines each table was supplied with a spirit lamp, glass beakers, and covered baskets. Mr. Jager stood at the front of the room, head down, shuffling through a stack of notes. He didn't have Mr. Bellows's commanding presence and his students were obviously taking advantage of his distraction to gossip with one another.

Helen waved for me to come join her at a table at the front of the room with Daisy, Cam, Beatrice, and Dolores. I suspected Helen had chosen our seat to be near the Jager twins, because they would be able to help us the most with the work. It was a good idea. I had no idea what went on in a science class in a regular school, let alone a school that trained its students to fight fairies and demons. Would we be concocting magic potions? Turning each other into toads? Crafting explosive devices like the one that had killed Tsar Alexander II in Russia? My gentle mother had never taught me such things. I would need all the help I could get. But instead of joining my friends at their table I took a seat at the last table in the back, which was empty except for Nathan.

He narrowed his eyes at me. "Why aren't you sitting with your friends?"

I shrugged. "They don't look as if they need me."

"And you think I do?"

I met his icy stare. "Helen told me about your sister."

"And did she tell you that we're not allowed to talk about her? That once a girl goes missing at Blythewood her name is struck from the rolls and never mentioned again? That they believe to say the name of a *lost girl* is to conjure the black-hearted monsters that stole her?"

I shook my head, struck dumb by the hostility in his voice. I'd thought yesterday that Nathan's cool demeanor was a pose he adopted to seem more alluring to girls, but I saw now that the flirtatiousness was a pose that he wore over his icy resolve—there to get what he needed, gone when it would do him no good. I turned away from his cold glare and wondered if it was too late to change seats, but Mr. Jager had collected himself sufficiently to begin class—or at least he had stopped shuffling papers and was looking up at the room, a dazed expression in his watery brown eyes as if he wasn't sure why two dozen girls were sitting in front of him.

Mr. Jager cleared his throat and said something inaudible under the hum of the girls' voices. A girl in the second row giggled. Beatrice glared at her and made a loud shushing sound. Mr. Jager looked mournfully at the girl and waved a large bony hand, as if to say it was no matter to him if we listened or not.

Instantly the girl's hands flew to her mouth and she made a muffled noise. I couldn't see from where I sat what had happened to her but I saw the horrified expressions of the other girls as she jumped to her feet and ran from the room with one hand clamped over her mouth. Something was dribbling from between her fingers. Something red. A drop fell on the floor by my feet. I cringed away from it, but Nathan reached across me to pick it up.

"Jelly beans," he remarked.

"Ja," Mr. Jager said with a sigh. "My daughters tell me that American children enjoy zese trifles and that I should consider giving them out as rewards for good behavior. Would anyone else . . . ?"

We all shook our heads close-mouthed, not wanting to find our own mouths full of jelly beans, apparently Mr. Jager's idea of suitable punishment for talking or laughing in class.

"No? Good. I will commence my talk on magic, then. Ahem!" Mr. Jager cleared his throat, held up his rumpled notes, and launched into a long-winded, convoluted discourse on the nature of magic. I understood about every fifth word. It didn't help that he spoke with a thick Viennese accent or that he held the pages so close to his mouth that his voice was muffled or that many of the words I did hear—*prestidigitation, psychometry, necromancy*—I didn't understand. One would need to be a magician to decipher them. After about ten minutes he lowered his notes and looked out at us, his large melancholy eyes growing sadder as they took in our utter confusion.

"Perhaps, Papa," Beatrice said softly, "if you explained in your own words?"

Mr. Jager sighed. "Very well. You see there are four kinds of magic in the world, each related to one of the essential elements—air, earth, fire, and water. Air magic is what the fairies practice . . ." He paused to see if we were following along. Beatrice nodded hopefully and we all followed suit. "Basically, it's sympathetic magic. I create a bond between two things, say between Mees . . . er . . ." He looked down at Daisy.

"Moffat," Daisy squeaked. "Miss Daisy Moffat of Kansas City, Kansas, sir."

"Er . . . yes. I create a bond between Mees Daisy Moffat of Kansas City, Kansas . . ." He reached down and plucked a hair from Daisy's head. "And, say . . ." He dug into the basket on the front table and came up with a pair of embroidery scissors. He held them up in one hand so we all could see him wrap Daisy's hair around their handle. "The basis of fairy magic is that all things are connected by air. I can reinforce that connection by blowing on the object while thinking of the person I want to connect it to."

Mr. Jager glanced between Daisy and the scissors and then blew on the scissors. Daisy shivered . . . then giggled. "It tickles!" she announced.

"Hmph." Mr. Jager frowned. "Ja, I suppose it does. That was a piece of your soul leaving your body. We can all take comfort in the fact that our final parting of soul and body will . . . *tickle*. It should mean that I've created a bond. Let's see." He held up his hand. The silver scissors seemed to be trembling. I thought it was because Mr. Jager's hand was shaking until the scissors stood upright on its sharp points. A halo of glitter surrounded the scissors. Mr. Jager lowered his hand and the scissors took two dainty steps onto the table.

"Aw," Daisy said, tilting her head, "it's cute."

The scissors tilted one empty circle of its handle in the same motion, eliciting coos from the circle of girls.

"Sympathy for the simulacrum is natural," Mr. Jager said in a mournful voice. "But to be avoided." He blew on the scissor creature and Daisy's hair puffed out behind her. Daisy laughed. He filled a beaker with water and emptied it on the scissors. This time Daisy gasped, spitting water out of her mouth. "Hey!" she squawked. "That's not . . ."

Mr. Jager struck a match to the spirit lamp and reached for the scissors. Without realizing that I'd moved I was suddenly between Mr. Jager and the table. I grabbed the scissors, which writhed in my hands, snapping at my fingers. Behind me Daisy was flapping her arms.

"Stop!" I cried, not sure if I was speaking to Mr. Jager, Daisy, or the scissors. A bell was ringing in my head. Not the danger bass, but the treble. I closed my eyes and listened to it chime twelve times. When it was done, I opened my eyes. The scissors lay lifeless in my hands. Daisy sat in her chair, limp and damp, but unburned. The air around her was full of smoke and glitter.

"Very interesting," Mr. Jager said, almost smiling. "What time of day were you born?"

I gaped at him, furious but stunned.

"What does that . . . ?"

"Was it at midnight, by any chance? On the very stroke of midnight while the bells tolled the hour?"

I nodded, unable to speak. "How . . . ?"

Mr. Jager reached into the basket and withdrew a handbell. He rang it once. The chime cleared the smoke and glitter from the air.

"The second kind of magic, and the most important to the order, is earth magic. We learned that bells forged of iron, with a drop of human blood, could dispel air magic. Then we learned that by ringing the bells in certain patterns we could keep the fairies away—or draw them closer to kill them.

"Only certain people can use the bells—you all have been tested to see if you possess the ability—and only the rarest of people can use earth magic *without* a bell. You, Miss Hall, are one of those: a chime child, born at the stroke of midnight. You have special powers. You can hear things others can't . . . and *see* things others don't."

I thought of the smoke coming out of the mouth of the man in the Inverness cape and the crows circling the roof of the Triangle factory. I thought of the delusions I'd had during my stay at the Bellevue Pavilion for the Insane. Were those the kind of things Mr. Jager meant? I glanced uneasily behind me at the rest of the class, who were staring at me. Soon enough, they'd be telling everyone that Georgiana Montmorency had been right—I *was* a freak, just like the bearded lady at Dreamland in Coney Island.

"I'd wager that some of things you see are not pleasant," Mr. Jager said in an uncharacteristically gentle voice.

I nodded weakly, tears springing to my eyes as some of those visions floated before my eyes—girls with fire in their hair, snakes made out of smoke lurking in the corners.

"That's the price that the chime child pays, but in exchange you are granted great powers. Out of all your class, you have the potential for the most power. Now, to move on. Let's discuss the two other forms of magic—water magic and fire magic, also sometimes called shadow magic. The latter is strictly forbidden."

Helen grabbed my arm on the way to Miss Frost's class. "Why didn't you tell me you were a chime child?"

"I didn't even know it was a real thing," I objected. "I thought if was just a fancy of my mother's. How do you know about them? I thought you didn't know anything about the magical side of Blythewood before you got here."

"*Everyone's* heard of the chime children!" she said, as if I'd expressed ignorance of which fork to use with salad. "My mother and her friends always compared what time their children were born. It was considered lucky to be born at the stroke of *any* hour—I was born at precisely four just as tea was being served—but most lucky to be born at midnight."

"I don't see how it's lucky," I said, noting the stares of a group of girls going into Miss Frost's class. "I hear these bells in my head and see . . . *awful* things."

"Oh well, that does sound unpleasant, but I'm sure they'll teach you how to control it here. Can you"—she pulled me aside at the door to Miss Frost's class—"read people's minds?"

"No!" I insisted.

Helen looked disappointed. "That's too bad. Maybe you can learn."

"Would you like me to know what you're thinking all the time?" I asked.

Her blue eyes widened and she blushed. "Oh, I suppose not. Not that I ever think anything improper." Her blush deepened. It occurred to me that it might be entertaining to *pretend* to Helen I could read her mind, but before I could imply the possibility, Sarah Lehman poked her head out of the classroom.

"This is the last class you want to be late for," Sarah hissed. "Trust me!"

Helen rolled her eyes. "I don't even understand what deportment can possibly have to do with our mission. And it's not as if *I* need any training on the arts of social courtesy."

I, too, had wondered what the deportment teacher could possibly have to share with us, but I soon learned that the world of Faerie was governed by etiquette rules even stricter than those of New York society and that it was Miss Frost's role to enlighten us to the nature and habits of the indigenous species as though she were instructing a group of missionaries about to embark on a trip to the Amazonian jungle, with the aim that we not get eaten by the natives. Lecturing in front of a deep burgundy curtain, she informed us that the fairies loathed the name "fairy" and would attack anyone calling them thus.

"They prefer to be called 'the good neighbors,' 'the old folk,' or, my personal favorite, 'the gentry.' The best way to gain control over a fairy, though, is to call it by its species name. That will stun it so completely you will have time to either run away or shoot it with an arrow. So, it is very important to learn the different types of fairy. For that purpose I have collected an array of . . . ahem!" Miss Frost cleared her throat while glaring at Sarah, who got up from her seat and dutifully approached one side of the burgundy curtains. "An array of specimens!" Miss Frost declared, with a flourish of her be-ringed hands.

The curtains swung open to reveal a glass-fronted bookshelf filled with colorful objects. The whole back wall seemed to be papered with a design of multihued butterfly wings that was reflected in an assortment of glass jars and trays. "You may find it hard to believe, but in my youth I was an avid naturalist and collector. Many of these specimens were collected by myself while accompanying my mentor, Sir Miles Malmsbury, the noted zoologist and explorer. It was Sir Malmsbury who pioneered the study of germ plasm in indigenous lychnobious creatures."

A faraway look entered Miss Frost's eyes as she glanced at a framed photograph on the wall of a middle-aged man with bushy mutton-chops in a safari jacket, standing with one foot propped up on a dead rhinoceros. Sarah brought her back by asking if she'd like her to bring out the specimens now.

"Haven't you done it already?" Miss Frost snapped.

Flinching at the reprimand, Sarah opened the case and removed a tray and a large glass jar. She handed them to girls on either side of the room and asked them to pass them around. Helen, Daisy, and I had taken seats in the back, so we were the last to get the tray and the jar. As they were passed around a heavy silence fell on the room, punctuated only by the screech of chalk as Miss Frost wrote out a series of Latinate words that all started with *lychnobia*—a word that I dimly thought had something to do with lamps—*lychnobia arvensis*, *lychnobia arborescens*, *lychnobia collina*, *lychnobia hirta*, *lychnobia orbiculata*, *lychnobia vallicola* . . . they sounded like varieties of some kind of flower.

"And my personal favorite," Miss Frost said as she wrote the last name on the board, "*lychnobia pruina*, for obvious reasons." She chortled and I saw the girls in front of me looking at each other in puzzlement.

"The frost fairy," Sarah said aloud. "You see, it's like Miss Frost's name."

A murmur of understanding went through the room, but I was still confused. What did a frost fairy . . . ? The tray arrived at our table. Daisy looked at it first and I saw all the blood drain from her face. I worried she might faint. Helen took the tray from her hands, looked down, and quickly passed it to me.

I thought, at first, that it was a tray of butterflies. Brilliantly colored wings were spread out and pinned on an ivory baize cloth. I felt a flutter in my stomach at the thought of the fragile creatures captured and killed to create this display. It reminded me of the moment in the fire when the girls ran to the windows to escape the blaze and were forced out into the open air, their arms spread wide.

I looked closer and saw that between the colorful wings lay tiny human-like bodies, like little wax dolls. *Surely, that's what they are—waxwork dolls,* I thought. But as I stared longer at them I noticed that in the center of each one's chest was a pearl hat pin and a small drop of blood. These creatures had been pinned while alive. Then I looked up and saw the jar that was being handed around. Bobbing inside, like a pickled egg, was a tiny figure, its multicolored wings floating in the brine like seaweed.

Bile rose in my throat. My head swam and dimly I heard the bell in my head again, only this time it was the bass bell tolling danger. What could the danger be? I wondered. These poor creatures were already dead. They couldn't hurt us and we couldn't hurt them anymore. But the bell was tolling louder and faster, clanging in my head. I had to get out of there.

I lurched unsteadily to my feet and headed toward the door. Behind me I heard Miss Frost's voice droning on. "*Lychnobia hirta*, or hairy fairy, is the most unappealing of the lot . . . Miss Hall! Where do you think—?" A shattering of glass interrupted her. The reek of formaldehyde filled the room as I fled, not looking back. I knew what I'd see—the glass jar holding the preserved fairy had shattered. The danger the bells had been warning me against was from myself.

16

I FLED THROUGH the nearest door, desperate for fresh air after the reek of formaldehyde, and into an enclosed colonnaded garden.

All my worst fears had been realized. I wasn't going to fit into Blythewood at all. I was a freak. Mr. Jager was wrong—it wasn't a gift to hear the bells in my head, it was a curse. If it had been a gift I would have stopped the Triangle fire and saved all those girls who died. I would have saved Tillie. My mother had changed the time on my birth certificate because she knew it was a curse. She must have been afraid that the bells inside my head would eventually drive me insane—and they nearly had. Hadn't I raved like a madwoman all those months in Bellevue hospital? Clearly that was where I belonged.

I'd almost rather be there than here, I thought, pacing the enclosed path and looking for a way out. The path was bordered with columns made of the same honey-colored stone as the bell tower and topped with capitals carved with monstrous creatures that leered and stuck out their multiple forked tongues at me. What kind of a place was this that decorated their walls with monsters and kept such grisly specimens? Yes, I knew that such specimens were collected of animals, but the bodies of the fairies looked *human*. And if they were human it couldn't be right to skewer them with hat pins and pickle them in brine.

The memory of the pickled fairy brought up a wave of nausea again. I ran behind a column and was sick in the rose bushes. When my stomach was empty I crawled a few feet away and huddled behind a rhododendron bush with my back against the stone wall.

The wall felt warm and solid on my back. I closed my eyes, exhausted by the events of the morning, and must have drifted off for a few moments. I awoke to the sound of a voice.

"You found my hiding place." I opened my eyes and found Sarah Lehman crouched next to me. "You look a little green," she commented.

"You do, too," I said, tugging on one of the waxy rhododendron leaves. "It's the light. What are *you* hiding from?"

"Miss Frost," she said. "If she sees me unoccupied for two minutes she thinks up a chore for me to do, like dusting her Cabinet of Gruesome Curiosities."

I shuddered. "Why do they allow her to keep those? It's so cruel!"

She nodded. "Yes, it *is* cruel. But no crueler than what those creatures do to us. Look, do you see the figures on the capitals?" She pointed up at the column above us. I looked up and saw that there were tiny sprites carved into the honey-colored stone. Their wings formed a delicate tracery in the marble. "Do you know what this place is?"

"This place?" I asked, confused. "You mean this garden?"

"It's a cloister," she said. "One of the original ones from the first abbey where the early sisters of the Order could walk in the fresh air behind thick walls because they dared not walk outside. If they did they might encounter the lychnobia, the lampsprites. They looked harmless enough, but they led girls astray into the forest, and once they were in the forest worse monsters would come to devour them." Sarah pointed up at another column. A hideous troll stretched his mouth open so wide that I could see inside where a human hand flailed.

I flinched at the horror of it and turned back to Sarah. Her face had taken on a greener hue that I didn't think came solely from the rhododendron leaves.

"That's what probably happened to Louisa after those *poor creatures* led her into the woods," Sarah said.

"You mean Nathan's sister? Did you know her?"

"She was my best friend," Sarah said, wiping a tear from her eye. "You see, I spend my holidays here because I've no place else to go. Louisa felt sorry for me and was kind to me— but then Louisa was kind to everyone. She even felt bad for the little sprites. She told me just two weeks ago that she was going to prove they weren't evil. And then she disappeared."

Sarah choked back a sob. "I think she must have followed them into the woods to prove that they weren't dangerous, but then she never came back. So what she proved was that they *are* dangerous." She turned to stare at me through the green gloom of the rhododendron bushes. "I think that must have been what happened to your mother, too."

"Why do you think that?" I asked. I was remembering stories my mother told me about will-o'-the-wisps. She'd always made them sound like lovely things. Would she have spoken of them like that if they'd led her astray in the woods?

"It's something I overheard Miss Frost saying to Dame Beckwith." She squeezed my hand, then added, "I overhear a lot of things in my various jobs. No one notices *Sour Lemon* in the corner dusting. If you'd like I could try to find out more about your mother."

"You could?" I asked, returning the pressure of her hand.

She smiled. "I'll keep my ears open . . . only . . ."

"Only what?"

"I won't be able to tell you what I find out if you run away from Blythewood."

"How did you know I was thinking of running away?" I asked, the blood rushing to my face. What else did Sarah know about what I'd been thinking? But her smile was reassuring.

"Because this is where *I* come when I'm thinking of running away. But then I look at these creatures . . ." She looked up at the hideous monsters carved on the column capitols. "And I remember why I'm here. We all come to Blythewood for a purpose. Are you really ready to give up yours already?"

I thought about my questions about my mother. Then I thought about Tillie Kupermann. If she were in my place would she run away? "No," I told Sarah, "I'm not ready to give up."

"Good," she said, smiling at me. "Then we'd best get you to your next class. It's all right you missed Latin—Mrs. Calendar is so blind she won't have noticed you weren't there—but you mustn't skip archery. Miss Swift has an eye as keen as a hawk's. I'm supposed to assist her today setting up targets, so if we don't get there soon we'll both be on her bad side."

I didn't want that. Sarah was the best—perhaps the only—

friend I'd made so far at Blythewood. The first friend I'd made since Tillie. I didn't want to risk losing her.

⋙→ ✦ ←⋘

Sarah showed me a door on the far side of the cloister, hidden behind the roses, that let out onto the gardens. "My little secret," she said. "It's the best way to get out of the building without anyone seeing you." The archery court was set up at the end of the gardens, so we were only a few minutes late for class. We found our classmates in a semicircle around Miss Swift, who was standing beside a marble statue of the goddess Diana drawing a bow. I slipped in between Helen and Daisy while Sarah began collecting stray arrows off the lawn and setting up targets.

"Thank the bells," Helen whispered. "Daisy was afraid you'd run away."

"So were you—" Daisy began, but was silenced by a glare from Miss Swift. Daisy's face turned bright pink. I'd already discovered today that Helen couldn't stay quiet for two minutes and Daisy had a horror being caught talking by our teachers.

"Behold Diana," Miss Swift continued, gesturing toward the statue. "The virgin huntress, a symbol of our Order. She dedicated herself to the hunt, forsaking marriage and children, as many of us here at Blythewood have."

"As if Miss Swift had many offers of marriage," Helen whispered beside me while Daisy, still blushing, glared at her.

"Why not?" I whispered. Miss Swift looked attractive enough to me, with a figure as lean and lithe as Diana. Only her mouse-brown hair, scraped back into a tight bun and fixed with an arrow-shaped pin, made her look a bit severe.

"Oh, everyone knows that Blythewood teachers don't marry."

"But what about Dame Beckwith? She was married."

"Oh, but she gave up teaching when she went away to be married, and then she came back when her husband died—"

Daisy stomped on Helen's foot to silence her and we all focused back on Miss Swift's lecture, leaving me to wonder if Dame Beckwith's sad eyes came from memories of her deceased husband.

"Some of you may have practiced archery with your friends and brothers, at your summer cottages and lakeside camps. Perhaps you like how the sport shows off your figure and you've taken prizes at your local competitions—"

"I came in first at Camp Wanasockie last summer," Cam announced proudly.

Miss Swift smiled. "Ah, that is precisely what I mean. Come up here, Miss . . ."

"Bennett," Cam said cheerily, pushing past the rest of us to stand between Miss Swift and the marble Diana. "Camilla Bennett. Cam for short." She grinned at the rest of us and winked at Helen, who grimaced. "I'm a crack shot, if I do say so myself."

"Uh-oh," Helen whispered. "She's in for it now."

"A crack shot," Miss Swift repeated, her upper lip curling. "How splendid. And what have you shot?"

"What? Oh, well, targets, of course . . ."

"Targets like these?" Miss Swift nodded to a tall blonde

girl, one of the Dianas, whom she introduced as Andalusia Beaumont. She carried a canvas target to the edge of the woods, about thirty feet away from where Cam and Miss Swift stood. "Would you like to demonstrate your prowess?"

She handed Cam a bow that was nearly as tall as Cam was, and an arrow fletched with black feathers. As Cam positioned herself at a right angle to the target, lifted the bow, and nocked the arrow in it, the sun struck the feathers. Prisms danced off them and I felt my stomach clench as I realized the feathers must be from a Darkling's wing.

When Cam released the arrow, it shot true and straight to the target and lodged with a satisfying *thwack* into the bull's-eye—a *thwack* that was echoed in the woods by an ominous crash. Cam was smiling and lowering her bow when the brush behind the target exploded. A blur of horns and fur trampled the target and headed straight toward Cam.

"What's the matter, Miss Bennett?" Miss Swift asked calmly, handing her another arrow. "You're a crack shot. Hadn't you better take aim?"

Cam's eyes widened. She took the arrow with a shaking hand and tried to nock it in the bow. Most of the girls screamed and ran for the cover of the garden wall, but Miss Swift and Andalusia Beaumont stood calmly beside Cam as the horned creature ran toward them. Helen, Daisy, and I stood rooted to the spot—not so much out of bravery, I think, as because we were too shocked to move. I looked from the horned creature, which I noticed with a sickening sense of horror had only one eye, back to Cam, who finally got the arrow nocked, drew, and shot—a good six feet wide of the charging monster.

Miss Swift nodded at Andalusia. The tall blonde coolly raised her loaded bow and shot the creature straight into its one eye. It slumped to the ground, twitched twice, and then stilled, thick blue gore pulsing from the arrow wound.

It's not human, I said to myself, forcing myself to look at the monster. It was like something out of mythology.

"Excellent shot, Miss Beaumont," Miss Swift said, striding toward the fallen goblin and placing one slim-booted foot on its chest. "A cyclops can only be killed with a direct shot to its eye. You see, girls, archery at Blythewood is quite a different sport from what you've been used to. I am not here to teach you to be archers." She wrenched the arrow from the cyclop's chest. "I am here to teach you to be *hunters*. Now, if one of you would please go find Gillie in the garden and tell him there's a bit of cleaning up to attend to, the rest of you can be measured for your bows."

The rest of the class was spent getting measurements taken and learning how to maintain our bows and arrows, but it was hard to concentrate very well while keeping an eye on the edge of the woods. I'd felt horrified at how human the lampsprites looked, but now I was horrified by how inhuman the cyclops looked—and at the thought that more creatures like that were roaming the woods. I think we were all relieved to go back into the castle, and to climb to the very top of the bell tower, for our bell ringing class in the belfry.

We all crowded by the windows to admire the views. To the southeast lay the quaint Dutch village of Rhinebeck. Trim Victorian houses lined the streets, many of them with glass greenhouses for growing the violets the town was famous for.

We could make out the train station and the tracks that led back to New York City. To the east lay a patchwork of farms—hay fields and apple orchards, and fenced paddocks in which horses, cows, and sheep grazed—a pretty, bucolic landscape like something out of a Dutch painting.

It was hard to imagine what could threaten such peace and order . . . until you looked to the north and saw the Blythe Wood crouched along the river like an animal tensed to spring out at its prey—deep, dark, and secret. Looking into it was like looking into a deep pool on a summer day that you wanted to dive into despite knowing that you might drown in it, or the eyes of a beast that drew you into its depths.

"What you feel when you regard the Blythe Wood, ladies—and gentleman," Mr. Peale began, bowing to Nathan, "is the magnetic pull of Faerie. The existence of that other world alongside ours is an anomaly, an aberration. Where that world breaks into ours it disrupts the flow of magneto-electro energy between our worlds, like a vacuum that pulls everything into its hungry maw."

"Hmm, Grandma, what big teeth you have!" Nathan whispered beside me. Helen slapped him on the arm and told him to stop being ridiculous, but her voice shook, and I recalled her fear of heights.

"To disrupt that energy we break up the sound waves with the bells. We have found that certain patterns interrupt the flow of malevolent energy. May I have six volunteers?"

To my surprise, Nathan volunteered right away—and volunteered me and Helen and Daisy as well. Beatrice and Dolores insisted on making up the six. Mr. Peale directed us to each grab one of the ropes that hung down into the square stone chamber. The ropes were so thick it took both my hands to span mine. I expected it to feel rough, but the rope had been worn smooth by many ringers before me. It thrummed with a tension as if it were tethered to an animal straining at its lead. As if the bells were alive.

Mr. Peale explained how the bells were numbered and counted us off so we knew our numbers. I was the sixth bell. "When I call your number you pull. For today I'll point, but eventually you'll remember when it's your turn."

He commenced calling numbers while circling us, demonstrating by grasping our arms how to pull down smoothly and let up with control. The sound of the bells right over our heads was deafening—at first just a cacophony of sound that drove all thought from my head. But slowly, the rhythm worked its way into my body, coming in through my hands and the soles of my feet where the sound vibrated upward from the stone. Soon I knew when it was my turn before Peale called my number. My whole body thrummed with the vibrations of the bells.

I caught sight of Nathan's face and he grinned at me. His cheeks were ruddy and healthy looking, the shadows beneath his eyes faded, his eyes bright. The haunted boy mourning for his lost sister was gone—perhaps because he wasn't alone anymore. I recalled what Gillie had said about ringing the bells—that you felt a part of something bigger than yourself. Even Dolores and Beatrice had cast off their habitual melancholy demeanor and were grinning.

I hardly noticed that Peale had ceased calling numbers or that we each knew when to stop. The peal had its own logic that led to its ending. When we stopped, the pattern seemed to go on, floating out into the air above the treetops. I thought I heard an answering call in a bird singing deep inside the forest, singing the same tune that we had played, and then came the echo of the last bell, tolling sweet and sonorous from beneath the river its plaintive cry. *Remember me*, it said, *remember me*. I looked around at my fellow bell ringers and saw that their ruddy cheeks were damp and felt that mine were, too, but whether from perspiration or tears, I wasn't sure.

"Excellent!" Mr. Peale exclaimed, his face shining and pink as though he had been pulling the bells himself. "Mr. Beckwith, you especially will make a fine bell master. Now, if you will all turn to your campanology guide and mark the first two dozen changes to memorize by tomorrow . . ."

17

WE RUSHED DOWN the stairs, late for our last class of the day, literature with Miss Sharp, held in the library so that we could have access to the Order's collection of great books. By now my arms ached, my ears were ringing, and my head was full of discordant facts that jostled against one another like riders on the Sixth Avenue streetcar at rush hour: Latin names for sprite species, the dates of the three great wizard wars, an antidote for centaur bite. Mixed up with all these were a dozen warring emotions: the horror of seeing Miss Frost's specimens, the terror of the cyclops attack, Nathan's grief over losing his sister, my fear of being exposed as a freak, but also the sense of belonging I'd had ringing the bells.

I wondered what I would find in the library. I had spent some of my happiest moments with my mother in libraries. I'd looked forward to seeing the one at Blythewood, but now I wondered how many more bloodthirsty stories were hidden behind the gilt-stamped leather spines on the floor-to-ceiling rows of books. No doubt Miss Sharp would soon explain that they held the secrets of evil fairies, and then she would assign two hundred pages to read and memorize by the morrow.

As we settled into our seats she stood at the front of class in a blue serge skirt and high-necked white blouse from which her slender long neck rose like the stem of a lily. Her abundant blonde hair was piled high on her head in the Gibson Girl style. She stood, still and tall as a candle, her golden hair the flame, regarding us. Then she turned away and walked to a window. She pushed open the heavy leaded casement, letting in river-scented air and the trill of a lark. Still looking out the window she began to speak, her voice somehow part of the breeze and birdsong.

> *"My heart aches, and drowsy numbness pains*
> *My sense, as though of hemlock I had drunk,*
> *Or emptied some dull opiate to the drains*
> *One minute past, and Lethe-wards had sunk."*

I had never taken opiates myself, but I had seen my mother's eyes dulled by the drug and I knew this was what she had felt. I felt that way myself right now, my brain over full of all the wonders and horrors of this strange and savage world I'd stumbled into. At least the poem was familiar. It was Keats's "Ode to a Nightingale," one of my mother's favorite poems

> *"'Tis not through envy of thy happy lot,*
> *But being too happy in thine happiness,—*
> *That thou, light-winged Dryad of the trees,*
> *In some melodious plot*
> *Of beechen green, and shadows numberless,*
> *Singest of summer in full-throated ease."*

Miss Sharp recited it as though she were addressing the bird outside the window but also, I felt, speaking to me directly. I felt the fatigue and confusion of the day fall away. On her voice I traveled past *the weariness, the fever, and the fret* and climbed on *the viewless wings of Poesy* to a tender night full of hawthorn, eglantine, and violets. When she got to the lines

> *"Darkling I listen; and for many a time*
> *I have been half in love with easeful Death . . . "*

I felt my eyes fill with tears at the thought that my mother must have felt this, too, perhaps as she drained the last drops of laudanum. It made me recall, as well, how I'd leaned toward the Darkling last night, wanting him to carry me away. Was it a spell they cast on humans? Is that how Louisa Beckwith had felt? Had she gone with her captor willingly?

I glanced guiltily around the room, hoping that no one had noticed my emotion, but each girl was gazing enthralled at Miss Sharp as if the teacher were speaking directly to her. And not only the girls. Nathan wasn't with us, but Rupert Bellows had come to the door of the library and leaned on the jamb, hands in the pockets of his rumpled tweed jacket, head back, eyes closed. He didn't look like the man who had lectured us on the evils of the fairies. He looked like a man who wanted to believe there was still beauty in the world.

There was one other listener in the room. Miss Corey the librarian, in the same hat and veil she'd worn last night at dinner, sat at one of the desks filling out index cards. When Miss Sharp came to the last stanza, the bells in the tower began to ring and I could see Miss Corey's lips moving beneath her veil, mouthing the words with her.

> "Forlorn! The very word is like a bell
> To toll me back from thee to my sole self!
> Adieu! The fancy cannot cheat so well
> As she is fam'd to do, deceiving elf.
> Adieu! adieu! Thy plaintive anthem fades
> Past the near meadows, over the still stream,
> Up the hill-side; and now 'tis buried deep
> In the next valley-glades:
> Was it a vision, or a waking dream?
> Fled is that music:—Do I wake or sleep?"

The bells had ceased as she came to the end, save for that ghostly echo of the seventh bell ringing in the river valley like a shred of the waking dream we'd all fallen into. Miss Sharp turned to us and leaned back against the window frame.

"After what you saw last night—and all you've heard and seen today"—she exchanged a look with the librarian and I wondered if she was thinking about Miss Frost's specimens— "you must wonder today whether you wake or sleep. What I'd like you to remember is that the world is beautiful despite—and sometimes because of—all the darkness in it, just as a white cameo is more beautiful against an ebony setting."

I startled at the image, reminded of how the Darkling's face had looked like a beautiful cameo set against the ebony of his wings. Had she, too, seen a face like that? I was jarred out of this reverie by the word "assignment" and reached for my pen to copy down the no doubt long list of pages we would have to read for tomorrow, but instead she only told us to "take a walk by the river, watch the sun set, and write a poem about what you see." Then she dismissed the class.

When we didn't move right away—three-quarters of the allotted hour for literature remained—she made a shooing motion with her hands as if we were a gaggle of geese. At last we all got up to go and drifted out of the class, each girl quiet and hugging her thoughts to herself. When I turned back, I saw that Miss Sharp had moved to the librarian's desk and perched on a corner of it. She leaned down to look at something in a book the librarian held up, and as she did her hair slipped out of its pins and fell in a golden waterfall. Miss Corey lifted her head and looked up. Caught in the light, her veil cast a dappled pattern across her face. Then Miss Corey moved the veil aside to see something in the book Miss Sharp held open for her, and I saw that the dapples weren't shadows from the veil but marks on her skin, like the spots on a fawn's pelt. She said something and Miss Sharp tossed her head back and laughed, the sound like the nightingale's song. I turned away—and nearly ran into Rupert Bellows.

"Oh, Miss . . . er . . ."

"Hall. Avaline Hall."

"Of course," he said, looking over my shoulder to where Vionetta Sharp laughed. "Are you off to write poetry by the river? Miss Sharp's recitation was very . . . er . . . inspiring, wasn't it?"

"Oh yes," I concurred, "but . . ." I hesitated, not thinking it right to criticize my teacher.

"But what?" Mr. Bellows demanded, his attention abruptly

focused on me and not Vionetta Sharp. "Spit it out, Miss Hall. I expect nothing less than honesty from my pupils."

"It's just that now there will be a dozen students walking along the riverside attempting to write a poem. It will hardly be a place conducive to writing poetry."

Rupert Bellows stared at me for a moment and then tilted his head back and laughed. "By Jove, you're right. My suggestion to you is to find your own brooding place. When I was at Cambridge it was on a punt in the River Cam. You'll need a place to yourself here or you'll go mad." He glanced at Miss Sharp as if he knew where his own madness lay.

"Thank you, Mr. Bellows," I said, "I think I know where that might be."

Rupert Bellows gave me a distracted smile, but I knew he hadn't heard me. Like the fellow in the poem, he was still in his own waking dream.

⤞ ✦ ⤝

Instead of going to the riverside, I climbed to the fourth floor and slipped out the landing window onto the catwalk. I'd noticed when I was out here with Nathan that there was a ladder leading up to the roof. What better place to brood, I thought, than up among the pigeons and chimneys. Rooftops had been my sanctuaries in the city; they could be here, too. But when I climbed to the top of Blythewood Castle I found I didn't have the roof to myself. I would have to share it with Gillie.

He was sitting on a stool outside a wooden shed built into the corner of the crenellated tower. The falcon mews, I guessed. Through the open door I could see two rows of falcons and hawks standing on their perches, their heads turning to me as I approached. The motion set up a jingle, which came from the bells attached to their talons. They were each wearing an elaborately tasseled hood, making them look like ladies in their best tea hats. The bird perched on Gillie's gloved hand, though, did not look like a lady in a tea hat. It was huge, at least two feet tall, all but dwarfing tiny Gillie, with downy white and silver feathers, talons the length of my ring fingers, a wide heart-shaped face, and great yellow eyes that followed my every movement. A barn owl, I thought, recognizing it from an Audubon print I'd seen once at the Astor library.

"Ah, Miss Hall," Gillie crooned as though I were another bird that needed to be settled. "I might have guessed you'd find your way up here. It was your mother's favorite roost."

"She often fed the pigeons on our fire escape," I said, my throat tight with the memory of my mother's face bathed in light as she leaned out the window murmuring to the birds. "And she talked to them," I added. "Was she . . . I mean, is *that* one of the things we learn here—to talk to birds?"

Gillie laughed in an eerie high-pitched tone that made the owl shift restlessly on his hand. "What do ye think, Blossom? Are ye up for a little polite conversation?"

"Blossom?" I asked, laughing at the incongruously cheerful name for the somber-faced creature.

"Aye, her proper name is Blodeuwedd, from the Welsh, but that's a mouthful even for me. It means 'flower face,' so I call her Blossom. I don't like to think what she calls me." He lifted his arm up so that the owl's face was near his own. She ducked her head and let out a long, mournful hoot that made me shiver.

"Ah, she's talking to you already. She likes you. Tell her something that ye'd not want to tell that gaggle of girls down below and see what she says."

Feeling foolish, I leaned closer to the owl, who cocked her head and regarded me with a yellow eye the size of a gold doubloon, and whispered, "I don't know if I belong here."

In answer, Blossom lifted her great wings and hopped from Gillie's hand to my shoulder, where she hooted into my ear. She was lighter than I would have thought, but her talons clutched my shoulder with an inexorable grip that I did not doubt could have broken my skin and crushed my bones.

"See, Blossom thinks ye belong and she don't take to just anybody."

"But not everyone thinks I should be here," I said, gingerly stroking the owl's feathers. "On account of my mother being expelled."

Gillie muttered something under his breath that I guessed was an expletive in his native Scots tongue. "Your mother was the finest, truest girl who ever trod the halls and paths of Blythewood and she had already decided to leave before those old biddies expelled her. She told me so herself, standing right where ye stand now. 'Gillie,' she said, 'I cannot stay in a place that persecutes poor, helpless creatures.'"

"Helpless creatures? Did she mean Miss Frost's specimens?"

Gillie scowled, his dark eyebrows swooping together like two hawks fighting over a morsel. "Aye, she didn't like to see the wee lampsprites splayed out like that—I don't like it myself. Not that they aren't dangerous. The sprites have led many a traveler into harm's way." Gillie lifted his dark head and looked north toward the Blythe Wood. "My job is to go after the girls that are led astray before they're caught by the bigger creatures. There are terrible creatures in the woods, Miss—goblins that will eat the flesh right off your bones, kelpies that'll drag you into the river and suck the last breath out of your gullet, boggarts that'll . . . well, never mind what the boggarts will do to you."

"What about the Darklings?" I blurted out.

Gillie frowned. "Have ye seen one of them?"

I nodded. "Last night on our way back from the Rowan Circle. One swept down and scared off all the other creatures."

"If it did that it was because it wanted you to itself. The Darklings are the worst of all of them put together. Some say the first Darkling was an angel that fell from heaven for love of a woman and that's why they're so cruel to the lasses."

"Gillie . . . I found one of their feathers beside my mother on the day she died. Is it possible—" I stopped, startled by how Gillie's face had darkened. Blossom, sensing her master's distress, ducked her head and hooted.

"They must've come for her at last, poor girl. I believe one caught sight of her in the woods and took a fancy to her. They say that once one of them demons fixes on a lass it won't stop until it has her—or she's dead. When she went missing that last year, they all thought she was gone for good, but I wasn't having that. I went into the woods and found her and brought her back."

"You found her?" I asked. "Did she tell you where she'd been?"

He shook his head. "She wouldn't say. But I think she'd been with the Darklings. She . . ." He leaned closer and whispered even though we were alone on the roof except for the birds. "She had a black feather in her hair. I think she left Blythewood to get away from them creatures, but one must've followed her." Gillie ducked his dark head in the same motion as Blossom. He even seemed to bristle like a preening bird. "The monsters must've gotten her at last."

18

GILLIE'S PRONOUNCEMENT ENDED my first day of classes on a somber note, but in the days that followed, I was too busy to brood, on the roof or elsewhere. In Mrs. Moore's boarding-school books the girls had plenty of time for cocoa parties and high jinks. But the teachers at Blythewood gave far too much homework. Each day was taken up with classes, archery practice, and bell ringing. Each night there was enough Latin to translate, spells to memorize, potions to learn, and history books to read to keep us swotting till lights out.

Even Miss Sharp, who had given us a break on the first day, assigned us *Great Expectations* for the first week and *Jane Eyre* for the second. I saved that reading for the last each night so I'd go to sleep thinking about Jane or Pip instead of Latin spells to disarm pixies or the secret history of the Crimean War.

If other girls were having difficulty adjusting to this odd education, they didn't let on. As for me, there was so much that was strange and exotic, so much to absorb of the rituals and mysteries of girls'-school living, that I wasn't sure what to be shocked by anymore—that Georgiana Montmorency received fresh boxes of kid-leather gloves each week because she never wore a pair twice or that fairies existed? That someone might take for granted the ability to borrow any book in the world at any time or that some of those books were grimoires filled with spells?

Soon I was so caught up in the rhythm of routine at Blythewood that I ceased to wonder at its strangeness and simply tried to keep up. I could never have done it without Daisy and Helen. Although Mr. Jager had predicted I had the potential to excel in magic because I was a chime child, my magical abilities were unpredictable and volatile. When I tried to make a porcelain figurine come to life it exploded into a million pieces. After that I was forbidden to try any sympathetic magic for fear that anyone I bound to an object would get hurt.

"It could be that the earth magic in you is so strong it cancels out all air magic," Dame Beckwith remarked one day at tea after I had broken all the teacups in the room.

My friends had clearer and more useful powers. Daisy, we soon discovered, was not only the best Latin student in our year, but also had a preternatural ability to memorize any fact or figure presented to her once.

"I used to memorize all the accounts at Papa's store," she replied after scoring 100s in all our first exams. "Mr. Appleby says I'd make a fine bookkeeper if ever we began our own business."

"Mr. Appleby will have to wait for your services," Helen declared. "You're going to be our secret weapon to get through midterms."

Helen, although not an exemplary scholar, turned out to be a Roman general when it came to organizing study sessions. She enlisted Dolores and Beatrice to help with species classifications and potions and Cam to drill us in bell changes and practice archery.

"I'm surprised she's so determined not to fail," Daisy remarked to me one day when Helen had run down to the lab to "nick" test tubes and Bunsen burners so we could practice conjuring, and then banishing, a goblin fog. "I thought she hated it here. If she fails won't she be able to go back to New York City for all the dances and parties she's missing?"

"I don't think Helen likes to be second best at anything. You saw her at archery when Charlotte Falconrath shot farther than her."

Daisy paled at the memory. Miss Swift often called one of the Dianas from their patrols on the edge of the woods to demonstrate a particular shot. It annoyed Helen because she felt that she was good enough at the sport that she should be called to demonstrate. She tolerated the experience when it was Andalusia Beaumont, whom even Helen admired, or Natasha Petrov, a Russian girl whose father had been the gamekeeper for the tsar. But if it was Charlotte Falconrath or Dorothy Pratt, both of whom Helen had grown up with, Helen would seethe with resentment. When Miss Swift asked both Charlotte and Helen to shoot together to demonstrate a technique for distance shooting and Charlotte's arrow went a yard farther, Helen stomped across the lawn to retrieve her arrow from the edge of the woods, past where we were allowed to go.

Since that first day, we had all kept a respectful distance from the woods. Only the Dianas, who patrolled the edge of the woods by day with their falcons, and Gillie, who patrolled by night with his owl, Blodeuwedd, went so close. But Helen, enraged by being bested by her rival, ignored Miss Swift's shouts and marched straight to the verge of the forest—so close she was in the shadow of a pine tree—grabbed her arrow and turned, brandishing it in the air like one of the angry Picts threatening the Roman legions we were reading about in Mr. Bellows's class. The blue-faced troll that leapt out of the woods behind her might indeed have been one of those ancient Picts. We all gasped while Miss Swift raised her bow and shot the troll between its eyes before it reached Helen. Then she gave Helen ten demerits.

The demerit system at Blythewood was designed to keep us from breaking the rules. A hundred demerits meant you were expelled. By the end of my first month, I had ten for being late to Latin class when Nathan blew up an experiment in science class and I had to change my shirtwaist. Daisy had ten for the same reason (it had been a *big* explosion) and Helen had thirty—ten from the troll episode, ten for being late to Latin after the explosion, and ten for egging on Nathan to set off the explosion.

Nate had eighty. Twenty for the explosion, thirty for tardies, ten for stealing Miss Frost's bustle and putting it on the statue of Diana, ten for sneaking into town at night and getting drunk at the Wing & Clover, and ten for throwing up on Miss Frost's shoes the next day.

We all wondered if Nate would make it through midterms. The only class he excelled in (and showed up for regularly) was bells. Helen, who hated bells because of her fear of heights, dismissed this as the one class where brute strength was an asset, but Nathan's skill at bell ringing came from more than his strong arms—which, truthfully, were weaker than Cam's when he started out. He had a good head for numbers and could memorize a complicated-change ringing pattern after seeing it once; he had a deep, powerful voice that could be heard over the bells; enjoyed bossing people around and so was a natural for calling changes; and, most importantly, he loved it and so it was the one class he applied himself to and never missed.

I thought I knew why he loved it so much. When you were ringing the bells you couldn't think of anything else. Your mind was blank except for the sound of the bells and the pattern of the change ringing. It was the only time I didn't think about my mother, or the fire, or being a chime child, or the Darkling who still flitted through my dreams. I suspected it was the only time that Nathan wasn't thinking about his sister Louisa.

But he wouldn't be able to keep ringing the bells if he flunked his midterms and was forced to leave Blythewood. He told me in October that although his mother had prevailed on the Council to let him attend Blythewood, she would have to send him back to Hawthorn if he didn't pass his exams.

"Weren't you expelled?" Helen asked one day while we were all studying in the Commons Room.

"Not exactly. I sort of left without permission, but the Headmaster says he'll have me back—not that I want to go."

"I don't know why you don't want to go there," Cam remarked to him. "I'd give my eyeteeth to be a knight!"

"It isn't what you think," Nate replied. "They don't teach any magic or swordplay or anything remotely interesting for a while. Initiates spend their first year sleeping on a bare stone floor in an unheated cell and bathing in an icy tarn. Mr. Bellows says it's all about subjugating the flesh and training the senses, or some such hogwash. They don't teach the good stuff until the third year, and I don't have time for that."

"I'm surprised you're not studying harder." The words were out of my mouth before I realized how they sounded. Nathan glared at me. "I mean," I explained, "if this is the 'stuff' you're in a hurry to learn . . ."

"But it's not," Nathan said, flinging his notebook to the floor. "All this nonsense about fairy phylums . . ."

"Phyla," Beatrice Jager corrected, earning a vicious glare from Nathan.

"Who cares?" Nathan cried, storming out of the library.

Nathan stopped coming to our study sessions, while our teachers kept piling on work as we got closer to the exam day on the first of November. Our stacks of notes piled up as fast as the autumn leaves falling from the trees and drifting across the lawn outside the window of the Commons Room, where we studied.

"I swear," I complained the day before the exams, "these facts are falling out of my head as quickly as they go in. Why do they keep giving us more to memorize?"

"To weed out the weak." The voice came from the table across the room where Georgiana, Alfreda, and Wallis were studying—or rather where Alfreda and Wallis prepared crib sheets for Georgiana and fetched her cups of tea and plates of cake. "Haven't you been paying attention in Miss Frost's class? Good breeding always shows in the end."

"She's been talking about lampsprites and other fairies," Daisy objected. "Not people."

"The same rules apply," Georgiana said, dusting the powdered sugar from a Victoria sponge cake off her fingertips. "It's even more important for the Order to keep our bloodlines pure. We've been entrusted with the hereditary make-up to resist and repel evil. That's why it's so important that we marry within our class. If we breed indiscriminately"—she looked pointedly at me—"we risk weakening or even perverting our race."

"Ava's mother is from one of the oldest families of the Order," Helen said, rising to my defense.

"Yes," Georgiana replied sweetly. "But does anyone know who her father was? Does *she* even know?"

I felt the blood rise to my face and heard the bass bell clanging in my head. "That's none of your business," I bit out between gritted teeth.

"Oh, but it is," Georgiana went on. "Miss Frost says it's our duty as women of the Bell to choose fit mates to protect the bloodline of the Order—or to remain unwed if no fit mate is available." Georgiana laughed as if that possibility was absurd for someone of her beauty and wealth. "In fact, she says that nature protects those of the best blood from undesirable matches because impure mates will appear repugnant to the truly pure woman."

"Are you implying," I asked, the bell ringing so loudly in my head that I could hardly hear myself speak, "that my mother chose an undesirable mate?"

"Well," Georgiana said, spreading her hands so that the light reflected off her diamond rings. "Why else do you have so much trouble doing magic? Why else is your power so . . . erratic? Why do things break around you?"

To punctuate her sentence, the teacup in Alfreda's hand shattered in perfect concert with the gong of the bass bell in my head. Alfreda squeaked, but Georgiana went on smiling. "You see? Temper, like madness, is an undesirable trait that's been bred out of the Order. Your father might have been a crude laborer, or even a mental patient."

The next teacup to break came hurtling across the room straight at Georgiana's head. Daisy gasped—I thought because I'd never made anything fly before—but then I saw she was staring at Helen, who was holding the matching saucer to the lobbed teacup. Helen's face was white with rage.

"How dare you insinuate that my roommate came from such a base union."

"Helen . . ." I began, but she was already stomping out of the room. I followed her out and caught up to her in the foyer.

"I cannot stay in the same room with that . . . that . . . *harridan*! In fact," she added, looking wildly around her, "I can't stay in the same house. I've had it with this place! I'm going into the village!"

Helen stormed out the front door just as Daisy, clutching an armful of notes and her reticule, came out of the Commons Room. "But we're not supposed to go to town without first asking permission! And we're not even supposed to leave the house on Halloween!"

Just that morning Dame Beckwith had given us a long speech on how dangerous Halloween night was, with demons and fairies coming out of the woods to roam the grounds.

"What should we do?" Daisy asked, so agitated she was shredding Beatrice's notes into ribbons.

"I'll go with her," I said. "I'll make sure she's back before nightfall. You can stay here if you like."

"Oh no, I'd be too nervous!" she cried. She gave one anxious look at her pile of notes and abandoned them on the hall table, holding on to her reticule—a small, embroidered bag her mother had made for her and that Daisy carried everywhere but rarely opened. Helen and I had debated what essentials it might contain. She clutched it now as we followed Helen, who was striding down the drive kicking at leaves as she went.

"The nerve of her," Helen said when we'd caught up to her. "She thinks that just because the Montmorencys are the richest family in New York she can treat the rest of us like dirt. The van Beeks are just as old, and a far nobler family. Papa says that Hugh Montmorency sold inferior lumber to the railroads and took over the lines when they failed. And Georgiana's great-grandfather was in trade!"

"It was *my* bloodline she was impugning," I pointed out as we turned onto River Road. We were soon passing fields where reapers were gathering in the last of the hay and orchards and village boys were picking the last apples of the season, which filled the air with their scent. It felt good to be outside the castle and the gates of Blythewood, even if we were breaking the rules.

"What a lot of rubbish!" Helen cried. "As if we were brood mares to be bred. Of course our families want us to wed wisely. Mother is always talking about finding me a proper husband, but Papa says he won't make me marry anyone I don't like."

"Which will no doubt be someone suitable since you're a well-bred young woman who wouldn't choose a crude laborer or mental patient."

"Pish!" Helen cried. "Your mother would never pick a crude laborer. She was a *Hall!*"

"What does she mean by a crude laborer?" Daisy asked. "Some of the very nicest people I know are farmers, and come, harvest we all pitch in. Mr. Appleby milks his family's cows before going to work at the bank. Does that make him a crude laborer?"

"My mother said all work is honorable work," I said, wondering for the first time if she said it so often because my father had been a blacksmith or a farmer—perhaps one of these farmers pitching hay in these very fields. I found I didn't really mind the idea. It was the other possibility that Georgiana had craftily tossed out—*mental patient*—that scared me.

"Don't worry," I reassured Daisy. "Mr. Appleby sounds very nice."

"Yes, indeed," Helen concurred. "And besides, it doesn't matter so much for you since you're not from the One Hundred. No one will care if you marry a country bumpkin."

"What do you mean a country bumpkin?" Daisy asked, her brow creasing with confusion. Most of the time Daisy seemed not to notice Helen's careless remarks. I had come to believe that she was so lacking in meanness herself that she hardly recognized it in other people. But she was very sensitive on the issue of Mr. Appleby. The last thing I wanted right now, though, was another argument. Fortunately I saw, as we came to the glass greenhouses on the outskirts of town, just the right thing to distract both girls.

"Isn't that Mr. Bellows coming out of that greenhouse with a bouquet of violets?"

"Oh!" Daisy said, instantly forgetting the slight to Mr. Appleby. "Do you think they're for Miss Sharp?"

"Well, I don't think he's buying them for Miss Frost," Helen replied. "There's one way to tell for sure, though. Let's follow him."

"Oh, my!" Daisy squeaked. "Do you think we should? I'd die of embarrassment if he saw us."

"I don't think there's much chance of him seeing anyone," Helen replied. "He doesn't look like he'd notice an Arabian Desert foot-licker demon if it jumped out and seized him by the feet right now."

I shivered, recalling that the demon, genus *Palis*, had been described by Miss Frost as a creature that attacked travelers at night in the desert and licked the soles of their feet until their blood was gone. Rupert Bellows, sauntering down the main street of Rhinebeck with a bouquet of violets in one hand, his head tilted up toward the clouds, and a carefree tune on his lips, did indeed look as though he could be prey to any number of the horrid creatures we had learned about in Miss Frost's class. He certainly didn't notice the drunken fellow who lurched out of the Wing & Clover tavern until he collided with him.

"Ho there, my good man!" Mr. Bellows exclaimed good-naturedly. "Steady as she goes."

The drunk belched in Mr. Bellows's face and careened toward us. Daisy let out a yelp that attracted Mr. Bellows's attention. He quickly inserted himself between the drunken man and us.

"Let's steer clear of the young ladies, sir," Mr. Bellows said, attempting to herd the man around us. But the man refused to be herded. Leering at the three of us he jutted out his grizzled jaw and shoved his face inches from mine. His eyes were bloodshot and watery, his breath smelled like gin.

"Young ladies, y'say? Witches more like! You can't fool auld Silas Trumble. I know what goes on up there at that accursed school."

"I sincerely doubt that, Mr. Trumble. If you did, I do not think you would trifle with me," Mr. Bellows said ominously, "or insult my charges."

Mr. Trumble's rheumy eyes swiveled toward Mr. Bellows and raked him up and down dismissively. Although we all admired Mr. Bellows's height and commanding presence in the classroom, I could see from the perspective of a rough character such as Mr. Trumble how he might not be much of an intimidating figure with his tweed jacket, gold-rimmed spectacles, and posy of violets in his hand. Mr. Trumble conveyed his opinion of Rupert Bellows by spitting on his polished brogues.

"*Redirezam tibi-zibus!*" Mr. Bellows muttered under his breath. Was that Latin? And wasn't that the speculative tense combined with the transformative case, which Mrs. Calendar had told us was the correct way to form a spell? Even as I ran through the conjugations and declensions in my mind the glob of sputum was rising in the air in front of the widening eyes of Silas Trumble. It rose slowly at first, trembling in the bright sunshine like a soap bubble, but then at another command from Mr. Bellows it flew into Mr. Trumble's right eye.

"Why you . . . !" I saw Mr. Trumble pull back his arm, his hand curled into a fist. Before he could swing his arm, though, I heard the sound of bells in my head. They tolled loud and clear, shattering the quiet of the sleepy town. Mr. Trumble's arm fell limply to his side and he bent over, his other hand clapped over his ears.

"Make it stop!" he cried, looking up at me. But I didn't know how to make it stop. The bells tolled twelve times and then, when they were done, Mr. Trumble gave me a wild look and ran across the street, nearly getting himself run over by a trolley.

"Well done, Miss Hall!" Mr. Bellows said, clapping me on the shoulder. "Strictly speaking we're not supposed to use magic on civilians, but no one's likely to believe a word Silas Trumble says."

"I hope not," I said, still shocked and a little horrified that the bells had worked so effectively. I hadn't meant to cause the man pain. "I didn't mean to hurt him."

"Oh, I'm sure Silas Trumble has hangovers worse than what you just gave him," Mr. Bellows said, taking out a handkerchief to clean off the tip of his shoe. "But say, what are you girls doing out of school? Shouldn't you be studying for exams? And isn't it against rules to leave the school grounds on Halloween?"

We exchanged guilty looks. "Please don't turn us in," Daisy pleaded.

"It was all . . ." Helen began, but Daisy interrupted her.

"My idea," Daisy interjected. "According to recent studies by . . . er . . . Dr. Freud, a change of scenery is stimulating to the brain cells. I thought a walk to the village would improve our memorization skills."

"Ah," Mr. Bellows said, pursing his lips and tapping his finger against them. "Does Dr. Freud saying anything about the effect of tea and scones on brain function?"

We all looked at him blankly.

"Because I'm headed right now to a very congenial tea party. Would you like to join me?"

Helen and I glanced at each other but Daisy answered for us without hesitation. "We'd love to."

"Very well, then," Mr. Bellows said, grinning. "Come along."

He held out an arm for Daisy and she, blushing bright red, took it. Helen paused to adjust her hat in the window of the Wing & Clover.

"What exactly did you do to that man?" she asked.

"I have no idea," I said truthfully. "I just didn't want to see him hurt Mr. Bellows."

"Hmph. Remind me not to get on your bad side. Come on now. Heaven only knows what boring function we've gotten ourselves committed to." Sighing, Helen began to turn away from her reflection in the window. Something caught her attention, though. She gave a little start and quickly grabbed my arm and pulled me away. Before she did, though, I saw what had startled her. Nathan Beckwith was at the bar, drinking a tall pint of ale. That wasn't what surprised me, though. Seated a few stools down was Miss Euphorbia Frost and, next to her, a man in an Inverness cape and Homburg hat.

19

IT COULD HAVE been any man wearing the same outfit as my pursuer in the city, I reasoned with myself as I followed Mr. Bellows and my roommates through the residential streets of Rhinebeck. Lots of men no doubt wore the Inverness cape, a style made popular by the illustrations in Mr. Conan Doyle's detective stories. It was none of my business if Miss Frost chose to meet one at the tavern in the middle of the day. As for Nathan being there . . . although I'd like to ask if he'd noticed the man drinking with Miss Frost, he'd probably interpret the question as a criticism—and then ask me what *I* was doing in the village instead of studying.

Shaking off the gloom the sight of that Inverness cape had cast over me, I focused on my surroundings instead. The village streets of Rhinebeck were lined with regal maple trees, their last red and gold leaves drifting down into the gardens of pretty Victorian houses painted in cheerful colors. I noticed, too, that many of the houses had their own glass greenhouses. So many sparkling glass roofs made the village appear to be a crystal fairy-land.

"Many of the residents have taken up the cultivation of violets," I heard Mr. Bellows explain to Helen and Daisy, "but none are so devoted as the Misses Sharp."

"Sharp?" I asked, catching up with my companions. "Are they relations of our Miss Sharp?"

"Her aunts. That's where I've been invited to tea ... ah, and here we are. As you can see, they're so enamored of the *Viola odorata*, commonly known as the sweet violet, that they have painted their house in its colors."

Mr. Bellows waved his hand in a flourish toward a gabled Italianate house painted in a rich violet hue, its molding and verge board trim painted white and yellow like the center of a violet. Two black cast-iron urns overflowing with unseasonably blooming violets stood on either side of the front door. A glass conservatory on the side of the house sparkled in the sunshine.

"Come along," Mr. Bellows said, opening up the front gate and leading us up a path bordered on both sides by banks of more violets blooming out of season. "Tea at Violet House is usually around four o'clock."

"Won't Miss Sharp's aunts mind unexpected guests?" Helen asked in a worried tone, which I guessed had more to do with the fear that Miss Sharp would reprimand us for leaving the school than the impropriety of showing up unannounced for tea. I'd noticed that Miss Sharp was the only teacher whose opinion mattered to Helen.

"I don't think so," Mr. Bellows said, turning and frowning at Helen. "I rather get the idea that the household is run on ... er ... rather spontaneous principles."

As if to illustrate that point, a gentleman in a rumpled cream-colored linen suit and broad-rimmed hat wandered out of the back garden at that moment, a book in one hand and a violet-patterned teacup in the other.

"Is it time for tea?" he inquired of Mr. Bellows. "I'm afraid my clock has stopped." He removed a small brass-plated clock from his jacket pocket and shook it. "Blasted thing! I was waiting for the bells to set it—" Just then the church bells began to ring the hour. "Ah, there they are! Do you know the rhyme?

"Oranges and lemons
Say the bells of St. Clement's
You owe me five farthings
Say the bells of St. Martin's."

"When will you pay me?
Say the bells of Old Bailey,"

Mr. Bellows eagerly chimed in. The two men walked up the porch steps, trading verses of the rhyme as the church bells tolled.

"When I grow rich
Say the bells of Shoreditch."

"When will that be?
Say the bells of Stepney."

"I do not know,
Says the great bell of Bow."

"Here comes a candle to light you to bed ..."

"'And here comes a chopper to chop off your head'!" the gentleman in white concluded triumphantly just as the front door was opened by Vionetta Sharp.

"Uncle always has to have the last line," Miss Sharp said. "Don't you, Uncle Taddie?" She gave him the sort of indulgent smile one might give a child.

"I've brought my teacup," Uncle Taddie said, handing Miss Sharp the violet-patterned cup. "Emmy says I can't have any more tea if I don't bring back the cups."

"That's perfectly right, Uncle, as we would soon run out of cups if they all remained in the tower with you, and then we wouldn't be able to have these lovely young women for tea."

"I found these three wandering the streets of the village being accosted by drunken sailors," Mr. Bellows announced rather loudly. I guessed that he had been composing the speech while walking here. "I thought it best to bring them along. I brought these, too," he added in a lower voice, thrusting the bouquet of violets toward Miss Sharp.

"Rather like bringing coals to Newcastle," a female voice remarked. The door opened wider and Miss Corey appeared. She was wearing a white lace tea dress rather than her usual plain shirtwaist and skirt, and a straw hat rather than the heavy cloche she usually wore. Although she still wore a veil, it was a lighter one, a rose-colored net that cast only a faint shadow over her face.

"Oh, Miss Corey," Mr. Bellows said in a subdued tone, "I didn't know you'd be here."

"Nor I you," Miss Corey replied primly. "And I certainly didn't expect to see any Blythewood girls. They're not supposed to leave the school grounds without permission, and I'm quite sure no one would have given them permission on Halloween."

"Well, now that they have they might as well have tea," Miss Sharp said, smiling, and then, in a lower, more ominous tone, added, "It will be better if we walk them back." Then she relieved Mr. Bellows of the bouquet as we stepped into a foyer paved with lilac and jonquil-yellow tiles and dominated by an enormous grandfather clock. She held the flowers to her nose and inhaled deeply.

"Ah, Parma violets, my favorite. Aunt Emmaline won't grow them because of an unpleasant incident with an Italian prince that occurred in Naples on her grand tour. I shall secrete them away until it is time to go." She slipped the violets into a carpetbag that stood on a marble-topped table. "Come along. Tea is served in the conservatory."

Miss Sharp led us to a glass-roofed room on the side of the house. Although it was a brisk fall day outside, the room was as warm as the tropics. Potted palms and aspidistras filled the corners of the room, ferns trailed from baskets hanging from the glass ceiling, and pots of violets stood on every available surface along with a great assortment of framed pictures and clocks. Brightly colored birds flitted inside wire cages or darted freely amongst the ferns and palm trees. Although the room was as cluttered as my grandmother's parlor in New York City, it was a great deal cheerier—and the plump woman in lavender silk and mauve lace sitting in a high-backed wicker chair, although around the same age as my grandmother, was a great deal more welcoming.

"I knew there would be unexpected guests for tea," she cried out at the sight of us. "Didn't I say so, Hattie?" she asked a tiny birdlike woman perched on a footstool to her right. The tiny woman—she was so small I wondered if she wasn't a species of fairy—looked up from her needlepoint and nodded.

"You did, and I promptly told the cook to make extra sandwiches and Victoria sponge cake, as you are always right about such things." She turned and looked over her beak-like nose at us.

"My sister Emmaline predicted the stock market crash of ninety-three and had father move all our holdings into gold. Come sit down, children. Doris will be in with the tea in a moment. We always have tea at four."

She glanced up at an imposing grandfather clock, the kind that has a sun and a moon that move around with the hour. This one also had a dial painted with an apple tree in varying stages of foliage—bare, budding, fully leaved, and blazing red—to represent the seasons. According to the clock it was a quarter past two, in the middle of the night, in the summer.

"Oh dear, that one's wrong," Aunt Harriet said, glancing at a smaller clock on the mantelpiece, which said that it was half past six. "Our father was an horologist, you see. He made beautiful, rather complicated clocks, but since he passed away we haven't been able to figure out how to keep the clocks going right. But never mind—the church bells have just gone four o'clock. Doris will be in soon."

We sat and introduced ourselves to Miss Sharp's two aunts. "I believe we are fifth cousins on the maternal side with your uncle Hector," Aunt Harriet remarked to Helen.

To me, Aunt Emmaline mentioned she'd been at Blythewood with my grandmother. "She was an excellent archer."

By the time the tea trolley was rolled in by Doris—an ancient woman even older than the two sisters—it was clear that the Sharp sisters were well acquainted with Blythewood's secret, but that their brother Thaddeus was not. Or at least the sisters preferred to think he was not. Whenever a detail about the school was brought up the sisters lowered their voices to a conspiratorial whisper and bent their heads together, but because they were both a little deaf they spoke so loudly anyone could have heard them.

"Is Euphorbia Frost still teaching deportment?" Aunt Emmaline asked loudly, and then in an equally loud whispered aside to her sister, "And still preaching about the evils of fraternizing with F-A-I-R-I-E-S?"

"As if any fairy would be caught dead fraternizing with her." Aunt Harriet chuckled.

I glanced at Uncle Taddie and saw that he was following the conversation avidly as he stuffed cucumber sandwiches into his mouth, his eyes bright as the hummingbird that had alighted to drink from a saucer of sugar water Aunt Harriet had put out. Did the two women really think he wasn't in on the secret? Miss Sharp gave her aunts a warning look when Emmaline tried to ask Daisy if she'd seen any lampsprites in the woods, and steered the conversation to more neutral topics, such as the new archery equipment ordered by Miss

Swift and a concert program being organized by Mr. Peale for Christmas.

Eventually lulled by this conversation—and the copious quantities of tea sandwiches, scones with clotted cream, and sponge cake—Taddie fell into a doze and began to snore. Taking that as a signal to abandon all caution, Emmaline leaned forward and asked us all what kind of fairies we'd seen on our first night and whether we'd caught sight of any since then. Daisy, who was the best at the classifications we memorized in Miss Frost's class, listed off the species we'd encountered so far. "Lampsprites, horn goblins, piskies, fenodorees . . ."

"Any boggarts or boggles in the house?" Harriet interrupted.

"In the house?" Daisy asked, alarmed. "What do you mean, in the house? The bells keep all the fairies out and the Dianas patrol the grounds . . ." She faltered and Emmaline smiled craftily.

"Ah, you see, why would the Dianas have to patrol if the bells kept all the fairies out?"

"It's because the bells don't work on all the fairies," Harriet said. "In our time there was a boggle living in the pantry. The cook tolerated it because it kept out the mice, but it also liked to play tricks on the girls."

"We'd wake up with cattails braided in our hair and our shoes full of tadpoles," Emmaline said, her eyes shining.

"It was a marsh boggle," Harriet explained. "It only did that to girls it liked."

"But I thought all the fairies were evil!" Daisy cried. "That's what Dame Beckwith told us. And that's what we learn in Miss

Frost's class." Daisy's voice shook when she mentioned Miss Frost. I knew she hated looking at the specimens.

"Of course that's what they teach you." Harriet patted Daisy on the hand and offered her a plate of bread and butter. "The mission of Blythewood is to protect the world from the creatures who wander out of Faerie. India thinks it would be confusing to teach that there are gradations among the fay from innocent mischief-making to unadulterated evil. And as for Euphorbia Frost—well, she wouldn't have the imagination to conceive of gradations of good and evil in her narrow worldview, let alone differences among the individuals of any one species. She's a very closed-minded person who worshipped her mentor, Sir Miles Malmsbury, and slavishly adheres to the old ways, which teach us that *all* fairies are evil and that in order to destroy them we must obey a set of rigid rules invented in the fifteenth century!"

"You mustn't get so upset, Hattie," Emmaline cut in. "You'll bring on another bout of dyspepsia. My sister feels things very strongly," she explained to us. "And some of the Order's rules are rather . . . *limiting*."

"Limiting?" Harriet spluttered. "Try draconian! Their rules on marriage, for instance . . ."

"I'm sure these girls are not old enough to be worried about marriage yet, Aunt," Miss Sharp said with a warning look at her aunt. And then to us: "My grandfather Thaddeus Sharp began to question the old ways before he died."

"He believed that young people ought to be trusted with the truth," Aunt Harriet averred with a thump of her walking stick.

"I agree entirely," Mr Bellows said, jostling the teacup on

his knee in his excitement. "As a historian I am committed to the truth. I believe our girls are mature and intelligent enough to appreciate shades of gray. I was shocked to learn that there are certain books in the library that are removed from the shelves to keep students from reading them." He cast a reproachful look at Miss Corey.

"Don't look at me," she said, her veil trembling. "It's not my choice. If it were up to me I'd make all information available to every student. But the Council tells me every year what books I must place in the Special Collections Room."

"*That's* what's in the Special Collections?" Helen asked. "I thought it was a bunch of moldering antiques."

"Many of them *are* moldering," Miss Corey replied, "but most are there because they are deemed too . . . *controversial* for students."

"What controversy?" I asked, recalling the discussions I'd overheard Agnes having with Caroline Janeway and Vionetta Sharp and how Agnes had looked bitter when she referred to the "old ways." What I really wanted to ask was whether their father had thought the Darklings were completely evil, but Uncle Taddie chose that moment to snort loudly and startle awake. The aunts exchanged a look and Emmaline asked Taddie if he wouldn't mind going into the greenhouse and gathering three poesies "for the girls before they left." When he'd gone Aunt Emmaline told us Taddie's story.

"As we mentioned before, my father believed that young people ought to be trusted with the truth, so even though Taddie was deemed too frail to attend Blythewood—let alone Hawthorn—our father took him into the Wood for the initiation. Taddie became so frightened that he ran off and was lost in the woods for three days. When we found him he was quite . . . *distracted*. He never would say what happened to him and he was never the same again. We try not to talk about the fairies around him. The incident quite devastated Mother and had unfortunate consequences for us all." She looked nervously at her sister, who was suddenly intent on tidying the tea things, and then continued. "Of course Father couldn't very well continue proposing that Blythewood change their policies when his own son had been so . . . damaged by his encounters with the wee folk."

"Unfortunately there are scores of such incidents recorded in the annals," Miss Corey said to Aunt Emmaline. "As I've said before, I'd be happy to do some research into what treatments have proved useful in handling such cases."

Aunt Emmaline sighed. "That's very considerate of you, dear, but Father brought Taddie to all the experts in Europe. He spent a year at a sanatorium in Marienbad that specializes in *psychical traumata* brought on by encounters with the fay. It only made him worse. What calms him now are working with the violets and tinkering with Father's old clocks—although, frankly, I'm afraid that he's made rather a mess with the clocks. I believe Father was attempting something more complicated than telling time, but I don't think anyone else will ever figure out exactly what he was doing with them . . . Oh, here's Taddie now. What lovely poesies you've brought for the girls, Taddie!"

Uncle Taddie presented us each with a bouquet of violets surrounded by heart-shaped leaves and bound with lilac ribbon. Taking this—and Mr. Bellows' anxious consultations of his pocket watch—as a cue to leave, we made our farewells.

Aunt Emmaline gave us each a parcel of cakes to take back with us and told us not to mind what her sister Hattie had said about boggles. "I'm sure they're better about keeping them out these days, although you need to be especially careful tonight because of its being All Hallows' Eve. You'd best hurry back before nightfall."

Before we left, Emmaline pulled me aside in the foyer and whispered to me, "You're a chime child just like me, aren't you?"

"How . . . ?"

"One chime child can always recognize another once you've learned how to use the bells . . . but you haven't learned yet, have you? You come see me one day and I'll show you how to find an object to focus the bells."

I thanked her and said I would like that. Then I hurried after my party, who were being escorted down the path by Uncle Taddie. He seemed sad to see us go, and I half thought he might follow us back to the school. But when we got to the gate the church bells began to ring the hour and he froze on the path as if they were the signal to go no farther. Nodding his head, he held one finger up and recited a rhyme to go with the rhythm of the bells. I did not think that this verse was part of the original poem, though.

"*Violets and Monkshood,*
Say the bells of Blythewood.
Here comes a lampsprite to lead you astray,
And here comes a Darkling to steal you away."

20

WE WALKED OUT of the village and onto River Road. Miss Corey walked on ahead at a brisk clip, glancing anxiously at the western sky, where the sun was sinking over the mountains on the other side of the river. Miss Sharp walked between Helen and Daisy, and I trailed behind with Mr. Bellows, who seemed too busy checking his pocket watch and whistling the bells tune he'd sung with Uncle Taddie to talk. Helen, too, was distracted, peering ahead on either side of the road as if she was looking for someone. For Nate, I guessed. She must have been wondering if he had already left the village or would be stranded on the road after dark.

Only Daisy felt compelled to trade social niceties. "I liked your aunts, Miss Sharp," she said.

"Yes, they're old dears. I'm sure they liked you, too."

"It's sweet they take care of their brother."

"Yes, fortunate, too. I'm not sure what we'd do with Uncle Taddie otherwise."

"Is that why they didn't marry?"

Miss Sharp didn't answer right away. I could see Daisy fidgeting with her reticule nervously. "I'm sorry," she said after a few awkward minutes, "I didn't mean to pry."

"No, it's perfectly all right. As my grandfather would have said, young people deserve to know the truth. My aunt Harriet meant to marry. She was engaged to a young man of the One Hundred—a Driscoll, in fact—but when Taddie became . . . disturbed, the Driscolls insisted her fiancé break off the engagement. They were afraid, you see, that madness might run in the family. According to the old ways it's irresponsible to have children if there's a taint in the bloodline."

Beside me Mr. Bellows had ceased whistling, and up ahead Miss Corey had slowed down.

"But that's . . . that's . . ." Daisy spluttered.

"Unfair? Cruel? Yes. You can see why my aunt Harriet has no fondness for the old ways."

Even Daisy's repertoire of cheerful homilies was exhausted by this comment. She lapsed into silence. Miss Sharp resumed her inspection of the woods. Miss Corey walked on at an even brisker pace. Mr. Bellows walked with his head bowed, scowling at the ground. I kept my eyes on the lengthening shadows at the side of the road and thought about tainted blood. Aunt Harriet had only to have a brother who chattered harmlessly about fairies to be denied marriage. What if the Order knew about the dreams I had about the Darkling? Were they signs of madness? Or were they part of a spell the Darkling had cast over me to lure me into the woods? But would a sane woman be susceptible to the lure of a Darkling? Georgiana's mocking words came back to me. "Nature protects those of the best blood from undesirable matches because impure mates will appear repugnant to the truly pure woman."

So did my desire for the Darkling mean I was *impure*?

Tainted by impure blood? Had my father been mad? Is that why my mother never spoke of him?

Or was it my mother who was mad? After all, did a sane woman shun her rich relatives and live in poverty with her daughter?

Did a sane woman drink laudanum?

Did a sane woman hear bells in her head . . . ?

As I did now.

The bass bell had been chiming in my head for some moments now. But for what? There was no danger here. There was nothing in the woods but a large crow rustling its feathers as it alighted in the low-hanging branches of one of the giant sycamores that lined the road. It was joined by another crow . . . and then another. A dozen of them were amassing in the trees, like bits of the gathering dusk made visible. A flock of them—only that's not what you called a group of crows . . .

"A *murder*!" Vionetta Sharp said with a quick intake of breath. She had come to a stop a few feet ahead where the road curved just before the gate to Blythewood. She held out one arm to keep us back and with the other she reached forward to grab Miss Corey's arm, her fingers digging deep into the other woman's flesh.

"Ah yes," Rupert Bellows said, ambling forward. "My favorite of the collective nouns. A murder of . . ." His voice died as he reached the two women. I edged forward to see what they were looking at.

They were staring at the gate to Blythewood. The black wrought-iron scrollwork stood out starkly against the indigo and violet sky, especially the spikes on top.

Only there hadn't been spikes on the gate when we left this afternoon. I took a step closer and the spikes *rustled*. The top of the gate was lined with huge black crows, so packed together that they jostled against one another for purchase. There must have been fifty of them.

"Those . . . are . . . not . . ." Miss Sharp said slowly, carefully enunciating each word, "*ordinary* crows." She turned her head to Miss Corey, who was staring at the gate. "Lillian, I am going to do a mesmerism spell. When I've drawn them away, take the girls and run to the hall."

Miss Corey turned her head to her friend, opening her mouth to object, but she snapped it shut when she met Miss Sharp's eyes. She nodded once and turned to us. Helen and Daisy had reached me now and stood on either side of me. I felt Daisy's hand slip into mine as Miss Corey whispered to us.

"I want you three to stay perfectly still until I give you the signal. Then we will run straight for the house being very, very careful not to trip or to look back. Do you understand?"

We nodded our agreement. Helen grasped my hand and squeezed. I looked over Miss Corey's head to Miss Sharp. She and Mr. Bellows were whispering together. Mr. Bellows reached into the pocket of his tweed coat and drew out a long silver dagger, its hilt decorated with opalescent stones, its blade inscribed with strange runic designs. He handed it, hilt first, to Miss Sharp with all the aplomb of a knight handing his sword to his lady in order to be knighted. The crows stirred on the gate, black feathers rustling against each other with a sound like dry paper crackling. Miss Sharp swung the dagger into the air in a long graceful arc, as if she were swinging a tennis racket back to serve. A hundred pairs of jet black eyes followed the motion. She swung the dagger back down and around, drawing great looping patterns in the air. The runic inscriptions on the blade seemed to dislodge from the blade and float free in the clear evening air . . .

"Don't look at it," Miss Corey hissed in my ear. "You'll be mesmerized, too."

I dragged my eyes away from Miss Sharp and looked at the crows. They were swaying in unison, their eyes following the motions Miss Sharp drew in the air . . . and then they rose from the gate in one long black stream, like smoke rising from a fire, and swooped toward Miss Sharp.

"*Now!*" Miss Corey shouted. "*Run!*"

We ran under a stream of crows, so thick in the air that they darkened the ground, through the gate. Miss Corey was ahead of us. Behind us I could hear the birds' hoarse, raucous caws rending the air. There was something fierce in the sound—and angry—as if the crows knew they had been deceived. It seemed to grow as we ran instead of fading with the distance. Had Miss Sharp been successful in luring them away? Or were they following us? I itched to turn around and look, but Miss Corey had said not to.

We were climbing the rise, running so hard I could feel my heart pounding in my ears. Or was it the sound of the crows, gaining on us, about to swoop down and peck at the exposed flesh of our necks?

Daisy's hand slipped from mine and she let out a sharp cry. Helen was pulling me forward, but I broke away and turned to see Daisy stumble and fall, a black shape beating about her head.

I swatted the crow away and grabbed her hand. Something thumped hard against the back of my head. Daisy screamed and swung her reticule at the bird, but it clung to me, icy claws digging into the nape of my neck. I had the horrible feeling that the crow was clawing its way under my skin. I stumbled and began to fall, Daisy's face and the world around me going black, my ears ringing . . .

Bells were ringing in my head, but they weren't dispelling the cold wave rushing over my body, numbing me to the tips of my toes. I could see Daisy's face above me, her eyes wide with horror, lips moving, but I couldn't hear her. The world had gone quiet except for the bells. Dark shadows were creeping over the lawn where I lay, over Daisy's face, across my eyes . . .

I fell into the darkness as though falling down a well. It was very cold and full of echoes. I heard voices—or rather one voice, a voice that was somehow familiar—chanting a singsong rhyme to the rhythm of the bells inside my head

Violets and Monkshood
Say the bells of Blythewood . . .

It was the rhyme that Uncle Taddie had recited, but the next two lines were different.

Swallow the shadows down
To make them all drown.

Then the voice laughed—a horrible laugh that echoed in my ears. *That's what your mother did, only she was too late. The darkness was already inside her. Just as it's inside you, Avaline Hall.*

"No!" I screamed, thrashing out in the dark. "That's not true!"

The well filled with the sound of beating wings. My hands struck against something smooth and . . . *feathered.* The talon grip on my neck suddenly loosened and melted like ice water rushing down my back—cold, but instead of numbing me, it woke me up. I opened my eyes.

I was looking up into a darkened face surrounded by a halo of light. Enormous black wings blocked out the sun. Dark shapes wheeled in the glare—as if feathers from those wings had been torn loose and sent spinning through space. I heard bells . . .

Only this time they weren't in my head.

The winged creature turned his head to listen to them and I recognized his face in profile—the same face I'd seen carved white as a cameo, now carved out of ebony against the glare of the sun. It was the Darkling. *My* Darkling. He'd come for me—but what did he want?

His turned and his face was in shadow. I couldn't see his expression, but I could tell from the bend of his head that he was looking at me. His gaze felt like a warm bath after the ice claws of the crow—a warmth that was healing me from the attack. I wanted to move closer to that warmth. I reached out and felt his hand grasp mine. The shock of warm solid flesh shattered the last shards of ice from my body. I rose feeling light and free.

Then his hand was wrenched out of mine and he spun around. There was a flash of steel, then wings beat the air and knocked me backward. I was blinded by the flurry of black feathers. When I opened my eyes Nathan was standing over me. He was holding a fire poker.

"Nathan! How . . . ? What . . . ?"

I wanted to ask why he'd attacked the Darkling who was saving me, but my lips were still numb, my body still weak from the alternating waves of ice and fire I'd just been through.

"I was on the roof when I saw those birds attack you," Nathan cried, his voice full of the horror he must have felt at the sight. "I ran to the tower and rang the bells. It seemed to do the trick. They melted."

"Melted?" I asked, recalling the sensation of freezing water running down my back and the long cold plunge into the dark well. My mouth was full of a coppery taste. Had they melted inside me? Had I swallowed them?

"But then when I got down here I saw that monster crouched over you. I hit him with this." Nathan brandished the fire poker proudly, his face glowing. I'd never seen him with so much color in his face. Or looking so . . . *happy.* How could I tell him that the Darkling hadn't been trying to hurt me? He'd been the one to save me from the crows. Or at least I'd *thought* he was saving me.

"And a jolly good job you did!" Rupert Bellows had reached us. He clapped Nathan on the back and then looked down at me. Miss Sharp came up behind him and let out a little cry when she saw me. She knelt down and laid her hand on my forehead.

"Don't just stand there, Rupert, help me carry Avaline inside."

"I can walk," I objected, although I was none too sure that I could. The thought of being carried by Mr. Bellows, though, made me go hot and cold all over. I struggled to my feet with Nathan's and Miss Sharp's help. Stinging prickles ran up my legs as though I was standing in a briar bush. Helen was suddenly there, slapping dust away from my skirt, tugging my waistband straight and patting my hair neat. Ordinarily I would object to her fussing, but her brisk hands were bringing life back to my limbs.

"When I looked back and saw that you'd fallen I ran right back. But then that monster landed . . ."

Why did they keep calling him a monster when he'd saved me? I tried to correct her, but Miss Sharp cried out.

"Where is Lillian?"

"She went on to the hall to tell Dame Beckwith what happened," Helen said. "Look, they're coming now."

Everyone turned to the house except for me. I spied my posy of violets where it had fallen and knelt to pick it up. As I stood up I looked down the drive to the gate and felt my heart stutter in my chest.

Standing in the center of the open gates was a lone dark figure of a man in an Inverness cape.

"Look!" I said, turning to Nate. "It's the man who was in the Wing & Clover."

"What man?" Nate asked.

I turned back to point at the figure at the bottom of the hill but he was gone, melted away as quickly and completely as the murder of crows.

21

I WANTED NOTHING more than to go back to my room, wash my face, lie down, and think about what had happened in privacy. What were those crows? Were they the same ones I had seen circling the Triangle building the day of the fire? The Darkling had been there then, too—did he summon them? But it seemed that the Darkling had come to save me from the crows and I'd felt that rush of warmth in his presence. I'd *wanted* to go with him.

The confusion wasn't just in my head—it seemed to be in my body. Alternating waves of hot and cold broke over me as I remembered in turn the icy grip of the crows' talons and then the heat of the Darkling's touch. But there was no time to sort through my warring feelings. We were summoned to Dame Beckwith's study.

I'd passed the tall oak double doors to the headmistress's study in the north wing a number of times on my way to classes and noticed that there always seemed to be a few girls fidgeting nervously on a long narrow bench waiting for the summons to enter. I had hoped I might never be one of them.

Expecting the room to be forbidding, I was relieved to find a charming study, lined with books and bathed in the last lingering light of the sunset. Glass doors led onto a balcony overlooking the river. The sun had sunk below the mountains on the other side of the river, turning the ridges deep blue and purple. Wisps of cloud flared pink and lilac above them. Glancing at them reminded me of the Darkling's darkened face and the flash of his wings behind him. Those wings weren't entirely black—they held the iridescent colors of the sunset in them.

I was startled out of my reverie by a touch of a hand—cooler than the Darkling's hand and smaller, but no less firm in its grip. It was Dame Beckwith, who had risen from her desk and grasped my hand, her steady gray eyes gazing deeply into mine.

"Are you all right?" she asked me. "Are you sure you've come to no harm? I saw that monster hovering over you. I thought . . ." Her voice cracked. I was shocked to see her strong, firm jaw tremble as she fought back tears. "I thought we were going to lose you."

"We might have if Nathan hadn't rung the bells," Miss Sharp said, stepping forward, "and attacked the Darkling."

"It was just lucky I grabbed that poker," Nathan said. "I ran down to fight the crows. I didn't know the Darkling was there until I reached the lawn."

"He wasn't at first," Miss Sharp said. "It was just the crows. But then he showed up."

"It was when the crows attacked Ava," Daisy said, her voice small in the presence of Dame Beckwith. "I saw that beastly crow sink its claws into Ava's neck. I tried to get it off . . ." Daisy's voice cracked.

I let go of Dame Beckwith's hand and reached for Daisy.

"You were so brave!" I said. "I saw you swing your reticule at the crows. And I know how much you love that bag!"

"It has all of Mr. Appleby's letters in it!" she blurted out.

I stared at her for a moment, then felt something bubbling up inside of me. I wasn't sure if I were going to laugh or cry until I heard Helen giggle, and then I began to laugh, too, helplessly and a little bit hysterically. The adults all stood around staring at us, wide-eyed and open-mouthed, until the door opened and the housekeeper came in carrying a heavy silver tray loaded with teacups, teapot, creamer, and sugar bowl.

"Oh thank goodness, Bertie," Dame Beckwith said, "that's just the thing. I'm afraid these girls have had a terrible shock and are now having an attack of nerves. They need hot tea with plenty of sugar."

Helen, Daisy, and I were made to sit down. Shawls were draped over our shoulders and we were each given a cup of hot sweet tea as if we were invalids. Although I would have thought I'd had enough tea for one day I gulped the hot liquid gratefully. I could feel the chill in my bones dissipating with each mouthful, but laughing with Helen and Daisy had chased the cold away even more effectively than the tea.

"Now," Dame Beckwith said briskly, "let me have the whole story from the beginning, one at a time. Why don't you go first, Miss Sharp, as I believe you saw the shadow crows first?"

Shadow crows? Was that what they were? I wondered as Miss Sharp explained how she had realized right away that the crows were a "malevolent manifestation." She described in some detail the mesmerism spell she had employed to divert them. "I had to use shadow runes," she said in a low whisper.

Shadow runes? Hadn't Mr. Jager said that shadow magic was strictly forbidden?

"Perfectly acceptable under the circumstances," Dame Beckwith said briskly.

Mr. Bellows, when it was his turn, lavished praise on Miss Sharp's brilliant deployment of the spell and added that all but three of the crows were effectively mesmerized.

"But those three broke away?" Dame Beckwith asked.

"Yes, they flew up the hill and attacked Daisy and Avaline. Thank goodness the bells rang."

Nathan was then asked to describe what he had seen from the roof. He explained how he had recognized the crows as shadow demons because we'd read about them in Mr. Bellows's class, and remembered that they could only be banished by the tolling of the bells. He'd run to the belfry and alerted the bell ringers on duty to ring a shadow-dispersing peal; then he'd run down, grabbing a fire poker from the fireplace in the Great Hall, and dashed out to see if he could help out on the ground, which was when he saw the Darkling standing over me.

"The Darkling must have summoned the crows," Mr. Bellows said. "The birds must be their minions. I'm afraid we may have to call out the Hunt."

"Wait," I said, interrupting Mr. Bellows. "The Darkling wasn't trying to abduct me. He *saved* me!"

Dame Beckwith's eyes narrowed. "And what makes you say that, Miss Hall?"

I stared back at her, desperately trying to think of some way of explaining how I felt about the Darkling without giving away how we'd first met. But if I didn't say something,

Dame Beckwith would call out the Hunt to destroy him.

"Because he did it once before," I said, trying to keep my voice from shaking. "He saved me from the fire at the Triangle Waist factory."

I saw Helen and Daisy staring at me and then exchanging a look.

"I'm sorry I never told you," I told them. "But since I've come here, I've tried to forget about it. At the hospital, they tried to convince me that I'd imagined the boy with the wings who'd saved me, but I recognized him the first night when I saw him in the woods, and today I recognized the man in the Inverness cape who I saw at the Triangle factory."

I told them everything then: about seeing the man in the Inverness cape at the factory, and how the fire had burst through the airshaft windows and raged across the factory floor—the flames like burning rats and the smoke like the crows we'd seen today. I found myself telling them about the girls pinned between the flames and the glass windows—how they'd been forced to jump or be burned alive. I told them about how the boy had helped me and Etta and Tillie up to the roof, but the crows had swooped down on us and the man in the Inverness cape had pushed Tillie off the roof and the boy had saved my life. I even told them about the months in the hospital and how I'd seen the man in the Inverness cape there, and again below my window at my grandmothers, and then today inside the Wing & Clover.

As soon as I mentioned the Wing & Clover, Nate blanched. I caught his eye and shook my head to let him know that I wouldn't give away that he'd been there, too, but he spoke up anyway.

"I saw him there—a man in a dark cloak and hat. His face was shadowed and somehow strange." Nate frowned and shook his head. "I can't somehow recall what he looked like."

"Did he speak to you?" Dame Beckwith asked, her eyes looking truly frightened.

"Yes . . ." Nate answered haltingly, as if trying to remember something in a dream. He scratched his head, looking puzzled. "Funny thing, I can't seem to recall what we talked about."

"He mesmerized you," Dame Beckwith said, her voice trembling. "That *monster*!"

"You know who he is?" I asked.

"I know *what* he is," she said. Her face looked *stricken*, the firm smooth flesh sagging around her jaw and making her look, for the first time since I'd been here, *old*. "I-I can't . . . *explain*," she stuttered, the first time I'd ever heard her voice falter. "But I can *show* you. Come."

We followed Dame Beckwith through the winding halls of the North Wing to the library, barely able to keep up with her. Was she going to show us something in a book? She swept past the floor-to-ceiling shelves with the same intensity of purpose until she reached the enormous fireplace at the end of the room. I'd spent many a class staring at the intricate carving on the stone mantelpiece, following the pattern of interlocking spirals and strange creatures. Did the identity of the man in the Inverness cape lie in the pattern's labyrinthine maze? But Dame Beckwith didn't pause to examine the design. She placed her index and middle fingers in the eyes of a particularly frightful gargoyle and her thumb in its mouth. A horrible groan emanated from the stone, as if the gargoyle had indeed just had his eyes poked out, and the floor beneath my feet trembled. The great hearthstone in the fireplace was sinking as if the foundations of Blythewood were crumbling. A cloud of soot and ash rose into the room. When it settled, a great gaping hole had opened up inside the fireplace. Dame Beckwith took a lantern from the mantel and held it above the hole, lighting up a curve of spiral steps carved out of stone. Miss Corey was handing out lanterns to each of us.

"Oh my!" cried Daisy. "It's like something out of one of Mr. Poe's stories."

"Yes, the one in which the madman walls up his enemy in a dungeon," Helen said, shaking soot off her skirt, only the tremble in her voice giving away that she was afraid.

"Is that where we're going?" Daisy asked. "To the dungeons?"

"In a manner of speaking," Miss Sharp explained. "We're going to see something in the Special Collections, which happen to be in the dungeons. Watch your step. It's a long way down."

⋙— ✦ —⋘

We descended single file down the narrow, spiraling steps. I had the feeling that we were drilling our way into the ground. The walls on either side of the stairs were damp and, in the flickering lantern light, mottled with mold and crawling things. It felt like the well in my vision when the crow had dug its claws into me. Perhaps I was still in the well. The Darkling had never come to save me. My friends had never come to save me. Perhaps this was a punishment for asking who the man in the Inverness cape was. I wanted to shout that I didn't need to know anymore. Whatever it was that Dame Beckwith was going to show us down here in the bowels of the earth, I didn't need to see it. Daisy and Helen were behind me on the stairs, but I could push past them and run back up. I stopped, ready to turn, but before I could, Nathan looked over his shoulder at me, his eyes flashing silver in the lantern light.

"It's all right," he said, as if he knew what I was planning. And suddenly it was—not because of his reassuring tone, but because of the look in his eyes. He was afraid, too—maybe more afraid than I was—but he was ready to brave his fears to see what lay below. If he could do it, his look told me, so could I.

I nodded and followed him, wondering, as he turned, what he was so afraid of.

At the bottom of the stairs we passed through a corridor lined with filing cabinets and glass cases. Holding my lantern up, I saw that some of the shelves contained books while others held mysterious objects—shells, bones with runic inscriptions on them, clay figurines, bronze bells coated with a green crust-like algae, and long tattered tapestries embroidered with enigmatic figures. The Special Collections wasn't just a library; it was a museum of the Order's history. Dame Beckwith must want to show us some object from the collection. But she passed by the cases without a glance to either side. At the end of the corridor she asked Miss Corey to hold her lantern so she could remove a ring of keys from her pocket and unlock a door.

"Leave your lanterns in the hall," she told us. "You won't need them in here."

One by one we left our lanterns on a ledge beside the door

and passed into a room so dark it was as if we'd been swallowed by the earth. Then a light flared, a blinding pinpoint like an exploding star. It ignited other stars—a galaxy. When my eyes adjusted to the glare I saw that Dame Beckwith was lighting the candles of an enormous crystal chandelier hanging from a high domed ceiling. I'd seen chandeliers in the houses where my mother and I delivered hats, but I'd never seen one like this. It was crafted of concentric brass rings of candles and crystal bells, each bell carved with intricate designs that sprung to life as the candlelight touched them and cast shimmering patterns over the walls and domed ceiling. By the candlelight I could now see we were in a circular room, empty save for a round table directly beneath the chandelier.

"How beautiful!" Daisy cried.

"Yes," Helen agreed. "It's bigger than the chandelier in the Vanderbilt's Hyde Park mansion."

"It's a candelabellum," Miss Sharp told us, her voice hushed in awe. "One of only three that the six bell maker's daughters made. This is the only one that's survived."

"And even this one is missing some of the original bells," Dame Beckwith said. "But it's intact enough to tell its story."

"Its story?" I asked, staring at the glittering crystal. It was dazzling to look at, but the patterns carved into the crystal bells were abstract and enigmatic. I couldn't see how anyone could read a story in those patterns.

"Yes, a story!" Mr. Bellows cried, leaning so close to the candles that I thought he was going to singe his eyebrows. "The candelabellum was designed so that the vibrations of the bells would move the rings in such a way that the light refracting through the crystal bells would cast a picture on a darkened wall. That's why the candelabella were always kept in underground vaults like this chamber. The room must be completely dark except for the candles, and have exactly the correct acoustics to control the vibrations of the bells. But one must know which bell to strike first."

"I know which bell to strike first, Mr. Bellows," Dame Beckwith said. "If you will all sit down I will proceed."

Cowed by Dame Beckwith's command, we all pulled out the heavy chairs and sat at the round table. I noticed that the chair back was shaped like a long bell—and was not particularly comfortable. When we were all seated Dame Beckwith lifted a slender metal rod and held it poised over the candelabellum.

"Before I begin, I must ask that none of you speak of what you see here. I only show this to you so that you know what evil you brushed against today and you do everything in your power to fight it."

As she spoke she looked at each of us in turn as was her wont while giving speeches, but her gaze came to rest on Nathan the longest. We all nodded our heads in agreement, even Nathan, and then Dame Beckwith raised the metal rod and struck one of the crystal bells.

The sound was pure and sweet and reverberated through the domed cavern, which was itself, I noticed now, shaped like an enormous bell. I could feel the vibrations in the floor traveling up my legs and spine to the top of my scalp. The bells in the candelabellum began to vibrate, and the rings began to spin. The bells played a mournful tune, and the crystal cast shards of light on the wall that grew into images of birds flitting across the walls like a great wheeling flock of starlings. Then they were swooping through a snowy woods and more images evolved: a wagon and horses and then, slipping out of the shadows as if they had been lurking all along in the recesses of the room, wolves running beside the wagon, which went faster and faster, around and around the room, until, in a great jangle of bells, it crashed, throwing into our startled faces sprays of snow so lifelike that I could have sworn I felt their icy kiss on my cheeks.

As one lone figure picked herself up from the broken wagon I understood that we were watching the story of the bell maker's daughters. Seven figures rang seven bells to scare off the shadow wolves that seemed so real I could swear I smelled the musk of them in the air. And why not? The wolves that stalked the girls were made up of shadows, and what were we watching but a shadow play like the shadow puppet shows I'd seen in Chinatown? Only in reverse—we were watching shapes made out of light moving on a ground of shadow. The more I watched, though, the more the shadows seemed to encroach on the figures carved out of light. The prince and his brave knights who rode to the girls' rescue, their horses' bridles jangling with the song of the crystal bells, seemed thin and insubstantial against the shadowy woods that surrounded them. Out of that blackness came an enormous winged creature that swooped over the youngest bell maker's daughter and plucked her up. Her flickering light was absorbed into the blackness. Then the blackness spread and formed into a gruesome shapes—goblins and trolls stalked the margins of the room, their high-pitched chittering echoing in the high bell-shaped dome.

It's just a shadow play, I told myself, but I knew that the combination of reflected light and chiming bells could not produce the images I was seeing and the sounds I was hearing. As it spun, the candelabellum used some magic to recreate the story that the bell maker's daughters had wanted to tell. Of their sister's abduction. Of their rescue. Of the flight back to the castle pursued by the shadow creatures. Of the knights' desperate attempts to fight back the shadow creatures.

When they drove their swords into the shadow wolves, the creatures exploded into black shards that floated up to the ceiling like the flakes of ash that rose from the fire at the Triangle factory. But these ash flakes grew as they rose. They sprouted wings and dove back down to attack the knights, who fought them off with shield and sword, keeping the bell maker's daughters safe until they reached the castle.

As the castle's gates opened to let them in, the mass of shadow crows swarmed toward it. The prince turned to keep them back while the others rode through. He stood on the drawbridge, battling each crow as it swooped toward him, swinging his sword in a pattern that looked familiar to me. It was the same pattern that Miss Sharp had used to mesmerize the crows, and the runic inscriptions on the sword were the same ones I had seen on the sword that Mr. Bellows had brandished. And just as Miss Sharp had been able to mesmerize the crows while we ran to Blythewood, so the prince saved his brother knights and the bell maker's daughters. But when he turned to join them, a terrible thing happened. A great winged creature appeared in the sky. A man with wings. A Darkling.

At the sight of him I felt my heart contract. Even in this shadow play I felt that this creature was *real*. And I didn't want to see what came next. I wanted to close my eyes. But when I did, I discovered the power of the candelabellum. Even with my eyes closed I saw the story unfold. The Darkling did not attack the prince. Instead it broke into a million pieces and each piece became a shrieking crow. They swarmed over the prince, sharp beaks pecking at the soft places between the seams of his armor, picking at each chain-mail link, rending flesh, shredding skin. The prince went down in a clamor of armor that rang so loud I thought the crystal bells of the candelabellum would shatter. I thought my own eardrums would shatter. It felt like the sound was inside me, as the ravening crows were inside the prince.

Because that's where they were. As the prince fell to the snowy ground the crows picked his body apart, opening it up and climbing inside. They burrowed into sinew and soul, eating what was left of him until he was a hollow carcass filled with the shadow carrion. And then, when they'd eaten their fill, the prince rose to his feet. Bristling with feathers, his movements jerky as if pulled by a puppeteer's hand. . . . I'd seen that jerky motion before when Tillie snagged the coat of the man in the Inverness cape and he juddered to a halt like a piece of machinery poorly oiled. That was how this creature moved until he shook himself once, feathers rustling and then smoothing into a familiar shape. A man with a cape where arms should be and a bowl shaped helmet where a head should be. The man in the Inverness cape. Only he wasn't a man at all. He was a bit of that darkness that grew and grew until darkness swept over everything in its path as the darkness swallowed us now, leaving us in an empty black pit.

22

IT TOOK ME a moment to realize that the candles in the candelabellum had burnt down. That's why we were in the dark. After a few moments of silence—we were all, I believe, stunned by the show we had seen—there was a rustling and the strike of a match. Miss Sharp and Miss Corey had fetched two lanterns from the doorway and set them on the table. The light shining up on our faces turned us all into frightful ghouls, Dame Beckwith most of all.

"But I don't understand." Daisy was the first to speak. "I thought the prince went on to found the Order." She sounded aggrieved, like a child whose favorite bedtime story has been changed.

"That is the story the sisters and knights passed down," Dame Beckwith said. "The real story was considered too frightening, but the sisters preserved the truth in the candelabellum so a select few would know of the danger that has always haunted our Order." She turned to Nathan. "The man you saw today is not a man at all. He's a creature made up of shadow that can control the shadows. He's the Shadow Master."

"Was he ever a man?" Nathan asked hoarsely. If I didn't

know better I would think he'd been crying. "I mean, the prince in the story was a man before the crows got at him."

"Yes," Dame Beckwith admitted reluctantly. "The creature you met today and who's been following Ava was likely once a man, but he must have been taken over by the shadows long ago. When he wishes he can dissolve himself back into the shadows—into the crows that attacked you today or into a giant winged creature—a Darkling."

"You're saying that the Darklings are made up of shadows, too?" I asked.

Dame Beckwith stared at me. "Weren't you watching, Avaline? Didn't you see the Darkling break into the shadow crows? It's one of the shapes they can take. That's what makes them so dangerous. The boy you saw at the Triangle who you thought saved you—how else could he appear to you without wings but by changing his shape?"

"But he saved me!" I cried.

"Did he?" Dame Beckwith asked. "Or did he bring you to the hospital where you were held captive and tortured?"

Her question—one I had asked myself many times—silenced me. Taking my silence as acquiescence, she nodded once at me and then addressed the group.

"I have shown you this so you know what evil you encountered today and how fortunate you were to escape it. You must avoid any contact with that man." Here she looked at Nathan, but then she switched her gaze to me. "Or with the Darklings. They are both creatures of the shadows, deceptive and seductive. They want to get inside us and destroy our power.

If the shadows infiltrate the Order, then there will be no one to stop the creatures of Faerie from coming out of the woods and swarming over the whole world. That's what the shadow creatures want: evil and chaos and despair. That's what they feed on. We must reinforce the magic of the bells that protects Blythewood and continue our war against the creatures in the wood. But you must avoid the shadow creatures."

"Avoid them?" Nathan cried. "Is that all you're going to do? Those demons might have taken Louisa—"

"Yes." Dame Beckwith cut Nathan off with a fierce look. "They most likely did. And that's why we have to avoid them. That's what they do when we get too close to them—they steal what's most precious to us." Nathan's eyes flashed and Dame Beckwith's tone softened. "All we can do is protect what we have left."

"But why not try to get her back?" Nathan demanded.

"Because she won't be the same," Dame Beckwith answered. "You saw what happened to the prince in the story. Do you really want to see your sister if that's what happened to her?"

Nathan looked pale in the lantern light, but he persisted. "Then why don't we destroy the lot of them!"

"We've tried," Dame Beckwith said. "We've sent in the Hunt to destroy them, but whenever we have we've lost more of our people than we've killed of theirs. And always there are the girls who vanish in the battle and are never seen again. I'd rather see a girl dead than taken by those creatures! Still, if these attacks persist we may have to prepare for a Hunt if it's our only option left. And if that's the case . . . may the Bells save our souls." She rose to her feet, but Nathan wasn't finished.

"Isn't there something in all those books and gewgaws out there"—he waved his hand to the corridor of glass cases we'd come through—"that could tell us how to destroy them? Couldn't this . . . *hoo-ha*"—he tapped one of the crystal bells and the candelabellum shivered with a sound that made my skin prickle—"tell us anything more?"

"We've looked through the books," Dame Beckwith replied. "And we've fiddled with the *gewgaws*, as you called them. Some of them are quite dangerous. Three of my classmates were killed fiddling with them. And as for the candelabellum . . ." She cast her eye on the glass and metal contraption. "It may once have told more than one story, but now this is the only story we know how to make it tell. Others have tried to tinker with it and coax knowledge from it, but they have come to ruin by doing so. You must never enter the candelabellum chamber alone. We believe the candelabellum is calibrated to pick up on minute vibrations of breath, heartbeat, even electrical pulses within the brain, and respond to individuals. There are stories of those who have entered the candelabellum chamber alone coming out mad. Even in a group, it is not . . . *healthy* to spend too much time down here watching the play of light and shadow. We've tarried too long already. It's time to go."

She picked up one of the lanterns and strode to the door. One by one we followed her. She waited at the door until we'd all passed through and then she locked the door behind her and pocketed the key.

"You lead the way," she instructed Miss Sharp. Surprised, Miss Sharp led us down the corridor. I started to follow, but

Dame Beckwith laid her hand on my arm. I was startled by how icy her fingers felt.

"Hold back a moment, Ava. I want a word with you."

My stomach clenched as Daisy and Helen helplessly looked over their shoulders at me and then vanished into the gloom.

"There's something you're not telling me," she said.

"Y-yes," I stammered, wondering how on earth I was going to tell her about the dreams and how I felt about the Darkling. "I didn't mean to keep it from you, but I didn't want to say in front of the others."

"Of course not. I respect that. I don't believe in publicly airing the behavior of my faculty."

Faculty? What was she talking about? Seeing my confusion Dame Beckwith narrowed her eyes at me. "There was someone else in the Wing & Clover, wasn't there? I understand you protecting my son, but if there was a faculty member there I must know."

"Oh!" I cried, relieved that she didn't know about the dreams after all. "Yes, Miss Frost was there. I didn't want to . . . well, I didn't want to get her in trouble."

"Your concern is touching, but not wise. I think you can see that keeping secrets here is not a good idea. Secrets thrive in shadows." She glanced meaningfully at the dark passage. The rest of our party was already on the stairs. Only Dame Beckwith's lantern lit the gloomy hall, throwing looming shadows on the walls. For a terrifying moment I thought she might extinguish the lantern to give me a lesson, but she only turned to go, saying as she did, "And the shadows thrive on secrets."

»→ ✦ ←«

I followed Dame Beckwith up to the library, where I found Daisy and Helen waiting for me. Mr. Bellows and Nathan were gone. Miss Sharp was helping Miss Corey dust soot off the bookshelves. Dame Beckwith whispered something to Miss Sharp and then left.

What was the point of warning me about secrets, I wondered, when she kept so many? As I joined Daisy and Helen I saw them exchange a look. They had been talking about me, no doubt reviewing all they'd learned about me—the Triangle fire, the fact I'd seen the Darkling before, and that I'd spent months in a mental institution. All the things I'd kept from them because I was afraid they would recoil in horror from me if they knew. They were not recoiling now, but the look of pity in Daisy's eyes and the questions in Helen's were suddenly more than I could bear facing.

"Daisy!" I cried. "Where's your reticule?"

Daisy gasped and looked down at her empty hands. "I must have left it in Dame Beckwith's office! Oh dear, what if she reads Mr. Appleby's letters? I'll have to go back for it. . . ."

"I'll go for you," I said, getting to my feet. "There's something I need to ask her anyway."

I left before Daisy could object, but not before catching Helen's suspicious look. But I *did* have a question for Dame Beckwith. I wanted to know if what had happened to the prince in the candelabellum story was what had happened to my mother. Had she been devoured by the shadow crows? Is that why I had found the black feather by her body? I hated the thought of those . . . *things* invading her body, but worst of all I hated what Dame Beckwith had said had happened to the prince—that the shadows ate his soul. I couldn't bear to think that that had happened to my mother, but I needed to know if it had.

When I got to her office door, though, I hesitated. What if the feather really did mean my mother's soul had been taken by the shadows? Did I *want* Dame Beckwith to know that?

"I tell you it's that girl. She's the one who's drawn the shadows here!"

The voice came from inside Dame Beckwith's office. I recognized the plummy outraged tones of Miss Frost. And I was pretty sure whom she meant by *that girl*. I should either knock and announce my presence or leave . . . but then I heard Miss Frost add, "It's little wonder, given what happened to her mother."

Euphorbia Frost knew what happened to my mother? Any thought of leaving gone, I looked up and down the hall to see if anyone was near and then moved closer to the door.

"We don't really know what happened to Evangeline," Dame Beckwith said, her voice angry—and loud enough for me to hear through the door.

"We know that she vanished in the woods," Miss Frost said. "And that when she came back she was covered with black feathers! She was never the same."

"She's not the only one who was changed after she came back from the woods."

A silence followed these words and then a long sigh and a creaking of springs. I could picture Miss Frost sinking into the deep armchair in front of Dame Beckwith's desk. But what did Dame Beckwith mean? Who else had managed to come back from the woods? Then I heard a strange fluting noise, like the call of a wild loon calling for its lost mate. It took me a moment to realize it was the sound of Miss Frost weeping.

"There, there, Euphorbia, you know I don't like to mention it. And I know how hard you try to immerse yourself in your work."

"Only for *his* sake!" Miss Frost cried. "I swore to myself that I would honor Sir Malmsbury's memory by continuing his work. It's the least I can do after . . . after leaving him behind!" Another bout of high-pitched sobs followed, punctuated by soothing words from Dame Beckwith from which I gathered that Sir Malmsbury had been lost in the woods on a collecting expedition and that Miss Frost blamed herself. I wasn't sure what was more surprising—that imperious Miss Frost blamed herself for *anything* or that Dame Beckwith was so indulgent. But after a few minutes her tone became firmer.

"Now, Euphorbia," I heard her say," I *do* understand your little trips to the Wing & Clover, but if I'm to continue paying your tab I must have a full account of who you meet there. Ava says she saw you with a man."

"I'd never speak to a strange man without a proper introduction!"

"Not even after a few snifters of brandy?"

A spluttering sound erupted, followed by another sigh of springs and a low murmur. I only caught a few words—"not sure . . . a fine Madeira . . . no, I don't think so . . ."—and then in reply to another query, her voice rose in agitation. "I can't remember! All I remember is finding myself out on the street and then, luckily, Sarah Lehman came along and found a cab to take us back to Blythewood. I had a terrible headache."

"It sounds as though you were mesmerized," Dame Beck-with said.

It sounded to *me* as if Miss Frost might have simply drunk too much and once again Sarah had had to come to her rescue.

"Yes, I believe I was. It's all a bit of a blur, but I do remember one thing he asked."

"Yes?" Dame Beckwith asked. "Did he ask about Blythe-wood? Did he try to wrest from you the secrets of the Order?"

"No," Miss Frost said. "He asked about Avaline. He said he knew her father."

»→ ✦ ←«

I waited to hear Dame Beckwith tell Miss Frost she must be mistaken—or that it must be a lie. Surely a soulless creature couldn't be trusted. But instead I heard a flurry of furtive whis-pering, as if what they were saying was too awful to speak aloud even in the privacy of the headmistress's office, and then footsteps approaching the door.

I fled. I couldn't let them know I'd heard them talking about me or my father—my *illegitimate* father. The shame of it made my cheeks burn and hurried my steps back to the library. When I got there I found Helen and Daisy still seated at the table, joined now by Sarah and Nate, drinking tea. Hadn't everybody had enough tea by now? I wondered irritably as I sat down.

"Did you find it?" Daisy asked.

"Find what?"

"My reticule!" she cried.

"Oh blast your silly reticule!" I snapped. "Do you think anyone cares about your letters from Mr. Appleby with everything else that's going on?"

Daisy's upper lip trembled. Sarah, Helen, and Nate stared at me. Finally Sarah patted Daisy's hand and, looking at me strangely, said, "We'll look for it tomorrow. We should get to work now. You've still got midterms in the morning. Miss Corey has volunteered the use of the library," she explained to me. "Since clearly Nathan couldn't study in your dormitory room and we thought that you might be besieged by questions in the Commons Room."

"I thought you didn't care about passing your midterms," I said to Nathan.

"I do now," he told me, winking. "Things have gotten exciting around here."

I stared at him, dumbfounded that his response to all that had happened today was that it was *exciting*, and then I suddenly laughed. The girls stared at me for a second and then joined me.

"What's so funny?" Nathan asked.

"Don't you see?" Helen replied, gasping. "It's taken an attack of killer crows to turn you into a scholar!"

"Come on, then," I said, squeezing Daisy's hand and whispering that I was sorry. "We'd best get to work."

↠   ✦   ↞

Miss Corey had left us there with a night's supply of lamps, firewood, tea, and biscuits. Sarah drilled us on declensions and spells, history dates and fairy phyla, hunting terms, and potions, making up rhymes and acronyms to help us remember them.

"You're so good at this," Daisy enthused. "Do you plan to be a teacher yourself?"

I was glad to see Daisy had recovered from my outburst. I'd been trying all night to make it up to her, which had the extra advantage of taking my mind off what I'd overheard in Dame Beckwith's office.

"Perhaps," Sarah said, biting her lower lip. "I want to do something that makes a real difference. There's so much to be done in the Order—not just here at Blythewood, but out in the world."

"What *does* the Order do out in the world?" Daisy asked, frowning. "I mean, I understand that we're meant to know how to guard the Blythe Wood and keep the fairies and demons from getting out, but what about the Blythewood graduates. What do they do?"

"They're meant to keep a lookout for demons and fairies that have infiltrated the outside world. They're all over." She lowered her voice to a low conspiratorial whisper. "What they haven't told you yet is that there are fairies who look just like us and pass as humans. They're the most dangerous ones. We really should be doing more. All we do here at Blythewood is maintain the status quo. But I think it's time for us to take a more active role and eradicate evil."

Her fervor reminded me of Tillie and the suffragists I'd heard speaking from soapboxes in Union Square. I was also reminded of the whispered argument I'd overheard between Agnes and Caroline Janeway.

I wasn't the only one moved.

"Exactly," Nathan said, his eyes shining at Sarah. "We can't just sit around doing nothing."

"But what can *we* do?" I asked.

"*We* can continue studying and pass our exams," Helen said reprovingly, glaring at Sarah. I don't think she liked the way Nathan was looking at her. "Now can you please go over the bell changes for repelling sprites once again? I never can keep them straight."

Sarah complied, but when Helen wasn't looking, I saw Sarah passing Nathan a note. He smiled when he read it and tucked it away in his pocket. I tried to concentrate on the two hundred changes we were supposed to have memorized by tomorrow and not think about what the note had said—or feel a pang of jealousy at the way Nathan had looked at Sarah.

We studied through Halloween night, keeping the fire stoked and the curtains drawn. Even if we had gone to bed it would have been impossible to sleep. The bells rang every hour; to ward off any creatures that might try to stray from the woods, Sarah told us. I felt that we were doing our own part to keep away the demons, reciting our spells and declensions, forming a bond against the dark forged out of the camaraderie of a shared task. I was banishing my own demons, too—my questions about my father and what his connection might be to the awful Shadow Master—with the laughter and warmth of my friends.

It seemed cruel to schedule exams after such a sleepless night, but Sarah explained that it was so we'd get used to performing under pressure. It certainly was grueling. The exams took up the whole next day. Hours of essay writing and answering questions left us all covered in ink splots and splashes of potions from the practical section of the science exam. Whenever I felt my energy flagging one of my friends was there with an encouraging smile or a grimace of shared toil—and not *just* my friends. A girl I'd never noticed before offered me a pen when mine broke; another made room for me at her lab table. In between exams I noticed girls whispering in knots. I feared at first that the details of my past life that I'd told in Dame Beckwith's office had gotten out and they were whispering about me working in a shirtwaist factory or being locked in a mental institution, but when we were heading into our last exam—in Miss Frost's class—one of the girls came up in the hall to ask if it were true that we had saved the school from a shadow crow attack.

"Yes," Helen answered for us. "I personally slew a dozen of the creatures and Daisy here beat off an entire murder with her reticule." Helen motioned to the embroidered bag, which Daisy hadn't let go of since it had been restored to her this morning by Sarah. "But the real hero was Ava. She mesmerized the birds with the power of the bells in her head. If not for her, the entire school would have been overrun. There's talk of erecting a statue of her."

"Personally," Georgiana sniffed, "I would be worried if I heard things in my head."

"Personally," Nate said as he strolled over, "I'd be surprised if there were anything in your head."

Georgiana was about to utter a retort when Miss Frost appeared, Sarah struggling in her wake with an armful of trays, and commanded us all into the classroom. When we were all seated, Sarah began distributing the trays.

"After the calamitous attack on Blythewood yesterday, Dame Beckwith required my consultation late into the night. I was therefore unable to prepare the written section of the exam."

Cam Bennett, sitting behind me, broke into a cheer that was taken up by the whole class.

"Yes, yes, there's no need to thank me for my service to the school. As my mentor Sir Miles Malmsbury would say, 'Steady sails the ship of science.' The events of yesterday have driven home to me how vital it is for us to understand our enemy. So, in lieu of a written exam, you will dissect a lampsprite, identifying each anatomical—"

"No."

The voice came from my right, but I hardly recognized it as Daisy's. She was standing, her reticule clutched in both hands before her as if she were drawing strength from Mr. Appleby's letters inside.

Miss Frost stared at her, her face turning the same purple as her dress. "How dare you talk to a superior in such a fashion, Miss . . . er . . ."

"Moffat," Daisy said in a loud, clear voice. "Miss Daisy Moffat from Kansas City, Kansas."

"I do not care what your name is, girl, or from what provincial backwater you hail. You will sit down and do as you have been told."

"No," Daisy said again. "It is cruel to treat the lampsprites as you have. Even back at our farm in Kansas we treat our animals better, and these are *not* animals. I have been reading about them. They're—"

"They are devious, dangerous demons!" Miss Frost cried, shaking her fist at Daisy. "It was a lampsprite that led Sir Malmsbury astray on his last mission, from which he never returned. I will tolerate no sympathy for the creatures. If you do not sit down and dissect the little demon I will personally see to it that you are expelled and sent back to the farmyard pigsty from which you came."

Would Miss Frost really have that power? I wondered. She was a sour, drink-addled woman, and yet Dame Beckwith had seemed oddly tolerant of her in the conversation I'd overheard yesterday.

"Miss Frost," I said, rising to my feet beside Daisy, "I think we all understand how important it is to honor Sir Miles Malmsbury by continuing his work." I'd only meant to echo the words that Miss Frost had used yesterday to remind her of Dame Beckwith's patience with her in the hope she would show a similar patience with Daisy, but as the blood drained from her face I saw that she guessed I'd overheard her. She was looking at me with such hate that I heard the bass bell ring an alarm in my head. Very well then, I thought, hardening my heart to her, let her think that. I went on in measured tones that were punctuated by the slow toll of my inner bell.

"But would Sir Malmsbury really want us to mutilate the specimens he worked so hard to collect? Wouldn't he prefer that we, er, honor his work by, perhaps, drawing and diagramming them instead?"

When I finished the bell was ringing so loudly in my head I was sure that everyone could hear it. Any minute now I would be denounced for practicing magic on my teacher. Wasn't it obvious? Miss Frost had cocked her head and was staring at me with a gaze as blank as the dead eyes of the skewered sprite. She swallowed audibly, then shook herself.

"Sir Miles *did* always admire a well-done sketch." She looked at the photo of her mentor on the wall. "As I was saying, girls, please draw a diagram of the sprite, identifying the genus and its distinguishing features. Sarah will collect the drawings. I've suddenly developed the most unpleasant headache."

As soon as Miss Frost left, the class broke out in applause. "Three cheers for Ava," Cam cried, thumping me on the back. "Hip, hip, hooray!" The class actually cheered.

"Thank you," Daisy whispered.

"It was nothing," I said, but as I bent my head down to my drawing I felt my cheeks burning as I thought of how proud Tillie would be of me. I'd finally earned Mr. Greenfeder's nickname—I was a fiery girl.

23

I SLEPT DREAMLESSLY that night and awoke the next morning to a world transformed. A storm had stripped all the last autumn leaves from the trees and glazed the bare branches with frost, like the icing on a cake. Autumn had become winter and our lives at Blythewood had changed just as dramatically.

The ordeal of the crow attack, the mysteries that had been revealed to us by the candelabellum, and our night studying together had forged a bond among Nathan, Helen, Daisy, and me. A bond cemented when Nathan drew us aside the morning after exams and asked us for our help with a special research project.

"A *research project*?" Helen scoffed. "Since when have you been interested in researching anything but gambling and drinking?"

"Since I learned that those demons took my sister," Nate replied, wiping the smile from Helen's face. "I'm going to get her back."

"But you heard what your mother said," Helen said. "Once a girl's taken by a Darkling she's . . . *changed*. You can't get Louisa back, Nate."

"Ava's mother came back from the woods. There might be

something in the Special Collections that can tell us how to save Louisa. As long as there's a chance, I'm not going to give up."

"What do you want us to do?" I asked.

"I want us to study in the library the way we did last night so that I can get into the Special Collections."

"That's all?" Helen asked, folding her arms across her chest. "But Miss Corey is always there. She's not going to let you just go down into the Special Collections."

"She will if Ava bell-mances her."

"I can't!" I cried. "I wouldn't do that to a teacher!"

"You did it to Miss Frost for Daisy."

"I didn't *mean* to. And Miss Corey is different. I like her."

"Fine." Nathan sighed. "You don't have to bell-mance her, just study with me in the library. I'll find my own way into the Special Collections."

To my surprise, Helen turned to me and Daisy and lifted an eyebrow. "What do you two think?" she asked us both. "Shall we aid and abet Mr. Beckwith with his illicit quest? If it turns out like most of his projects, we'll probably end up sacked from the school."

I expected that shy Daisy, who hated even to be caught talking in class, would object, but instead she said, "I think it's a very good idea. I'd like to know a thing or two more about the lampsprites to prove to Miss Frost that they shouldn't be treated as they are."

"I applaud your progressive zeal, Miss Moffat," Nathan said gallantly. And then, turning to me, "And what about you, Miss Hall? Anything you care to look up in the Special Collections?"

I thought about all I'd learned in the last twenty-four hours.

The boy who I thought saved me from the Triangle fire might be a soulless demon. My mother had come back from the woods covered in black feathers. The man in the Inverness cape said he knew my father.

"Yes," I told Nathan, "now that you mention it, there are a couple of things I'd like to look into."

»→ ◆ ←«

From then on the four of us met each day, after classes, in the library at the long oak table that stood between the fireplace, from whose mantel marble busts of Homer, Plato, and Sappho watched over us, and the diamond-paned windows that looked out to the river, where the ice grew thicker each day until the river itself seemed to stand still in time. Outside, the high-pitched cries of the falcons patrolling the woods and the ringing of the bells tied to their legs echoed in the chill air as though we were sealed under a glass dome. Inside the library, beside the fireplace, the books from the Special Collections mounted up on the table before us as steadily as the ice forming on the river.

I didn't have to bell-mance Miss Corey; Nate was able to convince her to give him access to some of the "more harmless" books from the collections. "Perhaps we'll find something in them that will help us ward off another attack," he argued.

Although Miss Corey insisted that "better minds than his" had combed through the books, he told her he'd heard what she'd said at Violet House about making all information available to every student. He even offered to help her bring the books up the spiral stairs. He was the first to sort through the books and hand them out to each of us. Gone was his attitude of boredom and cynicism. He seemed possessed by the desire to know more about the creatures that had stolen his sister.

Daisy also seemed possessed by a new fervor after her "revolt" in Miss Frost's class. "Are there any books by Sir Malmsbury?" she asked Miss Corey one day as the latter was helping Miss Sharp pick out books for a class project.

"Why yes," Miss Corey replied. "I'll get them for you as soon as I've done helping Vi—er . . . Miss Sharp."

"I'll fetch them," Nathan volunteered, jumping to his feet and opening the trapdoor mechanism.

"Well, um . . ." Miss Corey hesitated until Miss Sharp laid her hand on hers and asked whether the library had a copy of the secret fairy journals of Charlotte Brontë. Nate used her distraction to head down by himself and emerged some time later covered by dust and bearing a collection of leather-bound journals, which Daisy eagerly dived into.

Even Helen gave up complaining about missing the New York season and applied herself to all her studies. I suspected that it was not from love of poring over old books, which often made her sneeze and which she complained soiled her nice clothes, but from the time she got to spend with Nathan. Just as I suspected that Mr. Bellows's enthusiasm for spending time in the library stemmed in equal parts from scholarly ardor and the glow of Vionetta Sharp's smile when he brought her, as he did almost every day, a bouquet of violets from town. I think we all basked in that glow.

While Miss Corey and Nathan brought the books out from the Special Collections Room, Miss Sharp would stir the coals in the grate and put a kettle on for tea. She seemed at those moments like some ancient goddess of the hearth—the Greek Hestia, or Roman Vesta, or one of the Scottish hearth hobs we learned about in Miss Frost's class, fairies who lived in fireplaces. The honey-colored light that streamed in through the leaded glass windows bathed her face and turned her hair to liquid gold. As she handed out the teacups she had a kind word for each of us. As we read she would come around to refill our cups, tuck a shawl around Miss Corey's shoulders, brush crumbs off Mr. Bellows's jacket, save Helen's sleeve from an ink spill, tuck an errant pin into my hair, feed Nathan a biscuit, and straighten Daisy's collar—all her motions binding us in a warm glow that lessened the gloom of what we were reading.

The books Nathan brought us to read were all the ones that dealt with shadow attacks on the Order. There were many. The prioress of a Benedictine convent wrote in the fourteenth century that just before the Black Death ravaged the neighboring village she spied a murder of crows perched on the town walls, and that when she ordered the bell ringers to toll a peal they melted away "like smudges of ash" only to be replaced by a single figure of a winged man.

In a fifteenth-century bestiary I found a reference to "a Darknesse of Shadoes" next to an illustration of rats melting into black puddles. In the margin of the text was a drawing of a winged man. The scribe had written next to it "Angel or Shadoe?"

My circle of friends and teachers may have made it easier to deal with this grim material during the day, but at night the images—of crows flaking into ash and rats melting into puddles—made their way into my dreams. Worse, the images reversed themselves. I would be walking down Fifth Avenue with my mother, her boot heels clicking on slick cobblestones, and then her boot would land in a puddle and the puddle would turn into a nest of rats that swarmed over her, carrying her away from me. Or I was at the Triangle Waist factory, sitting next to Tillie, large flakes of ash floating through the air. When I looked up from my sewing and looked at Tillie I saw that the ash had turned to bats, which clung to her, sucking the blood from her veins. They were swarming over all the girls, tangled in their hair, I felt them in my hair, too, crawling over my skin.

I would wake up in a cold sweat, batting at the empty air.

One night I awoke and heard a pattering on the window-panes above my bed. Shadows flitted over the glass. I lay for a moment, very still, watching the shadows moving, feeling a cold dread creeping over me as I grew sure that they had come for me because I was part of them. The girl who went to classes, and laughed with her new friends, and worked so hard to impress her teachers was an illusion—a trick of the daylight. I didn't really belong at Blythewood. The real Avaline was the girl who carried laudanum home to her mother and worked in a factory. The real Avaline belonged in the Pavilion for the Insane. The real Avaline dreamed of monsters and *longed* for them. I belonged to the shadows and now they had come to take me back. I had only to lie still and they would take me.

A floorboard creaked, breaking my frozen spell. Daisy was standing beside my bed, her long white nightgown spattered with the moving shadows. I sat up to warn her away, but she was already crouching on my bed, her face pressed to the window.

"Look!" she whispered. "It's snowing!"

I crouched beside her and looked out. Fat snowflakes swirled through the night, lit by a half-hidden moon. Already the lawn was covered with a glittering white blanket. The hedges and statues in the garden had been transformed into fanciful ice sculptures; the great pine trees at the edge of the woods mantled in white looked like women in ermine cloaks.

"Isn't it . . . *magical*?" Daisy asked in a hushed voice.

"Yes," I agreed. More than all the spells and potions and bell changes we had learned, *this* felt like the true magic of Blythewood, as if a bit of Faerie dust had blown out of the woods and spread itself across the school grounds. Seeing the school like this felt like seeing its secret self. It made me feel like I belonged here.

But even that magic had its dark side.

In the morning Miss Swift, accompanied by Gillie and a hooded falcon, roused us all from our dorm rooms to gather on the lawn near the edge of the woods for a "tracking class." There in the pristine white snow we found the cloven hoof marks of centaurs, the long clawed scratches of goblins, and, most frightening of all, a trail of blood that ended with a long black feather.

"As we approach the winter solstice we must all be on our guard," she lectured us. "Like All Hallows' Eve, the solstice is a time when the barriers between the worlds grow thin. Fairies and demons slip though the gap and venture into our world. They're particularly brazen at this time of year and use the snow as cover for their incursions. Observe."

She nodded to Gillie and he removed the hood from the falcon's head. Immediately the bird was alert, eyes searching the ground. She cocked her head and strained at her jesses. Gillie made a clicking sound in his throat that sounded just like the falcon's trill, and released her. She flew straight off his hand and dove into the snow. She came up almost immediately with something in her talons. Gillie cast a feathered lure down to distract the bird away from her prey and quickly scooped up the struggling animal when the falcon released it.

Only it wasn't an animal. It was a tiny winged sprite like the ones Miss Frost kept pinned in her classroom—but alive. This one was covered in white down and had blue eyes. Gillie cupped it in his gloved hands as it beat its wings furiously.

"Who can identify it?" Miss Swift demanded.

"*Lychnobia riparia*," Daisy said breathlessly, "commonly known as a hyter sprite. They can't make themselves bigger like some of the other sprites. There's even a legend that they lead stray children home."

Miss Swift snorted. "Completely erroneous, as are all such legends of fairies helping children. There's a similar story about your namesake, eh, Gillie?"

"Aye," Gillie answered hoarsely. "The Ghillie Dhu was said to find lost children and lead them home, just like the hyter sprites. This one is just a wee thing. Shall I let it go?"

"And let it tunnel its way through the snow into the castle? That's what they do. They get into the root cellar and granary and eat up all the oats and apples. *Vermin*." She sniffed. "I'm sure Miss Frost will be happy to have it as a specimen. Bag it and give it to Daisy to bring to her."

Gillie lifted his black eyes up to Miss Swift. For a moment

I saw a flash of green in them and his hands opened to let the sprite out, but when it tried to fly up it landed with a thud back in his hands. "It's broken its wing," he said sadly, "and probably wouldna last the winter." He took a soft leather sack out of his hunting bag, popped it over the sprite's head, tied the sack shut, and handed it to a wide-eyed Daisy.

"Make sure Miss Frost is quick about it," he said gruffly. Then he whistled for his falcon and stomped off in the snow. Miss Swift rolled her eyes. "Very well. I suppose it's time for us all to go. Class dismissed."

I walked back to the castle between Helen and Daisy, Helen complaining about the cold and being up so early she hadn't had a chance to curl her hair, Daisy cradling the bag holding the condemned hyter sprite in her arms. When we got to the house, Daisy suddenly wheeled on Helen.

"How can you go on about your hair when this poor creature is about to die?" she cried.

Then before Helen or I could say anything she ran toward the North Wing classrooms, sobbing.

"What's wrong with her?" Helen asked. "It's not like the lampsprite's *human*."

"Do we really know that?" I asked. "I mean, no, they're not *human*, but they're not animals either. The reason Miss Frost hates them so much is because she blames them for leading Sir Malmsbury astray."

"Well, not that I generally agree with Miss Frost, but she does have a point here. The important thing to remember is that these creatures are not like us."

I stared at Helen, who had paused by a gilded mirror to fuss with her hair. "And just because someone is not like you, that means it's okay to torture and kill them?"

"Oh please, now you sound like those horrible radicals preaching from their soapboxes in Union Square."

"Some of those 'horrible radicals' were my friends," I said, thinking of Tillie, "and the people who they were speaking up for were people like my mother and me and all the girls at the Triangle."

Helen made a face in the mirror. "Everyone agrees that the Triangle fire was most regrettable."

"*Most regrettable?*" I cried. "You make it sound like a failed tea party. Girls were burned alive and all because no one cared enough about their lives to install proper fire escapes or trusted them enough to leave the doors unlocked—"

"Well," a voice came from behind me, "girls like that *do* steal. We had a maid once who stole my pearl earrings."

I turned and found Georgiana Montmorency standing with a cluster of girls. My argument with Helen had drawn a little crowd. These were the same girls who had cheered me a few weeks ago, but there were all looking at me queerly now.

"I had no idea you worked as a seamstress, Ava," Georgiana said, raising her eyebrows at Alfreda and Wallis. The rest of the girls were staring at me as if I'd suddenly sprouted horns. It was the way they looked at the lampsprites when they examined them. A factory girl was as much a different species as a lampsprite in their eyes. Georgiana, seeing that the tide of public opinion had turned against me, smiled sweetly. "I have some shirtwaists that need mending if you're looking to earn some extra money. Who knows? Perhaps they were made by your friends at the Triangle. I'm afraid they're rather slipshod."

I don't know why this insult was the one that finally broke me. I heard the bass bell in my head and instead of trying to slow it I made it speed up and, somehow, I made it change tone until it was a high screech inside my head. The mirror behind Helen shattered. I turned to see if Helen was all right. Glass shards glittered in her hair like new-fallen snow. Her eyes were wide and frightened. She was looking at me as if she saw a monster. I couldn't blame her; it's what I felt like. I turned and fled, the other girls scattering away from me in fear, and ran blindly through the halls until I turned a corner and ran into Nathan.

"Ah, Ava, I was looking for you . . ." He stopped when he saw the tears streaming from my face.

"Why?" I cried. "Do you have some mending for me to do? Or do you want a display of my freakish powers?"

He stared at me, open-mouthed, and then slowly smiled. "Neither," he answered. "I want to show you a display of *my* freakish powers." Then he grabbed my hand and dragged me into the empty library and before I could protest he opened the trapdoor behind the fireplace and started dragging me down the spiral stairs.

"Where are we going?" I asked. "We're not allowed down here without a teacher."

Nathan snorted. "Do you really care what anyone here thinks after the way they've talked about you?"

"You heard them?" I asked, glad that he was ahead of me on the dark stairs and couldn't see the blood rise to my face.

"Helen's little lecture on social inferiors and Georgiana's offer for you to slave over her blouses for a few pennies? Yes.

I heard that and much more. You think these girls are your friends just because they smile to your face? Do you think they'll ever see you as an equal?"

We'd come to the corridor at the bottom of the stairs. Nathan held up his lantern in front of the wall, lighting up a row of filing cabinets. "Do you know what these are?" he asked.

I shook my head.

"Genealogical records," he replied. "The Order has kept track of the bloodlines of their members since the original six sisters and six knights, down to the families that founded Blythewood and everyone who's joined the Order since. They've made careful notes of abilities and flaws so that they could breed a better warrior. Why do you think Sir Malmsbury studied lampsprites? So he could understand how to breed people."

"But that's heartless!"

"Yes, but can you tell me you're really surprised, with all Helen's silly blather about marriage and finding a suitable husband?"

"But what about girls like Daisy?"

"Outsiders? They bring them in when they find a desirable trait to introduce into the stock. If Daisy is deemed acceptable after three years here, she'll find herself matched up to a proper boy from Hawthorn. If not, well . . . the Order isn't totally heartless. They offer her employment."

"Like Miss Sharp?"

"Exactly. They would never allow Miss Sharp to marry because of the madness in her family—or Miss Corey because of that peculiar skin of hers, or Miss Frost because of a tendency to drink and corpulence." Nathan's voice changed, as it did when he was repeating something he'd heard or read.

"You've *read* the files?"

"Yes," he admitted. "At first I was just looking for mine." He opened a drawer and took out a slim manila folder and smiled at it ruefully. "Honestly, I just wanted to know more about my father. He died when I was so young, you see. So I don't recall much about him. Louisa used to tell me there wasn't much to know. He was a wealthy man from an old family. Simon Beckwith." He held open the folder to a chart with a family tree and pointed at the names of Simon Beckwith and India Montmorency joined together with a lowercase *m* and the date 1893. Below them were Louisa and Nathan's names and their birthdate, February 12, 1894.

"I didn't know you and Louisa were twins," I said.

"We were so unalike that people often forgot," Nathan said with a rueful smile.

"What are these symbols?" I asked, pointing to a bell and an eye next to Dame Beckwith's name and an acorn next to Simon Beckwith's.

"Traits. A bell means the ability to ring the bells—not as a chime child—the symbol for that is a circled bell, but as you see, that's very rare. My mother had the ability to ring the bells and to influence people with a glance of her eyes. I apparently got the bell-ringing ability from her, but not the fixing people with a steely gaze . . ." Nathan bulged his eyes out at me and I laughed, the sound echoing strangely in the underground corridor. I wasn't so sure he hadn't inherited something of his mother's penetrating gaze. "And I certainly didn't inherit my father's personality. The acorn is a symbol of steadfastness."

"Oh," I said, trying not to smile. "I didn't know your mother was a Montmorency."

"Oh yes, she's from the original founding families and so was Simon Beckwith. I must have been a disappointment to them. All I got was bell ringing, but look at Louisa. She got steadfastness, the penetrating gaze *and* bell ringing. Imagine their dismay to lose such a valuable breeder."

"That's not fair, Nathan! Your mother loved . . . *loves* your sister. I could tell from how she looked when she talked about her."

"Oh yes, I'm sure she was fond of her, but if she loved her would she have done this?" Nathan held the folder closer to the lantern. I noticed his hand was shaking and was afraid he might set it on fire. I had to steady his hand to make out what he meant. A faint pen stroke had been drawn through Louisa's name. Below it, in delicate script that I recognized as Dame Beckwith's handwriting were written the words "Lost in the Blythe Wood, August 1911. NLVBL."

"What does NLVBL mean?"

"I asked myself the same question. That's when I started looking though the other files to find that notation. I found it right away in Euphorbia Frost's file and your mother's."

"My mother's?"

He opened another drawer, retrieved a file, and showed me another chart. I glimpsed a long line of Halls intermingled with Rutherfords, Vanderbilts, Morgans, and Montmorencys (Georgiana and I were related!) that ended with my mother's name. The same florid pen stroke had crossed out her name with the notation "Lost in the Blythe Wood, 1893. NLVBL."

"But my mother came back!" I said. "Why doesn't it say that?"

"Because it doesn't matter," Nathan replied. "She was still NLVBL."

"But what . . . ?

"No longer viable bloodline."

I stared at Nathan, desperately trying to think of something else the initials could stand for, but I couldn't come up with anything.

"You see, that's why they haven't bothered trying to find Louisa. As far as they're concerned, she's already ruined. They've given up on her, but I haven't. I'm going into the woods to find her. And if I can't find her I'll take one of the Darklings and hold him for ransom until they give me Louisa back."

"Why are you so sure it was a Darkling that took Louisa?"

"I saw how that fiend looked at you that night in the woods and on the day on the lawn. If the bells hadn't rung he would have grabbed you. And what do you think those crows were about? The Darklings sent them. You saw in the candelabellum how the Darkling broke up into the crows. They're one and the same thing."

"But the crows felt . . . *different*."

Nate gave me a strange look. "They felt the same to me— same black wings and black beady eyes. And they both disappeared when the bells rang. And I bet they're both vulnerable to this . . ." He slid a silver dagger out of his pocket, identical to the one that Mr. Bellows had given Miss Sharp when we were attacked by the crows.

"That belongs to Mr. Bellows! How did you get it?"

"I took it from him when he was goggling at Miss Sharp. He didn't even miss it. It's not like he's making any use of it. Everyone here knows that those monsters are in the woods preying on innocent girls and no one's doing anything about it. Because they don't think it's worth saving a girl once she's been taken. They think she's worthless, just as they thought your mother was worthless. They banished her when she came back. Well, I don't think Louisa is worthless, no matter what's happened to her. I'm going to take a Darkling hostage and get her back."

I didn't think Nathan was strong enough to take a Darkling hostage, but I didn't tell him that. "Even if you could get Louisa back," I said instead, "you must remember that she might not be the same. She might be possessed by those shadow creatures . . . like my mother. She was never completely . . . *right*. She could never settle. She moved us from place to place. She never trusted anyone. And then she began drinking the laudanum . . ."

"But at least you had her," Nathan said. "At least she came back. I won't stop until I find Louisa . . . and make the bastards that took her pay. Everyone goes home for break in a few days. The solstice is considered so dangerous that they send everyone home and then cower in the castle, leaving poor old Gillie to patrol the woods. I can easily slip past him. I'm going into the woods and I'm not coming out until I've caught one of the Darklings and made them give Louisa back."

He glared at me, daring me to argue with him. But I didn't. Instead I told him that I'd go with him.

24

I HAD KNOWN for several weeks that I would be staying over the winter break. Early in December I had received a letter from Agnes telling me that my grandmother had decided to spend the winter in Europe.

> *I had hoped to get a chance to see you so we could have a good long talk about all that you have seen and done at Blythewood, but am afraid that will have to wait for the spring when we return. Caroline Janeway sends her regards and says that if ever you need to get away from Blythewood for a spell you are welcome to stay with her.*
>
> *I hope you will not be too lonely staying there over break. I stayed during winter break one year and rather enjoyed the solitude. Christmas at Blythewood is a magical time.*

Such hints were the only references Agnes ever made to the true nature of Blythewood. I guessed that she didn't want to commit anything sensational to writing and she was waiting for us to meet in person to talk about all I had learned since she left me at the Grand Central Station in September. I suspected from what Agnes had said about "the old ways" that she didn't approve of everything that went on at Blythewood. I wondered now if the old ways she had so despised had to do with the charts in the dungeons recording the family bloodlines. Had Agnes been deemed NLVBL and denied marriage? From the way Mr. Greenfeder had looked at her I didn't think he would agree. I would have also liked to ask her if *she* thought all the fairies were evil—especially the Darklings. She knew I'd found the black feather beside my mother. Did she think a Darkling had killed her? But until I could talk to Agnes, the only answer might come from the Darkling himself.

Which was another of the reasons I agreed to go into the woods with Nathan. All we had to do was wait for everyone to leave the school for break. Most of the girls left right after final exams on the Wednesday before Christmas in a flurry of automobiles and carriages, trunks and hatboxes, cheerful shouts and tearful partings. Watching them go it was hard not to envy the homecoming they were headed toward. They all *belonged* somewhere. But where did I belong?

For a little while I'd thought it was here, but since my argument with Helen I wasn't so sure. Although Helen tried to smooth things over I couldn't forget that I wasn't her "sort of people." Daisy, sensing the strain between Helen and me, had been acting like a skittish cat, unable even to be in the same room with the two of us. I almost would have been glad to see the two of them go, but Daisy had volunteered to stay an extra day to help Sarah Lehman catalogue Miss Frost's samples. Helen, because she lived so close, was waiting until her mother came up from their Washington Square brownstone to open the Hyde Park house for the holiday season.

"Mother says you're welcome to come," she invited me stiffly. "Although we will no doubt be treated to a boring array of old men my mother would like to marry me off to."

I thanked her just as stiffly for the invitation, but the last thing I wanted was to witness a parade of potential suitors for Helen. Although I had not peeked at the van Beeks' files (that would have been dishonorable) I was sure that Helen must be considered the cream of the Blythewood crop. She might complain about her mother lining up suitors for her, but at least she was considered marriageable. So I told Helen that I'd already promised to catalogue books for Miss Corey. I didn't mention my plans to sneak into the woods with Nathan.

"Will Miss Corey be staying here, too?" Helen asked.

"She and Miss Sharp are staying at Violet House, but they promised to check in on me."

"Won't you be terrified here all alone?" Daisy asked as we watched Gillie ferry the last coach to the train station and an eerie silence descended over the castle and the grounds. "Especially on the solstice."

"Gillie'll be here," I replied, perhaps not altogether convincingly, as I saw Daisy and Helen exchange a worried look, "and Sarah. As long as we all stay in the castle during the solstice we'll be perfectly safe." Of course I didn't mention that I wasn't planning to stay inside during the solstice.

The next morning we awoke to a couple of inches of new snow and predictions of another storm on the way—enough to make travel slow, but not to justify my roommates' reactions.

"I'm afraid I'll get stuck on a train somewhere in Ohio," Daisy said. "I've wired Mother and Father that it's best if I stay here."

"And I've told my parents that I want to stay over break and get a head start on my studies for the spring," Helen said.

"And they believed that?" I asked incredulously.

Helen smirked. "No. They think I'm avoiding the ancient groom Mother's picked out for me—and they're right. I hear he's twice my age and has a face like a dead mackerel. But he's also from one of the oldest families in New York—the van something-or-others—and rich as Croesus. Mother's so angry at me she's convinced Daddy to sail to Europe for the spring season. She thinks I'll mind missing Paris, but I don't. Really. Think how cozy we three can be here all on our own. It will be loads of fun."

I didn't think being stuck alone with Helen and Daisy all break would be cozy, nor did I believe my roommates' excuses for staying for a minute. They had clearly decided that I mustn't be left on my own, which made it very inconvenient to get away from them to go into the woods with Nathan. He was adamant that he needed to go in on Friday night—the night of the winter solstice. "All the creatures will be out that night."

I thought that was a good reason *not* to go into the woods on that night, but Nathan thought it made it more likely that he'd find a Darkling. I still wasn't sure how he planned to capture one of them, but I knew I didn't want him to go into the woods by himself.

Without the bustle and noise of students in the castle, we could hear the wind groaning through the acres of woods at the edge of the lawn. The woods felt, in fact, as if they had come closer to the house, as if the very trees knew we were alone and would creep up on us when we weren't looking. Eating dinner in the Great Hall with Nate and Sarah, Helen and Daisy, and only old deaf Bertie to wait on us, our little group seemed like a band of pilgrims who had wandered into a medieval castle seeking shelter from some dreadful disaster—plague or civil war. The great columns that held up the arched ceiling loomed over us like trees in a forest. Winds shook the panes of the stained-glass windows, rattling the swords and shields of the seven sisters standing guard between us and the woods. I thought I could just make out a tinkling sound that might have been ice crystallizing on branches, but that reminded me of the bells of the candelabellum beneath us in the dungeons, spinning their stories in the dark.

After dinner we played flush and trophies in the Commons Room until eleven, and then left Nathan and Sarah to go upstairs to our room. Our steps echoed strangely in the nearly empty castle. Daisy's and Helen's silly chatter sounded frail and thin as birdsong in the stairwell. Wind rattled the windowpanes on the landings as if it were trying to get inside. Our room was icy, but we were all too tired to build a fire. Instead we climbed into our beds under extra quilts.

I waited until Daisy's and Helen's replies to each other grew shorter and farther apart and then finally subsided. Then I waited through the midnight tolling of the bells before stepping out of bed. I'd worn wool stockings to bed under the navy-blue bloomers we wore for archery class, along with a navy-blue jersey and heavy socks. I carried my boots as I crept out of the room and down the back stairs to the back door by the scullery where Nathan was waiting for me, sitting on the bottom step beside a lit lantern, its wick trimmed to a faint glow.

"There you are," he whispered. "I didn't think you were coming. A few more minutes and I'd have gone without you."

"I had to wait for Daisy and Helen to fall asleep." I sat down to pull my boots on. "They took forever talking about whether Mr. Bellows would ask Miss Sharp to marry him and if she'd say yes, and if they got married would they have the ceremony at Violet House and what would she wear and would Miss Corey be maid of honor and would we be asked to be bridesmaids . . ."

"What utter rot," Nathan said.

"I know," I replied. In truth I'd been beguiled by the image Helen had conjured of Miss Sharp in cream Peau de Chine, orange blossom lace and an enormous bouquet of white violets, with us in her wake arrayed in lilac dresses. "The Order won't let her marry, will they?"

"Whyever not?"

The voice came from above us on the stairs and was decidedly female. Nathan flinched, sprung up the steps, and seized the intruder, who yelped and struggled as he held the lantern to her face. Helen, in the same navy outfit of jersey and bloomers as I wore, swatted the lantern away. "Get that light out of my eyes. Do you want to wake Sour Lemon? She'll turn us in for sure."

"What are you doing here, Helen?" Nathan demanded.

"I could ask you the same thing, Nathan Fillmore Beckwith, only I think it's obvious. I knew as soon as you'd gotten it into your head that a Darkling had stolen Louisa that you'd go running off into the woods the moment you had the place to your-self. When Ava insisted on staying here over break I thought something must be up. And then when she went to sleep in her bloomers I realized it must be tonight."

Nathan turned to glare at me. "I didn't think she noticed," I said, "or that she'd be caught dead in the things herself outside of archery."

Helen shrugged. "It's not as if anyone is going to see us."

"You can't come, Helen." Nathan bit off the words between clenched lips. "It's too dangerous."

"Nonsense! If Ava can do it, so can I. I'm a better shot and I've brought my bow." She demonstrated the bow and quiver strapped over her shoulder. "Have either of you even thought to bring a weapon?"

Nathan brandished his dagger.

"That's Rupert's!" Another voice came from higher up the stairs.

"Hell's bells!" Nathan swore. "Not you too, Daisy!"

Daisy crept meekly out of the shadows. Helen leaned over toward me and mimicked, "*That's Rupert's!* Since when are you on a first-name basis with our teachers?"

Even in the dark I could tell Daisy was blushing. "I was only shocked to see that Nathan had filched his knife."

"Stop it!" Nathan hissed. "Why do you think I didn't ask you two? Ava at least knows how to keep her mouth shut."

I was stung that my only recommendation was taciturnity, but bit back a retort. "Nathan's right," I said. "Sarah might hear us and tell Gillie what we're planning."

"And what *is* your plan to get past Gillie?" Helen asked. "He's got that creepy owl with him."

"Blodeuwedd's not creepy," I countered. "And she can't be everywhere. We'll wait until she passes and then sneak into the woods."

Daisy shook her head. "I've watched her. You'll never get past her . . . unless she's distracted by this." She reached into her jersey pocket and drew out something small and furry.

Helen squeaked and clutched Nathan's arm. "A mouse! You've got a mouse in your pocket! A live mouse!" She looked like she was going to clamber up on top of Nathan's shoulders.

"I rescued it from Miss Frost's specimen room," Daisy said, cradling the small creature. "I thought better a fast death out in the open than whatever terrible thing Miss Frost had planned for it. And at least it will die for the good of the group." She looked from me to Helen to Nate. Poor Daisy. Since my fight with Helen all she'd wanted was for us to be united again, like the time we all faced the goblins together in the woods. She didn't know anything about the bloodline records in the dungeons or that she and I would never really belong here at Blythewood. But then Helen did something very strange. She folded her own hands over Daisy's hand and held the mouse.

"That's a very noble sacrifice, Daisy. We all know how much you care about small helpless creatures."

I looked at Nathan, expecting him to mock Helen's sentiment, but instead I saw something shift in his eyes. The haunted look I'd seen since that day on the roof had softened. He reached out and took my hand and Helen's, linking the four of us together.

"All right," Nathan said, "we'll all go together, but only if you all promise to follow me and do what I say. We're going to find that Darkling and make him tell us what happened to my sister. And if I find out they've killed her . . ." He let go of Helen's hand to hold up the dagger and turn it in the light of his lantern. The dark runes carved on its blade leapt into life. For a moment I saw the runes floating in the air, casting shadows over the faces of my three friends, linking us together, but in what fate I didn't know.

⋯→ ✦ ←⋯

We could not have picked a worse night. The sky was crystal clear. Even though the moon was less than a quarter full, it reflected off the snow so brightly that it might have been daylight. I didn't see how we'd make it across the lawn without Gillie seeing us. But Nate pointed to the stone wall that edged the formal garden.

"If we stay in the shadow of the wall we'll be okay. When we get to the end of the wall we'll wait until we see Blodeuwedd, and then Daisy can toss out the bait and we'll run for the woods." He waited until we all nodded our agreement, Daisy looking wistfully at the mouse in her pocket. If we survived this, I swore to myself, I'd find her another to keep as a pet.

We crept along the garden wall, Nate first, then me, Helen, and Daisy, all of us keeping to the shadows. When we reached the end of the wall there was still a long expanse of moonlit snow, against which was painted a shadow of enormous wings. I clutched Nathan's hand, thinking the Darkling had come to meet us, but then I looked up and saw the white wings and wide pale face of Blodeuwedd lit up by the moonlight. Her solemn heart-shaped face seemed to look directly at me. I pressed myself against the stone wall, feeling helpless as the mouse in Daisy's pocket.

"Deploy the mouse, Daisy!" Nathan hissed.

"I don't think I can," Daisy cried.

"Oh, hell's bells!" Helen swore.

I looked back to see Helen putting her hand in Daisy's pocket, making a face. She flung the poor mouse out onto the grass, where it squeaked in alarm. Instantly, Blodeuwedd's remorseless face swiveled toward the noise and she plunged on soundless wings toward the mouse.

"Now!" Nathan cried. He ran for the edge of the woods. I followed, nearly stumbling because my legs were numb from crouching, but Helen caught my arm and pulled me upright. Daisy was on the other side of me, her face wet and shining in the moonlight. Relief swept over me when we reached the shadows of the trees . . . until I looked into those shadows.

Amidst the snow-dusted and icicle-hung trees stood looming figures of glowing white ice. My first thought was that they were statues from the garden that had been coated in ice, but if they were statues why was the bass bell clamoring in my head? Besides, they didn't look like any of the statues in the garden. Instead of beautiful, classical youths and maidens, these statues were of huge, shaggily bearded men holding clubs and grimacing through mouths full of sharp teeth.

"What . . . ?" I began, but then one of the statues snarled and took a lumbering step toward me.

"Ice giants!" Nathan shouted, grabbing my hand. "Come on, we have to reach the Rowan Circle."

"Why the Rowan Circle?" Helen shouted over the wind as we ran from the lumbering ice giants. On every side of us trees thrashed in the wind, spraying snow and icicles. Ice-coated branches reached out to block our way, and roots writhed under the snow to trip us. I could hear the lumbering steps of the ice giants pursuing us.

"It's enspelled to keep out fairies and demons," Nathan replied. "I read about it in one of the books from the Special Collections."

The whole woods seemed to be throwing itself in our way. Branches fell from the trees and roots erupted from the ground. A vine scratched my face. When I tried to brush it away sharp claws dug into my arm. A wizened face loomed in front of me, its mouth opened in a toothy grimace.

"Hunn . . . gree!" it cried.

I screamed and silver flashed in front of my eyes and blood splashed in my face. "Goblins!" Nathan shouted, drawing his dagger out of a limp, furry creature that had the face of a wizened old man. "Run!"

We ran blindly through the woods. I no longer knew if we were headed toward the Rowan Circle, only that I had to get away from the creatures at my heels. The sound of them alone was maddening—a chittering combined with sounds that might have been words. Could goblins talk? The one that had attacked me had said something that sounded like "hungry." If they could talk they weren't animals, but "hungry" seemed to be the sum total of their vocabulary, and I didn't have time to turn around and try to converse with one. Their smell, like rotten meat and fetid water, covered my skin with an oily film and crept down my throat, making me gag. Somehow I knew that the smell came from their last meal and that my flesh would soon join the rotting meat stuck between their teeth.

I doubled over, retching at the thought, and felt something snatch at my arm. I flailed out, but it was Nathan dragging me away from the snapping jaws of a tortoise-faced goblin and into the Rowan Circle. Letting go of me, Nathan spun around to face the creature, dagger flashing. Helen was beside him, an arrow drawn in her bow. Daisy reached into her pocket and drew out a handbell that had been stoppered with a handkerchief. She unstoppered it and rang the bell in a slow steady beat. My friends had all brought weapons to fight the enemy—only I had come empty-handed.

Or almost empty-handed. Reaching into the pocket of my jersey I found the black feather. I ran my fingers along its bristled vane and the bell inside my head slowed. I felt immediately calmer. I looked down at the feather and wondered if this was what Miss Emmaline had meant by finding something to focus the bells. Wasn't it odd, though, that it should be a feather from a Darkling? But I couldn't worry about that now. I held the feather up and watched it sway in the wind, proud and regal as the plume of a warrior going into battle. The chittering goblins, ringed all around us now, went silent. I felt the force of their yellow eyes all trained on the black feather.

Nathan, Helen, and Daisy followed the direction of their gazes to me. "Brilliant!" Nathan cried. "Are you doing a mesmerizing spell like the one Miss Sharp did?"

I had no idea what I was doing. My arm was moving in a definite pattern, but I wasn't controlling it. Light as it was, the feather was pulling my arm into wide swoops and flourishes, writing furiously on the air as if driven by the mind of a mad poet possessed by the muse. I could almost see the words it wrote rising luminescent into the night air and floating up into the trees, a desperate distress message sent out by a sinking ship.

The bell in my head was tolling to the rhythm of my swaying movement as if I were conducting a symphony. Even the goblins grew quiet watching the runic signs floating up into the air. Was this shadow magic? I wondered. If it was, how did I know how to do it? The wind stilled and all the creatures of the forest went silent, as small birds and mice grow quiet when a hawk is on the wing.

Into the silence dropped the sound of a long low whistle, followed by the thunder of feet pounding the forest floor—a hundred goblins running away from us and scattering into the trees as fast as they could go.

"They're all running away!" Daisy cried.

"Yes," said Nathan, "but what are they running *from*?" He turned from the woods to me and then tilted his head up. "Perhaps you'd better stop now."

But it was too late. Above us the moon and stars were blotted out by enormous black wings. The Darkling landed in front of me, its huge wings beating away Nate and Helen and Daisy. Out of the corner of my eye I saw Helen draw back her bow and Nate lunge forward with his dagger. Daisy was ringing her bell but the sound was drowned out by the whoosh of wings.

The Darkling paid no attention to any of them. He stepped forward and wrapped his arm around my waist, pulling me tightly against his chest. I felt the length of his body against mine, the steely power of his arms holding me, the beat of his heart against my breast, the long hard muscles of his legs bending and tensing as he sprang up.

And then we were airborne, rising above the Rowan Circle and into the dark.

25

I MUST BE DREAMING, I told myself, as we rose into the sky. I had had this dream so many times before. But in those dreams I hadn't felt the heat of the Darkling's skin, or heard his heart beating against my cheek, or noticed the long white scar that ran from his elbow to his wrist. Nor gotten a cramp in my arm from trying to hold on to him.

"Hold on a few more minutes," he shouted against the wind. "We're almost there."

There? Where was he taking me? To Faerie, where monsters would rip me apart and feast on my bones? We were still above the treetops, which looked like spearheads waiting to impale my falling body. I would wait until we reached the ground, I thought, and then run.

Only we didn't reach the ground. We flew lower to the treetops and then he suddenly folded his wings, tipped forward, and plummeted straight down. I'd watched hawks perform the same maneuver when they spotted their prey, always miraculously swooping back up before they crashed into the ground, but as branches whizzed by us, frozen pine needles brushing against my face, I was sure he meant to dash my brains out on the forest floor.

As quickly as our descent had begun, though, so it ended. His wings snapped out, cupping the air, and beat backward. We landed on a thick pine bough, scattering snow. The whole tree swayed with the impact, icicles in the branches clattering against each other like wind chimes. I felt the motion in the soles of my feet when they touched the bark, not the movement just of this tree, but of its neighbors swaying in sympathy, the whole forest moving from pointy treetops down to roots burrowing deep in the rich loamy earth. I felt a part of it all . . .

Until he let go of me. Then my arms flailed and my knees buckled. He laughed and steadied me with a wing. "You've got to get your tree legs. But until then, perhaps you'd better have a seat."

Still steadying me with his wing, he lifted up a needled branch and gave me a gentle push forward. I groped in the darkness until I felt solid wood beneath my feet. We were on some kind of platform built into the tree branches, but it was too dark for me to see how far it went. I stood still and looked up. Between intertwined branches I saw stars so bright and so close I felt I could reach up and touch them.

Then light bloomed around me as if one of those stars had exploded. I looked down and saw the Darkling crouched over a lantern, adjusting its wick. The light cast his winged shadow on the curved wall behind him and the sloping roof above us, painting the whole space with a delicate lace-like feather pattern.

He stood up and the space was filled with the beat of wings louder than the beat of my heart. I stepped back . . . into the wall. I could see how powerfully built the Darkling's chest and wings were. Taut muscles rippled under his marble-white skin. Ebony wings thrashed the air into a windstorm. One flick of those giant wings would crush me. Still I held my feather up between us as if I could use it to fend him off.

"What do you think you're going to do with that?" he asked, folding his arms over his chest.

"It summoned you, didn't it?" I asked, feeling suddenly foolish but determined not to show it.

His lips quirked into a crooked smile. "You think that's why I came to your rescue? Because you waved a feather in the air?"

"Rescue?" I squawked. "Is that what this is? It looks more like a kidnapping to me. If you were rescuing me why did you bring me to your . . . your lair?"

"Lair?" He raised an eyebrow. "Look around you. Does this look like a lair?"

I looked around. We were in a circular room with a floor laid with smooth planks, the walls and ceiling woven of tightly intertwined branches kinked and mortared with soft green moss. Even in the depths of winter, plants grew in the moss pockets—orchids and hanging ferns and fragrant herbs. Under the scent of pine I detected rosemary, mint, and something deliciously sweet . . . *violets!* Some were growing in the moss, but there was also a bouquet in a glass vase on a shelf beside a stack of books. A teapot and blue-and-white willow-pattern teacups were on another shelf along with an assortment of clocks, some of which had been taken apart, and other metal contraptions. *Violets? Clocks? Teacups?* He was right. It wasn't particularly lair-like.

"Do you . . . *live* here?" I asked. He started to laugh again but then he registered the look in my eyes. Slowly he stilled the beating of his wings and drew them in close to his back until they were folded neatly between his shoulder blades. Then, keeping his eyes on mine and moving with the same cautious pace as I'd seen Gillie use approaching a skittery hawk, he reached for a shirt hanging from a hook and put it on. I noticed the shirt had neatly sewn slits to allow his wings to come out. "It's okay," he said, "I'm not going to hurt you."

As he spoke I realized that the bell had stopped ringing inside my head. Did that mean there was no danger here—or was the Darkling able to silence it?

"Why should I believe you? You killed my mother."

This brought him up short. "Killed . . . ?" He looked genuinely puzzled. "Why would you think that?"

I brandished the black feather. "Because I found *this* by her side. Do you deny that it's one of yours—or one of your kind's?"

He stepped forward until he was only a few inches away. His wings were beating behind him, agitating the air. I felt the breeze from them on my face, and despite all of my reasons to fear this creature, I felt my fear dissipating.

He took the feather out of my hand and ran his finger along the vane, then held it up to his nose. "It's one of ours, but it's not mine," he said, handing it back to me. "Another Darkling must have come to your mother when she was dying, but he wouldn't have hurt her. Why do you think any of us would hurt you? I came to the Triangle to help you; I caught you when you fell from the roof."

"But you let Tillie die!" I cried.

"Is that what you think?" he asked angrily. "After all I've done to help you and your friends?"

Abashed, I remembered how he had helped Tillie and Etta and me up to the roof. But then I remembered something else.

"You took me to Bellevue!"

His face darkened and his wings began to unfurl again, but he tightened his jaw and drew his wings back between his shoulder blades. He took a deep breath and I saw his lips moving, as if he were counting to himself to master his anger. I wondered if he heard bells in *his* head. When he spoke his voice was icy and formal.

"I regret that you ended up in that awful place, but I don't understand why you think I brought you there. I laid you down on the sidewalk so that I could help the other girls. I saved a few, but there was only so much I could do." His lips trembled and he looked away from me. I saw the pain etched in his face. I suddenly understood that his anger wasn't directed at me—it was at himself for failing to save more of the girls and for failing to keep me out of Bellevue. Still, when he reached toward the shelf with the clocks and teapots and removed one of the metal contraptions, I jumped.

"What are you going to do with that?" I asked suspiciously.

"With this," he said, changing his icy tone to a menacing growl. "I'm going to make you a cup of tea."

⟶ ✦ ⟵

I sat on a low bench while my Darkling abductor performed the homely and practical chore of tea making. The metal object was a small gas stove. He lit it and poured water (melted snow, he told me) from a ceramic pitcher into an iron teakettle.

"I thought fairies couldn't touch iron," I said.

"I'm not a fairy," he replied, shaking a tin. "Earl Grey or Darjeeling?"

"Earl Grey," I said. "Are you a . . . *Darkling*, then?"

His lips quirked into that crooked smile again—they were full, finely molded lips, shaped like a bow—and he whistled softly under his breath. I'd heard the falcons in their mews make a similar sound. "Isn't it customary in your society to introduce oneself by name first before identifying one's *race*?"

"Oh," I said, feeling as if I'd been admonished by Miss Frost. "I didn't think . . ."

"That I had a name?" He asked, quirking one eyebrow up. "Well, I do. It's Raven."

"Oh! I'm pleased to meet you, Mr. Raven," I held out my hand to shake his, determined now not to neglect the social niceties. He laughed so hard he spilled water from the kettle.

"Just Raven," he corrected, taking my hand. As it had when he first touched me, I heard the treble bell chime inside my head, startling me so that I dropped his hand abruptly. He turned away and busied himself cleaning up the water he'd spilled. "As for what your kind call us—Darkling is one name for us. The Greeks called us *aggelos*, messenger, because we traveled between the worlds and carried the souls of the dead to the next world—the mortals to their afterworld and the fairy creatures back to Faerie."

"That rather sounds like what angels do . . . oh!" I said, clapping my hand to my mouth. "Are you telling me you're an angel?"

Instead of answering he lifted the kettle from the stove and poured a stream of steaming water into a brown glazed teapot. He swirled the water around and then dumped it into a moss pocket. He measured out tea leaves into the pot and refilled it with boiling water and placed it on a silver tray next to two blue-and-white china teacups, a sugar bowl, and a creamer.

(A *creamer*? I wondered. Wherever did he get cream?)

"That's your word for us," he finally answered. I wasn't sure anymore what I was more surprised by—that I was standing three feet away from an angel or that he had a supply of fresh cream (from a bottle labeled "Honeybrook Farms, Rhinebeck, N.Y.") and a tin of chocolate biscuits. "Later we were called nephilim or fallen angels because our wings were black instead of the pretty gold-and-white ones in paintings. Whenever we'd show ourselves to humans they thought we were demons. Then your lot came along and decided all creatures from Faerie were demons."

"Aren't they?" I asked. "Those ice giants tried to kills us!"

"Yes, the Jotuns are pretty vicious, but at least they're slow and they're only in the woods for a few months during the winter."

"Well, those goblins that were chasing us certainly weren't very nice."

He shuddered and his wings strained against his shirt. "No, goblins *aren't* nice. Sadly they developed a taste for human flesh."

"Hell's bells!" I swore, getting to my feet. "My friends! We have to go back and save them!"

"Calm down," he said. One wing stretched through the hole in his shirt, blocking my way. The feathers only grazed my arm but I stopped. There was something soothing in their touch, something that reminded me of my mother's hand when she stroked my hair when I'd had a nightmare. "Once I scattered the goblins they took off for their burrows. They won't show their rat faces for another fortnight. Your friends will be all right."

As he talked he continued stroking my arm with his feather tips, and then gently led me to a bench beside the tea tray he'd set up. He sat down on the bench beside me and tucked in his wing. His feathers rustled as he gathered them together until the wing was tucked back between his shoulder blades and nearly invisible. Then he poured tea, as if it were the most normal thing in the world: *fold wing, pour out tea, add sugar.*

The homely motions along with the soothing touch of his wings and the hot, sweet tea calmed me, but then I remembered what Dame Beckwith had said about the Darklings practicing mind control.

"Why should I trust you?" I asked. "Your kind has hunted down my kind. I saw it in the candelabellum. You abducted Merope and destroyed the prince. You turn into crows and eat the souls of your victims!"

"Ah, the candelabellum," he said, his lips twisting into a sneer. "Yes, it shows pretty pictures, but how do you know it tells the truth? I can show you a picture show as well. Finish your tea."

"What?"

"Your tea," he repeated slowly. "Finish it. It's for—"

"Shock. Yes, so everyone keeps saying. I am not in shock."

"I was going to say it's for a story. *Our* side of the story." His long fingers wrapped around the blue-and-white teacup, which suddenly looked tiny in his hand. He held up the cup and revolved it in the air, his tapered fingertips grazing the figures in the china pattern—a man and a woman in Chinese dress, a pagoda, a boat, two birds.

"I know the story of the willow-wear pattern," I said a little smugly, taking the cup in my hand. "A girl who's promised to another runs away with her lover and her jilted fiancé tracks them down and kills them, but they're resurrected as birds." I touched my fingertips to the two blue birds, their beaks locked in an everlasting kiss. Although I'd started out telling the story in a bored voice just to prove I knew as much as him, my hand trembled as I touched the birds. I was remembering my mother telling the story, and how her voice would fill with emotion whenever she got to the part about the lovers transforming into birds, how she would place the cup in my hands and say, "Nothing can keep true lovers apart."

I felt Raven's hand slip beneath mine, cradling my hands just as my hand cradled the teacup. Suddenly my hand felt just as fragile as the delicate china, and my body as hollow. His other hand splayed over the cup, fingertips resting lightly on its rim.

"Look into the cup," he said, his voice a husky purr next to my ear. "This is our story."

With a flick of his wrist, he twirled the cup. It began spinning in my hand like a top, only when it should have stopped, it spun faster, the blue-and-white pictures blurring like muffled shapes moving through a snowstorm, flakes of snow gusting past them, so hard and fast I felt its sting on my cheeks and saw the whirl of flakes all around me, so dizzying that I couldn't tell if I were watching snow rising from the spinning cup of if I was *inside* the cup watching the snow falling down . . . or if I were the one falling.

I fell into the snowy woods. Only Raven's hand still gripping mine kept me from tumbling to my knees into a waist-high drift. We were standing in a snow-filled woods. A bell was ringing—not the bass danger bell, but the sweet treble, tolling out its forlorn tune. *Remember me, remember me.* I squinted through the driving snow and made out the figure of a girl slumped over a large bronze bell—a girl no older than me and much thinner and slighter, and yet she rang steadily with hands that were white with frostbite and raw with blood. Around her lay her sisters, each beside a bell, too exhausted to keep ringing, and around them . . .

I flinched as a shadow slunk behind me. Raven gripped my hand tighter as I turned to look at what surrounded the grove. Shadow crows filled the trees like a second snowfall made out of ash. Long trails of soot wound around the tree trunks—shadow wolves prowling the edges of the grove, tightening the circle as Merope's bell grew weaker. It was only a matter of time before they overcame her. Even now the shadows were creeping toward her, nosing at her flesh. A crow dislodged from a branch and landed beside her, then another and another, each one coming closer, talons scrabbling over snow, beaks darting toward soft flesh . . . I lurched toward her to stop them, my legs rubbery in the deep snow, but Raven pulled me back.

"Wait," he whispered in my ear, his breath the only warmth in this frozen world. His arm grasped my shoulders and he pointed at the sky. "Look."

Huge black wings spread over the grove, scattering the crows. They beat the snow into a lather of white, flecked with the torn feathers of the carrion crows and drops of blood.

The shadows . . . bleed? It was a thought so horrible I couldn't even say it aloud, but in the teacup snow globe Raven heard me and whispered back, his voice as filled with horror as my thought.

Yes, inside every shadow creature is a bit of the animal—or person—it once was.

The huge winged creature cleaved his way through the bloody and smoldering crow carcasses to reach Merope. When he reached her she had already been pecked and torn by crows, but she was still alive. He lifted her up, blood dripping from her torn flesh and filling the hollow impression where she had lain through the night. But I saw her arms wrap around her winged savior and her eyes fasten on him. I heard the treble bell ring out, not the one on the ground, *or* the one in my head. I heard it ringing inside *her* head.

"She knew him!" I cried. "And loved him."

Raven clamped his hand over my mouth to hush me. Why? Weren't we just spectators here?

I heard Raven's answer in my head, not in words but in images. Merope and Aderyn—I heard his name in Raven's voice—

loved each other, but it was forbidden. A Darkling could not love a mortal. But he could not let her die. When he rescued her and took her as his bride the Darklings were cursed. They could ferry souls to the mortal afterworld and Faerie, but they themselves could never cross into Faerie again. As this part of the story fell into place, I felt Raven's sorrow and his longing—but whether that longing was for the world his kind had lost or for the love that Aderyn and Merope had, I couldn't tell. And there was no time to ask.

Aderyn rose with Merope in his arms just as a jangle of bells filled the clearing and the knights arrived, their horses steaming the air, their shouts scattering the shadow creatures. They gathered up Merope's sisters, who cried and screamed when they saw the bloody shape in the snow, but who were too weak to do much else but cling to the backs of their rescuers as they rode out of the grove, trailed by the shadows.

Come.

Before I knew what was happening, Raven had lifted me up—as Aderyn had Merope—and we were winging through the driving snow, following the route of the knights and the rescued sisters. They were pursued by the shadow creatures on land and in the air—a thick stream of crows and wolves. At the edges of the shadow stream, though, I could make out other creatures—lampsprites and goblins and trolls—fighting back the shadow creatures.

"They were trying to help," I said.

"Yes," Raven replied, his voice mournful. "The creatures of Faerie are no friends to the shadows. They've battled them for eons. Wherever the shadows are, the fairies try to fight them. Sometimes they lose and the shadows take over their forms."

I saw a goblin fall under a cloak of shadow crows that pecked holes in his tough hide. He screamed out to his companions—and in the spell of the teacup what would have normally sounded like jibbering grunts turned into words.

"Kill me!" he cried. "Slay me rather than let the tenebrae eat my soul!"

I watched, horrified, as another goblin threw himself on his companion and ripped out his throat with his teeth. I looked away and heard Raven's voice in my ear. "This is why your kind think that the fairies are aligned with the shadows. But look, even the Darkling who rescued Merope tried to save her sisters."

I saw that another Darkling was flying beside us, the girl perched on his back calling instructions into his ear and pointing to the figures on the ground. The knights had reached the castle gate. They formed a guard around the sisters to get them through the gate while fighting off the shadows. It was the same scene I'd witnessed in the candelabellum, only now from my aerial vantage point I could see what I hadn't before—on the edges of the battle goblins and sprites fought off the shadows and from above Aderyn staved off the attack of the crows. If not for Aderyn and the fairies, the knights and sisters would not have gotten to safety, but they were not able to save the prince. When the last of the crows landed on him I wanted to look away. I didn't want to see him ripped apart again. But I couldn't look away. I was drawn to the cluster of darkness that formed around him as if it were a magnet that pulled me toward it, its power growing greater as each shadow filled the hollow shape of the struggling prince.

Watching, I grew limp in Raven's arms. He landed beside a rampart of the castle and braced me against the wall. I felt his breath in my ear, but I couldn't hear what he was saying. The toll of the bass bell was too loud in my ears. I hadn't heard it when I watched this same scene in the candelabellum, because that had been a shadow play. This wasn't. Whatever magic ruled the teacup, it was stronger. This wasn't a play I was watching; it was real. The prince was being ripped to shreds in front of my eyes. The shadow crows were burrowing beneath his skin, devouring him from the inside. I could see the crows squirming and bulging beneath his skin. I moaned aloud at the horror of it.

And the shadow-thing turned toward me. Its face was a mass of roiling, raw flesh, but its eyes were already sentient and they were fastened on me. They *saw* me. His mouth opened and smoke curdled out as he spoke.

I screamed. Raven squeezed my hand so hard I felt my flesh rend . . . and then we were back in Raven's nest and I was crouched on the floor, Raven's wings mantled over me, one arm around my shoulder, the other cradling my closed fist. Blood spilled from between my clenched fingers.

"It's all right," he was saying, his voice audible now that the bass bell wasn't ringing. "I'm sorry, I didn't realize your magic was so strong you could make the scene real. I had to do something to break the spell." He was prying my fingers apart, picking shards of broken china out of my shredded flesh, murmuring over and over again that he was sorry and that it was all right until his words blurred into a cooing like the sound pigeons made on the windowsill in the city. Dimly I felt him cleaning and wrapping my hand and then he was wrapping me in a blanket because I couldn't stop shivering and then he was laying me down on the pallet, which was surprisingly soft, like a feather bed, and he was covering me with his wings because I *still* couldn't stop shaking because a part of me was still standing in the snow watching the shadow-thing turn and fix me with its red eyes, open its mouth, and say my name.

26

I AWOKE TO the calls of mourning doves. With my eyes still closed I could imagine myself in our Fourteenth Street apartment, my mother spreading breadcrumbs on the window ledge and talking to the pigeons, her voice low and murmurous as the birds. I used to lie in bed listening and imagining I would learn my mother's secrets by eavesdropping on her morning talks with the birds, but she spoke so low I never could catch a sound.

Only I wasn't in my apartment on Fourteenth Street. As the events of last night came back I felt a slow, dawning horror creep over me. I'd been taken by a Darkling. He had cast a spell over me. He had made me see visions in a teacup. My hand was cut and bandaged. I was in his lair now. The Bells knew what he was planning to do with me. I opened my eyes.

Raven was perched on a window ledge holding out a handful of crumbs to a flutter of doves, their wings a blur as they crowded around him.

"There's plenty for everyone, dovelings," he murmured. "What was that?" He tilted his head as if to listen to a fat gray dove that had landed on his shoulder. The dove puffed up its chest and trilled a long histrionic tune. Raven listened gravely.

The dread melted from my bones. A boy who was this

gentle with birds wasn't going to hurt me. And the visions I had seen in the teacup last night were real.

"Can you really understand what they're saying?" I asked, sitting up.

Raven turned to me, his lips quirking into a smile at the sight of me. Too late I realized what I must look like. I patted my hair and found it a tangled mess full of twigs and feathers. He looked politely away as I tried to put it to rights, giving his attention back to the doves.

"Mourning doves are quite easy to understand. They usually say the same three things over and over again: 'Woe is me,' 'Where's the worm?' and 'Who are you?' This one, though, is upset about the shadows she's seen massing in the forest. She's afraid it means that it will be a hard winter. I'm afraid it means something worse than that."

He stroked the dove's ruffled feathers until they lay flat again. "Don't fret, doveling. I'll go into town and buy extra seed to see your entire *dule* through the winter."

The dove bobbed its head, cooed contentedly, and then took off in a flutter of wings. Raven brushed his hands together to scatter the remaining crumbs out the window and turned to the kettle that had begun to whistle on the stove. While he made tea I finger-combed the twigs out of my hair, picked feathers off my jersey, and straightened my clothes, none of which solved the more pressing issue of my toilette.

"I thought we'd take the tea in a thermos flask groundwise and have our breakfast there," he said, pouring tea into a silver flask. "You might . . . er . . . like to be on solid ground."

"Yes, that would be nice," I replied, embarrassed but relieved.

"There's a ladder right there." He tilted a chin toward an opening in the floor I hadn't noticed last night. "You go on ahead. I'll catch up."

I slithered through the hole, found worn but solid ladder rungs with the tips of my toes, and climbed down, trying not to hurry. When I reached the ground I danced around until I found a downed tree that afforded me some privacy and gratefully crouched behind it. Raven's tree house was cozy, all right, but I'd miss indoor plumbing.

When I was done, though, I looked around the forest and saw how beautiful it was in the early-morning light. A thin layer of ice coated each branch, giving a pearly sheen to everything. The first rays of the sun streamed slantwise through mist, turning the ice to fiery opals. Birdsong filled the upper canopy—a sound that made me feel curiously safe.

Because the birds wouldn't be singing if there was danger nearby.

When had I leaned that? I wondered. Was it something Miss Swift had taught us? *The hunter must become the thing she hunts,* Gillie had told me. That's why we studied birds. But when had it become second nature to think like one . . . ?

A branch snapped behind me and I turned to find a doe standing only a few feet away nibbling the lichen off a fallen tree. She lifted her head and looked at me out of gold-flecked eyes. Her fur was the color of the last brown leaves clinging to bare branches and the rough bark of the trees. Her eyes were the color of the sunlight streaming through the morning mist. I didn't feel like a hunter. I felt as much a part of the forest as she was.

"She likes you."

Raven's voice came from close behind me. I hadn't heard him approach. So much for my survival skills.

"Why isn't she afraid of me?" I asked.

"Because you smell like the forest." He plucked at my sleeve and held up a black feather, one of his that had been stuck to my jersey. "You smell like a Darkling and the creatures here know we won't hurt them." He reached inside the canvas bag strapped across his chest—he was wearing a shirt, wings tucked beneath it—and brought out an apple. He held it out toward the deer. Her black wet nose twitched and then she stepped forward, delicate as a ballet dancer *en pointe*. She stretched her long graceful neck toward Raven's hand. She pulled back her lips, revealing white blunt teeth, took the apple out of his hand, and crunched into it. The crisp scent of apple made my mouth water.

"Here, we might as well share our breakfast with her." He sat down on the fallen log where the deer had been nibbling and took out the thermos flask from his canvas bag and poured milky tea into two tin cups. I sat beside him and took the cup and a roll stuffed with cheddar cheese. We sat side by side, eating our rolls and cheese and apples in quiet, the doe crunching her apple companionably beside us, as the bands of sunlight widened in the morning mist.

"It's hard to believe it's so peaceful after all I saw last night."

"But you know it was real, don't you?"

I looked down at my bandaged hand. "Yes," I said. "I do. I

know because that man . . . that *thing* . . . I've seen him before. He was at the Triangle."

"The Shadow Master," Raven said in a low growl that frightened the deer away. "Yes, the creature who came for you at the Triangle was the same kind of monster, only in a different body—a body taken over by the shadows, or the *tenebrae* as we call them. The Darknesses."

"What are they?" I asked, shivering.

"Pure evil," he answered. "Hatred, murder, envy, greed, disembodied evil that has lurked on the edges of the world since time began. They lodge in animals, especially crows and wolves and snakes, but then can lodge in anything alive, human or fairy, as long as there's already a chink of darkness to let them in."

"What happens to the creatures they take over?"

"Usually the *tenebrae* burn out their host in a few years, but sometimes they find a vessel strong enough for them to live in side for decades, even centuries. That creature you saw became a shadow master—he can control the *tenebrae*, drawing them into other life forms and controlling them. The prince became a shadow master who ravaged the countryside for years, infecting the creatures of Faerie and the Darklings. Only the knight and sisters were able to fight them off with their bells—that's why your Order thinks that the fairies are evil. They don't understand that it's the shadow master controlling them—not even when the *tenebrae* infected one of their own kind."

"What happened?" I asked, chilled at the thought that the shadow creatures could creep through the stone castle walls and spells of the Order.

"Merope destroyed him. Only a chime child can destroy a shadow master. That's why this one is trying to capture you before you can become strong enough to destroy him."

"Capture me?"

"If he'd wanted to kill you, he would have. He set the factory on fire as a distraction to snatch you. I should never have let you out of my sight for a minute." He swore under his breath. I stared, horrified.

"A distraction? A hundred and forty-six people were killed! Are you saying it was all my fault? And why were you there? To snatch me away before he could?" Raven laid a calming hand on my arm, but I shook it away and stood up. "And what will you do to me now?"

Raven stood and faced me. His wings were struggling to unfold beneath his shirt. "I will not *do* anything to you. All I've ever done is try to keep you safe. But yes, you're valuable to us—and to the Order and to the Shadow Master."

"So that's why you took me last night? To use me as tool against the Shadow Master?"

"I was also trying to save you from those goblins."

"Oh, it's pretty convenient, isn't it, you always being around when I'm in trouble!" I wasn't sure why I was so angry. Perhaps it was because it sounded like Raven was only interested in me because I had some special ability to defeat the Shadow Master. Which shouldn't have bothered me. So why was I storming off from him as if it did?

"Ava," he called as I plunged through a mote-filled sunbeam. "Wait!" He grabbed my arm and held me back. Although my feet were planted in several inches of snow I was teetering on the edge of a green meadow surrounded by gently swaying willows and starred with a million wildflowers.

"A bit of Faerie," Raven said softly. "At this time of year the barriers between this world and Faerie are thin. Look, you can see the Riding of the Gentry."

The sunbeam widened to reveal a procession of men and women on horseback. The horses were all white and decked out with gold saddles and bridles and silver ribbons braided in their manes. A beautiful woman in green rode on the lead horse. Her hair was the same color as the horses' manes and braided with bells that made a lovely sound, a silver tinkling that was nothing like the iron clanging of *our* bells. The sound was so lovely I was drawn to it. I stood up and took a step toward her . . . but Raven's hand tightened on my arm.

"Unless you don't mind leaving your friends behind for a hundred years, I wouldn't go any farther. Time is different in Faerie—in fact, they don't have 'time' as we know it. Once you go in there, there's no telling when you'll come out again—if ever."

I longingly watched the procession as it passed by me. The woman in green turned her head and looked at me out of slanting green cat's eyes. Looking into those eyes I felt everything I had learned at Blythewood slipping away. It wasn't that those eyes looked innocent—far from it. Those eyes saw everything. They saw *me*: my doubts and fears and everything that had happened to me. They saw my mother laughing and telling me fairy stories and they saw me going to the chemist for her bottle of laudanum. They saw Tillie Kupermann flirting with the law students and the Triangle girls jumping from the ninth-floor windows. They saw the cocoa parties with Daisy and Helen, and Miss Frost's specimens. They didn't judge. The woman in green came from a place that was beyond time—and therefore beyond judgment of what we called good and evil.

As I gazed at her I heard her voice inside my head. *Come, chime child,* she said, *this is where you belong.* I wanted with all my being to go with her—to belong somewhere finally—but Raven held me back until the procession had moved by us. Following the men and women on horseback were many other creatures—the tiny lampsprites, fur-covered goblins, lumbering trows. And at the end of the procession walked a slim girl dressed in a flimsy white dress with wispy blonde hair falling loose around her shoulders who looked up at me out of wide gray eyes and opened her mouth to say something . . . but then the sunbeam dissolved into mist and once again I was looking at the winter woods.

"That girl," I said, turning to Raven, "I think she might be Nathan's sister. Her name was Louisa. Her brother thinks she was abducted by one of you."

"Nathan? Is that the frailing who tried to stab me with his little blade last night?" Raven asked, his voice thick with disdain.

"Only because he thought you were going to hurt us," I said, not liking to hear Nathan so summarily dismissed. "And because he thinks one of your kind took his sister. Is it true?"

"No!" Raven got up abruptly. "A Darkling would never take a human girl against her wishes." He brushed crumbs from his trousers and stuffed the thermos and cups into his bag and started walking briskly away. "As I will demonstrate by taking you back right now."

"You needn't get all huffy," I said, getting up. "You can't blame Nathan for wanting to find out what happened to his sister. And after all, all our books tell us that you are dangerous—"

"Not all your books. There's a book called *A Darkness of Angels* that tells the truth about the Darklings and how our curse can be lifted. He stopped when he saw my startled look. "What?" he asked. "Have you heard of it?"

"Yes, that was one of the books my mother used to ask for at every library we went to—and then later she would send me to the library to find—only they never had it."

"You see," Raven said. "Your mother was looking for it to prove the Darklings aren't evil. It will also tell you how a chime child can use her power to destroy the *tenebrae* and it might even tell you how to get your friend's sister out of Faerie and how to lift the Darkling curse."

"Is that what you want?" I asked. "To be free of your curse so you can go back to Faerie?"

He studied my face, not answering right away. In the morning light I saw that his eyes, which had looked black last night, were really a deep midnight blue with swirls of gold inside them. Looking into them was like staring into a night sky full of stars. They made me feel a little dizzy. I'd almost forgotten my question by the time he answered.

"I suppose it's what the sisters of your Order would want—for us to leave this world forever. And it's what my elders want.

There is less and less room for us in this world. But for myself . . ." He faltered and looked away.

"What?" I asked, reaching out to touch his hand. "What do you want?"

His wings rippled beneath his shirt at my touch. We had reached the edge of the woods. He turned to answer me, but then the bells of Blythewood began to ring the matin changes—the peal to banish the shadows of the night. Raven looked toward the tower. His wings strained beneath his shirt as if he wanted to take to the sky.

"Do the bells scare you?"

He shook his head. "No, they merely make us sad. They remind us of all we've lost." He looked down at me, his dark eyes studying me. Then he reached out his hand and ran one finger down the side of my face. "It doesn't matter what I want, Ava. Try to find the book. Just be careful. We think that the Shadow Master has a spy at Blythewood."

I should have asked how the Darklings knew there was a spy, but instead I asked, "Will I see you again . . . I mean . . . in case I have news?"

He smiled. "I'll figure out a way." Then his wings fanned out behind him, blue-black and iridescent as a peacock's tail in the morning sun. The sudden rush of wind from their movement blinded me for a moment. When I opened my eyes he was gone—a flicker of darkness in the pine boughs as he soared upward. I stared into the shadows of the pinewoods for a moment longer, reluctant to turn my back on them. But then I recalled that he was somewhere in those shadows watching and felt reassured.

I walked across the snow-covered lawn toward the castle, which glowed honey gold in the morning sun like an enchanted castle in a fairy tale. The last echo of the last bell rang through the valley, tolling not Merope's death, if I believed what Raven had told me, but her farewell to her sisters. Although I'd spent only one night in the woods I felt as though it had been a hundred years since I'd left Blythewood. What if I had strayed into Faerie and been gone twenty years, like Rip van Winkle, And all my friends had grown up and gone away without me?

But here were Daisy and Helen running across the lawn toward me, their faces shining with relief. I felt a corresponding leap of joy in my heart and rushed to meet them, nearly slipping in the snow.

"Oh, thank heavens!" Daisy cried, flinging her arms around me. "We were so frightened! If you weren't back after matins we were going to have to tell Gillie."

"I knew you would rescue her," Helen said, looking over my shoulder.

I whirled around, thinking that Raven had reappeared, but it wasn't Raven behind me; it was Nathan. The tips of his fair hair were heavy with ice, his skin nearly the same blue as his eyes. He looked like one of the ice giants we'd run into last night, and for a moment I was afraid that he'd been turned to ice by them—that when the sun struck him he would shatter into a million pieces.

"Ava didn't need me to rescue her," he said with a smile that chilled me to the bone. Had he seen me with Raven? Would he tell Helen and Daisy that I had spent the night with a Darkling? "In fact, *she* rescued *me*. We spent the night huddled in a hollow tree. See"—he held up my bandaged hand—"she scraped her hand on a thorn bush."

He fixed me with an icy stare that I understood completely: *Go along with the story or I'll tell them you spent the night with a Darkling.* I hadn't even thought through how much I would tell my friends, but one look at Helen and Daisy told me that they would never understand—at least not until I could prove that Darklings weren't evil. And for that I needed to find the book—*A Darkness of Angels.* So I smiled back at Nathan and lied.

"Yes, that's what we did. We're frozen clean through." I shivered, not having to pretend; I did feel suddenly cold. "I'd kill for a cup of hot cocoa."

"Of course, let's get you both inside." Helen took Nathan's arm and led the way for Daisy and me. As I watched them walking in front of us I realized that Nathan's lie hadn't only hidden where I had spent the night—it hid where he had as well.

27

THE DOVES WERE right about the winter: it was a hard one. Not just because of the bitter cold, relentless winds, driving snow, and day after day of gray skies with barely a glimpse of sun. Along with the awful weather, a pall had settled over Blythewood like an icy fog that had fallen between the rest of the world and us. The Jager twins seemed to go into a virtual hibernation, and even chipper Cam Bennett came back from vacation unusually subdued.

"It was just so peculiar to have to keep secrets from Mater and Pater," she told us at the welcome-back dinner.

Even Georgiana Montmorency was too listless to think of rumors to start about me.

The lawns were too icy for us to practice archery. Our only exercise was walking up and down the interminable stairs and bell ringing. Gone, though, were the sprightly tunes we had practiced for the Christmas concert. Instead we rang changes that sounded like funeral dirges. They were designed, Mr. Peale explained, to beat back the ice giants that inhabited the Blythe Wood at this time of year. Recalling the monsters I'd encountered in the woods the night of the solstice I couldn't argue. The frigid wind that blew through the belfry felt as though it had come straight from the Arctic Sea. The rime-covered trees at the edge of the forest looked like frozen sentinels—an army camped at our doorstep. Whenever I glanced at the woods—from the belfry tower, the landing windows, or the rooftop mews—it seemed as if the woods had moved closer to the castle, hemming us in a little more.

I confided my impression to Gillie one day when I had volunteered to help him imp a wounded bird. I was holding a young tiercel, *gentling* it, as Gillie had instructed, by playing the bells in my head. The falcon had responded almost immediately by going limp in my arms so that Gillie could clip off her broken wing feathers and graft on new donor feathers. When I told Gillie I thought the woods were moving closer I expected him to laugh off the idea, but instead he glanced uneasily over his shoulder.

"Aye, them Jotuns are wee tricky devils. They can take the shapes of trees or rocks and bide their time till some unwary traveler passes too close by. Y'see the ice on the river?" He pointed his clipper toward the Hudson, which was now entirely frozen over. Along the banks great chunks of ice had piled up. "I've heard tell that an ice giant can assume the shape of an iceberg and lie in wait for a ship to pass, then it seizes the hull in its teeth and drags it down to the ocean floor along with all its crew and passengers."

The falcon stirred restlessly in my arms, shaking the bells on her jesses, and I realized I'd let the bells in my head speed up in the same jangly rhythm.

"Aye, Jessie, you watch out for those devils now." He released the wing he had been working on and nodded to me to let the bird go. Jessie hopped onto Gillie's gloved hand and stretched out her repaired wing. "Good as new," Gillie said. "You see, lass, we're none of us doomed to be just one thing. We can change our feathers just like Jessie here." He swung his arm forward, releasing the falcon into the sky. She soared across the lawn toward the woods. Gillie held his hand over his eyes to shade them from the glare of sun on ice. In the shadow of his hand his eyes looked mournful. "I wish all broken things were so easy to fix," he said, leaving me to wonder what had broken in Gillie's life.

With the ice so impassable, the Dianas no longer patrolled the lawn. Instead they stalked the halls, restless as housecats kept indoors. One day I found Charlotte Falconrath sobbing in a broom closet. When I asked what was wrong she told me that her father had arranged a match for her and she was to be married just after graduation.

"I only just met him at Christmas! He's old and fat, but Mother says he comes from good blood!"

I thought of the bloodline charts in the dungeon and felt a chill go through me. But when I tried to comfort Charlotte, she snapped, "What do you know of it? With your history they'll never make *you* marry!"

Not everyone was quite as sympathetic to the Dianas' stress. "Why do I feel as if they're on guard to keep us *in* more than to keep anything out?" Helen remarked one frigid February evening in the Commons Room over an interminable game of flush and trophies.

I glanced around the room and noticed one of the Dianas, Augusta Richmond, a statuesque brunette from Charleston, at the entrance to the Commons Room, bow drawn, eyes alert. Beyond her in the hallway, Charlotte Falconrath was standing at the foot of the stairs. Her bow was drawn as well—which was alarming considering Charlotte's poor aim and precarious mental state lately.

"Who would want to go out in *this*?" Daisy said, shivering. The wind rattled the windows of the Commons Room as if in reply.

"They're afraid of winter fever," Beatrice informed us after laying down a flush of spades and calling trophy. "I read about it in *Sieges and Campaigns of the Dark Ages*. It's what happens when an Order is under siege in its castle. Sometimes a girl goes crazy and runs out into the woods and throws herself right into the hands of the demons."

"I thought *Sieges and Campaigns* wasn't assigned for another month," Daisy said.

"I read ahead," Beatrice replied with a smirk. "There's an account of a nunnery in the Pyrenees that was cut off from the outside world for three months. When the villagers reached them after the spring thaw they found them all dead except for one girl who had holed herself up in the belfry. She claimed that the nuns had gone crazy and started killing each other."

"Ugh! I knew it was unhealthy to wall up so many women together," Helen said.

"The men aren't any better," Beatrice said smugly. "An order of monks on an island in Scotland got it in their heads that they were being attacked by ice giants. They set fire to the monastery to melt them."

I recalled what Gillie had said about the frost giants disguising themselves as icebergs. Maybe the monks hadn't been crazy. But I kept that thought to myself. We all became, I think, a little wary of expressing ourselves too freely in case a careless word or snappish response would be seen as a symptom of winter fever.

The one person I could have talked to, Raven, was as unreachable as the Pyrenees. The frozen woods were off limits. He'd said he would find a way to see me, but weeks went by without any sign from him. During the day I paced the quiet halls of Blythewood, staring out the windows for a trace of him in the winter sky. At night I tossed and turned, worrying that he had frozen to death in his treetop nest—or that he had better things to do than come looking for me. He was an otherworldly being entrusted with the ferrying of souls and I . . . I was an ex–factory worker and schoolgirl. So maybe I was also a chime child who was supposed to be able to defeat the shadow master, but I couldn't even do that unless I found *A Darkness of Angels*, and so far I'd had no luck.

I spent as much time as I could in the library, seeking an opportunity to sneak into the Special Collections, but with no one going out it was hard to do. Worse, our little group in the library had grown irritable. Since break there seemed to be some unspoken tension among our teachers. Miss Sharp still stoked the fire, set out biscuits, and poured tea, but she moved around the room like a trapped bird in a cage, trying to divide herself evenly between Miss Corey and Mr. Bellows. She would pour half a cup for Mr. Bellows, then catch a glance from Miss Corey and jerk the teapot toward her already-full cup, splashing tea across the stacks of ancient books, setting Miss Corey fluttering over the books like a mother hen gathering her chicks under her wing.

Only Nathan was quicker to protect the books. He had taken himself off to a window seat overlooking the river and made a nest of books like a peregrine on a cliff. Since coming out of the woods on the solstice he had been devoted to reading. I tried to ask him where he had spent the night in the woods, but he had brushed off my question.

"I could ask you the same thing, Ava."

Before the night in the woods I might have confided in Nathan. The boy who laughed about opium dens and teased me about how many books I read might have understood that the Darkling boy Raven wasn't evil. But not the Nathan who had come out of the woods. He no longer laughed or teased or played pranks. He was like the boy in the fairy tale who gets a splinter of the goblin's evil mirror in his eye and whose heart turns to ice. All he did was hole himself up in his window seat and read. I was afraid that if I told him that I'd seen Louisa in Faerie he would go running off into the frozen woods to save her. Without knowing how to get her out, he could get himself killed by the Jotuns or wind up trapped in Faerie himself.

I thought of talking to Miss Sharp or Mr. Bellows about Nathan but they were both so distracted I hated to bother them. Helen insisted that Nathan was just in one of his usual funks. Daisy asked if anything had happened the night we spent in the woods to change him, but without confessing that I hadn't been with Nathan that night I couldn't answer the question truthfully.

My friends, as if knowing I was keeping a secret from them,

became secretive themselves. Helen received long letters from her parents every post, which she read with unusual concentration and covered up whenever Daisy or I walked near her. She hid them in a locked trunk, an uncharacteristic worried look settled over her brow, and she nearly bit Daisy's head off when Daisy accidentally spilled a bottle of ink on her shirt cuff.

"D'you think I'm made of money?" she cried in an aggrieved voice that sounded as if it belonged to someone else.

Daisy began making herself scarce from our room. She said she was doing work for Miss Frost, but when I looked for her once in Miss Frost's specimen room she wasn't there.

"That flibbertigibbet!" Miss Frost exclaimed. "She's always late and she lost one of my best specimens. I ought to fire her."

"I could help Ava look for her friend," said Sarah, who was standing on a stepladder dusting the floor-to-ceiling glass case of pinned sprites. "I've finished organizing the sprites by genus and phylum."

"I need you to pick up my physic from the chemists, girl."

"Yes, ma'am," Sarah replied. When Miss Frost turned her back, though, Sarah splayed herself against the glass, spreading her arms wide, dropping her head and letting her tongue loll out, mimicking the pose of the pinned sprites. I suppressed a giggle, the first bit of merriment I'd felt in a while.

Sarah had been helping with my homework since Helen and Daisy were both acting so strange. I'd also seen her tutoring Nathan, which made me a little jealous, but I tried not to mind because I enjoyed her company. She was the only girl I could talk to about my days in the city, the only one who knew the vaudeville theaters and the sweatshops and the food carts like

I did—and the longer I was at Blythewood, the more I found I missed them. I also learned that her own mother had died a few years ago—of a dysentery outbreak in Five Points.

"I remember that," I told her. "My mother brought food and fresh water to the sick."

"What a valiant woman your mother must have been!" Sarah said, and then when she saw the tears in my eyes, she asked what she'd said wrong.

"She *was* valiant, but then she changed." I told her about my mother's strange obsessions and drinking laudanum, but I couldn't confide to her that I'd spent a night with a Darkling—not until I found the book that proved that the Darklings weren't evil.

The only way I could think of to get into the Special Collections was to volunteer to help Miss Corey carry books up. Now that Nathan was so distracted with his own reading, Miss Corey always carried the lantern downstairs and held it up while pointing to the books she wanted brought up, making it difficult to search for *A Darkness of Angels* on the shelves. A layer of dust covered the spines, and many of the shelves were double stacked. The day I left Sarah dusting specimen cases, I had the idea of volunteering to dust the books so Miss Corey wouldn't get her clothes so dirty.

"Perhaps that's not a bad idea," she replied. "Vi *is* always saying I look like a chimney sweep. But won't you mind being down here all alone?"

"Not at all," I lied. "Why should I?"

"It's just that it's so close to the candelabellum." She looked nervously toward the door at the end of the corridor. Now that

I looked toward the door it *did* give me a strange feeling to think of those bells hanging in the dark, the pictures lurking in them like sleeping dragons. As I stared at the door I thought I even heard a faint tinkling.

"It *is* peculiar," I said, "to think of the founding families bringing over the original dungeons with the castle."

"These rich people," Miss Corey said irritably, "who can ever understand why they do the things they do? Why does Rupert Bellows buy violets every day for Vionetta when she could get them for free from her own aunts' greenhouse? Go ahead and dust, if you like. I'm sure Vionetta and Rupert will prefer that we don't look like grimy paupers."

It had never occurred to me that Miss Corey might not be as well off as Miss Sharp or Mr. Bellows. Truthfully, I hardly thought about my teachers' lives beyond Blythewood. Someday, though, I would have to make my own way in the world beyond these walls. I didn't know whether my grandmother intended to help me financially, or what strings might be attached to any help she offered. And as for marriage . . . what if Charlotte Falconrath was right and no one would marry me because I was a freak? Better to remain unmarried, though, than to be matched up like a prize cow or to trade a dowry for a house in town, summers in Newport, and a handsome dress allowance.

I'd wager the Darklings didn't talk about dowries and bloodlines when they married. If they married.

"My mother always said it was better to be a pauper than a slave to money," I told Miss Corey.

Miss Corey gave me a startled look from under her veil. "Evangeline was very wise," she said, squeezing my hand.

"Thank you for offering to dust the books, Ava. I'll bring down an extra lantern and some dust cloths."

I spent the rest of the afternoon down in the Special Collections Room carefully dusting and inspecting each book, but I didn't find *A Darkness of Angels*. I did find, though, a catalogue of special collections in other libraries run by the Order. I discovered it just as Miss Corey called me to come up for tea. I slid the catalogue behind one of the shelves and hurried up the spiral stairs, promising myself that I'd look through it later. At tea I casually asked Miss Corey if she'd ever worked at any other libraries.

"I worked at the Order's library at Hawthorn," she replied, "until the head librarian absconded with all the funds and several priceless books."

"Oh, I remember that!" Miss Sharp exclaimed, sipping her tea. "What a scandal! Did they ever apprehend him?"

"No, but they recovered the books when he tried to sell them in London. They're back in the special collections at Hawthorn. I worked at the Order's library in London after that, and then I came here."

"Can't imagine why you'd leave London for this backwater," Mr. Bellows remarked.

"If you don't like it here," Miss Corey replied, "I hear there's an opening at Hawthorn."

I didn't follow the rest of their conversation. I bided my time through tea and then waited for everybody to leave. Nathan took forever, rearranging the books in this window seat and making Miss Corey promise not to disturb the order of his stacks.

"I have a system," he said. "I think I'm on to something."

"That's fine, Nathan, but they'll all have to go back in the Special Collections by spring break."

"I'll be done with them by then," Nathan assured her. "Or else it will be too late."

He left without explaining what he meant. I offered to help Miss Corey straighten and lock up. She seemed touched by my offer. "Perhaps you might want to be a librarian, Ava. You'd make a fine one."

"I would like that very much," I said, feeling guilty as I slipped the library key from its ring before handing her keys back to her. "I do love libraries."

"I'll talk to Dame Beckwith about having you assist me. Perhaps she could even pay you a small salary. Then you'd feel a bit more . . . *independent*."

I was so touched I almost confessed and gave her back the key, but I couldn't bear to ruin her good opinion of me. And I wanted to get another look at that catalogue. After dinner Daisy disappeared, stuffing a roll and apple in her pocket and making a vague excuse that she'd forgotten something somewhere. Helen, rereading a letter from home, didn't even look up when I said that I'd forgotten my Latin textbook in the classroom in the North Wing. Charlotte Falconrath tried to stop me as I passed through the Great Hall, but I distracted her by telling her that Cook had put out fresh-baked cookies in the Commons Room.

I hurried past the empty classrooms, which looked eerie in the moonlight. Someone had left a window open, letting in an icy breeze that ruffled the large maps that hung in the history room. I thought I heard footsteps behind me and turned to see the shadow of wings on the corridor wall. I ran to the window, hoping that it would be Raven, but it was only Blodeuwedd flying past a window with a long mournful hoot. I rushed on to the library, my hands shaking as I fitted the key in the lock.

"If you want to become a librarian, you'll have to learn to be quieter."

I nearly shrieked at the voice inches from my ear. I whirled around. For a second I thought one of the ice giants had found a way in from the forest. A figure pale and still as a frozen statue stood in the moonlit corridor, its eyes cold as ice chips. Then the figure moved and I recognized Nathan.

"You were spying on me!" I accused him.

"I wanted to know where your sudden interest in library economy came from. Now I see that you're really interested in a career in book thievery."

"I am not," I hissed. "I just wanted to have a look at something."

"Something you couldn't look at with everyone else here?"

"As if you don't hoard your books to yourself, too, Nathan. I've seen you hunched over them like a hawk mantling its prey."

Nathan laughed at the image. For a moment he looked like the old Nathan, but then his eyes turned chilly again. "I suppose you know all about birds of prey now," he said.

"So you *did* see me with the Darkling that night," I said, glad it was too dark where I stood in the hall for him to see me blush. "Why didn't you tell the others?"

"Because I saw other things in the woods that night that I'm not ready to tell anyone about. I'm willing to hide your secret if you're willing to hide mine."

I knew it was a deal I shouldn't make, but my fingers were itching to get a look at that catalogue. Once I'd found *A Darkness of Angels* I could prove the Darklings weren't evil and find a way to rescue Louisa from Faerie. Then I could tell Nathan everything and find out what he was hiding. "Fine," I said. "I suppose you ambushed me here so I could let you into the library, too."

"Actually, I don't need you for that," he said, taking a ring of keys out of his pocket. "I stole these from my mother months ago. I just thought it would be fun to give you a scare."

If Nathan had looked like he was having fun I would have been angrier, but it was clear he was in the throes of winter fever, pursuing his mysterious obsession. "Then let's go in, shall we? I won't bother you if you don't bother me."

He unlocked the door and waved me in. "Ladies first," he said with mock courtesy.

The moonlight was bright enough to light the library, but I would need a lantern to go down to the Special Collections. Descending those spiral stairs with the moonlight pouring down them felt like climbing into the well I'd envisioned when the crows had attacked me. I was relieved when Nathan offered to go down with me.

"So what was worth fooling Miss Corey for?" he asked when we reached the bottom.

"It's a catalogue," I said, taking the book out of its hiding place, "of other libraries belonging to the Order. I thought I might find a book I'm looking for." I flipped through the pages, searching the alphabetical list . . . and found it. *A Darkness of Angels* by Dame Alcyone. *Alcyone.* That was the name of one of Merope's sisters. There was a copy in the Hawthorn School library in Scotland.

"Hm," he said, looking over my shoulder. "Are you going to Scotland to find it?"

"Hardly," I said, "but I can write to the librarian at Hawthorn. The address is on the first page." I flipped to the beginning of the catalogue and copied down the address. I was closing the book when I heard a noise from the candelabellum.

I turned to Nathan to see if he had heard it, too. I wasn't sure what would be worse—if I was imagining noises in the candelabellum chamber or if something was making the bells move on their own. The minute I saw Nathan's frightened face, I knew which was worse. I thought of the figures we'd seen in there—shadow crows and shadow wolves, but worst of all, the prince who'd succumbed to the shadows and become a shadow master. What if *he* were in the candelabellum chamber?

The door knob turned.

Nathan extinguished the lantern, plunging the archive into darkness save for the circle of moonlight coming down from the stairwell. He pushed me behind a filing cabinet and squeezed in beside me while the door creaked open, making so much noise it covered the sound of our breathing and my heart beating—out of fear, I told myself, not from the warmth of Nathan's body pressed against mine.

A lumpen figure loomed in the doorway, cast in shadow by a ruddy wedge of light that angled toward us. I thought of the red eyes that had fixed onto mine in the teacup vision and imagined the light came from them. The figure lumbered into the corridor and paused, holding a lantern up to one of the shelves. I was afraid he would find us when the light reached us, but evidently the intruder found what he was looking for. He took something off the shelf and turned to go, pausing in the circle of moonlight. He looked up . . . only it wasn't a he. Shining greasily in the moonlight was the face of Euphorbia Frost.

She stared at the open doorway to the stairwell for several long seconds. Then she looked around the corridor, peering into the shadows. She was staring straight at us, her eyes shimmering red in the light from her lantern, which, I saw now, was shaded by a red silk scarf. I was sure that she'd seen us, but then I remembered that she was nearsighted. She groped for her lorgnette, but she was holding too many things in her hand to raise it to her eyes.

"Careless!" she muttered, clucking her tongue. Then she lifted the thing she'd taken from the shelf. Something glimmered glassily in the moonlight and the room was suddenly full of the smell of spirits. Miss Frost lifted the bottle to her mouth and took a long swallow of the clear liquid. Then she smacked her lips, belched, and went back into the candelabellum chamber.

When the door had closed behind her, and the sound of her retreating footsteps had faded, Nathan exploded in a paroxysm of giggles. I elbowed him in the ribs to hush him, but laughter was bubbling up in my own mouth.

"She hides . . . her liquor . . . in the dungeons!" Nathan managed through bursts of hilarity. "All the most valuable secrets in the world—the location of the fountain of youth for all we know!—and she uses it for her liquor stash."

"Well," I said, "I suppose for her it *is* the fountain of youth. She's certainly well . . . *pickled*."

Nathan collapsed against me giggling. It was so good to hear him laugh like his old self that I added, "Perhaps she stores the stuff here to age it like fine wine."

"I sincerely doubt she leaves it long enough to age it," Nathan replied, wiping his eyes. "Imagine what we could do with this knowledge. We could switch her liquor for one of Jager's potions. Turn her hair lavender . . ."

"Or give her a shape-shifting potion that makes her grow horns," I spluttered.

But Nathan had stopped listening. He had spotted a book on a shelf that interested him. As soon as he plucked it off the shelf the hunch came back to his shoulders and all the merriment drained out of his face.

"Yes, that would be droll," he replied absently. "Well, if you've got what you want, then, I'm going upstairs to do some reading. You can let yourself out." He drifted up the stairs, leaving me alone in the dark.

I went to the shelf from which Miss Frost had removed her bottle and saw that there was an empty space between the books. I'd just dusted this shelf so I knew that it held forbidden books on contacting evil spirits. What would Miss Frost want with those?

Unless she was the spy Raven had warned me about.

28

I WROTE A letter to the head librarian of the Hawthorn School in Scotland, whose name, I learned from Miss Corey's files, was Herbert Farnsworth. I considered pretending to be one of my teachers, but in the end I told him that my mother had been looking for the book *A Darkness of Angels* before she died. Generally all the girls posted their letters by leaving them in a basket in the front hall, where they were collected by Gillie and then taken to the town post office. I'd seen Miss Frost idly rifling through these letters, though, tsking over bad penmanship and improper modes of address. If she were the spy, I couldn't take the chance of her seeing that I was writing to the librarian at Hawthorn, so I decided to walk into town and post it myself, even though it was against the rules to leave the grounds without permission. I waited for a morning when Daisy had vanished again (to wherever it was she went) and Helen was busy writing a letter to her mother, and then snuck out and walked the mile into town myself.

It felt good to get out of the castle and into the crisp, clean air away from all the whispers and secrets lurking around the halls of Blythewood. It was cold, but I was wearing my Christmas present from my grandmother, an oxblood-red wool coat with black passementerie embroidery on the sleeves and hem and plush black fur at the collar and the cuffs. It had come with a matching fur hat and muff that Agnes had said in a separate note were just like the ones the youngest tsarina wore. I *did* feel like a Russian princess in the ensemble.

But I still didn't feel like I fit in at Blythewood. If the girls at school knew what I was really like they would turn away in horror—even Sarah, who'd been so kind to me these last few months, would never understand my feelings about one of the creatures she blamed for abducting her best friend. I would be expelled, as my mother had been. And then where would I go? My grandmother wouldn't take me in after a second humiliation to the family name. Even Caroline Janeway might not be able to employ me if I'd embarrassed myself at Blythewood when she depended so much on the school for her trade.

No wonder my mother had drifted from place to place. When you didn't fit in anywhere, you had to keep moving.

By the time I reached the post office I'd worked myself into a tizzy. The salutary effects of the fresh air wore off as I stood on line in the snug, low-ceilinged building. I was sweating under my Russian princess coat, my shoulders and back itching against the wool. When the postal clerk looked up from my letter and said, "All the way to Scotland, eh? Have you family there?" I almost burst into tears.

"No," I managed hoarsely, "no family."

Outside on the street the cold air snaked under my loosened collar and spread its icy touch down my damp shoulder blades. It felt as if someone had laid his hands on my back. And then I heard a bell tolling inside my head. I whirled around. A shadow moved on the front porch of the inn next door to the post office. I squinted at it, the bright winter sun glancing off the glass windows of the inn momentarily blinding me. I shaded my eyes and saw him—the man in the Inverness cape. He was standing beside a column, facing me, his face shadowed by his Homburg hat.

Then he tipped his hat and smiled at me. A wisp of smoke curled out of his mouth.

I wanted to scream. I wanted to run. But suddenly I was tired of running. My mother had spent her whole life running, and look where it had gotten her.

I straightened my back and felt the ice along my shoulder blades turn to steel. I strode up the flagstone path, straight toward the man in the Inverness cape. Two women whisked their skirts out of my way and whispered behind their fur muffs. Let the great Shadow Master take me on here in front of the good people of Rhinebeck. Let him loose his crows at me and turn into a writhing smoke monster. Let him . . .

He bowed low in front of me, sweeping his hat out in an arc. I stopped abruptly, my boot heels screeching on the bluestone flags. I held my breath as he lifted his head, steeling myself for a monster.

Instead, a handsome gentleman of perhaps forty-odd years with refined features smiled at me. He had a long narrow face, an aquiline nose, and dark hair brushed back from a high forehead with two silver streaks at his temples that looked like wings. His eyes were dark—almost as black as Raven's, but flatter and colder. One eyebrow was raised archly in query.

"I do not believe I've had the pleasure of your acquaintance, Miss. Was there some way I could be of assistance to you?"

Did I have the wrong man? Had I imagined that wisp of smoke?

"I . . . er . . . I thought you were someone else," I stammered.

"Ah, I am relieved. You approached me as if you had a vendetta against me. I would not like to be the man who crossed you so. Allow me to introduce myself."

He held out his hand. As if lifted by a string, my own hand floated up and found itself in his. It was like dropping my hand into ice water. The iciness spread from my hand, up my arm, and into my chest—a cold so intense it *burned*. I looked down, expecting either a block of ice or a charred lump where my hand had been. My gloved hand lay lightly in his gloved hand, but I could no more have removed it than if it had been trapped inside a metal vise. I lifted my eyes back to his.

"Judicus van Drood," he said.

"Avaline Hall," I replied, feeling as if someone else was speaking. The numbness had reached my lips. I had a horrified feeling that anything might come out of them—shocking improprieties, bawdy songs, gibberish.

"Ah, I believe I knew your mother," he said. "You have her eyes. My condolences for her untimely demise."

"Thank you," I said through frozen lips, "for your sympathy." Inside I was screaming. I would rather have shouted obscenities than trade polite niceties with the man who had hounded my mother to her death.

"Such a shame," he continued, clucking his tongue as though my mother's death was a broken vase. "For such a lovely woman to die so young. I'm afraid that her constitution was weakened by too much intellectual stimulation. Education can have that unfortunate effect on the frailer sex. Even after she left Blythewood she wasted her time reading foolish books, didn't she? In fact, those last few years she was engaged in a search for a particular book, was she not?"

I tried to clamp my lips shut, but the words came bubbling up. "Y-yes . . . she sent me to the library for s-s-some books . . ."

Hot tears sprung to my eyes, but they froze before they could fall. The burning ice had risen to my eyes. Soon it would be inside my brain and then I would be his entirely.

"I just hope you're not following in your mother's footsteps, Ava. I was very concerned to hear that you've been looking through the Blythewood special collections."

I wanted to ask how he knew that, but the words would not come out of my mouth. He smiled, parting his lips, and a puff of smoke slipped out of his mouth. Before my horrified eyes, I watched it form into the shape of a crow that flapped its wings and settled on his shoulders. I wanted to turn my head and see if anyone else could see it, but I couldn't move.

"Never mind who told me that you've been looking through the special collections. I know you haven't found it there. But I *am* intrigued about this little trip to the post office. Have you located a copy of the book? If so, I'd very much like to know where."

Mr. Farnsworth's name and address were on the tip of my tongue. I bit the inside of my cheek to keep them from spilling out. The taste of blood momentarily melted the ice in my mouth. Iron and blood, Mr. Jager had once told us, were our best defenses against other magic. But it wasn't enough. The name was still coming . . .

The church bells began to ring the noon hour. Van Drood

swiveled his neck toward the sound. The minute his eyes were off mine I felt a loosening of the ice. I wrenched my hand out of his, but I still couldn't move my legs. He snapped his head back toward me.

The ninth bell rang. If I didn't get away before the toll ended I would give him Mr. Farnsworth's name and something terrible would happen to him. The bells tolled ten and I heard it echo within me, the iron of the bell reverberating in the iron of my blood. The bells tolled eleven. The sound was inside me, a part of me. I was a chime child. The bells belonged to me.

The bells tolled twelve.

Judicus van Drood lifted his hand and reached for me.

The bells tolled thirteen.

His eyes widened, black pupils swelling over the whites.

The bells tolled fourteen.

His hand was frozen midair. The shadow crow on his shoulder shattered into shards and the ice that held me shattered with it.

The bells tolled fifteen. How many more chimes did I have? I should bolt.

I looked into van Drood's eyes. The black pupils had totally overrun the white. That darkness seethed like smoke. A vein throbbed at his temple so angrily it looked as though it was going to explode.

I smiled. "My mother always said that men who oppose women's education are afraid of women becoming too strong because they themselves are too weak. You have a weakness, Mr. van Drood. I will find it and destroy you for what you did to my mother. Good day."

I turned and walked back down the bluestone path. Pins and needles stabbed my legs as my limbs slowly came back to life. I had to concentrate on not falling and strive very hard not to break into a run. The bells were still tolling. Men and women stood on the street staring up at the church's bell tower, some walking toward the church.

I didn't know why the bells were still ringing, but I knew I had to get as far away from van Drood as I could before they stopped. The streets were crowded now, full of townspeople wondering why their church bells were tolling as if for a funeral or a fire. I crossed the street to get farther away from van Drood and picked up my pace as my legs warmed up. At the corner of Livingston Street I bumped into a short plump woman.

"Pardon me," I said, trying to get around her, but she grabbed hold of my hand. I let out a yelp and pulled away, frightened of being touched so soon after van Drood's hands had been on me.

"It *is* you!" The little woman cried. "I knew it! I told Hattie that only a chime child could do this."

I looked down into Emmaline Sharp's kind plump face.

"Are you in danger?" she asked.

I nodded and began to shake.

"You poor child, your hands are like ice. Come along to Violet House with me."

"But the bells," I said, looking back down Main Street. Van Drood was no longer standing in front of the inn. "If I started them mustn't I stop them?"

"They'll stop when you feel safe again. Come. We'll sit you by the fire and get some hot tea into you." She steered me down

Livingston Street, past houses where people stood on their porches and in their yards, talking about why the bells were ringing. Harriet Sharp stood in front of Violet House with her brother Thaddeus. She was stroking his arm, murmuring something to him. His sparse hair was standing up in disordered clumps and he was rocking on his heels, clearly agitated. When he saw me with Emmaline he began to hop in place.

"Be gone, say the Bells of Rhinebeck," he yelled out at the top of his voice. *"Shadows fly back to Hell's Gate!"*

Hell's Gate? Where was that? Could Uncle Taddie know what had happened from the sound of the bells?

"Yes, yes, Taddie," Aunt Harriet said soothingly. "The shadows are all gone. And here's Ava come to have tea. Why don't you go to the greenhouse and pick her a posy?"

Taddie grinned at me. "A posy for the chime child who banished the shadows. Yes, yes!" He turned and zigzagged across the lawn to the greenhouse. Aunt Harriet turned to her sister.

"I see you were right, Emmy, it *was* Ava! She must have been in terrible danger. But," she turned to me, "you're safe now. Come on in. Emmy said there'd be company for tea, so Doris baked a Victoria sponge cake."

I was ushered up the porch steps and through the front door by both aunts. The house was warm and smelled of violets, tea, and cake. I breathed in the comforting warm aroma and willed my heart to stop racing. *You're safe, you're safe*, I told myself, but still the church bells rang. Would I ever feel really safe again?

Hattie and Emmy bustled me into the conservatory, where a fire crackled on the hearth. They sat me down in an overstuffed chintz chair and draped a cashmere shawl around my shoulders as I falteringly told them about my encounter with the Shadow Master, whose name, I now knew, was Judicus van Drood. I thought I saw the aunts exchange a meaningful look when I mentioned his name, but then Hattie quickly poured another cup of tea and Emmy threw another log on the fire. Still the bells rang.

Doris brought in a silver tray laden with hot buttery scones and golden sponge cake. Taddie came in from the greenhouse with a bouquet of violets and laid them on the tea tray. The entire household bustled around me, but still the bells rang.

A floorboard creaked behind me and the aunts and Taddie looked up. "Oh," Emmy said, "I'd almost forgotten. You haven't met our new boarder..."

The last thing I wanted was to meet a stranger. I looked up at the tall dark man entering the room, wondering how on earth I was going to manage polite conversation... and my mouth fell open.

"Avaline Hall, allow me to introduce you to Mr. Corbin," Harriet said.

The dark-haired young man bowed his head in greeting. His hair was slicked back and he wore heavy horn-rimmed glasses, a bulky tweed jacket, and a barely-suppressed grin. Despite his urbane appearance I had no trouble recognizing Raven.

There was an awkward silence as I stared up at him openmouthed. Then Taddie broke the silence by turning to his sisters.

"Listen," he cried, "the bells have stopped!"

29

MY SECOND AFTERNOON tea at Violet House was a stifled affair compared to the first one. I could barely string two words together after the shock of finding Raven in the Misses Sharps' conservatory dressed as an ordinary mortal—and a rather fussy one at that. He even had on spats and braces! I wondered if the latter might have something to do with keeping his wings in place. I found myself peering at his back every time he leaned over to pour out the tea.

Thankfully, the Sharp sisters attributed my muteness and jumpiness to the shock I'd had. It was soon clear to me that they had no idea that their boarder was a Darkling—and that they were entirely enamored of him.

"Imagine our luck!" Hattie enthused, accepting a cup of tea from Raven, "to find such a suitable boarder. Mr. Corbin is an apprentice clockmaker. He's helping Taddie fix all of Father's clocks."

"Raymond says I have a sharp eye for working with mechanical things," Taddie said with an adoring look at Raven.

"Raymond?" I repeated, lifting an eyebrow.

"Yes," Raven said, "but all my friends call me Ray. If it isn't too impertinent, I'd be happy if you did, too, Miss Hall. Even though we've just met I feel as if we've known each other for ages."

I saw the aunts exchange pleased smiles. "Oh, we're so glad you're getting on," Aunt Emmy said. "I had a feeling"—she winked at me—"that you would. Mr. Corbin . . . *Ray*," she corrected herself after a mock stern look from Raven, "is interested in all the things you are, Ava—books, poetry, bird-watching—why, he's even made a study of bells!"

"You're too kind, Miss Emmaline. My study of bells is only a component of my interest in clocks. After all, what good's a clock that doesn't chime the—"

As if on cue, all the clocks in the house began to chime the half hour. They each played a different tune, but those tunes somehow added to each other to create a lovely symphony, just as Mr. Sharp must have originally planned. The two sisters listened with their hands clasped and eyes closed. When the chiming ended, Miss Emmaline wiped a tear from her eye. "We haven't heard them all chime together like that since Father died. We are so very grateful, Mr. . . . Raymond."

"And I am so grateful for the hospitality all three of you have shown me," Raven said, looking down at his teacup. "It means so much to me to be made to feel so . . . at home." He looked up and I saw a genuine look of gratitude on his face.

"But," he said, getting to his feet, "I'm afraid I must go. I have to stop by a house on the River Road to attend to a clock that needs fixing. Perhaps if Miss Hall is ready to go back to school I might accompany her."

"Oh yes, that would be best," Miss Emmy said. "Ava met a most disagreeable man at the post office. We wouldn't want her to encounter him again. But first she must come in the . . . er . . . library with me for that . . . er . . . book I promised to send back to Vionetta." She turned to me and screwed up one eye in such a peculiar fashion I thought she must have something stuck in it, but then I realized she was winking at me.

"Oh yes, the book! Miss Sharp will be disappointed if I forget it!"

As I got up to follow Miss Emmy into the library, Raven bowed formally and asked Miss Emmy if she needed any help retrieving the book. "I'm very good at getting into high places," he added mischievously.

"Oh no, no!" Miss Emmy chirped, her hands fluttering like agitated birds. "You wait here. We'll only be a moment."

As soon as we were in the library—a snug octagonal room with more violet pots, antique clocks, and figurines than books—Miss Emmy confessed there was no book. "It was a ruse I made up to get a moment alone with you. I feel quite awful tricking that sweet young man."

"I'm sure you wouldn't have done it unless it was important. Did you have something that will help me focus the bells?" I looked around the bookshelves, wondering if *A Darkness of Angels* could possibly be here amongst the aspidistras and china shepherdesses. But instead of a book, Miss Emmy produced a pocket watch from her pocket.

"My father made this for me," she said, cradling it in her plump palm. Its gold case was etched with a design surrounding a small enamel watch face. At the top of the watch face were two bells. Two figures flanked the bells—a woman and a man with wings. They were each holding a small hammer poised above the bells. When Emmaline pressed the stem at the top of the watch, the two figures struck the bells, producing a faint, tinkling tune. A familiar tune. It was the same tune that the Blythewood bells rang when I first heard them.

"It's an automaton repeater," Emmaline said. "My father programmed it to play certain protective tunes and also to repeat whatever tune was in my head so that I could learn how to make the bells in my head ring to my command."

"And have you learned how to do that?" I asked.

Miss Emmy smiled. "I've learned to slow the bass bell—the one that signals danger—to calm myself and others. It works wonders with Taddie when he gets agitated. But I've never been able to hear more than one other bell. Papa said there was a book somewhere that explained how."

"*A Darkness of Angels?*"

"Yes, that was the one. He looked for it everywhere but never found it."

"I may have found a copy." I told her about Mr. Farnsworth.

"Oh, Papa was good friends with Mr. Farnsworth. They looked together for the book. Perhaps he has found it. But in the meantime you hold on to this." She pressed the watch into my hand.

"But it was from your father!" I cried. "I couldn't."

"He would want you to have it."

"But don't you need it?"

She shook her head, her curls trembling. "Oh no, I have that tune memorized and all the clocks in the house are here to remind me now that Raymond has fixed them." She wiped a tear from her eye. "You need it more than I do." She squeezed my hand closed around the smooth gold watch. I could feel it ticking, like the beat of a bird's heart.

"Thank you," I told Miss Emmy. "I promise to take good care of it."

"Just take good care of yourself . . . oh, and here . . ." She plucked a book off the shelf. It was a guide for the cultivation of violets.

"What's this for?"

"Why, it's our alibi!" she said, attempting another wink. "So Mr. Corbin doesn't think we lied to him."

"How clever of you," I said, smiling at the thought of Miss Emmy thinking she was fooling Raven. She turned to leave, but I thought of one other question.

"You said you learned to summon one other bell. Which one?"

"Oh, Merope's bell," she replied, blushing. "But I didn't *summon* it. It summoned me." Lowering her voice, she whispered, "It's the one that rings when you fall in love."

⊪→ ✦ ←⊪

Raven escorted me down Livingston Street, my arm tucked firmly under his elbow, as if he were my suitor walking me home from the Sunday church picnic, smiling and tipping his hat at the good townspeople of Rhinebeck. My heart fluttered in my chest like a trapped bird. What if Raven's wings suddenly burst free of his tweed jacket? What would those good townspeople think of me then?

"How do you do it?" I asked quietly.

"Do what?"

"Play a part so . . . *convincingly.* You've got the Sharps completely bamboozled."

He laughed. "They're sweet, trusting people. Why shouldn't they believe I am what I say I am?"

"But Emmaline is a chime child. Shouldn't she . . . *sense* there's something wrong with you?"

His arm muscles tensed under my hand. "*Wrong?*" he echoed, an edge of anger in his voice.

"I didn't mean it like that. I meant *different.*"

"A chime child senses danger. If I meant the Sharps any harm—which I don't—Emmy would sense it. What about you? What do *you* feel with me now?"

Lightheaded? Giddy? Airborne? All occurred to me as possible answers, but instead I replied primly, "Confused. I mean," I added when he cocked one eyebrow at me, "I don't understand what you're doing at the Sharps pretending to be a clockmaker's apprentice."

"I *am* a clockmaker's apprentice," he snapped. "I've signed papers with Mr. Humphreys for a year's apprenticeship after I demonstrated my expertise. I've been practicing, you see, for some time. I like fiddling with clocks and I'm good at it. So why shouldn't I have a job like anyone else? Do you think I want to live in a tree the rest of my life?"

I stared at him, open-mouthed. We'd reached the corner of Main Street and had to pause to let a streetcar go by. Raven was staring at the traffic as though he'd like to vault over it. "But you're a . . ." I lowered my voice at his warning glance. "A *Darkling.* You can carry souls across the worlds. You can *fly*! Why would you want to live an ordinary life?"

He stared at me for a long moment, those dark eyes resting on me with a touch soft as velvet. His arm, though, was rigid as steel beneath my fingertips and I could see the cords in his neck tensing and his jaw clenching. I felt the ripple of muscles from arm to back. He was holding himself tight to keep his wings from unfurling and breaking through his jacket. There was so much pent-up energy inside him that I could see it, rising off him like heat waves on a sultry day. Then the ripple passed and he let out a soft sigh.

"You're right," he said through tight lips. "Why would anyone want to live an ordinary life with a monster like me—?"

"Wait," I said, "that's not what I meant."

But Raven ignored my interruption as he steered me across the street and headed us north on Main Street. "I have other reasons to be at Violet House. Thaddeus Sharp was quite the inventor—and he was a friend to the Darklings. He understood that the Darklings weren't the enemy, but that the *tenebrae* were. I believe the clocks in the Violet House were designed to repel *tenebrae*. I'm studying them to see if I can understand how they work."

"I think you're right that Thaddeus Sharp was trying to find a way to repel the shadows with his gadgets. Emmy gave me this."

I took out the pocket watch and opened it up. Raven stopped dead in the street and cupped my hand in his as the watch played its tune. The touch of his bare hand made me feel warm all over. I heard the treble bell in my head and thought of what Emmy had said it meant—but who knew if she knew what she was talking about. And besides, when had she been in love?

When the tune had played out Raven folded my hand over the watch to close it and then abruptly dropped my hand. "An automaton repeater. Interesting. Yes, I think that will help protect you—and you'll need it if you're going to take on the Shadow Master on the streets of Rhinebeck. What did you do to draw him out, by the way?"

Ignoring the sharpness of his tone—and glad that he had looked away so he wouldn't see the blush that had risen to my face—I told him how I'd found *A Darkness of Angels* listed in the catalogue, written to the librarian at Hawthorn, and decided to post the letter in town.

"He was waiting for me. He knew that I'd found something in the Special Collections and come to town to post a letter. I would have told him who the letter was to if the bells hadn't rung! When he touched me I felt this burning ice creep through me."

"*Tenebrae.*" Raven hissed the word. "I've heard that's how they feel when they get inside you—first cold, then burning, and then, after they burn through you, a dead numbness. If you hadn't gotten away you would have become his slave."

"I was able to break his hold on me," I said. "But I can see how he does it. Perhaps his spy is someone he took over . . . someone weak. I think it might be our deportment teacher, Miss Frost." As if saying her name had summoned her, the lady herself emerged from the door of the Wing & Clover just as we passed.

"There she is!" I hissed, pulling Raven into the doorway of the greenhouse next door.

We needn't have been so secretive. Miss Frost did not look

as if she would notice an elephant parading down the main street of Rhinebeck. She stood blinking in the sunlight, swaying unsteadily on her feet, her face as flaccid as blancmange. I felt an unexpected pang of pity for her in her confused, helpless state, but that sympathy vanished when she was joined on the sidewalk by Judicus van Drood.

Raven pulled me deeper into the doorway, shielding my body with his. I felt the rustle of his wings beneath his jacket straining to break free. I placed my hand on his back, between his shoulder blades, and willed the bell—which had begun tolling inside my head as soon as van Drood appeared—to slow and its vibrations to travel from my body to Raven's, just as I had done with little Etta at the factory. I held Emmy's pocket watch in my other hand. The bell slowed in my head, but Raven's wings still beat, tearing at the heavy tweed of his jacket. Then I remembered that with Etta I had held her bare hand in mine.

I slipped my hand under the collar of his jacket and touched his bare neck. His skin was hot and he was trembling. I stroked his back, listening to the bells in my head and felt the taut cords in his neck slowly relax. His wings subsided beneath his jacket. I took a deep breath and craned my neck around Raven to see what was happening.

Van Drood was standing next to Miss Frost, whispering in her ear, his unnaturally red lips nearly touching her skin. I shuddered at the sight . . . and then saw something worse. His lips parted and he spit out a writhing stream of black smoke that snaked into Miss Frost's ear. I felt my knees buckle and I gasped.

Van Drood must have heard the sound. He lifted his head away from Miss Frost's ear and swiveled his neck like Blodeuwedd when she heard a mouse squeak—only his eyes were colder than any owl's. I felt the chill of them move over our hiding place, saw the blood-red lips pull back over blackened teeth. My hands turned slick at the sight. I nearly dropped the pocket watch . . . and somehow hit the stem, releasing a tinkling chime. *Now he'd be sure to find us!* But instead of pouncing on us, the black eyes fogged over as though a mist had risen in them—a mist that had also risen around Raven and me. In my hand the watch continued playing its tune—a different one, I noticed now, from what it played before. I wondered if the mist would continue to conceal us when the tune was over. But before it finished I heard a familiar voice calling Miss Frost's name. Van Drood snapped his head toward it. Sarah Lehman, in her threadbare black coat, a thin scarf wrapped around her face, was crossing the street.

"Miss Frost, do you need me to find you a cab?" she called, making straight for van Drood.

I wanted to call out and stop her, but Raven held me back. Van Drood tipped his hat to Sarah. "You are just in time, Miss . . ." Sarah stopped a few feet away and stared at van Drood. "You must be one of Miss Frost's students whom she was just praising so highly. I am afraid she has overexerted herself and suffered an attack of . . . um . . ."

"Neurasthenia," Miss Frost blurted out as if she were one of the automaton figures on the repeater come to life. "It's my neurasthenia. Yes, I had better return." She looked around her as if unsure of where she was.

"To Blythewood," van Drood supplied. "Please allow me." He raised his cane to summon a passing hansom cab. It stopped with a screech of breaks and van Drood opened the door, guiding—nearly pushing—Miss Frost inside. He pressed something into Sarah's hands—cab fare, I imagined—then, bowing low, strode briskly north on Main Street, swinging his cane. Sarah stood at the cab door staring after him.

"Come on," Raven said, pulling me out of the doorway, "this is your ride."

"But why?" I began to object, but Raven ignored me and marched straight up to Sarah Lehman.

"Excuse me," he said, tipping his hat to Sarah. "But are you going back to Blythewood? Would you mind taking Miss Hall with you? She's feeling a bit faint."

Sarah stared at Raven—and then me. "Ava?" she said. "What are you doing here?"

Raven answered for me. "She was having tea at Violet House, where I am a boarder. Raymond Corbin, clockmaker's apprentice." He held out his hand.

Sarah placed her hand in his. "Sarah Lehman," she said.

"Oh yes, Miss Hall has often spoken of you."

Had I? I wondered. But Raven was speaking so quickly I didn't have time to remember. He was chattering on, explaining to Sarah how I'd nearly fainted in the street and he'd helped me into the greenhouse for a rest, when I'd recognized Sarah and Miss Frost and he had suggested I share their cab back to the school. Within minutes it had been settled and Raven was bustling me into the cab, his eyes already scanning the street, with only a hurried whisper in my ear to "keep an eye on this one."

Of course, I realized, he wanted to go after van Drood and needed to get rid of me first. I felt like a parcel that has been delivered as I squeezed up against Miss Frost's bulky—and inert—form. She had fallen heavily asleep and was already snoring. Sarah perched on the jump seat across from me and looked out the back window as the cab drove away. I craned my neck around and saw that she was following Raven's progress down the street.

"What a charming young man," she said when I turned back. "Have you known him long?"

"Oh no!" I nearly shrieked. "I only just met him at the Sharps."

Sarah tilted her head and looked at me quizzically. "But he said you'd spoken of me *often* and you two seemed . . ." She wrinkled her brow. "As though you'd known each other longer somehow. Almost *intimate*."

Blood rushed to my face. Had Sarah seen us in the greenhouse doorway, pressed close together, Raven's arm around my waist, my hand on his bare neck? My blush deepened as I recalled the moment. A slow smile dawned on Sarah's face.

"Ava! You're blushing! Is he a secret beau?"

There was something so gleeful in Sarah's expression that I hated to disappoint her. Of course I couldn't tell her the real story, but I could tell her something close to it.

"I met him in the city," I said. "In Washington Square Park while walking to work. His . . . um . . . the clock shop where he worked was nearby . . . on Waverly Place," I added, recalling that there *was* a clock shop on Waverly. "We passed each other often and one day he spoke to me. . . ."

As I embroidered the details a picture began to take shape in my head—a moving picture like the ones that played in the Automatic Vaudeville House in Union Square. It was my old life of working in the factory overlaid by a gauzy construction—walking through the park with Tillie, who might have urged me to talk to the handsome clockmaker's apprentice we saw each morning. *He likes you*, Tillie would have whispered in my ear. With her encouragement, perhaps I would have been so bold as to let him walk me home from work one day. He'd have brought me flowers. Perhaps he would have bought me an ice from one of the Italian stands on Mulberry Street. Eventually I might have agreed to accompany him to Coney Island one Sunday. . . .

"How romantic!" Sarah cried, her voice breaking into my little daydream. I'd barely realized I was saying it all out loud. "And now he's followed you up here to Rhinebeck!"

"Oh," I said, "I'm not sure. I suppose it was the opportunity to work with Mr. Humphreys."

"Nonsense!" Sarah leaned forward and lowered her voice, even though Miss Frost's snores assured us of her comatose state. "He's come for you. Why else would he be staying at the Sharps, where it will be easy for you to find excuses to meet?"

"I don't know about that," I said, suddenly nervous at the turn Sarah's imaginings—or rather *my* imaginings—had taken. If it got around that I was seeing a strange boy in town, how long would it be before Raven's true identity came to light?

Sarah's eyes widened at my obvious discomfort. "Don't worry," she said, grabbing my hand and squeezing hard. "I'll keep your secret. I could even carry messages for you if you ever need me to. I'm always going into town on errands for *her*." She slid her eyes over to the recumbent Miss Frost.

I looked into Sarah's wide brown eyes, as trusting and hopeful as a spaniel's, and realized how happy I'd made her by taking her in my confidence. Perhaps few other girls, if any, shared gossip with "Lemon." And I might need to get in touch with Raven. He had told me to keep an eye on Miss Frost. I would do that—and report back to him.

"And you won't tell anyone else?"

Sarah's eyes shone. "Your secret is safe with me," she said solemnly, pressing my hand in hers over her left breast.

"Secret . . ." Miss Frost's voice blearily echoed Sarah's words.

Sarah rolled her eyes and, giving my hand one more squeeze, let it go. "We're almost back at school," she said loudly to Miss Frost. "Shall I help you to your room? I have a new dose of your physic." Sarah held up a parcel from her bag and shook it. The sloshing sound seemed to revive Miss Frost.

"Be careful with that," she snapped, reaching across me for the parcel. As she leaned over me I was nearly overwhelmed by her odor—the familiar scent of tea rose, gin, and formaldehyde, now overlaid by something new. The stench of something *burnt*.

30

I WALKED UPSTAIRS trying to sort through all that had happened today—van Drood's appearance in Rhinebeck, what I'd done with the bells, Raven showing up as a boarder at Violet House, Miss Emmy's gift of the magical repeater pocket watch that seemed to have the power of raising a concealing mist, and confirmation that Miss Frost was the spy. The last revelation was the one that most worried me. Shouldn't I go to Dame Beckwith and tell her? But would she believe me? All I'd seen was a wisp of smoke as van Drood whispered in Miss Frost's ear. I'd need more proof than that to convince Dame Beckwith that her old friend was a spy. Better that I watch her as Raven had told me to.

In spite of all the tumult of the day, I smiled when I thought of Raven at Violet House. *Because he's safer there than in the woods,* I told myself, pausing on the fourth-floor landing to look out at the frozen woods. It had been horrible to think of him out there with the ice giants. Far better to think of him taking tea with the Misses Sharp and tinkering with clocks with Uncle Taddie at Violet House . . . where I could visit.

That was the real reason I was happier with Raven at Violet House, I admitted as I turned away from the window and continued to my room. Now I knew where to find him. It would be easy to send a message with Sarah, or go into town to visit the Sharps, perhaps even visit the shop where he worked. It would be not unlike the little story I'd made up for Sarah. And why shouldn't a story like that come true for me? I might not be rich like Helen van Beek, but a clockmaker wouldn't require a huge dowry. . . .

"You certainly look pleased with yourself."

Helen's voice startled me out of my daydream. I'd walked right by her without seeing her at her desk, where she was huddled over some papers. "Where were you? In the woods again?"

"No," I said sharply. "I went into town to post a letter . . . and then ran into Emmaline Sharp, who invited me to tea. Then I took a cab back with Sarah and Miss Frost." With the subtraction of van Drood and Raven, my afternoon sounded innocent enough for me to meet Helen's gaze with only the slightest of blushes. And boring enough to allay even her curiosity. It would never occur to Helen that I might meet an interesting male at the Sharps'. It probably wouldn't occur to her that I'd meet an interesting male *anywhere*.

"Oh," she said, looking back down at the papers spread out on her desk. "You might have told me you were going to the post office. I have some very important letters to mail."

In other words, more important than anything I would be sending.

"I'm not your maid, Helen," I said, my voice shaking. I turned to hang up my coat and fur hat and muff in the wardrobe so she wouldn't see the color flare in my cheeks. "I know you're used to having servants at your beck and call, but you're going to have to learn to do for yourself while you're here at Blythewood. You can't always lean on Daisy and me."

"I wasn't aware I was *leaning* on you," Helen said, her voice cold and haughty. I turned to see that she was gathering up the papers on her desk and getting to her feet. "Or on Daisy, whom I barely see anymore. But I will endeavor not to be a burden."

"I didn't mean—" I began, sorry I'd spoken so sharply to her.

"No, you said exactly what you meant," Helen interrupted. "And you're right. I have to learn to 'do for myself.' So that's what I'm doing—going to be by myself." With that she turned and swept out of the room before I could say anything else.

And what could I say? Helen and I came from two different worlds. She couldn't understand mine and I couldn't begin to understand hers. Perhaps it was better if we spent less time together.

As I hung up my coat my hand lingered on its fur collar, the silk plush of it reminding of the touch of Raven's wings. But when I brushed my cheek against it I smelled smoke and ashes.

⟫→ ⟡ ←⟪

The castle had lots of unused rooms, and it was big enough that everyone who wanted to be alone could find a place of their own—which more and more seemed to be what everyone wanted. I assumed Helen had found some little nook to study and write her letters in. Daisy was always off on some unspecified mission, only stopping by meals long enough to stuff her pockets with rolls and apples like a squirrel hoarding nuts for the winter. Even gregarious Cam would often vanish to an indoor target practice that she said some of the Dianas had set up on the sly—"strictly against the rules," she announced in a loud stage whisper, "so I can't tell you where it is." Dolores and Beatrice were doing research "for Papa" in the labs.

Between classes and meals, all the girls of Blythewood scattered into their separate nooks and crannies like beetles scurrying into the woodwork. Sometimes walking the deserted hallways I felt like they had all vanished and I was the last person left in the castle.

Except for Sarah. I was always running into her on her errands for Miss Frost. No matter how busy she was, she would take time to chat with me and ask if I had a message to send to my "beau" at Violet House. The problem was that I had nothing to report to Raven. After our encounter outside the Wing & Clover, Miss Frost had taken to her room on the third floor of the North Wing with a bout of ague.

I made it a point to walk with Sarah when she brought up meals and her medicine to check that she was really bedridden. When Sarah unlocked the door ("She has a horror of being disturbed," Sarah confided), I was nearly overwhelmed by a wave of hot, camphor-laden air. "She likes to keep it warm," Sarah whispered as I followed her in. "And the camphor fumes are good for her lungs."

At first I could barely see. Heavy drapes were pulled over the windows. The only light came from a low fire in the hearth and the flickering flames of spirit lamps, on which small copper basins of liquid bubbled and steamed up a brew of camphor and strong-smelling herbs. A heavy fog hung in the air. Miss Frost lay in the center of it like a beached whale on her four-poster bed.

"Have you brought me my medicine, girl?" she asked querulously as Sarah approached the bed.

"Yes, Miss Frost, and a visitor. Avaline Hall has come to say hello."

"Ah," Miss Frost said, struggling to sit upright and find her lorgnette on her nightstand. "Is she still here? I'd have thought she would have vanished like her mother by now."

"I'm still here," I said, my nose prickling at the rank odor of the bedclothes as I stepped closer. "I'm not going anywhere."

She regarded me through her lorgnette, her eyes magnified into grotesque bloodshot orbs, and sniffed. "Well then, you might as well make yourself useful. I'm afraid your friend Miss Muffat—"

"Moffat," I corrected.

Miss Frost waived her hand dismissively at my correction. "I'm afraid she's making a mess of my specimens while I'm indisposed. Go down and check for me—"

"I can do that, Miss Frost," Sarah interrupted, giving me an apologetic smile.

Miss Frost shifted her gaze from me to Sarah. As her eyes moved I noticed that there was a film over them and that a vein twitched at her temple. She stared at Sarah as if she didn't recognize her. Was she going blind? I wondered. But then she blinked and the film cleared. "You do too much," she rasped hoarsely. "You . . ." A coughing fit kept her from finishing.

"Not at all, Miss Frost," Sarah said, pouring a teaspoonful of the medicine she'd brought. "I'm happy to be of service. Here. Drink this. It will help your cough."

Sarah leaned over and deftly inserted the spoon into Miss Frost's mouth. The coughing slowly subsided, leaving Miss Frost exhausted. "There, that's better," Sarah said soothingly, pulling up the counterpane. Then to me she mouthed, "We'd better go."

We tiptoed out of the room. Before we left, though, I heard Miss Frost murmuring something. It sounded like "Miles."

⋺→ ✦ ←⋲

I wrote a message to Raven that evening. "E.F. looks too ill to do anything dangerous, but I plan to keep an eye on her tonight." I sealed the note, borrowing a bit of Helen's sealing wax because that was something the girls in Mrs. Moore's books did when they sent secret notes. I smiled to myself at the memory of the girl who used to read girls'-school adventures at the Seward Park library. She seemed a much more innocent person than the girl who was spying on her teacher.

While I was putting back the sealing wax a slip of paper fell out of one of the desk's pigeonholes. Putting it back, I couldn't help notice that it was a bill from a dress shop. I tucked it back in with several other bills. I recognized Miss Janeway's letterhead and the trademarks of several of the stores I'd gone to on Ladies' Mile. As I'd suspected, Helen's correspondence was mainly to do with clothing orders. Nothing as weighty as my note to Raven.

I slipped the note to Sarah at dinner. I needn't have worried about being so secretive. Cam had left early for her clandestine archery practice, Bea and Dolores had their heads together over a textbook, Helen was reading a letter, and Daisy was intent on cutting up her beefsteak into tiny pieces.

"I'm going in the morning to pick up a new physic for Miss Frost," Sarah whispered. "I'll deliver it then."

After dinner I waited until everyone had gone off to their separate hideouts and then crept up the back stairs in the North Wing to the third floor. I didn't have much hope of catching Miss Frost doing any spying, but I wanted to be able to tell Raven that I'd at least tried, and if I did see anything important I'd go myself to Violet House to tell him. I'd wear the new dress my grandmother had sent me from Paris. It was a lovely forest green that brought out the red in my hair, which I thought would remind Raven of his treetop nest.

I was so engrossed imagining myself in the dress—and Raven's reaction to it—that I didn't notice the two people coming down the stairs until they were almost upon me. I ducked behind a tall highboy on the third-floor landing just before Miss Corey and Miss Sharp reached it. Luckily they were too deeply engaged in an argument to overhear my hurried retreat.

"I don't know what you're so upset about, Lil," Miss Sharp was saying as they walked by. "I was merely agreeing with Rupert that there needed to be certain changes. I know you think so, too. I've seen how you look at Miss Frost's specimens."

"Of course it's horrible what she does to those poor sprites," Miss Corey cried out, "but the question is how best to bring about change. I just don't see where Rupert Bellows comes off storming in and demanding that we make changes."

"Because he's a man?" Miss Sharp inquired archly.

"Well, yes, since you mention it. Why can't the men run Hawthorn and let *us* run Blythewood?"

"You know that's not how it works, Lil. We must all work together as the knights and sisters did."

"In the old ways? Really, Vi, not you, too! And what if they tell you to marry some decrepit old man?"

"They won't," Miss Sharp answered, her voice bitter.

Miss Corey lowered her voice and whispered something, her voice warbling, as though she were fighting some deep emotion, but they were too far below me on the stairs for me to hear them. I thought I knew where this argument was going anyway. It sounded like the one that Agnes had had with Miss Janeway. At the time, I'd thought it was to do with the women's vote, but now I realized it was about the Order. It seemed as if everyone wanted to change the way things were done but they were afraid of making things worse—the way the girls at the factory were afraid that if they spoke out against the bosses they would lose their jobs. And look what happened to them. I felt a great pang then, missing Tillie. *She* would put the Order to rights if she were here.

A floorboard creaked. I pushed myself deeper into the space between the highboy and the wall and waited. I heard the sound again, coming from the third-floor hall. Someone was approaching, perhaps Sarah coming from Miss Frost's room . . . but these footsteps were softer and more erratic than Sarah's purposeful, boot-heeled stride. An odor of gin and camphor soon announced who it was. I peeked out and saw Miss Frost, barefoot in her nightgown, her long gray hair hanging loose and tangled down her back, careen onto the landing.

"Must check on my specimens," she muttered as she passed me. "Can't trust that girl."

She stumbled on the stairs going down and I thought she was going to plunge headlong to her death, but she grasped the banister and righted herself and kept going, muttering as she went.

I followed her, staying far enough back so she wouldn't hear me, although I don't think she would have noticed a scurry of goblins or a berg of ice giants thundering down the steps in her condition—nor did I have much trouble following her. Even without Miss Swift's tracking classes I could have tracked her by her scent.

On the ground floor, she veered down the hallway into her classroom. I crept carefully to the doorway and peered in. She was standing in a patch of moonlight, in front of the glass specimen cases, looking down at a square of glass.

"I will never forget what they did to you, never!" I thought she was talking to one of the specimen trays until she hung the object back on the wall and I saw it was the silver-framed photograph of Sir Miles Malmsbury. She touched her fingertips to her lips and then pressed them to the photograph. Sighing heavily, she turned back to the specimen case, lifted her hand to a brass handle, and turned it. Instead of the glass door opening, the whole bookcase swung inward on silent, well-oiled hinges and Miss Frost disappeared inside it, leaving the case slightly ajar.

A secret passageway! The answer of what she was doing for van Drood—and proof of her duplicity—might lie inside. I crept into the classroom and looked through the secret doorway. Moonlight illuminated stone steps leading steeply down into the dark. Pitch dark. Looking into it was like looking into the well I'd fallen into during the crow attack. What if van Drood was down there? I didn't know if I could face him and summon the bells in the dark. I stood uncertain on the threshold, remembering the eerie feeling of being down in the dungeon near the candelabellum. I could wait until tomorrow, tell Raven about the passageway, and ask him to come with me—but what if tonight's meeting was important? What if they were making plans to do something awful to Blythewood—or to the Darklings? I had to know what Miss Frost was doing down there.

I turned back to the room and snatched up one of the spirit lamps. Lighting it with the matches she kept in her desk and shielding the flame with my hand, I followed her into the dark.

31

EVEN WITH MY little lamp, I felt as though I were being swallowed by the dark. It had a texture like the heavy crepe my mother used to trim mourning hats and a smell like cold ashes. I could taste it in my throat, growing thicker as I went farther into the bowels of the castle. I wanted desperately to flee back up into the light, but I kept going, determined to find out what Miss Frost was doing.

At the bottom of the stairs a stone-paved corridor sloped even farther down. Water dripped down the walls and splashed under my feet. The more I walked, the more I wondered if the corridor was really a tunnel that led down to the river. A squeaking sound made me fear it was a passageway for rats—or worse. Miss Swift had said that the lampsprites tunneled through the snow and into the castle. Might other creatures from the Blythe Wood also use this underground passage?

A loud creaking noise startled me so badly I nearly dropped my lamp. I pressed myself into a niche in the stone wall and listened. It sounded like metal grating on metal, rusted hinges groaning, a gate being opened . . . and then a low murmurous voice like ghosts whispering. I inched closer, the hair on the back of my neck standing on end, skin prickling. The only reason I wasn't running back in the other direction was that I didn't hear the bell in my head. So there must not be any real danger. Besides, I had Miss Emmy's repeater. I could use it to raise a concealing mist to hide from Miss Frost if I had to.

The murmurous voice came from behind the door. I carefully peered around it.

I was more surprised than if I'd come upon a room full of ghosts. The low-ceilinged chamber was paneled in dark wood and lined with glass-fronted bookcases. A small leather-upholstered campaign desk was fitted into one corner, a cast-iron stove into the other. Miss Frost had opened one of the cases and was moving small white objects around on a shelf, dusting them with the hem of her nightgown. At first I thought they were seashells, but then she held one up to the light and I saw that it was a tiny skull. A human-looking skull.

I let out an involuntary gasp. Miss Frost wheeled on me, her eyes wide and glassy in the lamplight.

"There you are!" she cried, holding out the tiny skull. She had spied me before I had a chance to conceal myself. "You've let them get dusty! I told you they have to be kept in order for Sir Malmsbury when he returns. This is his life's work!"

I looked around the room at the thick ledgers, wicker baskets, butterfly nets, glass bell jars, microscopes, paraffin lamps, hanging diagrams of skeletons, brass microscopes, shelves of skulls and other bone fragments—and one embroidered reticule. It was a naturalist's study perfectly preserved as a shrine to Miss Frost's lost mentor, Sir Miles Malmsbury. But what did it have to do with van Drood?

"Well, don't stand there gawking, girl! There's cataloguing

to be done!" She pointed to the desk on which lay a large leather-bound ledger, next to a lit gas lamp and a box of matches. Clearly Miss Frost thought in her confusion that I was Sarah. Since I didn't want to disabuse her of the notion, I sat down and took up the fountain pen beside the ledger. As I pulled up my chair I felt something stir against my feet beneath the desk and heard the squeaking I'd noticed before.

I looked up to see if Miss Frost had noticed it, but she only handed me a tray of bone fragments, each one labeled with a small Roman numeral. "You can start with these," she said. Then, with a wistful glance around the study—as loving as if the grisly assortment of bones had been love tokens—she left. I sat for a moment wondering if I should go after her, but another squeak from beneath the desk decided me. I crouched down, lamp in hand. Two pairs of frightened eyes stared back at me.

"She's gone now, Daisy," I said. "You can come out."

"How did you know it was me?" Daisy asked, crawling awkwardly out of her hiding spot and cradling something in the crook of her elbow.

"Your reticule," I said, helping Daisy to her feet and staring at the creature nestled in the crook of her elbow. It was a lampsprite, with white wings tipped with silver, covered in a fine white down that formed a sort of dress on her slim body. As she shook her wings free of the dust, I saw that one of her wings was broken.

"It's the sprite Blodeuwedd caught in Miss Swift's class," I said. "The one you were supposed to bring to the specimen room."

"I told Miss Frost she escaped. I couldn't let her be killed . . . she's a *person*."

The little sprite hopped onto Daisy's shoulder and brushed her wings over Daisy's cheeks, leaving a light silvery powder, then trilled at Daisy in a high, squeaky voice.

"And you're keeping her *here*? Weren't you afraid Miss Frost would find her?"

"Featherbell wanted to be close to her departed sisters."

"*Featherbell*?" I asked.

The sprite whistled a long fluty tune and Daisy giggled. "Well, actually that tune you just heard is her real name. In her language it means 'feathered-one-whose-voice-rings-like-a-bell,' but I can't pronounce *that*, so we agreed on Featherbell as the closest translation."

"You can understand her?" The sprite's whistles and trills sounded like the sounds the hawks made in their mews.

"Oh yes, you can, too, if you let her brush her wings on your face. The sprites communicate with a combination of the powder on their wings and sound waves directly to your brain. They call it *powdering*—or actually 'the-speech-which-uses-powder-instead-of-voice,' but I—"

"Couldn't pronounce that. Got it. Okay, I'll try it."

The sprite looked from Daisy to me, tilting her head and blinking her large blue eyes. She chirped uncertainly. "She's really okay," Daisy assured her.

The sprite still looked uncertain but she hopped from Daisy's shoulder to mine, landing light as a butterfly. Her wings brushing against my cheek felt like cobwebs. When she sang I felt a vibration inside my brain that resolved into words.

"Greetings, friend of She-whose-name-means-a-flower-and-brings-food. Please do not blame your friend for hiding me and keeping secrets from you. I would not like any harm to come to her for rescuing me. She has been kind and good."

I looked at Daisy, who was smiling proudly at the little sprite, and felt as though I hadn't really looked at her properly for months. She'd subjected herself to Miss Frost's temper and forced herself to handle specimens that were repugnant to her so she could take care of this wounded creature—which wasn't a creature at all, but a person with thoughts and feelings. I had been as blind about their nature as I had been about Daisy's.

"I know," I said to the sprite, but smiling at Daisy. "She *is* kind and good. I won't let any harm come to either of you. In fact . . ." I held out my hand for her to hop on and studied her wing. "I think I know someone who can fix your wing."

↦ ✦ ↤

The lamp I'd brought with me was nearly out of oil, but we didn't need it. With a flick of her unbroken wing, Featherbell emitted a strong steady glow that lit up the stone corridor in more detail than I cared to see. The walls were covered with a slimy green mold, the floors running with black oily water from which rose noxious vapors that twined around our ankles. When the vapors touched me I heard the bass bell toll in my head. I clasped the repeater in my pocket and pressed its stem. A tinkling chime played and the vapors retreated.

"How can you stand to be down here?" I asked Daisy.

"It wasn't this bad at first. I think it's been worse since the snow's been melting and seeping down through the stones. The vapors started a couple of weeks ago—and they always seem worse after Miss Frost has been down here."

"A couple of weeks ago?" That would have been when I'd seen Judicus van Drood breathe smoke into Miss Frost's ear. Could these noxious vapors be *tenebrae*? The thought made my skin crawl. With Featherbell's light I saw now that there were other passages that turned off this main one. From one of them I thought I heard the tinkling of bells. The candelabellum must be that way, I thought, recalling that Miss Frost had come out of the candelabellum chamber the night Nathan and I saw her in the Special Collections Room. She must have used the candelabellum chamber as a shortcut to get into the Special Collections.

I hurried past the passage, the thought of the shadows moving in the bell-shaped chamber somehow even more unnerving than the creeping vapors, and sprinted up the stairs. I checked to make sure that Miss Frost's classroom was empty and then signaled Daisy and Featherbell to come through. Daisy closed the bookcase behind us. As it swung shut I thought I saw a wisp of smoke creep through the gap at the bottom, but then it seemed to evaporate. I was relieved until Featherbell hopped on my shoulder and swept her wings across my face.

Tenebrae. The word rang in my head. I didn't say anything out loud, though, because I didn't want to alarm Daisy, who was nervous enough as it was.

"Are you sure we can trust Gillie?" she asked as we crept

along the corridor, Featherbell tucked in her reticule.

"Remember how sorry he looked when he gave Featherbell over to you? I'm sure he'll help us."

I wasn't really as sure as I sounded, but I didn't know what else to do. It wasn't healthy for Daisy to be spending so much time down in the dungeons with the *tenebrae*, and she wouldn't abandon the sprite until she was well enough to fly back to the woods on her own. I couldn't be sure that Gillie wouldn't turn us all in, but I was hoping that his compassion for wounded creatures would overcome his loyalty to Blythewood regulations. I just hoped we could find him. I'd never gone looking for him at night.

I knew that Gillie had a room in the south tower, near the mews. To get there we had to go across the Great Hall, up to the fourth-floor landing of the South Wing, and climb out onto the catwalk, up a ladder to the roof, past the mews, and into the tower. As we passed the mews I heard an excited fluttering from the hawks inside and an answering thump from inside Daisy's reticule.

"I think she's afraid of the falcons," Daisy said.

We continued on past the mews to the tower. There was a low door barely as high as my head, with a brass knocker shaped like a stag's head. Daisy and I exchanged a worried look, and I lifted my hand to the knocker. Before I could lower it the door opened. Gillie stood, framed in lamplight, in a long-sleeved red wool undershirt and loose corduroy trousers, black hair standing on end. He gripped either side of the door with his hands, barring both our entry and view of the room beyond. In the low doorway Gillie suddenly looked taller than he was—and more imposing.

"What are ye girls doing here?" he growled. "Haven't I said often enough that my quarters are off limits?"

"Y-yes," Daisy stammered, already backing away. I grabbed her arm to keep her from fleeing.

"We're very sorry to bother you, Gillie, but someone's hurt who needs your help."

"Who's hurt ye, lass?" he demanded. "I'll have the bastard's head—"

"It's not me," I said quickly, surprised at the fervor of Gillie's response. "It's . . . well . . . a *smaller* someone. You might as well show him, Daisy."

Daisy stuck her hand in her reticule and lifted Featherbell into the light. She sat cross-legged on her hand, arms crossed over her tiny chest, glaring up at Gillie.

"We know it's against the rules . . . " I began.

"But I couldn't let Miss Frost kill her," Daisy broke in. "She's a person with thoughts and feelings and a family back in the woods. And she doesn't mean us any harm."

Gillie reached for the sprite. Daisy started to pull back her hand, afraid, as I was, that Gillie meant to capture Featherbell. But he only held his hand out palm up, the way you'd hold an apple out to a nervous horse. Featherbell sniffed cautiously, stood up, swept her uninjured wing over Gillie's hand, and trilled off a long musical tune that I only half understood—my powder must have been wearing off. It seemed to be some complicated formal greeting involving bloodlines, clan obligations, and an ancient treaty. At the end of it, Gillie bowed his head. When he lifted it his eyes were shining.

"Aye, little one, I havena forgotten. You are welcome here. You two as well." He looked at us. "Ye might as well come in, but ye have to promise not to breathe a word of what ye see here. Keep my secrets and I'll keep yours."

"We promise," Daisy and I said at the same time.

Gillie stepped aside to let us in. As we stepped into the small, low-ceilinged room I thought we'd entered an aviary. A dozen brightly colored winged creatures fluttered around the room or perched on roof beams over our head.

But they weren't birds. They were lampsprites.

Featherbell let out an excited trill and hopped from Daisy's hand to the back of a tufted chintz settee where a young male sprite covered in brown feathers embraced her. All the other sprites in the room were soon crowding around her, trilling and brushing their wings together until a cloud of multihued glitter rose around them—or at least I thought it was glitter until it floated back down and burned tiny holes in the upholstery and rugs. Gillie quickly beat out the sparks with his bare hands and let loose a stream of Scottish that I suspected included expletives, from the way he blushed when he saw us staring at him.

"The wee things have near set my house on fire a dozen times," he complained. "They don't call them a conflagration of sprites for naught."

"Does Dame Beckwith know about this?" Daisy asked, goggle-eyed as three sprites landed on her shoulders and brushed their wings along her cheeks.

"Are ye daft, lass? The mistress would boot me out on my

ar— articles if she knew. She and I dinna see eye to eye on the wee sprites. They're harmless, as long as ye keep them from setting the place on fire. And the puir things are having a hard winter, what with the Jotuns in the woods. I try to leave out food for them, but I found this whole conflagration near starved to death, so I brought them here. It's only until next week when spring begins. Now, let's see what we can do for your wee friend . . ."

"Featherbell." Daisy gave her name as the sprite jumped into Gillie's hand.

"Pleased to meet you, Miss Featherbell," Gillie said, his lips twitching into a crooked smile. "Let's see what ye've done to your wing."

He gently stretched out Featherbell's injured wing and inspected the broken feathers. "Ah, this won't be hard to imp, but I'll need replacement feathers."

"Could we use ones from Miss Frost's specimens?" Daisy asked.

At Miss Frost's name the sprites trilled and fluttered agitatedly, raising a cloud of angry sparks. The sparks landed in my hair and I made out—while extinguishing them—the word *murderer*.

"Can ye do it without attracting Miss . . . er . . . the lady's attention?" Gillie asked.

"She's staying mostly to her room," I said. "Except for wandering down to the dungeons at night. I could keep an eye on her while Daisy steals the spec—I mean, the departed sprite."

"I'd have to watch for Sarah, too," Daisy said. "She tells everything to Miss . . . *her*."

"She's just afraid of losing her job," I explained to Daisy. "But I have an idea to distract her as well. We'll do it first thing in the morning, just after breakfast when Sarah brings up her tray. I'll go with Sarah and you can get the feathers for Gillie."

"I'll have Miss Featherbell fixed in a trice, then," Gillie said. "She should be able to fly back to the woods with her conflagration on the first day of spring . . . which can't come soon enough," Gillie added in a gruff voice. "I'll be glad to have the nuisances out of my hair."

One of the sprites flew past me, grazing my cheeks with her wingtips, and landed on Gillie's shoulder. "We nuisances are grateful for your shelter, Ghillie Dhu, protector of all the injured and lost," she trilled. "You have cared for the creatures of the woods and all who stray into it from time immemorial. If you ever tire of serving your human mistress, you will have an honored place among us."

Gillie's moss-green eyes grew wide and bright, then he scowled, wiped the fairy dust off his face, and nodded curtly to the sprite. Looking up he caught my eye. He must have seen the streak of dust on my cheek and realized I'd heard what the sprite had said.

Gillie wasn't human. He was a Ghillie Dhu, an ancient guardian of the woods and all who got lost in it. But how had he managed to come to live within the walls of Blythewood? And who of the Order knew what he was? It was a mystery I couldn't unravel, but if I tried I knew I might bring harm to Gillie—and as I watched him tending to the sprites I knew that I would never be able to do that.

32

AFTER BREAKFAST THE next day it was easy enough to make sure Sarah and Miss Frost were out of the way while Daisy stole a specimen. I merely offered to help carry the tray, silently mouthing that I had a message for her to deliver.

"Another one so soon!" she remarked when I gave her the sealed note I'd written last night to Raven. "Aren't you afraid you'll seem . . . overly eager?"

I blushed at the thought, but answered, "He won't mind. I have important news for him."

"Really?" Sarah asked. "Have you come up with a plan to meet?"

"Y-yes," I stammered, though I hated to lie to Sarah. I had written to tell Raven that the *tenebrae* were in the dungeons. I had no idea how to smuggle Raven into Blythewood. After all, he was quite a bit bigger than a lampsprite.

But it turned out that Raven made my lie true. He wrote back that very day (Sarah passing me the note at dinner) that he had a plan to come to Blythewood the next week on the first day of spring.

"Hold on until then," he wrote. "The *tenebrae* bring out the worst in people. Keep a careful eye on your friends for strange behavior."

Strange behavior? Like Helen becoming increasingly secretive about her letters from home and Nathan walling himself into his library window seat like the victim in Mr. Poe's "Casque of Amontillado"? There seemed to be nothing *but* strange behavior at Blythewood the last week of winter—during which an icy rain fell, turning the snow to slush—as if the promise of release made the captivity of winter seem even more unbearable.

"Aye," Gillie said when I mentioned it to him. "This is the most dangerous time of the winter, when the scent of greening stirs the blood. Even the sprites are tearing each other's hair out."

I witnessed Miss Sharp snapping at Mr. Bellows for bringing her violets, Beatrice reprimanding Dolores for being a "chatterbox," and Alfreda Driscoll refusing to fetch Georgiana a cup of tea and telling her she was "not her maidservant." Georgiana retaliated by starting a whispering campaign that Alfreda's mother was the daughter of a tradesman and not one of the One Hundred at all. I caught myself spitefully thinking that at least someone else was getting a taste of Georgiana's medicine and then felt guilty when I found Alfreda crying in the same closet I'd found Charlotte in a few weeks ago.

As for the Dianas, they seemed oddly distant and fierce. One night at dinner old Bertie went to remove a plate from the Dianas' table and Andalusia Beaumont snatched it away from her, sinking her nails so deeply into Bertie's arm that Gillie had to be called to make her release her grip.

"They've gone into 'Hunt training,'" Sarah told me on the eve of the equinox. "Best stay away from them. If I was you, I'd go into town and visit your fellow," she added wistfully. I often thought Sarah wished she had her own "fellow" to visit, and that she was taking a little vicarious pleasure in my fictitious relationship.

"He says he's coming tomorrow," I confided to her, weary of the secretive atmosphere. I'd begun to fear that Raven wouldn't come and that I'd be stuck in this stultifying mausoleum forever.

But when I woke up the next morning, I felt a change in the air coming in through the window beside my bed. It smelled . . . *green*. Like living things. I sat up in bed and looked out the window. Overnight all the slush had melted from the lawn. The river had broken free of its ice and shimmered in the morning sun. Even the dark menace of the Blythe Wood was lightened by a sprinkling of tender green amidst the darker green of the pines.

"Look!" I called to Daisy and Helen. "It's spring!"

Daisy and Helen crowded into bed with me and pressed their faces against the window. "Isn't that funny," Daisy said, her breath steaming up the windowpanes. "Today *is* the first day of spring. It's as if the woods *knew*."

I shivered at the idea of the woods *knowing* anything.

"High time," Helen said, dismissing Daisy's fancy with a flip of her braid. "Daddy sent me a new spring dress from Paris."

At breakfast there was a posy of violets at each table, with a handwritten note that read "Happy Spring! From the Sharps of Violet House." While the girls exclaimed over how kind it was of Miss Sharp's aunts to send us flowers, I stared at my place setting. Lying on my plate was a letter postmarked from Scotland. I picked it up with shaking hands and nearly cut myself with the butter knife I used to open it.

"Ava's gotten a love letter," Helen remarked drily.

But this was even better than a love letter.

Dear Miss Hall, the letter read,

> *I was most interested to receive your enquiry about the book* A Darkness of Angels, *especially coming from Evangeline Hall's daughter. I knew your mother well and I was most terribly grieved to hear of her death. I thought of her recently when I found a copy of* A Darkness of Angels *here at Hawthorn. I believe she would have wanted me to bring it to you personally. As luck would have it, I am planning a voyage to the colonies in April. I think it is best that I bring the book with me. I will wire to you when I have embarked and make arrangements for our meeting. In the meantime, I urge you to tell no one about our correspondence. For reasons I will explain later I prefer that no one know I am travelling with the book. I look forward to meeting you in April.*
>
> *Yours,*
> *Herbert Farnsworth*
> *Archivist, The Hawthorn School*

"Ava!" Sarah's voice at my ear penetrated my daze as I was reading the letter over a second time. "Dame Beckwith is making an announcement."

I looked up to see Dame Beckwith standing on the dais commanding the room to attention with her penetrating gaze. I caught her eye guiltily and stuffed the letter into my pocket. She nodded as if she'd been waiting expressly for my attention to begin.

"I would like to wish you all a happy first day of spring," she said. "The weather has certainly cooperated with the calendar. In honor of the day I have decided to suspend normal classes."

A great shout went up in the hall, a spontaneous release of all the tension that had built up during the cold months. Even Dolores Jager let out a little yip of excitement. Dame Beckwith waited for the noise to die down before adding, "I've asked for our teachers to hold a class on the signs of spring in the gardens instead."

There was a perfunctory moan, but it wasn't heartfelt. One class wasn't much and at least it was outside. Dame Beckwith looked around the room with that way she had of seeming to meet each girl's eyes and see into each girl's heart.

"I understand that it's been a difficult winter for some of you, perhaps especially for those of you who are new here or have suffered losses." Her gaze had paused on Nathan. "But I hope you will take these early signs of spring as a token that the darkest days are past us. We have survived another winter. As Cicero tells us, *Dum spiro spero*. While there is life there is hope of a new beginning."

She moved her eyes away from Nathan, and I saw that they were shining with unshed tears. Perhaps she was telling Nathan that even though she had lost a daughter she was able to go on because she still had him.

"There's a little ritual we enact here at Blythewood on the first day of spring to mark that new beginning. We reset and wind all the clocks . . . ah, here is our clockmaker now." She lifted her chin and waved her hand to the back of the Great Hall. I turned with everyone else, my heart thudding. Could it be . . . ?

At first my heart sank with disappointment. A stooped old man tottered into the hall, his back bowed under the weight of a heavy toolbox.

"Mr. Humphreys will be making his way around the place all day. Please stay out of his way, girls, and make him and his assistant feel welcome."

Assistant?

Coming in behind old Mr. Humphreys, carrying two more toolboxes, a tweed cap pulled low over his eyes, was a tall strapping young man in a canvas smock. He glanced around the room, sunlight reflecting off the round lenses of his spectacles, until he found me. The smile he gave me felt like sunlight piercing the drear fog of the last few weeks.

"Do you know that *workman*?" Helen asked, her lip curling on the word *workman*. I looked at her to see if she really didn't recognize him. But all Helen saw was a lowly servant sent to fix something. She would never look past the worker's smock and recognize the Darkling we'd met in the woods. I glanced at Daisy, but she was busy pilfering food for the sprites. Only Sarah guessed that the clockmaker's assistant was my "beau," but that was all right. She didn't know that he was a Darkling.

Relieved, I turned back to catch Raven's eye again and somehow convey that I'd find him—but I saw that someone else had recognized him. It was Nathan, who was glaring at the clockmaker's assistant with a look of pure hatred. Nathan glanced from Raven to me, his lip curled in a cruel grimace. Then he fled the hall into the North Wing.

Raven stood watching him go while Mr. Humphreys talked with Dame Beckwith. My tablemates were cheerfully discussing what changes of wardrobe they needed to make for the outdoor class.

"Come along, Ava," Helen was saying to me. "I know your grandmother sent you a new dress from Paris because my mother said they went shopping together. We might as well make ourselves look pretty even if the only males to see us are an ancient workman and his assistant. Nathan seems to have disappeared as usual."

"Someone should go after him," I said, getting to my feet. I saw Raven bend down and whisper in old Mr. Humphreys' ear. Then with a sharp glance toward me, Raven followed Nathan into the North Wing. Was he trying to tell me to follow him? Or had he gone after Nathan to keep him from revealing his identity? Either way, I had to go find them.

"I don't need to change," I told Helen. "I'll meet you in the garden later."

"If you're going after Nathan perhaps I should go, too," Helen remarked querulously. "I've known him longer."

Mercifully, Sarah restrained her. "I think it's better if Ava goes alone," Sarah said, giving me a knowing look over Helen's head. Clearly she thought I had an assignation with my *beau*. "Why don't I help you unpack that dress? You might need help pressing its ruffles."

I shot Sarah a grateful look and hurried from the hall into

the North Wing. With classes cancelled for the day it was deserted. I started down the hall, but halfway down I heard a noise coming from Miss Frost's classroom. Miss Frost hadn't budged from her room since the night I'd followed her into the dungeons, so I doubted it was her. I peered cautiously around the door frame and found Raven standing in front of the specimen cases, his face drained of color.

"I know," I said, coming quietly into the room. "It's awful . . ."

He turned to me, his eyes wide and glassy. "It's an abomination. What kind of monster would do this to poor innocent creatures?"

I shook my head. "Miss Frost seems to think that she's somehow honoring the memory of her mentor—"

"*Honoring?*" Raven spit the word out of his mouth as if it were a piece of rotten meat. "Do you honestly think *this* has anything to do with *honor*?"

"No!" I cried, stung by the way he was looking at me. "My roommate saved one of the sprites and we brought her to Gillie last week to have her wing fixed. Gillie has been tending a whole conflagration in his quarters. And a lot of people in the Order think this is wrong."

"And yet they let it go on," Raven said in an icy voice. "Do you know what happens to a lampsprite's spirit if her body isn't allowed to disintegrate back into the air?"

I shook my head, but Raven wasn't looking at me. He was opening one of the glass doors and gently unpinning a sprite. As he cradled it in his hands a tear dropped from his eye onto the creature. He crossed to the window, opened it, and brought his hand up to his lips so close I thought he meant to kiss the tiny creature, but instead he gently blew on it. The sprite fell apart into dust that swirled in the air. A bit of it landed on me and I heard a voice piping inside my head.

Thank you for releasing me, Darkling.

A translucent image of a sprite flickered briefly in the air above our heads and then vanished into the breeze. I felt a tremor, as if the earth below my feet was shaking, and then *I* was shaking, trembling uncontrollably. Raven turned to me, startled, then wrapped both his arms around me and pulled me tightly to his chest.

"I'm sorry," he murmured into my ear. "I forgot the effect a spirit's passing could have on a human. You're feeling the space between the worlds. It will pass in a moment."

His hands moved over my back and arms, brushing off the sprite dust and warming my skin. The chill vanished, but his hands felt so good on me that I didn't tell him that. Instead, when he brushed his fingers across my face I covered his hand with mine and leaned my cheek into the bowl of his palm. I felt as though he held all of me in his hand—as he had gently cradled the tiny sprite—and as if I might as easily disintegrate at a touch of his lips.

Then his lips were on mine, and instead of disintegrating, I felt heat surge though me, from my lips to my toes, lighting up every molecule in my body. I'd never felt so . . . *whole.*

His hand moved to the back of my neck, gently cradling my head to bring me closer to him. I wrapped my arms around his back and felt the soft velvet of his wings straining against his smock, ready to burst through the thin fabric. I wanted them to; I wanted him to carry us away from here, back to his nest. But then I remembered why I'd called him here: the *tenebrae* lurking in the dungeons. I needed him to help me get rid of them.

Reluctantly, I pulled out of his embrace, put one hand on his chest and one on his lips. As I did I saw something flicker over his shoulder. Had his wings broken free?

But then the flicker resolved into a flash of steel—a knife blade slashing through the air toward Raven's throat.

I screamed and struck at the blade with my bare hands. Cold steel sliced into my skin. Raven whirled around, his wings now splitting his smock and unfurling so fast they knocked me backward against the windowpanes. My vision blurred for a moment. When it cleared I saw Nathan holding a blade to Raven's throat.

"You've taken enough of our women, fiend! You can't have Ava—and you're going to give me back my sister!"

"We don't have your sister, frailing! She wandered into Faerie."

"It's true, Nathan. I saw her there on the solstice."

"As did I," Nathan said, shifting his eyes toward me without moving his dagger from Raven's throat. "This monster has been holding her prisoner there. Now he's going to show me how to get her out."

"But if he lets you in, you'll be trapped. And he can't get Louisa out."

"Is that what he told you?" Nathan said scornfully. "You've been beguiled by his lies."

"They're not lies, Nathan. There's a book that tells the truth. Raven says it will prove the Darklings aren't evil—"

"*Raven?*" Nathan sneered, pressing the blade deeper into

Raven's throat. I saw him flinch and his wings flex. Why didn't Raven knock the blade from Nathan's hands? I knew he was strong enough. But then I noticed a trail of smoke rising off the blade and winding around Raven. "I didn't know you monsters *had* names. But I have learned a lot about you." He twisted the blade and the coils of smoke tightened around Raven, making him wince in pain. "I've even learned to use the shadows to entrap you."

"Shadow magic is strictly forbidden, Nathan. Don't you remember what Mr. Jager said?"

Nathan sneered. "Do you think I care about the rules when it comes to getting my sister back? You wouldn't care either, Ava, if this monster didn't have you under his sway."

"He's not a monster and I am not under his *sway*."

Nathan turned to me, his gray eyes clouded over, something dark writhing behind them. "Then you're a traitor. You've betrayed us," he snarled, his upper lip curling away from his teeth, letting out a wisp of smoke.

"You stupid boy," Raven said coldly. "You're the one who has betrayed your kind. By using shadow magic you've let the *tenebrae* inside you—and let them into Blythewood."

"Shut up!" Nathan cried, twisting the dagger. Raven let out a cry and sank to his knees. "You're lying. You're going to get Louisa back for me. Now!"

"Nathan . . ." I took a step forward but Nathan twisted the blade and snarled at me.

"Stay back. If you come any closer I'll make him pay. I can't trust you not to try your chime magic on me." He looked wildly around the room, his eyes coming to rest on the glass specimen case. "There." He waived the blade in the direction of the case. "Open it up."

"I don't know what you—"

"Stop lying! I saw you go in there one night. Open the case. You can stay down there until I get back with Louisa. Then we'll see if you're just this monster's victim or a traitor. Open it, I say, or I'll make this fiend wish he were dead." He twisted the blade and Raven writhed in pain. I quickly ran to the case and opened it. A dark shape billowed out of it, filling my mouth with smoke. I turned to beg Nathan to reconsider, but he was already shoving me into the choking darkness. I fell to my knees and heard the door slam behind me, sealing me inside with the shadows.

33

I POUNDED ON the door, screaming for help, until I realized that no one was coming for me. Everyone was outside in the gardens, enjoying the spring sunshine, while I was trapped underground with the *tenebrae* and Nathan dragged Raven into the woods on a fool's mission to save Louisa. If Nathan forced Raven to show him the door to Faerie it was likely he'd enter it—and never come out. The other alternative was that Raven would refuse and Nathan would kill him. I couldn't bear to think of either scenario. I had to get out of here, find help, and go after them. But how?

I turned away from the door to face the dark stairs and immediately felt a wave of panic sweep over me. Without a lamp I was in complete darkness. I could feel the *tenebrae* writhing around me, pressing their way into my mouth and nose . . . and into my mind.

I was back in the Triangle fire, smoke billowing around me, choking me, forced between two choices—death by fire or by jumping. I had two choices here, too—I could let the *tenebrae* inside me or I could throw myself down the stairs and hope my neck broke. Those were the choices my mother had faced. I saw now that she had done the harder thing. It would be easier to let the Darknesses inside me. They were already whispering to me, telling me how easy my life would be with them at the helm. No more difficult choices. They would steer me toward a life of riches and power. I'd never have to worry about money or work again. And I wouldn't have to choose between Nathan and Raven. Nathan was already with the *tenebrae*, and Raven—Raven was an illusion. What future could there be between a Darkling and a human? I only felt the way I did toward him because he had beguiled me, seducing me with his kisses.

But at the thought of Raven's lips on mine I felt a warmth that beat back the *tenebrae*. *No*, that kiss had been *real*. The memory of it was like a sweet bell ringing in my head.

The bells. I had used them to break free of van Drood. I could use them now to fight the *tenebrae*—and I had the repeater to help. I took it out of my pocket and pressed the stem. The two tiny figures struck the bells, playing a tune. At first the bells sounded tinny and faint, like funeral bells whose clappers had been muffled. I thought it was because the *tenebrae* were already in my head and they were muffling the bells, but as I focused on the sound it became clearer . . . and louder. As they rang I felt the *tenebrae* retreating down the stairs from me.

And as my mind cleared I remembered the passage that led through the candelabellum chamber to the special collections. If I could find my way there I could reach the library and get out through the trapdoor. Of course, it meant going through the candelabellum chamber by myself . . .

But I wouldn't think about that now. I started down the steps, keeping one hand on the damp wall and one on the repeater, which now played a tune that was echoed by the bells in my head. When I reached the bottom of the stairs I felt panic rising as I realized I had no light to guide my way. It was pitch black in the tunnel—as black as the well I'd fallen into after the crow attack. Even now the *tenebrae* could be crawling inside me . . .

Unless they're already inside you.

The voice was an insidious whisper at my ear. *Unless they've been inside you all along, making you mad.*

"No," I said aloud. "I'm not mad."

Aren't you? What kind of girl falls in love with a demon?

"Raven's not a demon," I cried. "He showed me the truth about the Darklings."

The truth? In a teacup?

How did the shadows know about what Raven had shown me in the teacup?

I heard laughter.

We know because we were there. Inside you. We've always been inside you, just as we were inside your mother. We passed from her blood to yours. Tainted blood. That's why you don't fit in here at Blythewood. They all know your blood is tainted. If you don't believe us, look . . .

Somehow I had found myself in a doorway. The *tenebrae* had led me forward. I should run back. But where to? Then I caught a whiff of gin and paraffin. I'd found my way to Sir Malmsbury's study, where, I recalled, there was a lamp and matches on the desk. I felt my way into the room, dreading the thought of the cases full of tiny skulls leering at me in the dark, and found the lamp and matches next to the open ledger, just where I remembered them. With fumbling hands, I struck a match, lighting up a roomful of snakes.

I screamed and dropped the match, plunging me back into the dark with the horrible creatures.

Not snakes, I told myself, *tenebrae*. I needed to drive them back with the bells. The repeater was still playing in my pocket, faintly and slowly, as if the mechanism was running down. I reached into my pocket and pressed the stem. Focusing on the tune, I lit the match again. The *tenebrae* recoiled into the corners of the room as the match flared, still snake-like, but at least now they were retreating. I lit the lantern and braced myself to go back into the corridor. I would find the passage that led to the candelabellum and pass through it.

Where all those shadows dwell?

Just pictures on the wall, I told myself, just as these writhing coils were just smoke and shadow. They couldn't get inside me if I kept listening to the bells. I held the lantern high and focused on the sound of the chimes coming from the repeater. The *tenebrae* shrank away and pooled around the desk, fingering the pages of the ledger as if flipping through them, looking for something. . . .

A page turned, and then another, and another, making a sound like dry leaves scraping over gravestones . . .

Over your mother's grave. You wanted to know her secrets. You wanted to know who your father was? Look!

In spite of my resolve not to listen to the *tenebrae*, I couldn't resist. I went to the ledger and held the lantern up to look at the page. At first I wasn't sure what I was looking at. It was a com-

plicated chart, like an octopus with a hundred tentacles—
moving tentacles. The *tenebrae* were swarming over the page,
encircling a name at the bottom. *Evangeline Hall.* My mother's
name. What was it doing in Sir Malmsbury's chart? Sir
Malmsbury had disappeared twenty years ago. My mother
would have been only a girl of fifteen, younger than I was now.
I put my finger on her name and traced the line above it to
where my grandparents' names appeared: Throckmorton Hall
and Hecatia van Rhys. Next to my grandmother's name and my
mother's name were drawn tiny bells with circles around
them—the icon for a chime child. Sir Malmsbury had drawn a
line from one bell to the other. Tracing that line upward I saw
that it connected circled bells from generation to generation.
This was a family tree—of my family. A note in the margin
read, "The chime child germ plasm travels through the matri-
lineal line, but may be strengthened by breeding to males
descended from chime children."

By breeding? Bile rose in my throat. Sir Malmsbury was
talking about my family as if we were cattle. He had studied my
family—and others, I saw from the other branching diagrams
on the page—just as he studied lampsprites, to figure out how
we came by the ability to hear an inner bell and use the power of
the chime child. I saw other family names on the chart—Sharp,
Driscoll, Montmorency . . . He was trying to determine which
family produced the most chime children. There were a few
in the Sharp lines, but there were also several crescent moon
symbols. I looked around the page for a legend to the icons and
found a small box at the bottom. The crescent moon, I read, de-
noted a "tendency toward lunacy."

With a pang I saw that there was a crescent moon drawn next to my mother's name. I scratched at it with my fingernail, wanting to strike it out, but as I did I scratched off a narrow strip of paper that had been glued next to my mother's name—and connected to my mother's name with a hyphen, as husband's names were connected to their wives'. Beneath the strip was my father's name! But why was it covered up?

Because your father's name was stricken from the ledgers.

Perhaps because they weren't married (I didn't see the low-ercase *m* that signified a marriage), but I didn't care about that. I still wanted to see . . .

The name was written in stark black ink, darker than the other writing on the page, as if Sir Malmsbury had pressed the pen harder—or perhaps it looked darker because the whole world around the name had grown dim by comparison. The name written where my father's name should be was Judicus van Drood.

"No!" I said aloud, my fingernails digging into the page. "That monster is not my father!"

I looked closer at the entry. There was no date of marriage. Sir Malmsbury had disappeared when my mother was only fifteen, three years before she would have been married. The notation had been made because of a betrothal—a thought that still roiled my stomach—or because Sir Malmsbury *thought* they should marry.

Yes, that must be it. I looked over the chart again and understood. Sir Malmsbury was figuring out how to produce a chime child through breeding, and he'd come up with the pairing of

Judicus van Drood and my mother. It didn't mean they'd ever married.

But I *had* been born a chime child.

A coincidence?

Or had my mother fallen in love with someone else with the chime trait?

The answer to who that was might lie in this chart.

I ripped the page out. The tearing sound scattered the *tenebrae*. The repeater was chiming madly, as if it had grown as agitated with my discovery as I had. I stuffed the page into my pocket, muffling the sound of the repeater. Holding up the lantern I strode from the room, scattering *tenebrae* in front of me. They were fleeing . . . or perhaps they were leading me on. I found the passage to the candelabellum chamber easily enough. At the door I hesitated. I pressed my ear to the door and listened, but there was no sound inside. It was only a room with bells. Dame Beckwith's warning not to enter the chamber alone—that those who had done so had emerged insane—echoed in my ears. But it was the only way out.

I turned the knob and entered the dark room, holding up my lantern, which cast the candelabellum's shadow onto the wall and showed me the door on the other side. I had only to cross the room. I lowered the lantern, not liking the shadows it threw across the walls, and walked slowly over the stone-flagged floor, careful not to bump into the chairs and table, hardly daring to breathe. Halfway across the room, my hand brushed against my skirt, and the page I'd torn out of Sir Malmsbury's ledger crackled.

A crystal bell shivered in response. I froze and drew my shaking hand away from my skirt. The paper crackled back louder, as though it had caught fire. The bells of the candelabellum tinkled as if ringing an alarm. I gasped—and the intake of my breath stirred the delicate brass rings into motion. The bells began to play a tune that was different from the one they had played when Dame Beckwith had struck them.

The candelabellum plays a different story depending what bell is struck first. What bell had *I* struck? What story would it tell?

You don't have to watch it, I told myself. I was only a few feet from the door. I could reach it with my eyes closed. I didn't have to listen to the bells, which were playing a tune that sounded like the song my mother had used to sing me to sleep. . . .

Could the candelabellum tell me my mother's story? But how? It was made hundreds of years before my mother was born.

Because the candelabellum contains the pieces that all stories are made of. All it had to do was rearrange the pieces and it could tell every story that ever happened and every story that would ever happen. It *knew* my mother's story.

I raised the lantern so fast the flame flickered. For a heart-stopping moment I thought it would go out, leaving me alone in the dark, but instead the flame pulsed and shot up, bursting the glass case of the lantern. I dropped it and it crashed onto the table. The fire gusted over the wood as I remembered the flames bursting through the windows of the Triangle and pouring over the examining tables, hungry for fuel. The fire soared up and lit all the candles at once.

The rings moved faster, the bells rang my mother's song, and the shadows leapt up on the walls and ceiling. A young man and woman. It might have been Merope and the prince, but it wasn't. It was a young girl here at Blythewood, ringing the bells, learning to shoot arrows, flying a hawk, reading a book in the library. There was a young man with her in the library. He looked familiar, but just when I thought I recognized him his face would merge with the shadows, slipping in and out of the dark. I saw him walking with my girl, giving her a book, and then a letter . . . but she gave back the letter and the book. I saw her walking away from him, and then running away into the woods, where a great winged creature swept down and stopped the other man from following her. As the man turned away, shadows leapt up around him, twining about his feet, growing wings and plucking at his sleeves, his hair, his skin. I saw him retreating to his library, to his books, walling himself up behind his books. I saw another woman trying to pull him away from his books, looking on with a worried face, but there was a wall of shadow between the young man and her. I saw him going down into the dungeon and to the candelabellum, where he watched the shadows whirl round and round. I could make out the girl's face among those shadows, and wings. As the shadows grew, there was less and less light to see them by. They *swallowed* the light, just as they were swallowing the young man's soul. They were filling him up, pouring in through his eyes as he watched the shadows, through his ears as he listened to the bells, his mouth as he gasped his beloved's name.

Evangeline!

The bells played my mother's name, and then I heard my mother's voice, as clearly as if she had been in the room with me, give back his name. Then the shadows swallowed him and the music stopped. I was alone in the dark room with only the echo of a man's name in my mother's voice.

Judicus.

»→ ✦ ←«

I'm not sure how long I sat there. Dimly I remembered that somewhere up above me Nathan was dragging Raven into the woods, but that seemed like another story that the shadows were playing.

It *was* another shadow story. The reason the man in the story looked so familiar was that he reminded me of Nathan. The way he retreated into the library and hid behind his books. The way he snuck down into the candelabellum chamber and watched the shadows . . .

Of course. That's what Nathan had been doing. He had access to the dungeons. He wouldn't have been able to resist the lure of the candelabellum, especially if he thought it could tell him how to find Louisa. But the stories the candelabellum told weren't entirely reliable. They were made of light and shadow, and so the story changed depending on what you focused on— the light *or* the shadow. Nathan had been lured into the shadows, into believing that Raven held the key to finding Louisa. It wasn't just Raven who would be destroyed if I didn't find them. Nathan, too, was in danger of being swallowed by the shadows, just as Judicus van Drood had been.

I got to my feet and crossed the darkness to the door. When I opened it, light poured in through the corridor beyond, which meant that the trapdoor to the library was open. I breathed a sigh of relief and turned to close the door to the candelabellum chamber. As I closed the door I heard the faint tinkle of bells— a last remnant of the song my mother used to sing to me, calling to mind the story I'd just watched. A story made up of light and darkness. Which had I focused on?

Feeling as though I'd missed something, I turned and walked toward the light.

34

AS I WALKED up the stairs to the library I heard a murmuring voice.

"Glory be to God for dappled things—
For skies of couple-colour as a brindled cow."

Miss Sharp was reciting a poem. It wasn't one I'd heard before.

"For rose-moles all in stipple upon trout that swim;
Fresh-firecoal chestnut-falls; finches' wings;
Landscape plotted and pieced—fold, fallow and plough.
And all trades, their gear and tackle and trim."

It was a poem that celebrated the unusual, the marred, the imperfect—things neither light nor dark, but somewhere in between. It seemed a fitting anthem to my return from the dark into the light.

"All things counter, original, spare, strange;
Whatever is fickle, freckled (who knows how?)

> With swift, slow; sweet, sour; adazzle dim;
> He fathers-forth whose beauty is past change:
> Praise him."

I reached the top step at the last line of the poem. Miss Sharp and Miss Corey sat at table, a tray with teacups and scones to one side. Both their heads, one gold, one russet, were bent over the same book. Miss Corey was not wearing her hat and veil. Without it I could see the dappled pattern that spread across her face. Miss Corey's face was as mottled as the brindled, freckled things the poem celebrated. She looked like an exotic creature, as strange in her way as the fairies that populated Blythe Wood, but also quite lovely, which must be why Miss Sharp was reading a poem that celebrated such "counter, original, spare, strange beauty." Miss Corey was certainly looking at her with gratitude—so intently that she didn't see me. But when Miss Sharp looked up from the page, she startled, her eyes widening.

"My bells! What's happened to you, Ava? You look like you've been . . ."

"In a fire," Miss Corey finished, closing the book Miss Sharp had been reading from with a decisive snap as if she could erase what we had heard by closing the book on the poem.

"Your face is covered with soot." Her eyes grew even wider. "And there are feathers in your hair!"

I patted my hair and plucked out a black feather—one of Raven's from when we kissed. I blushed at the memory of it.

"You've been with a Darkling," Miss Corey said.

"Yes," I admitted, "but I can explain. He's not evil. He's been explaining things to me since we met on the winter solstice—"

"You've been seeing him since then?" Miss Corey hissed. The blood that had suffused her cheeks a moment ago had drained away now, the strawberry-colored stains on her face standing out vividly against the white. Her eyes slid away from mine when I looked at her. Was that how it was going to be from now on? Would my reputation be so besmirched by my association with a Darkling that all my friends would turn from me? I didn't have time to worry about that.

"This is not the point!" I cried. "Nathan has taken him to the woods."

"Nathan has taken him?" Miss Sharp asked. "Don't you mean the other way around?"

"No, she doesn't." The voice came from the doorway, where Helen and Daisy stood. "We saw Nathan leading the clock-maker's apprentice into the woods," Daisy went on. "Only he's not an ordinary apprentice, is he?"

"He's a Darkling," Miss Corey answered before I could. "They're devious creatures—ruthless, cunning, and inhuman."

Miss Sharp winced at the harshness of the last word. "Really, Lil, I thought you were more tolerant. You sound like the social Darwinists."

"We're not talking about different sorts of people, Vi. You have no idea what these monsters are like. One of them killed my grandmother."

"Are you sure?" I interrupted. I hated to see two of my favorite teachers arguing. "Raven says that the *tenebrae* can disguise themselves as anything. Maybe it was one of them that killed your grandmother."

"Or maybe you've been mesmerized by the demon. When they found my grandmother she'd been ripped to shreds by one of the creatures, but she died begging my grandfather to open the window so she could see him one last time."

"Like Cathy in *Wuthering Heights*," Daisy murmured, "begging Heathcliff to open the windows so she can smell the heather on the moors."

"Life is not a romantic novel," Miss Corey said, wheeling on Daisy. Then turning back to me, "And the Darklings aren't misunderstood romantic heroes. Life is a lot crueler than you can possibly imagine. You might as well learn that now."

"What a terrible thing to say, Lillian!" Miss Sharp said, her eyes blazing. "You're the last person I would have thought would be cruel because someone was different."

All the color had drained out of Miss Corey's face, leaving only the dark mottling of her skin, which now looked like an angry rash instead of the beautiful "dappled things" praised in the poem. "Perhaps I'm just trying to protect her from nightmares," she said.

"Protect whom from what nightmares?"

The question came from the doorway. Mr. Bellows stood there, an apple in one hand, a book in the other. He looked innocently from Miss Corey to Miss Sharp and then to me, taking in my bedraggled state. "Ava certainly looks like she's taken a fright."

"Ava's been with a Darkling and Nathan is missing," Miss Sharp said quickly, waving him into the room and shutting the door behind him. "We're trying to decide what to do. Ava claims that Nathan took the Darkling."

"Whyever would Nathan do such a thing?" Mr. Bellows asked. "And how could he control a Darkling? I'm quite sure we haven't covered that in the syllabus."

"He has your dagger!" I cried impatiently. "He's been practicing shadow magic with it. I'm afraid Nathan's been taken over by the tenebrae."

"Then we must find him immediately," Mr. Bellows said, his face pale.

"We'll have to tell Dame Beckwith . . . " Miss Sharp began, but Mr. Bellows shook his head.

"She's not here. Gillie drove her to Rhinecliff this morning after breakfast to take the train to the city for an emergency meeting of the Bell & Feather. She won't be back until tonight. And then imagine her horror on hearing that her son is lost in the same woods where her daughter disappeared. She'll send in the Hunt to flush out any Darklings in the woods—"

"We can't let her do that!" I interrupted. "Raven helped me. I can't be the reason he and his kind are hunted down and killed!"

"If we begin the search ourselves *now* we might find Nathan before Dame Beckwith returns."

"And how do you plan to get past the Dianas and their hawks?" Miss Corey demanded.

"Wasn't Gillie going to hold a workshop on imping the falcons' tail feathers today?" Mr. Bellows asked. "The Dianas will be in the mews with their birds all afternoon."

"They leave one on duty," Miss Corey objected.

"But today it's Charlotte Falconrath," Mr. Bellow's replied. "And she's . . . well . . ."

"A ninny," Helen put in. "One of us could easily distract her while the rest of us sneak into the woods. I suggest Daisy do it. No one would suspect Daisy of subterfuge."

"The rest of us?" Miss Corey repeated. "You don't think *you're* going, Helen? We can't afford to lose another student in the woods."

"I have to go to watch over Ava so she doesn't run off with her Darkling paramour."

"My what . . . ?" I began to object to Helen calling Raven my paramour, but Miss Corey had raised another objection.

"Why must we bring Ava?"

Helen let out an exasperated sigh. "Because Ava's been meeting the Darkling since Christmas. She'll know where to find him."

I stared at Helen aghast.

"What?" she said. "Did you think I'm blind? You do know where he lives, don't you?"

I didn't think it was the right time to say he was presently living at Violet House. Besides, I knew where they were going. I pushed past Helen to get to the window seat, where Nathan had stacked his books. I picked up the top one. *To Elfland and Back* by Thomas the Rhymer. The book below it was entitled *Oisin's Travels to Faerie.* I quickly sifted through the rest of the books. Most were books about travel to Faerie, but there was also one on using shadow magic.

"They're almost all about traveling to Faerie," I said. "Nathan saw Louisa in Faerie on the solstice. That's why he's taken Raven. He's going to make him open the door to Faerie and let him in."

"Can a Darkling do that?" Miss Sharp asked.

"Yes," I said. "They can open the door but not go through it. And they can't help anyone out. If Nathan goes to Faerie . . ."

Mr. Bellows finished the thought for me. "He might not return for a hundred years."

⇥ ✦ ⇤

Miss Sharp insisted that we gird ourselves for the expedition rather than rushing in willy-nilly. She sent Miss Corey to the mews to prolong the imping of the birds to give us more time.

"You have a way with Gillie," she said, attempting, I thought, to put their quarrel behind them. But Miss Corey only seemed offended anew to be shunted off on a secondary errand while we armed ourselves for a mission into the woods.

"Miss Swift won't have taught you expedition protocol yet, so we'll have to cover this quickly. The most important thing to remember is bell, spell, and bow. Strap these bells around your wrists. You can use them to ward off the lesser fairies, and we can track each other by the sound of the bells. If you fall into Faerie, follow the sound of the bells *out*." She demonstrated two separate ringing patterns for warding off fairies and for signaling to someone trapped in Faerie.

"So it is possible to go into Faerie and come right out again without spending a hundred years there?" I asked.

"The hundred-year phenomenon—or Rip van Winkle effect—is rarer than people think," Mr. Bellows replied, leaning back in his chair and rubbing his chin. "Time is different in Faerie, but if you carry a reliable timepiece . . ." He took out of his vest pocket a gold pocket watch inscribed with the Bell and Feather insignia, "you can find your way out."

"Will this do?" I asked, taking out the repeater.

Miss Sharp's eyes widened at the sight of the watch. "That's one of my grandfather's watches," she said. "Yes, it should work *most* admirably. But you must also remember not to eat anything there or play any games."

"It was the game of nine pins that did old Rip in," Mr. Bellows commented.

"Dancing is also to be avoided," Miss Sharp added. "That's what beguiled Oisin into his two-hundred-year stay. It's understandable. The music there is divine."

I saw Daisy staring open-mouthed at our instructors. I, too, was surprised. "You sound as if you've . . . *gone there*," Helen said.

Miss Sharp and Mr. Bellows regarded each other guiltily. "You're not supposed to know about it until the senior-year field trip," Miss Sharp said. "Everyone at Blythewood has to go once to Faerie before they graduate. It's required for induction into the Order. We're carefully prepared and trained to get each other out. If Nathan hasn't eaten anything, or danced, or played any games . . ."

"Or kissed anyone," Mr. Bellows added with a rueful smile. "The natives can be quite . . . *flirtatious*."

"Why, Rupert!" Miss Sharp exclaimed with a mischievous smile. "Did someone flirt with you on your journey?"

"A siren," he answered, blushing. "She employed all her feminine and fay wiles, but I resisted by conjugating Latin verbs. The magic of Faerie, you see, is incompatible with logic. If you concentrate on something logical—and dull—you can't be seduced. Besides, fairies *hate* Latin."

"I can see why," Helen, whose least favorite class was Latin, remarked. "I don't think conjugations will work for me."

"Try reciting the Social Register," Daisy suggested. "You'll bore them to death."

"I suggest you both use the spell against enchantment you learned in Miss Calendar's class. *Defendite me artes magicas.*" She made us repeat it three times. "Excellent," she said. "And if that doesn't work, shoot the creature with these." She gave us each a quiver full of iron-tipped arrows. "We'll pair up teacher and student. I'll go with Helen, as she's such an excellent archer and I'm not. Ava, you'll go with Rupert."

"What about me?" Daisy asked, clearly unhappy not to be paired up with Rupert Bellows.

"After you've distracted Charlotte Falconrath, you can meet up with Lillian. Together you can watch the woods for our return. If we're not back by the time Dame Beckwith returns from the city, you should tell her where we've gone." She gave me an apologetic look. "There will be no choice then. Dame Beckwith will send in the Hunt and flush the woods of the Darklings."

⋺→ ✦ ←⋉

At noon Gillie whistled the falcons up to the rooftop mews. We watched from the library window. They came flying to him from across the lawn, their shrill cries rending the air. The Dianas came in their wake, trailing behind their birds as if they were tethered to them and not the reverse. "Dame Beckwith will tell ye that the falcon is trained to its mistress," Gillie once told me, "but it's just as true that the girl is trained to her bird. The falconer becomes a little bit a falcon, just as the hunter becomes the thing he hunts."

But here at Blythewood we hunted fairies. Did that mean we each became a little bit fay?

I didn't have time to ponder the question now. Miss Sharp gave Helen and me the signal to follow her and Mr. Bellows. We each had a pack basket strapped to our backs. Our story, should anyone challenge us, was that we were going to the gardens to collect flowers and herbs that had appeared in Shakespeare's plays.

Luckily, most of the girls had retreated to the house for lunch. The day that had begun so warm had grown chill. Only Charlotte Falconrath stood on the lawn, her small kestrel perched on her gloved hand. Daisy was already approaching her. We could hear her voice through the still air exclaiming at how pretty "the birdy" was and Charlotte's bored patrician drawl responding that it was a hunting animal, not a pet, and that he'd bite Daisy's fingers off if she weren't careful.

"More likely that Charlotte will bite Daisy's fingers off," Helen remarked as we crossed between the greenhouse and the mews. "I can't say I envy Daisy her job. I'd rather converse with fairies and demons than Charlotte Falconrath. Although I think *I* ought to be the one to go with Mr. Bellows. We two are the best archers and can go on ahead to clear the way for you and Miss Sharp."

"Why, Helen, I thought Daisy was the one with the crush on Mr. Bellows!"

Helen scowled. "She is. Do you think I'd give a fig for a *schoolteacher*?"

"He's not just a teacher, he's a knight of the Order," I objected, not sure why I felt offended on Mr. Bellows's behalf.

"That's all well and good, but he still only makes less in a year than my dress allowance. No, I simply think we'll make better time and find Nathan sooner if I go on ahead."

"Ah," I said, understanding at last, "you want to be the one to save Nathan. And what's Nathan's yearly income? He *is* the son of a schoolteacher, after all."

Helen looked at me aghast. "The Beckwiths are one of the wealthiest and most prominent families in New York. If I have to be stuck in this uncivilized wilderness I might as well set my cap at the only eligible bachelor in the place. It's better than ending up with the ancient van Groom my mother has in mind for me."

I thought of the charts and files in the Special Collections Room—of the page still crumpled in my pocket—and wondered how much choice Helen would have about whom she married. Perhaps I should try to warn her. "Do you really think that Nathan, with his proclivity to loitering in taverns and opium dens, is marriageable material?" I began, but one glance at Helen stopped me. Her cheeks were flushed, her eyes burning, her hair slipping out of its pins. She wasn't fretting over Nathan because of his income, but because she genuinely cared for him.

"Very well," I said. "If they don't object, you go with Mr. Bellows and I'll go with Miss Sharp. There—he's signaling for me now."

Our teachers had reached the edge of the woods. Miss

Sharp was standing watching the lawn a few feet away from where Mr. Bellows was peering into the trees. I pushed Helen forward and went directly to Miss Sharp. By the time I reached her, Mr. Bellows and Helen had already vanished beyond the tree line.

"What happened?" Miss Sharp asked. "Why didn't you go with Rupert?"

"Helen wanted to," I said simply.

Miss Sharp rolled her eyes. "Another of Rupert's conquests, eh? Didn't you want to contend for the honor?"

I shrugged. "Honestly, I'd just as soon go with you. There's something I wanted to ask you."

"Of course," she said briskly. "But you'll have to do it as we walk—and keep your voice low. The Bells know what's watching us from in there." She slid her eyes toward the tree line and I saw for the first time that she was frightened, which made *me* frightened. I'd already been in the woods twice, but as we passed from the sunlit lawn into the thick dark shadows beneath the trees I felt a tingling on my skin that was different from anything I'd felt before—a pulse of magic.

"Why does the magic feel stronger now?" I asked.

She glanced over her shoulder at me, brows furrowed. "You feel it?"

"How could I not? It's like I'm standing in a bath of fizzy water."

"Interesting," she replied, turning back to the path to follow the sound of Helen's and Mr. Bellows's bells. "Not all the girls at Blythewood do, you know. No matter how much we train you, we can't teach you to feel magic. There has to be a little bit of it in you. I suspected you had it at your interview when you saw the board members turn into crows."

"You *knew* about that?" I asked, surprised. I'd never mentioned to anyone what I'd seen and nowhere in my classes had anyone mentioned that we would be learning how to turn into birds.

"I wasn't supposed to but I saw it out of the corner of my eye. The higher ranks of the Order are able to transform themselves into the creatures we hunt, but it's not something we're supposed to tell the students. The Order has grown up alongside the fay. Would it be surprising that we have each grown a little like each other?"

"The hunter must become the thing she hunts," I quoted.

"Precisely," she replied. "Only that frightens some of us."

"Like Miss Corey?"

She sighed, a sound like a mourning dove's coo. If Miss Sharp turned into a bird, I thought, that's what she would become. "Lillian's family history is complicated. The Coreys have been fay and demon hunters for centuries. She was raised to hate and mistrust all the creatures of Faerie equally."

"Weren't you?" I asked. "I mean, aren't all the members of the Order?"

"I was raised by my grandfather, and he was different. He thought that some of the creatures of the woods might not be evil."

"Then there's a chance that what Raven told me is true?"

Miss Sharp stopped and turned to me at the edge of a small clearing where a tree had fallen, making a hole in the canopy through which vertical bands of sunlight stood like glowing pillars. In her white dress and with her golden hair she looked like a Grecian goddess against that backdrop.

"You want to believe that, don't you? This creature . . ."

"Raven."

"This *Raven* was kind to you?"

"Yes!" I cried a bit too fervidly. "He rescued me from the fire at the factory. He saved me on the winter solstice and did nothing to hurt me. He wants to be a clockmaker and live an ordinary life."

Miss Sharp laughed. "Ah, an ordinary life. I'm not sure I know anymore what that would look like." She smiled sadly. "But if you feel he is good I am willing to give him the benefit of the doubt. Sometimes I think we of the Order have been too quick to condemn what we don't understand just because it is different. My own experience has encouraged me to be more tolerant."

She squeezed my hand, her smile widening. A band of sunlight touched the back of her head, turning her hair the blazing gold of an angel's halo. A tightness in my chest relaxed and I felt sure that if Vionetta Sharp could come to believe that the Darklings were redeemable, then they *would* be redeemed.

I smiled back at her. Satisfied, she turned, stepped into a bar of sunlight, and vanished.

35

I STOOD PERFECTLY still, staring into the mote-filled sunlight, sure that if I didn't move Vionetta Sharp would reappear. I called her name—first *Miss Sharp* and then *Vionetta*. In the silence I heard doves cooing and then the faint chime of a bell.

Bells! That was what I was supposed to do! I lifted my hand and shook my wrist in the pattern she'd taught us. Then I listened. The woods, which had been buzzing with birdsong a few moments ago, had gone strangely silent as if all the smaller creatures had fled in the wake of a raptor's shadow. Then, faintly, I heard an answering chime coming from the center of the clearing, which was empty of everything but sunlight that filled the circle now like water filling a well. I was inches from the edge of the light. If I took one step I would fall into it—and into Faerie. I might find Miss Sharp, but then who would find me?

I sounded the chime again—for Miss Sharp, but also for Mr. Bellows and Helen. They'd been only a few yards ahead of us. Shouldn't they hear the bells and come back?

Unless they had fallen into Faerie, too.

In which case I was their only tether to this world. I rang the bell again and heard a faint echo of its chime coming from inside the empty well of sunlight—fainter than before. Miss

Sharp was straying farther away. I had to find her. I ventured one toe into the sunlight . . . but something yanked me back.

"What do you think you're doing?" It was Raven, his wings stirring up the air into a whirlwind of sun motes and feathers. "You'll be gone for a hundred years!"

"What happened?" I demanded. "Where's Nathan?"

"The fool insisted I open the door to Faerie for him, so I did."

"Couldn't you do anything to stop him?"

Raven stared at me. "He had me completely at his mercy with that blade of his. Should I have let him kill me?"

"No! Only now Miss Sharp's gone into Faerie, too. I saw her vanish in there but I can still hear her bell."

I shook my wrist and the bells jangled in a crazy rhythm. An even more frenzied peal sounded from the empty glade. Raven snorted. "Did they teach you that at your school? Don't they know that fairies will echo any sound you give them—like mockingbirds. Listen." He whistled a complicated tune. After a moment the sound came back. "Do you think your teacher did that?" he asked.

My eyes filled with tears. "But I know she went in there. I have to follow her!"

Raven stared at me. His wings beat slower and I felt my heartbeat slowing with them, the air stirring against my face gentle as a caress.

"No! You can't stop me! Let me go!" I cried, even though he wasn't holding me back or even touching me.

He sighed. "There is one way. As long as I hold the door open you can come back into *this* time."

"You can do that for me?"

His eyes skidded away from mine, but he nodded. "You have to be quick. Find your friends and come straight back. You mustn't eat anything, or play any games—"

"Or kiss anyone, yes, I know the rules. I promise I'll come back."

He nodded again, still not meeting my eyes. His face was taut, jaw clenched. "Stand back," he barked. "When I've opened the door you can slip underneath my wings."

I moved to the side. Raven stepped to the edge of the light. He closed his eyes, bowed his head, his lips moving in some silent prayer. Where the light from the glade touched his skin it shimmered into an iridescent glow. He winced, then flexed his wings so suddenly I stumbled backward. When I regained my balance, I saw him silhouetted against the blazing light, black wings stretched wider than I'd ever seen them, each feather tip limned in fire. His wings weren't black at all, I realized now— they held every color in the rainbow. I was so mesmerized by their beauty that for a moment I couldn't move. Then I heard someone scream from inside the glade. I ducked underneath Raven's wing and plunged into the light.

⇥ ✦ ⇤

It was like stepping through a waterfall. I emerged feeling clean and shining, like I'd been scoured and polished. I looked down at my skin and saw that it was glowing. I turned around to look back at Raven. His eyes were closed tightly, as if he were concentrating to keep the door open. Not wanting to disturb his concentration, I turned back to look for Miss Sharp and Nathan.

I was standing at the edge of a grassy meadow that sloped

down to a riverbank lined with green willows. Wildflowers of every imaginable color dotted the grass. White and pink blossoms floated from flowering trees through the air. I stepped toward one of the trees and saw that there were ripe apples amongst the pink blooms. How could it be, I wondered, that the tree bore flowers and fruit at the same time? It was as if it were spring and fall and summer all at the same time. Then I remembered what Raven had said about the timelessness of Faerie. Looking down at the ground, I saw spring violets growing beside late-summer goldenrod, all glowing in the golden light that flowed around me like honey.

I looked up into the lavender sky but could find no sun. The honey-colored light bathed everything evenly. It wasn't just that time was different here; there was no time at all—or *all* time *all* the time. Spring, summer, fall—even winter, I noticed, as I looked into the surrounding pine trees and saw icicles hanging from their boughs—were all happening at once, as were all the times of the day. The grass was wet with morning dew, the sky as bright as noon, the edges of the meadow shadowy with dusk, the woods dark as night. All of time was here at my fingertips, for me to pluck as easily as I might pluck the red-and-gold apple from the tree.

I *did* pluck it, my thought turning into action as swiftly as a hummingbird's wings. The apple was in my hand, firm and round, so fragrant it made my mouth water . . . I could almost taste it already . . . perhaps I had tasted it already. Time meant nothing here. I had already done everything I ever would and everything I ever had. If I bit into the apple I would be merging with all time. I could move within it freely. Perhaps I could even go back and undo what I had done. Perhaps I could go back to the day of the fire. I could warn the girls not to go to work that day. Or I could go back even further, to the day my mother died. I could stay home with her and fight the *tenebrae* with the bells inside my head. . . .

"It doesn't work like that."

I looked up from the apple into my mother's face.

I dropped the apple. It rolled over the grass toward my mother and cracked open at her feet. She knelt, picked it up, and held it out for me to see. Inside, the pulp was black with rot. The sweet, sickly odor of decay rose into the air between us.

"You can no more go back and make me live than you can make this apple whole again. But"—she tossed the apple away and stepped closer to me—"I can enjoy your company for a few moments." She held out her arms and I rushed into them.

She was real—solid and warm, indeed, more solid than I remembered her from her last months when she'd grown so fragile. When I buried my face in her neck and inhaled she smelled like violets and rosewater, not laudanum.

"Yes, it *is* really me, my dearling Avie." She stroked my hair and then tucked a strand behind my ear, the touch so familiar I burst into tears.

"Don't cry, dearling, I'm all right now." She held me at arm's length to look at me. "To see you looking so well is all I need for an eternity of peace. I was afraid the shadows would find you . . ."

"I led them to you!" I cried. "It's my fault you died."

Her face, which had looked so radiant and peaceful a moment ago, darkened, and the light around us dimmed as well.

"Oh no, Avie dearling, it was I who led them to you! I had sunk so deep in my own fear and despair that I'd become easy prey. When I saw Judicus on your birthday I was frightened they would take you from me."

"You knew him, didn't you? Judicus van Drood. You were engaged to him."

A shadow of pain crossed her face—even here where there were no shadows. "Yes, the Order arranged the match. At first I didn't mind. I cared for him . . . but then he changed. Or maybe *I* changed and it was my fault that he became lost in the shadows. I ran away when I should have faced him . . . and then I lost myself in the shadows. I'm sorry for that, dearling. I should have been braver, but sometimes the hardest thing to do is to remain yourself. When the *tenebrae* came for me I knew that if I let them in they would destroy us both. I did the only thing I could to defeat them."

"You drank the laudanum before they could get inside you?"

Her eyes widened and gleamed. "No, dearling, I let them in and *then* I drank the laudanum. It was the only way to destroy them so they wouldn't get you. I would never have willingly left you otherwise." She stroked my hair back behind my ear and cupped my face with her hand. I felt the hard calluses on her fingertips from years of sewing and trimming hats to feed and shelter us. All other signs of age and care had fallen from her face, but not those signs of wear.

As if she'd heard my thought she held her hands out, palms up, between us. "Here in Faerie we keep the marks we're proud of. I am proud of these calluses I got working to keep you safe. But I'm not proud of the fears I let prey on me, so I've let those go. Remember that, Avie, remember the strong things I did and forgive the weak ones. . . . Oh, there's so much I have to say to you, but there's no time!"

"I thought there was all the time in the world in Faerie," I said, surprised to feel a smile on my lips.

She returned the smile, but sadly. "Yes, we in Faerie have all the time in the world, but your friends don't." She took my hand and pulled me down the hill. "Vionetta has been trying to get Nathan to leave with her, but . . . well, you can see why he won't."

Below us on the banks of a river that looked much like the Hudson, Vionetta Sharp stood above two figures sitting on the rocks. I recognized one as Nathan and the other as the girl whom I'd seen before in Faerie.

"Louisa! He's found her!"

"Yes, but it's too late for Louisa to leave. Look . . ."

The girl was hunched over, looking intently at something laid out on the flat rock where she sat. I moved closer and saw that she was staring at a line of playing cards. She turned one over and let out a little yelp. "The queen of hearts! Exactly what I needed."

"Patience?" I asked. "She's playing patience?"

"Not just patience," Nathan said. "La Nivernaise. She's working through all the solitary card games in *Lady Cadogan's Illustrated Games of Solitaire or Patience*. Klondike, fortress, General Sedgewick, La Belle Lucie . . ."

"Light and shade is next," Louisa said. "That's a really hard one. But I've gotten very good at it."

"She ought to have," Nathan said. "She's been playing for seven months."

"Isn't there any way to make her stop?" I asked, sitting down next to Nathan.

"Not that I know of," Miss Sharp said. "Playing the game has bound her into the fabric of Faerie. If she breaks those bonds . . . well, it might break something inside her mind."

"Anything is better than *this*!" Nathan cried. "I can't just leave her here playing cards for all eternity."

"There might be a way."

The voice came from behind us. I turned and found a tall middle-aged man in a pith helmet and tattered, brightly hued rags. He looked familiar.

"Sir Miles Malmsbury?" I asked tentatively. Although he looked like the photograph in Miss Frost's classroom, that man had had trim muttonchops and wore a neatly pressed khaki safari jacket and trousers. *This* man had a full-grown beard and long straggly hair braided into a long queue. His jacket appeared to have once been a khaki safari jacket but was covered with tiny brightly colored feathers. But the biggest change was in his eyes. The man in the photograph had looked out at the world with a haughty, superior expression. *This* man's eyes were humbled, and more than a little bit mad.

"At your service," he said, saluting and attempting to click his heels even though he was barefoot. "I assume from your Bell and Feather insignias that you are members of the Order. May I ask who is in charge of this expedition?"

Nathan and I stared at each other, but Miss Sharp stepped forward and returned Sir Malmsbury's salute. "That would be me, sir. Vionetta Sharp. I teach English literature at Blythewood."

"Ah, Blythewood . . . " he said with a misty look in his eyes. "I had a most promising student at Blythewood . . . but no matter . . . we don't have much time. I observed the boy enter Faerie and engage with the girls. He hasn't taken part in her game or eaten anything, so he may leave."

"I won't go without Louisa," Nathan growled.

"So I understood. Admirable of you, son. I myself would never abandon a team member in the field. Luckily, I have been carefully observing the customs of the country during my . . . er . . . sojourn here in Faerie." He took out a worn notebook from his canvas bag. "With the help of the lychnobious people, who have been most kind considering my past unfortunate treatment of them, I have learned that the feathers of the *lychnobia* protect the unwary traveler from becoming trapped in Faerie. I gave this young lady a feather as soon as she arrived."

We all looked down at Louisa and saw that she was wearing a necklace of brightly colored feathers.

"So she can leave?" Nathan asked.

"Yes," Sir Malmsbury replied. "However, I cannot vouch for the time shift that may have occurred during her—or your—stay here. The *lychnobia* have a poor sense of time."

A lampsprite landed on Sir Malmsbury's shoulder, flicked its wing across his face, and chattered angrily.

"Excuse me," Sir Malmsbury said, looking quite abashed, "I was guilty once again of a hominid-centrist judgment. The lampsprite's sense of time is *different* from ours."

"But that's all right!" I cried. "Raven is holding open the door for us. He said that we'll be able to return to our time as long as a Darkling holds open the door."

"A Darkling is holding the door open for you?" Sir Malmsbury asked in awed tones. "Why, then, this is *my* chance to go back! We must all go at once!"

Nathan grabbed Louisa's hand and tried to pull her up, but she screamed and clutched the cards to her chest.

"I know something that might help," my mother said. She knelt down beside Louisa and gently laid her hands over Louisa's. Louisa looked up, her eyes vague and clouded. "There's another game we used to play at Blythewood," she said to Louisa. "Perhaps you remember it? It's called flush and trophies."

A flicker of recognition passed over the girl's face. "Oh yes, we played it after dinner in the Commons Room . . . only I don't recall the rules. . . ."

"But I do," my mother said with the same gentle smile she'd given me when I was frustrated that I'd forgotten a tense in Latin or a stitch for trimming a hat.

"And so do I," Vionetta said, sitting down next to Louisa and reaching for the cards laid out on the rock. Louisa flinched when Vionetta swept the cards up into a pile, but Nathan quickly diverted her.

"Flush and trophies! My favorite!" Nathan said with false enthusiasm; I was quite sure he loathed the game. "We all four can play."

"I thought we weren't supposed to play any games in Faerie," I whispered into Miss Sharp's ear as I sat down.

"All except this one," she replied as my mother dealt out the whole deck to Louisa, Nathan, Miss Sharp, and me. "Flush and trophies was designed to break the spell of Faerie."

"The game is quite simple," my mother was explaining

to Louisa. "The object is to get all of one suit—hearts, clubs, spades, or diamonds. The trick is figuring out which suit your opponent is trying for—to flush them out, so to speak—and keep them from getting all of their suit before you can claim the trophy. Each turn you discard a card. If anyone has the same card in a different suit they can trade it for you. Vionetta, you're north. You go first."

Miss Sharp laid out a two of clubs. I had a two of hearts, but I'd already noticed that I had more hearts than any other suit so I didn't offer to trade. Louisa would have beat me to it anyway. She slapped down a two of spades.

"She's looking for clubs," my mother whispered in my ear. "All we have to do now is keep feeding them to her."

Nathan obligingly laid down a queen of clubs next. Louisa made a face. She must not have any queens. It was my turn next. I laid down a jack of clubs. Louisa immediately reached for it, but Miss Sharp deftly knocked the card off the rock. It fluttered over the grass like a butterfly. Louisa sprung to her feet and went after it. Nathan and Miss Sharp got up and followed her, cards in hand. I followed with my mother and Sir Malmsbury. The rest was simple. All we had to do was keep laying out clubs and tossing them closer to the place where Raven was holding open the door.

"But you're not playing!" I said to my mother as we got closer. "Can't we use the game to free you, too?"

My mother regarded me sadly. She brushed back a lock of my hair and cupped my face with her hand. "Avie, dearling, I died in your world. A Darkling carried me here to Faerie because I wanted to come here instead of the mortal afterworld. But I can never go back to your world."

"Of course you wanted to come here," I said. "It's so beautiful! Can't I stay here with you? There's nothing for me back there."

A faint smile fluttered over her lips. "Nothing? Look . . ."

Nathan and Louisa had reached Raven, who still stood like a marble statue holding open the door to our world—only the marble was streaked with veins of fire now. He looked like the lampsprite had just before it exploded. His eyes were still shut, his jaw clenched, the muscles in his arms and chest straining like Atlas holding up the world. "It looks as if the light is crushing him!"

"It is," my mother replied. "A Darkling can only hold the door between worlds open for so long before he's crushed between them. This one must care for you greatly to do this for you, Ava."

"Then Ava was telling the truth, Evangeline?" Miss Sharp asked my mother. "The Darklings aren't evil?"

My mother shook her head sadly, her eyes still on Raven. "The Darklings are cursed, but no, not evil. You can trust them, especially this one. But he's not the only one who cares for you."

She nodded her head toward Nathan, who was holding Louisa's hand with one of his and an ace of clubs in the other. All he had to do now was lead her under Raven's wings back into our world, but he had turned and was looking back at me. The light behind him turned his fair hair into a golden halo. He looked more like one of the Botticelli angels than dark-haired Raven, but the light also threw his face in shadow. The *tenebrae* still lurked under his skin.

"Nathan doesn't care for me," I said.

"I wouldn't be so sure of that. But what I am sure of is that without you the shadows will claim him forever. So unless you care nothing for him . . ."

I shook my head, my body denying the statement before my mind knew what I felt. "I can't be the only one who can help him."

"Avie, all the years the shadows preyed on me, the one thing that kept them from claiming me was you. I had only to think of you and I was able to fight them off—until the end when I knew I had to sacrifice myself to save you. The only thing that gave me solace as I died was that you would be strong enough to go on without me . . ."

I began to object but she held up a hand to silence me. "You have no idea how strong you are, Avie. You're a chime child . . . and so much more! With training you, and you alone, will be able to banish the shadows—from Nathan and from your world."

I looked away from my mother to the two men who stood on the threshold of my world. One light, one dark . . . I wasn't sure which was which, only that both would perish if I didn't go back.

I turned to my mother. I could see by her face that she already knew what my decision was.

"Will you be all right here?" I asked.

"I will be now. Now that I have seen that you are," she replied, wiping the tears from my face. Then, before I could change my mind, I turned and ducked under Raven's wing.

36

AS SOON AS we had all passed through, Raven collapsed on the ground, his wings crumpling around him like charred paper. When I touched them my hands came away black. His face was gray as ash, soot-black lashes fluttering over sightless eyes.

"I didn't know it would hurt him like this!" I cried. "What can we do to help him?"

"There's nothing *we* can do," Sir Malmsbury said, "but his own kind can help him. Look: they're waiting for us to leave to take care of him."

I looked up into the trees to where Sir Malmsbury was pointing. At first I didn't see anything, only pockets of shadows in the pines, but then as my eyes adjusted to the dimmer light of this world, I made out the shapes of winged figures perched in the trees. An old man, two old women, a young girl, many young men . . . all their eyes trained on Raven. His flock.

"Can you help him?" I cried. My voice sounded hoarse as a crow's caw.

Wings fluttered in answer. Miss Sharp tugged on my arm. "They won't come down until we leave. And we need to get Louisa back to the house. She's not . . . *herself* yet. If she sees an opening to Faerie she may try to slip into it."

I looked back down at Raven. His eyes fluttered open and seemed to focus on me for a moment. I touched my hand to his cheek. "Thank you," I said.

His lips, cracked and seamed with ash, parted. "My . . . pleasure," he croaked, with a smile that turned into a wince. Then Miss Sharp was pulling me away.

The Darklings descended as soon as we were out of the clearing. The sound of wings was deafening, a black rain that fell like a curtain between us, obscuring Raven from my view. As if he were being devoured by the dark. How could I leave him to that darkness?

"Let me go," I cried, struggling against Miss Sharp's grip. "You can take Louisa back. Let me stay with him."

"I can't," she said, taking me by the shoulders and turning me away from the clearing. "Listen."

My head was so full of the sound of wings I couldn't hear anything else, but then I heard it: the bells of Blythewood tolling a peal.

"It's the Hunting Peal. Can't you see how dark it's gotten? Night is falling. We've been in Faerie all day. They've called out the Hunt to find us. If we don't stop them they'll ravage these woods. In his weakened state Raven won't be able to escape. He'll die and his flock will die trying to protect him."

I knew she was right, because along with the toll of the Blythewood bells I heard my own bass bell tolling an alarm inside my head. Still, I couldn't bear to leave Raven. "You can stop them while I warn the Darklings."

"They won't stop the Hunt if any one of us is still in the woods. You have to come with me."

I took one look back, but already the woods were too dark to make out the Darklings. Joined with the bells now came the sound of hunting horns. Their blare sent chills rushing down my spine. I wanted to flee from them, but I made myself run toward them with Miss Sharp and Sir Malmsbury. Louisa and Nathan had gone on ahead. "What about Helen and Mr. Bellows?" I cried.

Miss Sharp turned her head, her eyes flashing in the dark likwe an owl's. "Perhaps they're already out . . . look! They are, they're with the Hunt. Come on, there's not much time."

We'd reached the edge of the woods, where Nathan and Louisa stood. Louisa was pulling on Nathan's hand, crying and begging to be let go. She was trying to run back into the woods. When I looked out at the lawn I didn't blame her.

A wave of fire was rolling across the lawn toward the woods, dark at its base and crested with flame. An unbroken line of black-cloaked figures holding torches strode forward, their steps synchronized to the toll of the bells. With them came a crunching sound, like the surf churning through shells. I recalled a poem we'd read in Miss Sharp's class that described the surf's

> melancholy, long, withdrawing roar,
> Retreating, to the breath
> Of the night-wind, down the vast edges drear
> And naked shingles of the world.

Only this surf was made up of bows and arrows and swords rustling beneath cloaks. This wave would roll through the woods devouring everything in its path—or it would be destroyed itself. With the hunting lust upon them, the Order of Blythewood would fight to their deaths. I could see now why Dame Beckwith had not ordered a Hunt before this. She knew that she would lose her own teachers and students in the fight.

"Oh dear," Sir Malmsbury said, "and I'm covered in lampsprite feathers! Your Dianas and their hawks will tear me limb from limb. Perhaps I should have stayed in Faerie."

"Too late for that," Miss Sharp snapped, pushing Sir Malmsbury forward. "You'll have to explain what happened. Dame Beckwith will listen to you."

"Actually," Sir Malmsbury replied, hanging back, "India and I never quite saw eye to eye. I'm not sure I'm the best man for the job."

Impatient with their argument, I stepped out of the woods and in front of the hunt, my arms spread wide. For a moment I thought they would roll right over me. The faces I saw beneath their hoods were stony, eyes glazed. But then one of the figures cried out.

"Look, it's Ava!" The voice was Helen's. Mr. Bellows was right beside her.

The line came to a halt and the figure at the center stepped forward holding a torch high in the air. She lowered her hood and I saw that it was Dame Beckwith.

"You can call off the Hunt!" I cried. "We're all safe—Miss Sharp and Nathan, and look . . ." I stood aside so Dame Beckwith could see Louisa. "We found Louisa. She was never taken by the Darklings. She had strayed into Faerie, but Nathan found her." I urged Nathan forward but he was too busy struggling with Louisa to keep her from running back into the woods. Dame Beckwith was staring at Louisa as if unable to believe that it was her daughter. "And we found him," I continued, "and a Darkling held the door open for us so we wouldn't get stuck there—"

I realized my mistake right away. As soon as I mentioned a Darkling another figure stepped forward. I was shocked to see Miss Frost out of bed and seemingly recovered, her only sign of weakness that she was leaning heavily on Sarah Lehman's arm. "A Darkling *helped* you?" she shrieked. "That's impossible! You must have been seduced by the creature."

"Euphorbia? Is that Euphorbia Frost's voice I hear?" Sir Malmsbury stepped out of the shelter of the woods. "My dear, how you've . . . er . . . grown up. Do you remember your old teacher?"

Miss Frost gasped and staggered. Sarah struggled to keep her upright. "Sir Malmsbury? Is it really you?"

"Yes, dear Euphorbia, it is. I've come back from my expedition. And wait until you hear all I've learned in the field! I'm afraid my original notions were quite wrong."

"You are covered in feathers!" Miss Frost cried, her eyes wide. "It's just as I suspected—you were taken by lampsprites!"

"No!" Miss Sharp said, stepping in between Miss Frost and Sir Malmsbury. "Can't you all see, we were wrong about the fairies. I saw a Darkling hold the door open so we could get out, and the lampsprites gave Sir Malmsbury their feathers to protect him."

Dame Beckwith's eyes flashed over our little group—Nathan still struggling with Louisa, who showed no signs of recognizing her mother; Sir Malmsbury in his feathery attire; Miss Sharp defending the Darklings and the fairies. When her eyes came back to me she nodded, her decision made.

"Seize them!" she shouted. "They're not in their right minds."

Robed figures on either side of her stepped forward, two for each of us. Euphorbia Frost dug sharp nails into my arm, her breath reeking of ashes. I flinched away but other hands were waiting for me.

"Take them back to the castle," Dame Beckwith ordered our guards when we had been corralled. "We will sweep the woods. No matter what the cost, it's time we destroyed the Darklings once and for all."

Miss Frost pushed me forward, her fingernails digging deep into my arm. Sarah's arm was gentler on my other side, a light weight. I could easily wrench my arm away . . . but then do *what*? If I could get away, I could run into the forest to warn the Darklings that the Hunt was coming, but how far would I get? The Dianas were arrayed in front of me, bows drawn, arrows nocked, their faces stony, their eyes yellow in the flickering torchlight. I recalled Miss Swift saying that when the Hunt was called the Dianas entered a sort of trance. Their eyes, I saw now, weren't just yellow from the torchlight; they had become the yellow of their falcons' eyes—and just as inhuman. If I made a break for the woods I didn't doubt that they would shoot me. Right now, I wouldn't be surprised if they flew at me and tore me limb from limb as I'd seen the falcons do to their prey.

I felt anger bubbling up inside me—for what Dame Beckwith was planning to do to the Darklings, but also for what she'd done to these girls, turning them into hunters and robbing them of their youth and innocence. The anger tingled on my skin, from the nape of my neck, down my shoulder blades, to the tips of my fingers, which were still lightly coated with sprite dust. What had my mother just said to me? *Sometimes the hardest thing to do is to remain yourself.* My mother had been a Diana. Is that why she had fled Blythewood—because she didn't want to become a mindless hunter like these girls? *The hunter must become the thing she hunts.* From the time she fled Blythewood until her death, my mother had been hunted until she was finally caught and killed. Leaving one thing behind.

My hand stole into my pocket, unhampered by Sarah's light touch on my elbow. As soon as I touched the black feather I felt a spark, as if it had come alive.

I dug my heels in so abruptly that Miss Frost stumbled. At the same time I whipped the feather out of my pocket and brandished it in front of Dame Beckwith and the Dianas. Sparks flew into the air, erupting into firecrackers from sprite dust clinging to the feather, the edges of which began to glow as Raven's feathers had glowed when he held the door of Faerie open.

Thinking about Raven—what he had sacrificed to help me and how he was threatened now—fueled my anger . . . and apparently my magic. The feather glowed like a firebrand. In its light I saw Dame Beckwith's eyes flare.

"Ava, you don't know what you're doing!" she said.

"I know I can't let you destroy the Darklings," I said. "They're not our enemies—the *tenebrae* are." As I said the word I felt a prickling at the nape of my neck. The Dianas, entranced as they were, took a step backward. Dame Beckwith looked suddenly terrified.

"It's the Darkling feather," she said, her voice low and urgent. "It's summoned *them*."

Them? I turned slowly, still holding the blazing feather in front of me. Its glare blinded me at first. The line of trees loomed black against the purple sky, their shadows distorted by the light of the blazing feather and the torches behind me. But then I realized that the shadows were not distorted. They were alive.

They were taller than the tallest tree in the forest and bristled like pines, but unlike the trees they could move. They lumbered out of the forest now, each step shaking the ground beneath my feet.

How could shadows shake the ground?

Because these are shadows made of flesh, a voice inside my head answered. It was a familiar voice. I had heard it before, after the crow attack when I had fallen into the dark well, on the streets of Rhinebeck when its owner had held me captive, and in the dungeon when the tenebrae had swarmed around me. The voice belonged to Judicus van Drood, the Shadow Master. Only the creature in front of me wasn't a man. I It was an amalgam of oozing shadow that was capped by a belled shape—like a short cape topping a long coat. It was the man in the Inverness cape made huge. I lifted the blazing feather higher in a shaking hand to unmask his face . . . only there was no face, only shadows roiling in the dark. This creature was a projection of the Shadow Master's mind.

I wouldn't underestimate that, Ava dearling, the voice said inside my head. How had it gotten there?

You let me in.

I could feel the voice, like a snake slithering through my brain, nosing at my thoughts, memories, feelings. . . .

"No!" I screamed aloud.

Yessss, it hissed, the shadows writhing with the pulse of his voice. *You watched the shadows tell my story. I felt you watching. It felt so good to have someone see how she led me on and then turned her back on me.*

"That's not what I saw," I cried, but I could feel him inside my brain, prying at the memory of what I had seen inside the candelabellum room, releasing the images from the recesses of my brain as a beater flushes game from the brush. The shadow pictures flew upward and then began to spin inside my brain as though my head was the candelabellum chamber. I saw my mother as a young woman at Blythewood, running up the steps, laughing with her friends, ringing the bells, her face rosy with the exercise—yes, I could see the peaches and-cream color of her skin, the bright red of her hair, the flash of her green eyes. The shadow pictures had taken on hue and flesh in my head as I watched them. I was hungry for them, for memories of my mother before she had grown thin and wasted, haunted . . .

Haunted by what she had done to me.

I saw her with a young man, a familiar-looking young man, sitting together in the library, their heads bent low over a book. She was reading aloud, something in Latin, and he was nodding along to the rhythm of the poem, holding up a finger now and then to correct her.

"You were her teacher."

Yes, but hardly older than her. I'd just finished my training at Hawthorn.

Images of a young man fencing and running through a rugged landscape flashed through my brain and I recalled Nathan's disparaging comments about Hawthorn's rigorous regimen.

Yes, it's quite brutal. By the time I arrived at Blythewood imagine how grateful I was for feminine companionship—and how susceptible! Evangeline was everything I could want in a wife and helpmate, but I was circumspect. I followed the protocol as established by the Order, inquiring with the proper authorities into the suitability of a match.

I saw the young van Drood speaking to a young—and quite beautiful—Dame Beckwith, the two of them consulting the ledgers. She, I realized now, was the other woman I'd been shown by the candelabellum, the one who had tried to draw van Drood away from the shadows—but had failed.

"But that's awful!" I objected. "Arranging a marriage as though mating animals!"

Yes, I couldn't agree with you more, dear Ava. If I had spoken of my feelings directly to Evangeline . . . if I had spoken sooner, things might have been quite different. But by the time the Order approved the match, your mother had fallen in love with someone else.

I saw van Drood and my mother standing in the garden, beneath a rose arbor, silhouetted against a sunset sky like two figures in an engraving. He held a small jewel box in his hand and she was shaking her head. He reached for her. She withdrew. They looked like the automaton figures on the repeater performing a dance. But then the picture flew apart into black shards spinning through the sky like a startled flock of crows.

My mother ran toward the woods. Van Drood followed her, but before he could reach her he was set upon by the black crows. They swarmed over him, as they had the prince in the Merope story, devouring him.

And why not? van Drood whispered, his voice almost gentle inside my head. *What did I have left? Why stay with the Order when I had lost the one thing that made being a part of them worthwhile? When their rules and regulations—their damned old ways!—had cost me the love of my life? I left. I learned the truth behind the Order. And learned how to destroy them. They're such fools that they don't understand that the things they hunt are what keep the world free of the shadows. Without the Darklings, the balance between shadow and light will be destroyed. The shadows will rule. I will rule! They've already made themselves into vessels with all their training. Look at them! They're no better than puppets!*

I heard a gasp from behind me and turned to see the Dianas' bows trained on Dame Beckwith.

Fools! They don't realize that their training makes it easier for me to get inside their heads. They've made it very easy over the years for me to turn them into slaves, just as I've made this one my servant.

Someone behind me stepped forward and grabbed my arm, trying to wrest the feather away from me.

I spun around to face Euphorbia Frost—because who else could he have meant by *my servant*—and came face to face with Sarah Lehman instead. She smiled at me . . . and black smoke poured out of her mouth.

"Sarah!" I cried. "Why . . . ?"

"Why should I be loyal to these people who treat me like a slave?" she asked. "Why should you? These are the women who drove your mother away because she'd polluted herself by contact with the Darklings."

"I gave her a choice," Dame Beckwith said, her voice firm but her eyes riveted to the bows of the Dianas. "Stay and renounce the Darklings or go. She chose to go."

"She gave Louisa the same choice the day she ran into the woods," Sarah said. "She'd fallen in love with a Darkling, too. It was easy to lead her into the woods promising to take her to the Darklings—easy to lead her into Faerie instead."

"*You* led her into Faerie?" Dame Beckwith roared.

"Yes, me!" Sarah turned on Dame Beckwith, smoke now billowing out of her mouth and eyes and fingertips. The smoke filled and surrounded her, the shadows cloaking her like a cape. She was the one who had called the *tenebrae* into Blythewood and she was their beacon now. Van Drood wasn't here in the flesh; he was acting through his servant, Sarah Lehman, and through the *tenebrae* she had summoned.

"She said she was my friend, but she was happy to leave me for her Darkling lover. She left me all alone with *you*." She swept her finger in a wide arc at the crowd of teachers and students, smoke gushing from her mouth, fire sparking off her fingertips. Her gaze fell on Dame Beckwith and her voice suddenly changed. "I was your slave!" she cried in a voice that made Dame Beckwith cry out like a wounded bird. It wasn't Sarah's voice any longer. It was Judicus van Drood's.

He was inside her as he'd been inside me a moment ago. I'd let that voice inside me because I'd let a bit of darkness inside me as I watched the candelabellum and doubted my mother— or maybe that bit of darkness had first gotten inside me the day she died, when I first thought that if she had really loved me she wouldn't have killed herself. That darkness had been growing since that day, feeding on every bad and ungenerous thought— my jealousy of the girls who had more than me, my fears of being despised, of going mad. I'd let the shadows inside me, just as Sarah had. If I didn't expel them now they would devour me, just as they had devoured Sarah and threatened now to destroy everyone at Blythewood.

A wall of smoke billowed over Sarah's head, heading for the front line, for Miss Frost and Mr. Bellows, Miss Sharp, Miss Corcy and my friends—Helen and Daisy, Beatrice and Dolores, Cam . . . everyone at Blythewood. Looking at them now, torchlight flickering on their faces, shadows looming around them, I saw a mottled ground of light and dark, like the dappled things in Miss Sharp's poem—light and shadow, *a dazzle dim.* I saw Helen's vanity but also her loyalty, the Jagers' gloom but also their stalwart hearts, Miss Frost's cruelty but also her love for her old teacher. Even Daisy, who shone like a beacon in the shadows, had a flicker of darkness inside her, a doubt that she still loved Mr. Appleby after all she'd seen and learned at Blythewood. And even Sarah, so consumed by darkness, still had a spark of light within her: the love she'd had for Louisa.

I turned then and looked at the woods. The light of the blazing feather in my hand burned through the wall of shadows. I could see past the line of Darklings to the lampsprites and gob-lins and all the other creatures of Faerie, strange and horrible and sometimes beautiful. They, too, dwelled in shadow and light, neither wholly good nor wholly bad.

And then there were the Darklings. A line of them stood between the shadows and the woods. Their black wings glinted in the torchlight, their faces like carved marble. I saw Raven's face alive with anger and love. They, most of all, possessed both shadow and light. They stood in between. They kept the balance. Without them the world would be overrun by shadows.

That's why van Drood wanted them destroyed—and he was using the Order to do it.

Behind me I could hear the Dianas drawing back their bows. In front of me I could hear the rustling of the Darklings' wings and beyond them the growl and chitter of goblin and trow. The shadows writhed between them, hungry for blood on both sides. They were growing stronger at the mere antici-pation of bloodshed. Once they'd fed on blood they would be unstoppable. Van Drood would be unstoppable. I felt him, even though he wasn't here in the flesh, feeding off the shadows, just as they fed off the anger and hate in the crowd. The shad-ows needed his hate as a channel just as I used the repeater as a channel for my bells.

The repeater. Could I use it to channel my bells now to de-feat van Drood? But how? All it did was repeat the bells in my head. Could I get it to repeat the danger bell in my head?

As I drew out the watch and pressed the stem, the repeater

played back the bass bell, but it sounded weak and tinny on the little watch. I heard van Drood laughing inside my head. *That only worked on me in the village because I was unprepared. You can't hurt me with your bells or that pathetic device.*

It was true. What did I have in my little repertoire of bells? The treble that I heard when I was with Raven . . .

The repeater played back the treble bells, intermingling it with the bass bell.

Van Drood laughed again in my head. *Do you think you can fight me with love?* he mocked. No, I hadn't . . . but did van Drood's laugh sound just a little bit frightened? Was it possible that he was still susceptible to love? And a little bit frightened of it?

He laughed again—a laugh that echoed in the rattle of bows and the growl of goblins. If I could look again on van Drood, would I see a spark of light left in him?

"Is that why you're not here in the flesh?" I asked aloud. "Because you don't want me to see that spark of light left in you?"

"There is no spark left in me!" he roared, his voice suddenly filling Sarah's mouth. "Your mother made sure of that!"

The rage he felt for my mother made the bass bell ring louder, but also the treble bell. There was still a spark of love in all that rage. I knew now what I had to do. Although it was painful to use it like this, I played the tune my mother used to sing to me in my head. I heard her voice—and then I heard it echoed in the repeater, strong and clear now.

"Do you think that silly ditty means anything to me?" he snarled from Sarah's mouth.

But I thought I heard something in his voice that told me it *did* mean something to him. And not just to him. Out of the corner of my eye I saw Dame Beckwith's face crease with pain as if it brought up painful memories for her too. I played the tune over in my head, concentrating on my mother's voice, picturing my mother's face as she sang. When the repeater played the tune again, it was piercingly loud and unbearably sweet. I could have sworn I heard my mother's voice in the chimes. It brought tears to my eyes . . . and silenced van Drood. Then I heard him utter a low moan that shook the trees and made the shadows shrink away.

It was working! He was withdrawing his presence, and without his guiding force the shadows were losing substance and his influence was waning from his servants. The Dianas put down their bows, Miss Frost wavered on her feet—Sir Malmsbury leapt forward to catch her—and Sarah seemed to shrink two inches. She clutched her chest as if the wind had just been knocked out of her. She stared at me, her eyes wide and liquid in the torchlight.

"It's all right," I said softly, as if gentling a hawk. "He's gone."

"He's gone!" she shrieked, her voice so horrid that even the shadows recoiled from her—and then gusted back, hungry for the waves of anger rising from her. "What am I now without him but a pathetic servant? You . . ." She pointed at me. "You took him from me!"

She leapt so quickly I didn't have time to think. Instinctively, I thrust out my arm to keep her from me—only I had the blazing feather in that hand. The shadows writhing around her caught fire like a cone of spun sugar. A pillar of flame surrounded Sarah. I heard a wild shriek of pain and smelled hair and flesh singeing. She was on fire, and just like the girls at the Triangle, she would burn to death, all because van Drood had come for me. I couldn't let her die this way. I lunged at her, determined to smother the flames that were engulfing her with my own body, but as we hit the ground I heard the sound of wings. The Darklings, I thought. They've come to take my soul away. I felt something heavy fall, a wall of darkness, and I knew nothing else.

37

THE WORLD WAS born in fire and ice, Mr. Bellows had taught us in the mythology section of his class. According to the Norse myths the fires of Muspelheim mingled with the frosts of Niflheim to create the frost giant Ymir, out of whose body the earth and all its creatures sprung. In the weeks that followed the Night of the Shadows—as it came to be known in Blythewood lore—I had an inkling how Ymir must have felt. My body was a battleground between the warring forces of fire and ice: the fire I had raised out of the Darkling feather and the black ice let loose by the shadow creatures.

Miss Corey, who sat beside my bed for the two weeks I lay unconscious, told me afterward that the flames from my feather torch had ignited the shadow creatures. "They turned into a roiling mass of fire, shrieking and sizzling. What was most horrible was that inside the mass we could see struggling bodies and faces screaming in pain and terror—the souls of the beings who had been taken over by the *tenebrae*—including Sarah Lehman."

"What happened to her?" I asked, horror-stricken that I had killed the girl who had been my first friend at Blythewood.

Even though she had been van Drood's spy I had seen a spark of humanity inside her.

"We're not sure. Once you set them on fire, smoke rose into the sky. We saw shapes rising with it, and then the smoke was blown away, although there was no wind."

"The Darklings," I said, remembering a sound that had reached me in the depths of my darkness. "I heard their wings; they must have used them to fan the smoke away."

"Perhaps," Miss Corey said, busying herself then with the bandages on my hands. "When the smoke cleared we didn't see them. Dame Beckwith ordered a retreat. We had to get you back to the infirmary to treat your burns."

I looked down at my hands, which were swathed in white gauze. The worst of the pain was there and along my shoulder blades. I'd been afraid when I first saw the big clumsy bandages that they covered two stumps. But when the nurse uncovered them I was surprised to see that although the flesh was pink and shiny, my hands were whole and strangely unscarred. It still hurt to move them, but Miss Corey promised they would heal completely in time.

"If you hadn't thrown a cloak over me to douse the fire I wouldn't have survived," I said.

"I didn't throw a cloak over you," she said, looking away. "It was the Darkling. He flew straight through the flames and covered you with his wings. At first we thought he was attacking you. One of the Dianas shot him—"

"Shot him?" I cried, my hands flying to my own heart. "Was he . . . ?"

The corner of Miss Corey's mouth lifted. "It was Charlotte, and she only grazed his wing." The small smile faded from her lips. "He was able to fly away, but when he went back through the flames his wings caught on fire. I'm afraid . . ."

"You think he died in the fire?" I asked, fear searing up from my heart like the flames that had enveloped Raven.

Miss Corey took my hand. "I'm not really sure. I never would have admitted that one of those creatures could be . . . good. But I saw him risk his own life for you. If it's any consolation it's changed how I think of the Darklings."

"But it hasn't changed everyone's minds, has it?"

Miss Corey shook her head. "There was so much chaos. Everyone saw something different. Dame Beckwith believes the shadows were creating illusions. She said that when Sarah spoke she heard the voice of an old friend."

An old friend? Did she mean Judicus van Drood? I wondered. I remembered what I had seen in the candelabellum and how she had looked at van Drood. Would she believe me if I told her that Judicus van Drood was the Shadow Master?

"I have to speak with Dame Beckwith," I said.

"Of course. She would have come already but she was hurt in the retreat—she stayed behind until everyone was safe. Since then she's been busy trying to help Louisa regain her memories. I'm sure she'll come see you soon." She paused, as if uncertain about something, then went on. "You're probably wondering why no one's been to visit."

I wasn't thinking of that at all, but I nodded.

"I'm afraid your lack of visitors is my fault. Helen and Daisy have been begging to come—and half a dozen other girls as well. I just wasn't sure you were ready for visitors. You were delirious as first, calling out names, and then . . . well . . . I thought you might want to wait until . . . um . . ." Miss Corey's eyes, which had been skittering around the room, came to rest on my face.

"Oh," I said, a wave of heat rising to my scalp. With my hands bandaged I hadn't been able to inspect the damage done to my hair and no one had offered me a mirror. "Am I hideous?"

Miss Corey looked horrified at the question. *It must be because I am and she doesn't want to tell me.* Without a word she got up, crossed the room, and took down a small wooden-framed mirror from the wall. She brought it to the bed, but held it to her chest for a moment.

"Your hair caught on fire but the Darkling's wings put it out. We had to shave off what was left to apply the salve to your scalp. We were afraid at first that your hair might not grow back. . . ."

The look on my face made her pause. I was picturing myself bald as a boiled egg. "But it has!" she said. "And quite remarkably fast . . . well, look!" She thrust the mirror in front of me. Her hand was shaking so much at first I couldn't find my reflection—only a glimpse of wide startled eyes—but when her hand stilled I saw myself.

The light chestnut hair I'd been born with was gone. In its place was a fluff of deep garnet red the color of fire and the consistency of silk. It framed my face with feathery tendrils that made my eyes look bigger and greener and my cheekbones stand out more sharply.

I hardly recognized myself. I looked like a blade that had

been tempered in fire, burned down to its essential self. I looked, I realized with a strange pang, like my mother. I wasn't a monster; in fact, in the moment when I looked at the reflection as though it were someone else, I had to admit that I was . . . *beautiful*. A scary kind of beautiful, but beautiful nonetheless.

"You see, I thought you'd want to get used to your new self before you met your friends again."

I tore my eyes away from the strange creature in the mirror and looked up at Miss Corey. For the first time I realized that she was no longer wearing her veil. I remembered suddenly the morning—was it only a few weeks ago?—I'd come upon Miss Sharp reading that poem to her. *Glory be to God for dappled things*. The words had seemed to summon up a strange unearthly beauty in Lillian Corey's face. I had thought she kept it hidden under her veil because she was ashamed of the markings on her face, but now I saw that she was shy of the strange beauty she possessed. I understood then why she had kept my friends away.

"They're going to stare at me, aren't they?"

Miss Corey grinned. It made her look even more beautiful. "You're going to have to get used to quite a bit of staring, I think."

I smiled at her, and caught a glimpse of my reflection—of a girl who had come through fire and ice and seemed to possess a little of each. I remembered what Sam Greenfeder had called Tillie and me in the park. *Farbrente maydlakh*. Fiery girls. Now I'd really become one—a girl who'd come through fire twice. And if *I* could come through fire . . . maybe Raven had as well.

"Well then," I said, "I'd better start getting used to it."

Helen and Daisy came first. Helen screeched when she saw my hair. "It's the exact shade of the Countess Oborensky's hair when she was presented at court. However did you get it? Is it . . ." she lowed her voice, *"dyed?"*

"It just grew back this way after the fire," I replied.

"It will be lovely when it grows in," Daisy said diplomatically, eyes riveted to my scalp.

"I think I may keep it short," I said. "Perhaps I'll start a fad."

Daisy looked scandalized, but Helen only laughed. "I'm glad you came through the fire with your humor intact. You'll need it to bear the events Beckwith has planned for you—speakers, fêtes, high teas, parades. You're to get a heroine's reception once you're out of this cell. Why are you still here anyway? You look fit as a fiddle . . . rather better than you did before, as a matter of fact."

I smiled at Helen's backhanded compliment. "I still have some pain in my hands and along my back, but I'll be out soon. Catch me up on all the news, will you? I don't want to feel a complete ninny when I make my reappearance."

Helen readily obliged, as I knew she would. I was happy to have the attention focused away from my strange new looks and lingering injuries—and my mind taken off whether Raven had survived the fire or not—by Helen's gossip. I learned that not everyone was thrilled with my new status as heroine.

Georgiana Montmorency had loudly proclaimed at dinner one night that I had led the Darklings out of the woods with my torch and had been stopped by the Dianas. Cam had promptly risen to her feet and socked Georgiana in the jaw. A fight had broken out between Georgiana's friends and mine. Interestingly, not all of her friends had not come to Georgiana's aid. In fact, Alfreda Driscoll had been seen dumping a blancmange over Georgiana's head, effectively quelling the outburst—although Dolores Jager had gotten in one more jab at one of Georgiana's cohorts.

"Dolores? Really?" I asked, finding it hard to imagine the melancholy quiet girl taking part in a brawl.

"I wouldn't underestimate Dolores," Daisy said. "The next day Georgiana's hair turned green after using a soap I saw Dolores leaving in the showers."

"Well at least I'm not the only one with a new hair color," I said, smiling at the image of Georgiana with green hair. "But does anyone else think I was leading the Darklings to attack Blythewood?"

"Oh, no!" Daisy and Helen both said together. "The next day Dame Beckwith, after giving us all fifty demerits for fighting, announced that it had been Sarah Lehman who had summoned the Darklings and you were a hero for defeating them."

"But it wasn't the Darklings who were attacking; it was the shadow creatures—the *tenebrae*."

Daisy and Helen exchanged an uneasy glance. "Are you really sure?" Daisy asked, taking my hand. "When the shadows burned away we all saw the Darklings. It looked as if they had summoned the shadows."

"But they were trying to protect the woods from the shadow creatures. Nathan knows the truth . . . and Miss Sharp. What do they say?"

Daisy and Helen exchanged a guilty look. "Um . . . they've been busy," Daisy said. "And they've been staying at Violet House."

"Because of Louisa," Helen said softly.

I flushed, embarrassed that I hadn't asked about Louisa right away. "How is she? Has she recovered from her stay in Faerie?"

They looked at each other again and then Daisy said, "Not *exactly*. She only wants to play cards all the time and she has this vacant look in her eyes."

"That description could fit my mother," Helen said tartly.

I was about to tell her she shouldn't jest, but then she added, "But you should see Nathan. He sits with her all day playing cards. He's the only one who can keep her calm. That's why they're at Violet House—that and to keep Louisa from running back into the woods."

"Poor Nathan," I said, wondering if *his* shadows had been banished now that Sarah was gone. I recalled what my mother had said about him—that I was the only one who would be able to keep the shadows from claiming him. But how could I do that? "He worked so hard to get Louisa back."

"Yes, well things don't always work out as we plan," Helen said. "And speaking of plans . . . this letter arrived for you a few days ago. I saw it in the post and nabbed it before anyone else could see it and wonder why you're receiving mail from a strange man in Scotland."

I snatched the envelope out of Helen's hand and ripped it open.

"Why *are* you receiving mail from a strange man in Scotland, by the way?"

"It's from Mr. Farnsworth, the librarian at the Hawthorn School. He has a copy of the book I've been looking for—*A Darkness of Angels*. He says he's setting sail for New York in a few days—on April tenth. What day is it now?" I asked anxiously, realizing I'd completely lost track of the days.

"April fifteenth," Helen replied. "He should be in New York in a few days, then. About the time my parents are returning from their trip. I had a letter from Daddy a week ago saying they had run into your grandmother in London and that they were traveling back to New York together. Does he say what ship he's on?"

I flung the bedclothes away, ignoring Helen's questions. She probably wanted to gossip about who else she knew crossing the Atlantic. "I have to get up and start moving around so I'm ready to go into New York to meet him," I said.

Helen picked up the letter from the bed and read it. "Ah," she said, "he *is* coming in on the same ship as my parents and your grandmother."

"Are you sure?" I asked. "You can barely remember your declensions. How can you remember the name of the ship?"

"That's easy," Helen replied. "Everyone's heard of the *Titanic*. It's the ship built to be unsinkable."

38

THAT EVENING I had a nightmare. I was standing looking up at a range of great ice mountains, cliffs of black ice looming over me, making me feel smaller and smaller . . . because the cliffs were gliding steadily toward me to crush me in their icy maws. The worst part, the part that gripped me in an icy sweat, was when I realized that the cliffs were alive. They were ice giants come to smash me to bits and drag me to the bottom of the sea.

I awoke in the dark to find Helen sitting on the side of my bed, her face in the moonlight as white and immobile as one of the ice cliffs.

"It's sunk," she said, barely moving her lips.

I thought she was talking about my dream at first, but then she said. "The *Titanic* has sunk."

"But that can't be," I replied blearily. "You just told me it was unsinkable . . ." But already I knew it was true—that it was just as in my dream. The ice giants had come to destroy the ship that carried Mr. Farnsworth . . . and my grandmother and Agnes and Helen's parents.

I got up and got dressed in a numb daze, barely hearing what Helen—and then others who came and went—had to say.

There were conflicting reports. The *Titanic* was being towed into port by another ship, the *Titanic* was at the bottom of the ocean; everybody had been saved, nobody had been saved.

Somehow I managed to get myself ready to travel to New York. Daisy had packed for both Helen and me. She wanted to come with us, but I heard myself telling her to stay. "We'll need you when we get back," I told her, although I was not sure what I meant.

Then we were in the coach and Gillie was taking us to the train station. A fog covered River Road, just as it had on my first day at Blythewood—a cold fog that came, I felt sure, straight from the arctic sea where the ice giants had calved their lethal bergs and sent them to destroy the *Titanic*. Even now one might loom in the fog.

"Poor lass," Gillie said when he carried our bags down to the station. Helen stood like a statue, staring at the river as if watching for a ship to come out of the fog with her parents safely delivered.

"Yes," I agreed, "I hope her parents are all right."

"I hope so, too," Gillie said, "but it was you I was talking about. You're barely recovered from you own trials. How do your hands feel?"

"My hands feel fine," I said, flexing them under their light kid gloves. "My back still hurts, though, right along the shoulder blades. The fire must have run straight down them, but I'll be all right. To tell the truth, I'm glad to be up and away—not that I'm glad for the reason," I added, seeing that Gillie was staring at me oddly.

"Nay, you're right," he said, "better for you to get away. You let us know when you hear any news . . . as soon as ye see Agnes Moorhen . . ." His voice faded and my mouth went dry. *Agnes.* I hadn't even let myself think that Agnes might not be all right. Seeing the look on my face Gillie clamped his large hand to my shoulder. "She'll have come through all right," he said. "It would take more than a hunk of ice to sink our Agnes."

Helen was silent on the journey down, staring out the window at the fog-cloaked river. I'd never known her to go so long without uttering a word. When we arrived at the Grand Central Station she wanted to go straight to the White Star Line offices to get what information we could, but I convinced her we should go to her house first and wait for news. What news had reached the shipping offices now was likely not to be reliable.

We took a taxi to Washington Square. It was strange to be in the city again, passing familiar sights that no longer looked familiar, perhaps because I had learned so much about the world since I had last walked these streets, and now I suspected every shadow or wondered if all the people on the streets were entirely human. Or perhaps it was because I'd never looked at those streets from the window of a taxicab.

The van Beek townhouse was smaller than I had imagined it would be, a narrow brownstone with rooms painted in somber colors, the furniture draped in canvas looming out of the shadows like ghosts. The housekeeper apologized for not having the house ready and then burst into tears. I expected Helen to chide her but instead she patted the woman on the arm and said, "There, there, Elspeth," and asked if there'd been any news. There was a stack of wires and letters, mostly from friends and family asking if Helen had heard anything. I convinced Helen to go to bed, promising her that we'd get up first thing in the morning and walk over to the White Star Line offices to check the lists of survivors. Before we went to bed I made Elspeth promise to wake me first if there was any news.

The next three days were a blur of raised hopes, dashed expectations, and tortuous waiting. The early survivor lists were contradictory. Mrs. van Beek and my grandmother were listed as survivors on one and as victims on another. Agnes and Mr. van Beek weren't mentioned on either. Nor could I find Mr. Farnsworth's name on any of the lists.

Finally on the night of the eighteenth we heard that the *Carpathia* had been sighted coming into harbor with the survivors. We rushed down to the pier where she was expected to dock and waited in the rain with the largest crowd I'd ever seen assembled. When the survivors began to disembark, the crowd came to life. Names were called out. Men and women pushed through the crowd to embrace survivors. Some fainted. Helen stood, her face stony, until she spotted someone.

"Mama!" she cried, her face turning instantly younger. I could barely keep up with her as she pushed through the crowd. As we got nearer I saw that Mrs. van Beek was clutching the arm of another woman—my grandmother. I searched the faces around them, my heart sinking when I didn't see Agnes . . . but then, a little way back up the gangplank I spied, above the heads of the crowd, a navy feather.

"Agnes!" I cried. The feather twitched at the sound and a gloved hand shot up beside it. By the time I reached Helen and her mother and my grandmother, Agnes had reached them as well. I threw my arms around Agnes's neck.

"Well!" I heard my grandmother say. "I'm glad to see you're happy *one* of us is alive." I let Agnes go and threw my arms around my grandmother. Under her heavy wool coat she felt small and frail and her mouth seemed to be crumpling.

"Now, now," she tutted. "Let's not make a fuss. You didn't think Miss Moorhen would let me drown, did you? What do I pay her for if not to take care of such details?"

Agnes rolled her eyes and whispered into my ear. "You should have seen the trouble I had getting her to wear a life-jacket."

I started to laugh at the image, but then I saw Helen. She was looking around the crowd, her eyes skittering from stranger to stranger until they landed back on her mother.

"Where's Daddy?" she asked.

⌖ ✦ ⌖

I stayed at the van Beeks' through the rest of April and into early May, at first to see Helen through the early days of grief and then to help her sort through the morass of financial entanglement that descended on the van Beek household.

It seemed that Mr. van Beek had fallen deeply into debt over the last few years, something to do with a bad investment and then an attempt to recoup his losses that went even worse. Intimations of his losses had been coming for months. Having failed to prevail on his wife to curtail expenses, Mr. van Beek had confided his concerns to Helen to see if she might talk sense to her mother. That had been the subject of all the letters going back and forth between Helen and her parents.

The situation, though, was made far worse by Mr. van Beek's death. I couldn't make much sense of the explanations given by the men in dark suits who descended on the house like a murder of crows and, I saw, neither could Helen or her mother. So I called Agnes in to help. She came in a trim navy suit with a cerulean feather in her straw boater, and Mr. Greenfeder in tow. Together they marshaled the lawyers and accountants into order. Within a day she'd written up a clear report for Mrs. van Beek and sent Mr. Greenfeder on errands around the city to see what could be done to investigate the circumstances of Mr. van Beek's failed investments. When she was done, she left mother and daughter in the library and came out to talk to me in the parlor.

"Will they be all right?" I asked, noting that even the feather in Agnes's cap was wilting.

She sighed. "I've outlined a plan by which, if they are willing to cut back and be frugal, they should be able to manage. I'm afraid the rest is up to them. If the mother were able to be a little stronger for Helen's sake . . ." She faltered, perhaps remembering the example my mother set.

"It's all right," I assured her. "I've learned why my mother did what she did. She may have been weak in the months before she died, but in the end . . ." My voice quivered, but I went on. "In the end she did what she did for me. She drank the laudanum to destroy the shadows, not because she had given in to them."

Agnes's chin trembled and I reached out to squeeze her hand. It felt strange to be comforting the indomitable Agnes Moorhen. She must have felt it, too, because she smiled ruefully. "You've changed up there at Blythewood, and not just your new hair," she said, laughing. "Although I do think that it's quite fetching on you. But what I meant is that you've grown stronger."

I laughed. "Well, I didn't have much choice, did I?"

Agnes looked suddenly somber. "There's always a choice. And I'm afraid you're going to have to make some difficult ones in the future." She looked around the van Beek parlor, peering behind the aspidistras as if someone—or some*thing*—might be lurking in the shadows. "There's something I have to tell you about what happened on the ship. There was a man on board whom I recognized . . ."

"Was it Judicus van Drood?" I asked.

"How did you know?" Agnes cried, trembling at the sound of his name.

"Because he was the man in the Inverness cape who followed me and my mother."

"But why . . . ?" Agnes's eyes grew wide. "Wait . . . I remember when he taught at Blythewood your mother was his favorite student. There was some talk that they had formed an inappropriate relationship."

I shuddered, recalling van Drood's name on the chart betrothing him to my mother. Was it possible that he was my father? I pushed away the thought. "Why didn't you tell me?" I asked Agnes.

"Because I didn't believe it for a minute! Evangeline Hall would never have had an improper relationship with a teacher—not even with Mr. van Drood, whom all the girls liked so much . . . although I always thought he was a bit strange. When we met him on board I was quite sorry that Mr. van Beek invited him to our table."

"Helen's father knew him?"

"Why yes, the families have known each other for generations. Mr. van Drood had been advising Mr. van Beek on some business matters . . . oh! I should have thought of that sooner. I wonder if van Drood's advice led to the van Beek's financial difficulties."

"I wouldn't be surprised," I said. "What did van Drood talk about at dinner?"

Agnes shook her head as if trying to scatter cobwebs. "It's all rather a blur. I always had a headache after those dinners. I thought it was from the motion of the ship, but I don't generally get seasick, as I told Mr. Farnsworth—"

"Mr. Farnsworth! Mr. Herbert Farnsworth! The librarian of the Hawthorn School?"

"Why, yes! He sat at our table. He was quite . . ." She dimpled and colored. "*Learned.* We had some fascinating conversations about books."

I quickly explained that Mr. Farnsworth had been carrying a book for me.

"Ah," Agnes said, "that explains a few things. He carried with him a leather portmanteau strapped across his chest at all times because, he explained, he had some important documents in it that he could not risk leaving unattended . . . oh my!" Agnes turned pale. "I've just recalled that Mr. van Drood took quite an interest in Mr. Farnsworth."

My mouth went dry. "What happened to Mr. Farnsworth?" I asked as gently as I could.

Agnes shook her head and bit her lip. "I don't really know. Mr. Farnsworth and I were on the deck the night we hit the iceberg. We saw Mr. van Drood standing on the foredeck staring into the sea. Then the iceberg appeared . . . everyone was so shocked at its appearance, but not Mr. van Drood. I remember I had the strangest feeling that he had *summoned* it."

I recalled the dream I'd had about the icebergs coming to life as ice giants and what Raven said about the ice giants leaving the woods and going back north. Had van Drood somehow gotten control of the ice giants? Had he lured them to the *Titanic* to destroy the ship?

"What happened then?" I asked.

"Chaos! I had to go find your grandmother and Mrs. van Beek and help them get into their life vests. Mrs. van Beek wanted to retrieve her jewels from the safe! Can you imagine? Mr. van Beek said he would wait for the jewels and sent us on ahead. Poor Mr. van Beek—we never saw him again! I saw Mr. Farnsworth once more. He helped us find a lifeboat with space to take us. I wanted to go back and help more people but he lifted me bodily from the deck and placed me in the boat! Then he started to give me his portmanteau—"

"He was going to give you the book!"

"Yes, but then he looked over his shoulder and changed his mind. Instead he . . ." Agnes blushed. "Well, let's just say he gave me a very *fervid* good-bye. Then he was gone. I lost sight of him when the boat was lowered. That was the last time I ever saw him."

I squeezed Agnes's hand. "When Mr. Farnsworth looked over his shoulder, did you see what he was looking at?"

"No . . . I . . . well, now that you *ask* . . ." She furrowed her brow, trying to concentrate. "When I try to think about it everything gets all . . . *shadowy.*"

"Do you think it could have been van Drood?"

Agnes winced, as if in pain. Then she shook her head as if she were trying to clear water out of her ears.

"Yes!" she said suddenly, a look of determination replacing the fog on her face. "Yes! I don't know why I didn't remember earlier. That man! He was following Mr. Farnsworth even then . . . even with the ship sinking! And Mr. Farnsworth must not have given me the book because . . ." A sob burst from Agnes's mouth.

"Because van Drood would have pursued you for it," I said. "And no doubt drowned you and everyone in your lifeboat for it. He lured van Drood away from you." *Back onto a sinking ship,* I almost said, thinking of someone who had flown through fire to save someone. "What a brave man!"

"Yes," Agnes said, wiping her eyes, "but I'm afraid he must have drowned in his heroic efforts. I did not see him among the survivors on the *Carpathia.*"

"And did you see van Drood?"

Agnes shook her head. "No . . . at least, I don't think so . . . no, I'm *sure.* The only place I've seen that devil since is in my nightmares."

"Then let's hope he drowned," I said with as much conviction as I could muster. I had a dreadful suspicion, though, that it would take more than the *Titanic* sinking to destroy Judicus van Drood.

39

HELEN AND I left for Blythewood the next day. Mrs. van Beek insisted that Helen go. "Your kind Miss Moorhen and her friend Mr. Greenfeder have promised to look in on me and help me make some alterations in our domestic economy. You'd only be in the way. Best you go back to school. Who knows? Maybe you'll marry that funny Beckwith boy and support your old mother in her dotage."

Helen blushed at the reference to Nathan and chided her mother, but I could tell that it was the reminder of Nathan that decided her. She'd had a letter from him expressing condolences for her father's death that she must have read a dozen times on the train ride up to Rhinebeck.

"He says Louisa is making some progress. She plays games of patience most of the day, but she's willing to play bridge with the aunts and Uncle Taddie after tea. He says he's taking her to a sanatorium in Marienbad this summer."

"Perhaps they'll be able to help her," I said, wondering if it was the same sanatorium that had been unable to restore Uncle Taddie's mind entirely. "Does he . . . um . . . mention a boarder at Violet House?"

Helen looked at me strangely. "He did say his aunts had

a boarder who suddenly vanished. A clockmaker's apprentice . . ." Her voice trailed off. The old Helen would have grilled me on my interest in a mere apprentice, but she only looked out the window, her eyes growing as vague as the mist rising off the river.

Gillie met us at the train station. He took off his cap and bowed formally to Helen to express his sorrow for her father's death, then turned away when he saw she was struggling not to cry. She lost that struggle when Daisy greeted her on the steps of the school. We shuttled her quickly up the steps then, knowing she'd hate for the other girls to see her crying. As we unpacked Daisy kept up a constant chatter about her plans to get us through finals.

"I've organized all my notes and made a schedule," she said, demonstrating a thick ledger book with color-coded flags for each subject. "Dolores and Beatrice are going to prep you for science and I'm going to quiz you on bell changes. Cam has gotten Miss Swift to agree to drop your practical in archery, seeing how Ava saved the school with that feather trick of hers, and Helen . . ."

"And poor Helen's father died?" she asked, a bit of her customary tartness returning. "Am I to be passed out of pity?"

Daisy looked embarrassed. "Not at all. Miss Swift said she had no doubt you could shoot the tail feathers off the rest of the girls. She wants you to run the archery club next year."

"Oh," Helen said, abashed. Then recovering, she quipped, "Well, high time. I'll help you practice in exchange for all the work you'll be doing to get us through finals . . . and . . . er . . . thank you, Daisy. I can't imagine what we'd do without you."

Daisy beamed, dropped her ledger, then had to reorganize her colored flags.

Helen was right. We wouldn't have been able to get through finals without Daisy's help—or without Beatrice, Dolores, and Cam pitching in. Other girls helped, too—Alfreda Driscoll taught us a spell to help with memorization. Andalusia Beaumont lent me her lucky arrow for the practical, which I chose to take even though I'd been excused and even though my shoulders still ached when I drew the bow.

At first I thought they were all helping because of Helen losing her father, but I soon learned that my role during the Night of Shadows had spread throughout the school and I had become—at least according to Helen and Daisy—a Blythewood legend. I wasn't sure how I felt about that. Some of Blythewood's legends didn't turn out so well.

Judicus van Drood, for instance.

I wanted to talk to Dame Beckwith about the identity of the Shadow Master, but she had gone to Europe with Louisa and Nathan and wouldn't be back until the Fall term. By then perhaps I'd know more about what had happened to Judicus van Drood. If he had really perished on the *Titanic* perhaps there was no need to tell her that her old friend and colleague had been taken over by the tenebrae. Or if I did have to tell her, at least it would come after Louisa was better.

On the day the exam results were posted and we learned we had all passed, Miss Sharp threw a celebratory tea party in the Great Hall for the whole school, helped by her aunts, who were a bit at loose ends since Nathan and Louisa had left for Europe. There were cucumber sandwiches, bread and butter, scones with clotted cream and fresh raspberries, Victoria sponge cake, and iced cakes topped with sugared violets. It lived up to the most elaborate feasts in Mrs. Moore's girls'-school books.

But none of Mrs. Moore's feasts culminated in the strange spectacle we were treated to after tea. Euphorbia Frost stood up to make an announcement. I hadn't seen her since I'd come back, and I noticed right away how changed she was. She'd lost weight during her illness, and although her figure was still ample, she no longer looked stout. Color had returned to her face and she had stopped dying her hair that awful eggplant color. It had come in a soft, silvery gray that better suited her violet eyes.

"I have been consulting with my esteemed mentor, the eminent Sir Miles Malmsbury, since his return from the field, and he has convinced me that the practice of keeping specimens of the *lychnobia* is inhumane . . ."

"Do you think?" I heard Daisy mutter under her breath.

"And contradicts the burial habits of the lychnobious people. And so, today, Sir Malmsbury and I will return the lampsprites to their proper burial ground. If you would care to join us . . ."

Gillie had rigged up a pony cart with ribbons and flowers, which he led to the edge of the Blythe Wood. I peeked inside and saw that the sprites' bodies were laid out on white linen, the pins removed from their breasts. It was a sad sight, but when we reached the edge of the woods, a breeze stirred over their bodies and they began to disintegrate. The breeze quickened into a gust that picked up the sprite dust and carried it into the air. We all looked up to see a conflagration spreading across the sky. Some of the dust fell on our upturned faces. I felt the chill of their passing, but I warmed when I heard their song.

Remember us, they sang, *remember us.*

I looked around at my friends and teachers and saw tear-stained faces streaked with sprite dust. Would remembering the lampsprites change how they thought of the fairies? Would they ever accept that the Darklings weren't evil if I didn't find the book that proved it? I wasn't sure—but I knew we had all changed this year and that Blythewood would never be the same.

When the last of the sprite dust had vanished into the air, the crowd turned and headed back to the castle, all except Gillie, who stood gazing into the woods, his moss-green eyes the same color as the shadows beneath the trees. I noticed he had a sprite feather tucked behind his ear.

"That's where you come from, isn't it?" I asked.

He took so long to answer that I grew afraid that I'd offended him, but when he did speak at last his voice was gentle. "Aye lass, that is where I'm from, but your true home is with the ones ye love and I've come to care for the creatures on both sides of the woods."

"Do they know?" I asked, afraid for him.

"The Dame knows."

"But how can she teach that all the creatures of Faerie are evil if she knows you're not?"

Gillie smiled. "Folks can hold two opposite ideas in their heads at the same time, lass. Don't forget that. And don't stray too long in the woods . . ." He winked at me. "I'll only be able to cover for you for a little while." Then he turned to go, whistling

the same tune that the lampsprites had sung: *Remember me,*
remember me.

When he was halfway across the lawn I slipped into the
woods.

The trees on the edge of the forest were charred from the
fire, but once I got past them I was enveloped in a deep green
sea with flashes of sunlight flitting through the depths like
tropical fish. As I went deeper into the woods I noticed that
the flashes of sunlight had wings, and the birds, which had
gone quiet when I first entered the woods, were now calling to
each other. Were they warning their flocks that a hunter had
entered the woods—or were they sending a message to him?

Since Miss Corey had told me about Raven flying through
the fire to save me—and flying back again through it—I had
hardly dared hope he had survived. And while I'd told myself
that I had stayed out of the woods so far because of the patrols,
the truth was that I'd been afraid to learn that he hadn't.

I found the tree that held Raven's nest. I looked up, but the
canopy of green leaves was too thick for me to make out his
nest. I stood still and listened to the birdsong. It was sweet and
sad and reminded me of a funeral dirge. Where did Darklings
go when they died if they couldn't go to Faerie? I wondered.
Surely not into the shadows . . .

I felt the sting of tears on my face and lifted my hand to
wipe them off, but before my hand reached my face something
else brushed them away—a sweep of wings that cloaked my
back. I spun around, so fast the woods spun with me in a whirl
of green, and found him standing there, his dark eyes the only
steady beacons in a spinning world.

I rushed into his arms, desperate to know he was real. As he folded his arms and wings around me, I pressed myself to his chest. I could feel the heat of his skin through the thin cotton of his shirt. *Yes! He was real, he was alive!* But then I realized his skin wasn't just warm, it was *on fire*.

I stepped back and gingerly touched the collar of his shirt. His skin beneath was red and scarred. Looking up I saw that he was wincing against the pain of my touch.

"You *were* hurt!" I gasped.

Raven shrugged. I noticed now that he held one of his wings stiffly. "You were hurt, too, in saving us. How are your hands?"

I held them out for him to see. He took them both in his and I was glad he was looking down at them so he couldn't see the blush that had risen to my cheeks. I noticed how small my hands looked in his, like doves cupped in a nest. They fluttered like doves, too, until he covered them both between his two hands and looked up into my eyes. "I'm glad you did not suffer any worse injuries," he said so formally I almost laughed.

"My shoulder blades still hurt sometimes," I said, unnerved by the force of his gaze.

His brows drew together. "Your shoulder blades? I didn't see the fire reach your back."

I shrugged, embarrassed to seem as if I had been complaining. "It's nothing," I began, but he was already turning me around, his hands on my shoulders. I could feel his breath on the nape of my neck and, through the thin fabric of my shirtwaist, his hands running down my back.

His touch seemed to waken something inside me—a stirring that began in my chest and fluttered across my back. My skin felt prickly, as if it were stretched too tight across my bones. My heart beat so hard I thought it would burst out of my chest. After a moment he turned me back to face him. He was very close, his face hovering over mine, his lips only inches away. I felt myself leaning in toward him, but he stopped me by laying a hand on my chest.

"Ava, there's something you must know. It's about . . . your father."

My mouth went dry. I thought about the charts I'd found in the dungeons and the shadow play I'd been shown by the candelabellum and all that van Drood had told me about his courtship of my mother. Van Drood thought she loved him, and even my mother had said she had cared for him once. I didn't know much about how these matters, but I had begun to suspect that van Drood and my mother might have been . . . *intimate* before my mother broke things off.

"I'm that monster's child, aren't I?" I said with a horrible sinking in my chest.

Raven flinched as though I'd struck him. He clenched his jaw as if against some terrible pain. "What monster?"

"Van Drood. He loved my mother. She refused to marry him, but she must have loved him once and . . . *been with* him. That's why she ran away. She saw what he was becoming and didn't want to raise me with him. But that's why he was looking for me." I felt my chin wobbling, but I bit the inside of my cheek and forced myself to look Raven in the eyes. "That's why you've stayed away, isn't it?"

Raven gave me a long, level look.

"Do you think I would forsake you because of something like that?"

I felt a quiver of relief, but also a sinking in my heart. "So it's true."

"Where did you get this idea?" Raven asked.

"I saw it in the candelabellum."

"Tell me exactly what you saw," he commanded in an oddly stern voice.

I told him about the scene of van Drood and my mother in the garden and her running toward the woods, the crows chasing her, the wings dissolving into larger wings, and then vanishing. "Because she was swallowed up by the shadows," I said at last. "I'm afraid they were always inside her from then on."

"And this is what she told you when you saw her in Faerie?"

"No," I replied. "There wasn't time."

"Ava," Raven said, gripping both my shoulders in his hands. "What you saw in the candelabellum wasn't complete. When your mother disappeared in the woods she wasn't swallowed by the shadows. She was fleeing to her lover."

"Van Drood said she loved someone else, but I thought it was just his jealousy."

"No, she did love someone very much, someone she couldn't stay with."

"So van Drood's not my father!" I cried, so relieved I felt tears pour down my face. "The young van Drood looked so familiar to me."

"Yes, he would look familiar to you, because you know his son."

"His son? Who . . . ?"

But then I saw it—the way Dame Beckwith had looked at van Drood in the vision I had seen in the candelabellum and the way her face had changed when she heard his voice coming out of Sarah's mouth. She hadn't wanted to believe that the shadow creature was speaking with his voice because she had once been in love with him.

"Nathan is van Drood's son?"

"Yes. That's why I was afraid of you getting too close to him. He's half submersed in the shadows already."

"No!" I cried. "Just because Nathan is a monster's son doesn't make him a monster." I remembered what my mother had said, that I was the only one who could save Nathan from the shadows. I looked into Raven's eyes. He still gripped my shoulders, still stared at me.

"I'm glad you see it that way," he said. "It will make it easier for you. . . . You see, the man your mother loved . . . well, he wasn't a man."

"What . . . ?" But I was seeing the shadow play again, watching the swirl of wings. I could hear them in my head, almost drowning out Raven's words, but not quite.

"Those pains you feel in your shoulder blades are fledgling pains. We all feel them when our wings are emerging . . . You see, Ava, your father was a Darkling . . ." His voice faltered at the look on my face.

"No!" I cried, unable to disguise the horror in my voice.

"Is that so horrible?" he asked, his voice hoarse with emotion. "That you are becoming like me? Do you think I'm a monster?"

"Of course not . . . it's just I—I . . ." I stammered to a halt, searching for the right words, but before I could find them I heard Helen's and Daisy's voices calling my name. I turned and shouted to them that I would be there in a moment and when I turned back Raven was gone. I hadn't even heard his wings. For a moment I wondered if I'd imagined his appearance. Perhaps it had all been a dream and I wasn't turning into a Darkling after all. But when I turned back toward Helen and Daisy I felt the ache in my shoulder blades again and I knew it was true.

I walked out of the woods and found Helen and Daisy on the lawn standing a few feet from the edge of the woods.

"Daisy was worried, so we came looking for you," Helen said. Daisy opened her mouth to object but one look at Helen's drawn and anxious face made her close it again. "Yes, I was worried," Daisy said. "And Helen agreed to come look for you." She reached out her hand and took mine. "Come along or you'll be late for the farewell dinner."

Helen hooked her arm in mine and we all turned to walk back to Blythewood as the bells began to ring the dinner hour. They rang us all the way home and then, when they were done, the seventh bell rang from beneath the river, its tone clear and sweet in the spring air, only instead of saying *Remember me, remember me,* it tolled a different tune now. *You're not alone, you're not alone.*

Acknowledgments

I HAVE AN entire Order of *farbrente maydlakh* to thank for the creation of this book. First, my daughter Maggie's webcomic Penny Dreadful (PennyDreadfulComics.com) inspired the 1911 setting. My stepdaughter Nora was an invaluable source of historical detail, calling in her cohorts Barry Goldberg and Ben Hellwege to suggest sources for the period. Thanks to Dr. Richard LaFleur for his Latin consultation. Maggie's friend Sarah Alpert listened to many hours of world-building, gave invaluable suggestions on the manuscript, and invented Featherbell. My intrepid editor, Kendra Levin, saw me through many revisions and tirelessly pinned down the taxonomic hierarchies of Darkling and fairy.

Thanks, too, to Danielle Delaney, Nancy Brennan, and Janet Pascal at Penguin. My agent, Robin Rue, and her assistant Beth Miller, at Writers House, were fiery in their advocacy for this book.

Thanks to Wendy Gold, Gary Feinberg, Juliet Harrison, and Scott Silverman for reading early drafts.

And, as always, I couldn't do any of this without the faith and love of my husband, Lee.